Bantling

Bantling

Marlowe Russell

© Copyright Marlowe Russell 2023
No part of this book may be reproduced or transmitted by any means, except as permitted by UK copyright law or the author.
For licensing requests, contact the author at author@marlowerussell.com

Cover painting by Ron Russell
Untitled, 1962, oil on canvas, 17.5mmx25.5mm

Dedication

For my parents, Ron and Arda Russell,
and their friends, and mine,
Mary and Andrew Hyde

Contents

Dedication		v
1 Timmy. Peckham. 1926.		1
2 Violet. Southampton. 1923.		2
3 Ellen. Stockwell. 1923.		5
4 Violet. Southampton. 1923.		11
5 Ellen. Stockwell. 1923.		13
6 Violet. Southampton. 1923.		28
7 Ellen. Stockwell. 1923.		29
8 Ellen. Stockwell. 1923.		51
9 Violet. Southampton. 1923.		63
10 Ellen. Stockwell. 1923.		65
11 Violet. Southampton. 1923.		70
12 Ellen. Stockwell. 1923.		72
13 Violet. Stockwell. 1923.		94
14 Ellen. Stockwell. 1923.		96
15 Violet. Stockwell. 1923.		107
16 Ellen. Stockwell. 1923.		110
17 Violet. Stockwell. 1923.		116
18 Ellen. Stockwell. 1923.		118
19 Violet. Stockwell. 1923.		123
20 Ellen. Stockwell. 1923.		125
21 Violet. Stockwell. 1923.		130
22 Ellen. Stockwell. 1923.		131
23 Violet. Stockwell. 1923.		135
24 Ellen. Stockwell. 1923.		137
25 Ellen. Stockwell. 1923.		144
26 Violet. Stockwell. 1923.		155
27 Ellen. Stockwell. 1923.		156
28 Violet. Brixton. 1923.		171
29 Ellen. Stockwell. 1923.		175
30 Violet. Stockwell. 1923.		176
31 Ellen. Stockwell. 1923.		178
32 Violet. Stockwell. 1923.		186
33 Ellen. Stockwell. 1923.		189
34 Violet. Stockwell. 1923.		193
35 Ellen. Stockwell. 1923.		194
36 Violet. Stockwell. 1923.		201
37 Ellen. Stockwell. 1923.		202
38 Violet. Stockwell. 1923.		222
39 Ellen. Stockwell. 1923.		224
40 Violet. Streatham. 1923.		232
41 Violet. Herne Hill. 1926.		235
42 Timmy. Peckham. 1926.		236
43 Violet. Herne Hill. 1927.		239
44 Violet. Herne Hill. 1927.		240
45 Ellen. Stockwell. 1927.		243
46 Violet. West Norwood. 1928.		251
47 Timmy. Peckham. 1931.		253
48 Violet. Tulse Hill. 1931.		256
49 Timmy. Peckham. 1931.		257
50 Violet. Kentish Town. 1931.		260
51 Ellen. Stockwell. 1933.		261
52 Violet. Hull. 1934.		264
53 Timmy. Peckham. 1935.		268
54 Violet. Hull. 1936.		270
55 Timmy. Peckham. 1937.		271
56 Ellen. Stockwell. 1938.		280
57 Timmy. Whitechapel. 1939.		282
58 Violet. Hull. 1939.		294
59 Timmy. Peckham. 1939.		296
60 Sam. Stockwell. 1939.		305
61 Sam. Peckham. 1939.		313
62 Sam. Stockwell. 1939.		316
63 Violet. Hull. 1940.		321
64 Sam. Balham. 1941.		323
65 Violet. Hull. 1942.		336
66 Ellen. Stockwell. 1943.		337
67 Sam. North Atlantic. 1943.		340
68 Sam. HMAC Victorious. 1944.		344
69 Ellen. Stockwell. 1944.		347
70 Sam. HMAC Victorious. 1944.		352
71 Felix. Stockwell. 1944.		356
72 Sam. HMAC Victorious. 1945.		360
73 Sam. Sydney. 1945.		363
74 Sam. HMAC Victorious. 1945.		373
75 Sam. HMAC Victorious. 1945.		381
76 Violet. London. 1945.		386
77 Sam. HMAC Victorious. 1945.		391
78 Sam. Sydney. 1945.		399
79 Sam. London. 1946.		407
80 Sam. Stockwell. 1946.		418
81 Sam. Poplar. 1946.		427
82 Sam. Hull. 1946.		430
83 Sam. Poplar. 1946.		438
84 Violet. Hull. 1947.		446
85 Sam. Sydney. 1947.		448
86 Violet. London 1948.		457
87 Sam. Sydney. 1949.		460
Acknowledgements		467
Author's note		468

BANTLING

1 Timmy. Peckham. 1926.

The sweet soapiness of her nightie and the lovely warm smell of her. The up-down in-out breath of her, in-out up-down, the same as his, his breath for hers, hers for him, her front touch-touch-touching his back. They are one and the same. He is a leaf and she is the tide and they are bob-bob-bobbing towards the secret island. His magic shoes will take him to the castle in the sunny patch, where Ma and him will live, and Bertie and Doris can come and visit and they'll all eat jam roly-poly and chicken every day. But for now, it's as good as it gets, just being here with Ma, thumb in mouth, safe between her and anything horrid, and on guard too, against wicked shouting giants and smoky dragons.

BANTLING

2 Violet. Southampton. 1923.

Southampton, 10 January 1923, Dearest Stel, Four months or so to go & the Wriggler gets livelier every day. The festive holiday was not very jolly for me. I could not help thinking about Christmas a year ago, no clouds on the horizon back then & of course next year was on my mind too. All I could see was a dirty, lonely garret. To tell the truth, I understand why a girl might find a soft & comforting pillow, have a sleepy cup of cocoa & put her head into the gas oven. Don't get me wrong – I would not be that selfish nor do anything to hurt the Wriggler. Yet some nights, lying in my bed, I think that if I was never to wake up again it would be the easiest thing for all concerned. But every morning I get up and I go on, though who knows where. I wish I could see what the future holds. Then again, which of us knows what lies ahead? Nothing fits me, least of all coats & waterproofs so I am hardly going out & you know how I turn sour when I am cooped up. If I do manage to do a bunk for an hour or two, I look like poor Mildred, who we used to laugh at along the front in Shanklin, all shrammed up against the rimey chill, layered & bundled in never-mind-what or how it smells & just be grateful if it keeps out the wet & even if it don't. On my bad days I think of her and those luckless souls like her & find myself weepy about life's injustices. I picture myself & the Wriggler sleeping in doorways and under carts, though I know full well that

BANTLING

Mim & Da would not see me get that low. But how I am to look after the two of us I have only the faintest notion as yet. Who wants a book-keeper with a brat – which is how people will think of Wriggler, though I hope I never will. On the brighter side, these people here are likely sending me away to London before too long, to some place they know that will help me with my 'pie in the sky' (so almost everyone else tells me) idea to support and bring up the Wriggler by myself. They say it is about the only place in the country to have that sort of scheme. Perhaps there are not so many like me who are set on keeping their child. Most of the other girls here will stay here until the birth, then give their babies up for adoption. But if some folk in London will help, surely it is not as impossible as all that to do it different. Do you remember how we used to talk about London. Like they say, be careful what you wish for. You must think me ungrateful not to have mentioned your kind parcel. The olive oil works a treat on my poor itchy skin. Thank you also for the writing set. I shall take the hint & do my best to stay in touch, come what may. I will send you a postcard of Buckingham Palace too, where I will be expected for tea from time to time, don't you know. It's a funny old world & the gentle rain & frail moonlight fall on us all just the same. Here's hoping 1923 treats you as well as you deserve. Keep your fingers crossed for yours truly. Always with my warmest thoughts, Violet. P.S. If you bump into you-know-who (fat chance!), you can tell

BANTLING

him what you like, I don't care, but not a word to Stan. I'll deal with him as & when.

3 Ellen. Stockwell. 1923.

'I'm cold,' whispered Ellen. 'Put your arm around me. Please.'

From Felix, a sound, more than a breath, less than a sigh.

If it's your own husband, does it count as begging?

'Just a tiny cuddle, that's all. Nothing more, unless you ...'

He shifted away, just a tad, as if only fidgeting in his sleep.

She was marooned. She was cast adrift, here, in this high, chill bed on its sea of boards and linoleum.

She turned her back to him, rolling away from the soft, saggy middle of the mattress towards its cold edges, her nightdress dragging and winding around her waist and legs. A draught seeped down her neck. In the morning, she must ask Mrs Dawson about airing a second eiderdown for the bed. She would do it first thing, as soon as Mrs Dawson arrived for work. Small mercy that her mother could not see her own daughter reduced to a single daily-woman to help her run Felix's household. And that with all that being a vicar's wife implied.

She tugged the neck of her nightdress closer.

Felix had a nerve. Lying there for all the world as though he were asleep. He could not possibly think he could fool her. Far from it. He was an open book. He would pass wind horribly as he woke up and dip toast fingers into his breakfast egg forty-five minutes later. He would deliver an impassioned sermon on Sunday about love and duty while she sang and bent her head and thought about shopping lists and which rugs needed to be beaten on the Monday. Then he'd come back home to collect gravy in his moustache as he ate the roast.

This was what passed as marriage. A jumble of courtesies and banalities. They lived with each other respectfully, politely, cautiously, forever circling one another at a measured distance. They were so careful that Ellen had lost track of who she might have been.

She was like a shipwrecked sailor in this marriage, words becoming rusty, her tongue swollen and clumsy with disuse, and every now and then still dreaming of rescue.

When Felix had settled again to that rhythmic snuffling of his, she got out of bed. She could see the faint embers of last night's fire in the grate on his side of the room. Nothing seemed to warm the floor where she stood. Her feet were chilly already, which reminded her. She must speak to the coal-merchant tomorrow about the next delivery.

Here was the door. She ran her hands over it. The handle had disappeared into the shadows, wasn't where it should be. There are sprites that play in the dark and they amuse themselves by making mischief for humans.

BANTLING

Her fingers closed around the handle.

Move gently, Ellen, move as smoothly, as quietly, as your breath.

The latch clicked as it turned, the door caught for a moment on its frame. She must ask Mrs Dawson to oil all the latches and hinges when she had a moment. She opened the door only as much as she needed to slip into the passage.

She picked her way along the landing, staying away from the walls with their traps of small tables and trinkets. Sprites and goblins had stretched the space while she was in bed and played who knows what other tricks. Perhaps she was no longer in the upstairs hallway of her own home, but stumbling into a faerie place and time.

Better a goblin's malice than the thoughts running round her mind.

The newel at the head of the stairs appeared under her hand. One stair, two stairs, three stairs, four. On the fourth, she found the landing in its usual place. A softening in the shadows ahead must be the glass in the bathroom door. She opened the door, the click of it loud into the silence. Her feet burned on the cold tiles.

The crumpled glass of the window by the basin glittered with flecks of gold and silver from the street lamp beyond. The hem of her nightdress and the skin of her feet were mottled blue, grey, yellow by the weak light. For years, when she was still a little girl, she would creep secretly out of bed in a similar darkness and quiet, and watch the gas lamps being turned off in the street at dawn, one by one, the day starting before the night was done, with Ellen the sole witness. The magic and the solitude had made her special. Perhaps she had only done it for a few weeks. Mother had put a stop to it quick enough.

She sat down on the floor, pressing her back against the bath, wrapping her arms around her knees, her eyes adjusting to the dark, feeling the cold behind her, beneath her, all around. Greys and browns, slightly lighter, slightly darker, spread like lichens across the floor. Shadows shifted just out of sight. The nightdress's thick material held back some of the chill, but not for long. She waited until she shivered and could not stop shivering, the iciness touching the skin of her back, her feet, her face, her arms, spreading up her thighs, reaching her bones, numb and not numb all at once.

She pinched and twisted her nipple through the flannelette, hard, harder. As the pain rose and seized hold, she greeted a familiar friend.

She was standing on the edge of an abyss. She peered deep into it. There was no end or bottom to it. The abyss was inside her. Her foot was slipping. Any moment now she would keel over into it and be lost for ever.

This is no way to live.

You cross a line when a thought finds words.

This is no way to live.

BANTLING

You frighten yourself.

There was a towel hanging over the bath. She pushed it against her nose and mouth. It was damp and musty, overdue for a wash. She whispered into it, muffling the words, wanting, not wanting, to hear them. *This is no way to live*. She was shaking. She was a marsh, she was quicksand, shifting, deep and treacherous.

She said the words softly into the dark. *This is no way to live*, the words just as powerful for being in the open. They were outside her, invisible in the dark, and they were straining inside her. She said them again. She tasted them in her mouth, their strangeness, their rightness, their heft. Words that undid her moorings. Words that spirited away her marriage, ridiculed her future, unravelled the present. They were the fairies and goblins come out to play.

A light knock on the bathroom door.

'Ellen. Are you in there, dear. Are you all right?'

He would not come in without her say-so.

'Go back to bed,' she called. 'I'll be there in a minute.'

Her eye had grown used to the dark. She stood and watched the ghostly face in the mirror. Herself and not herself. What was hidden in the mirror, looking back out. She splashed cold water over her eyes. The pipes shuddered when she turned off the tap. She must remember to ask Mrs Dawson to arrange a plumber.

Felix had left a lighted candle for her in the hallway. In its flicker, she saw streaks on her nightdress bodice. Blood from her breast or a shadow masquerading. She held the cloth away from her body to prevent more chaffing. She let it drop again. Her bare feet felt like glass, heavy and clumsy, about to shatter and splinter against the floor.

In the linen cupboard she found her medicine, took a sip and felt its warmth blaze in her mouth and trickle down her throat until it reached her stomach.

By her bed was a glass of water. She licked the last of the medicine from her lips and took a gulp of water, swilled it round her mouth, swallowed. Cold as it was, it did not quite quench the earlier heat, now reaching her head.

He lifted the eiderdown for her and she got into bed. Her place was already cold. He patted her shoulder.

'Chin up,' he said.

She put her glass feet against his for warmth. He shuddered a little and pulled away. She turned on her side, her face away from him, and pinched her hurting breast with one hand to keep the malevolent sprites at bay. There was still the faintest taste of brandy in her mouth. The bed creaked and dipped as he shifted about. She felt his warmth at her back. With a little snatch of breath when their bare skin touched, he placed his feet around hers and so they settled to sleep.

BANTLING

4 Violet. Southampton. 1923.

Southampton, 20 January, Dear Mim & Da, I am keeping pretty well, all things considered, though I had a rough patch over Christmas & was much in bed, which is why you did not hear more from me. I am better now. I missed you all terribly & hope you had a fair enough time in spite of everything. They are decent Christians here & will see me on my feet again. They are trying to find a place in London I can go to, where I will be looked after & able to keep the little one also. It would be with a Christian fellowship. They set up such a scheme a few years ago, so I would not be the first. I am scared to think of going that far away to strangers, but if it comes off, it's the best offer I am likely to have. There would be a weekly charge for board & lodgings, but I can pay for most of it from my savings until I get another position, which they will help me do as well, so I do not think there will be a problem there. You have done so much already, but if you could see your way to helping me out with the doctor's & midwife's fees & other necessities, I would be everlasting grateful. I have gone over and over the figures & I will be short about ten pounds & seven shillings all in. I know it is a lot, but I will pay you back as soon as ever I can, I promise. I don't like to ask you this on top of everything else, but there is no-one else to turn to. The clergyman who delivers my letter to you will explain better than I can about the Fellowship. Please do not

BANTLING

blame Stan or take against him. It is not his fault, not in the slightest. I have let him down too. My predicament is because of my own foolishness. Please do not say a word to him if you can help it. Of course, I cannot ask you to go against your consciences, so you must do as you see fit if you run into each other. But as Da always says, I should do my own dirty work. I will write to Stan in due course, but have not the foggiest what to say to him just now. If he asks after me, please just tell him I have gone to London because I wanted a change. It's true. A clean break & fresh start will be best all round. I would say sorry again & again until my voice goes hoarse, but it would not change a thing. But I am your sorry daughter & send my sorry love to you, Violet.

5 Ellen. Stockwell. 1923.

Freshly-poured as it was, the coffee cup between Ellen's hands was already barely more than lukewarm. It could not be just her imagination that the weather was more severe than last January. At this rate, she would be wearing gloves by lunch-time to do her jobs around the house. She had to visit the coal-merchant. She wrote it down. Next, she wrote *make sure there is a fire built in Felix's study*. It was not good for him to sit for a long time in a chilly room. The pattern on the wallpaper looked even worse this morning, enough to give a person the goose-bumps. A most peculiar choice by the previous incumbent or his wife, though anyone could see that it had cost a pretty penny. She would have to get used to it. Felix would not waste good money repapering what was perfectly serviceable. Naturally – and who could disagree? – there were many more important matters to fret about.

There was nothing in the newspaper worth speaking of. The French and Belgians shaking their cock feathers in the Ruhr, as much at the British as at the Hun. Russia as tragic as ever. The Tsar's men still holding some ground in Siberia, such a long way east it surely didn't count as the same country. The Reds were killing people willy-nilly. Would they never come to their senses?

The letters that had arrived this morning were no

more cheerful. She opened one that was agitating again to raise the school-leaving age. There was a request from the Fellowship that she could do nothing about, though she wished them well, and yet another appeal to sit on yet another committee, this one determined to eradicate slums, those festering sores and disgraceful blights on a civilised society and so on and so forth. Felix would have her attending in a flash except it was way over in the East End of London and there was enough poverty on their doorstep to last a life-time. He'd flung himself into improving the lot of the locals from the start. She'd lost count of the times in the last few months he'd come back fizzing about what he'd seen over towards Nine Elms and Battersea and in those dwellings behind Stockwell Road. Dirt floors in some places and walls wetter on the inside than the out. It was eye-opening, without a doubt, but for herself, there had been more than enough to keep her busy in the immediate surrounds of the vicarage. Organising bazaars, baking and bottling for the same, appealing for blankets for the needy, rallying the choir; all those were more up her street.

'Can you imagine it? St Michael's Fellowship has asked me if I know a family that would take in a girl for several months before and after her confinement.' She was only making conversation for the sake of it.

She was nowhere yet near knowing who was good for what, who could be relied on for money or goods or time. Just remembering faces, putting them to names was a big job in its own right.

Extra blankets.

'That's somewhat irregular,' said Felix, barely looking up from his notes and scribbles. 'Surely your Fellowship has homes where they put their unfortunate mothers-to-be?'

'Generally speaking, you're right. This is a slightly unusual case and in the way of an experiment.' She gestured to her upper lip. He took the hint, for once, and wiped away the drips of egg and crumbs of toast clinging to his moustache. 'You know their interest is in keeping mother and child together.'

'Laudable, perhaps,' said Felix. 'Unconventional and probably impractical.'

'They certainly are not a rescue mission for destitute or fallen women,' said Ellen. 'They usually help young ladies from professional and upper-class families who can afford to support the young woman and her child within the family. This case is a bit different. They say here she's a well-behaved working girl, not up in the usual class of girls they assist, but well above that of the ordinary run of rescued women.' She read aloud, '... *a very clean girl. Having supported herself for some years as a book-keeper, she has no immediate need of professional training*.'

He glanced up. 'Other than moral instruction, one presumes.' He looked down again and tutted quietly. 'I've lost my train of thought. Ah, yes.'

Felix was hunching over his papers, his eyes and mind again on something quite other than her.

Wash towels?

The pain in her bruised breast anchored her. If not for that, she was as inconsequential as smoke haze.

'Are you preparing something in particular?' she asked him.

'Order of service for a funeral.'

'More coffee?'

Felix shook his head without looking up.

She had never expected to live like this.

She looked out towards the garden, ugly and disordered, blackened leaves clinging to dark branches, bare mud, ochre-coloured mist, funereal privet shrouded in the distance. The dead damp hand of nature. Years still to come of living in a place that might never feel like home.

She twisted the skin on the inside of her wrist. Just a little harder. There. Better.

Noisy pipes. Plumber.

Her finger pressed against the letter. 'What should I reply?' she asked.

'My dear, I bow to your expertise and tact.' He did not give a fig, was just humouring her. 'Presumably nobody springs to mind?'

Spring. Now there was a word and a half. It was still too early for buds on the trees or shrubs. Winter was barely half over. The roses would not be ready for pruning for weeks and weeks. Everything looked thin, untidy. Spring was still a world away, but the windows needed cleaning already.

'A little of your time to discuss this would be welcome. You are so much more familiar with our parishioners' circumstances than I am.'

He sighed gently. 'Bear with me, dear. I'm meeting with a bereaved family shortly. I have to show them something in return for my fee. Weddings, funerals, we can't do without them. I know I've only been installed here six months, but a city parish seems to cost so much more than a rural one. I have no idea where all the money goes.'

He worked hard, she gave him that, not that there was much to show for it. He minded more than he let on. They lived on a shoe-string, his superiors took no notice of him, the importunate demands came and came and his Chaplaincy at the maternity hospital hardly brought in two farthings. As far as his own wife and home went, he was a mean skinflint, but it was a different story where the parishioners were concerned. He was forever laying out for whitewash and medicine. In less than half a year he'd become their unofficial money-lender. She felt sorry for all those pinched-faced people, of course, anybody would. All the same. Loans, my foot. And she had to live with this nasty wallpaper. Still, it gave a purpose to his life. More than she could say for her own.

Her bruised nipple throbbed and caught against her underclothes. There was no real harm in what she did to herself. On the contrary, it stopped her floating away.

Piles of reproachful letters. Housework. A shipwreck of a bed. Ministering to Felix and his calling. It was not enough. She tore the slum letter into pieces and let them flutter onto the tablecloth.

Felix held out his cup to be refilled without so much as glancing up. She added milk, a lump of sugar.

'Don't you agree this house is a tad too big for us?' she said. It was a whim, nothing more, something to get a rise from him.

'It's a vicarage,' he said. 'It's useful to have a spare room or two. We use most of them one way or another.'

She flapped the letter from the Fellowship. 'Didn't you say your maternity hospital opens its door to young women exactly like this one?'

'I suppose so,' he said. 'They don't like to turn anybody away if they can help it, providing the girl seems unlikely to repeat her mistake.'

'Well, then.'

The Fellowship girl would never materialise, not in Ellen's house. But Felix took the bait.

He glanced up, but he'd made sure his face would give nothing away.

'You are surely not thinking of inviting the girl to live here?' It was gently said. He looked down again and wrote another sentence or two.

There was a demon inside her this morning. She

smiled. 'You always understand me before I understand myself.'

He shook his head. 'You are full to the brim with kindly sentiments, Ellen, but having one of those young women living here, it's not practical.'

'An unholy muddle, perhaps?' She tapped the Fellowship letter, wilfully misunderstanding him. Let him say what he thought for once.

'I wouldn't put it like that, but it might be, let us say, complicated.' He had finally put down his pencil. 'A push too far for some of our parishioners.'

'It would seem we were condoning immorality, perhaps?'

She poured herself another cup of almost cold coffee. It was quite possible Mrs Dawson had not heated the pot properly. She would speak to her about that when they discussed lunch.

'All those grumblers in your congregation who think the poor make their own misfortunes? Or are you worried about mass apoplexy at the sight of an unwed mother living here? Isn't it part of your mission to lead by example, to show that the best way to do Christian work is to get your hands dirty?'

He helped himself to the last of the toast.

'We shouldn't judge our flock,' he said. 'There are different ways to serve.'

She knew he meant that he relied on the most thin-lipped to fill the collection plate. All the same, she had him. He wore his hemmed-in look. He welcomed everyone who walked through his doors, including far too many robust men without employment as far as some better-off members of his congregation were concerned. Not just local men who'd fallen on hard times either, but itinerants who had taken to the road found their way to him, as though the vicarage flourished a beacon on its chimney pots. He'd had known their like, his lads, in the army, felt sympathy for them to this day. And who did Felix expect to feed them and send them onwards clean and shod?

The demon chivvied her along. 'What's one more unfortunate girl? With a mother-to-be here, we could set an example of how to love the sinner in spite of her sin. I thought that was at the heart of your ministry.'

She sipped her coffee. He sipped his. Drops of liquid settled on his moustache. She started to gather together the toast crusts, stood up to push one through the bars of Colbert's cage.

'The bishop would probably approve,' she added. 'The diocese has representatives among our Fellowship members.'

This time, he looked at her directly and smiled more warmly. It was the mention of the bishop that had done it. She knew him better than she had thought in the middle of the night. Those gloomy thoughts, just tricks of the shadows.

'You see, Ellen my dear, that's exactly why you're so valuable to me and my work. Your generous heart is coupled with such foresight, while here am I, my head knocking between the clouds of abstraction and the mire of pounds and pence.'

Her cheeks went red, she felt it. She was so easy to please. She could almost overlook a few toast crumbs still hanging among his whiskers.

'You flatter me,' she said, though there was more than a little truth in what he said.

He stared at the ceiling. 'Bishop or no bishop, I'm not convinced that having that sort of girl living here is practical. How long would she stay? What if she falls back on her old habits?'

She buttered one of the crusts on her plate. A smidgen of jam would do no harm either. She would most certainly put the rest of the crusts on the bird-table. Those poor little birds, shivering and hungry in the freezing cold. Lucky Colbert!

'It would be up to us to make sure she does not err again. The Fellowship's aim is to keep mother and child together by setting her on the path to earning a respectable living,' she answered. 'It usually takes six to twelve months, if it happens at all.' Mostly, she knew, those girls fell by the wayside or had to give up their children for one reason or another. Life proved too tempting or too hard. 'This young woman looks promising. She already has some qualifications and experience, but as you mentioned, she needs moral guidance to keep her resolve firm. Your forte, Felix.'

He put a dollop of marmalade onto his toast and chewed slowly.

'Perhaps, perhaps,' he said. 'All the same. Crying babies. Unpredictable young women.'

'One woman. One baby. Not a troupe of them.'

Listen to her. She sounded so convincing, so convinced.

He picked up his pencil again, but paused. 'Most of the responsibility for the girl and the infant would fall on you, on top of all your other responsibilities. It would be too much, I fear.'

Of course. He was worried he might be inconvenienced. All the same, he was chewing over this mad proposition of hers and she had held his attention for minutes on end now. Any moment now, he'd be encouraging the girl to move in.

She looked as though she was weighing up the pros and cons.

'She could help me around the house. If she is to be a mother, she will need to take on such responsibilities, to establish a routine.' Ellen glanced outside again, where the pretty beading of a spider's web caught her eye. 'Perhaps she cares for gardening.' Or perhaps she could negotiate the minefield of the flower-arrangement rota. 'To have something young about the house, Felix, think how wonderful that would be.'

She had gone too far. Felix's face registered alarm, then blankness again. Her demon retired satisfied. Neither Ellen nor Felix ever made any allusion, however faint, to that dreadful time of hers. Sadness he could not alleviate was not to Felix's taste. It had been easier to harbour her grief by herself.

He jotted down more notes, checked hymns, crossed out one number, wrote another.

Coffee pot, she wrote. *Heating thereof*.

He surprised her with his next words.

'There's no need to test yourself. Already, I sometimes think you are overdoing it.' He used his vicar's voice, as gentle as he would be with bereaved parishioners. 'For you, motherhood wasn't to be. That is all we know, and all we need to know.'

They were not many words, but more than he had said on the subject for half a decade.

She rang the bell briskly for Mrs Dawson to clear the table, and started to pile the crockery neatly in readiness. She scraped the butter from the sides of their plates back into the butter-dish.

There was something in her mind about the difference between filling her time being useful and having a proper purpose to her life. To be sure, actually having a child might not answer all life's ills, but being a mother supplied a woman with a purpose and a place. It gave her the right to hold up her head, no matter what.

'Back then was a long time ago,' she said after a little while. 'The best part of five years. They go fast, don't they? Time is a great healer, activity its balm, as Mother used to say, so I keep busy. I don't fritter away my life just because I can't bear children.'

There, it was said finally, although strictly speaking

she was not sure the fault lay with her. That there was nothing structurally wrong had been the doctor's judgement after all that embarrassing probing. The miscarriage was merely one of those accidents of nature that happened more often than one would like. It might well be different the next time, the doctor had said, though she and her husband should probably try again sooner than later. He'd been looking at her date of birth in her notes. There had seemed little point in passing this information on to Felix. He'd got it into his head that she was a fragile, damaged vessel, had made it clear he would consider himself a low brute to risk her health. And still her monthlies came, even more angrily now than before, but in her chaste shipwreck bed there was no chance of a last-minute surprise. It had occurred to her more than once that most husbands might take a less self-sacrificial view of the matter. It could be worse, she supposed. Felix did not maltreat her.

'There are many more ways you could support me in my work, if you have some time on your hands,' he suggested. 'From here in the vicarage, if you don't feel up to visiting a lot of homes.'

Perhaps he meant to spare her the sight of happy families, of healthy babies and mothers, or possibly their opposite, so she would not resent others doing poorly that which nature had denied her. In his mind he had relegated her making lists and jars of broth and to selling tombola tickets to save souls overseas. Piffling tasks without design or purpose. He was doing it again. Not listening, pushing his own vision down her throat.

'In any event, I hardly think you can speak of frittering away your life,' he continued. 'I could not ask for a better helpmeet. I am an extremely fortunate man in my choice of wife.'

He gulped the last of his coffee.

What did her husband know of her life?

Felix's faith cradled everything he did. All his actions, however trifling, were offered up as duty, as sacrifice, in peace as in war. He spoke often about duty, in the pulpit and out of it. His life had a meaningful pattern radiating from a faith-filled core, whereas hers was a blank, or so it must seem to other people. It certainly seemed so to her. A child would have loved Ellen without question, made Ellen the centre of its world. Everyone needed that, surely. It was not so much to ask.

The whole of her breast ached, and she imagined it purple and swollen and tender beneath her dress. The remnants of the marmalade went back into the pot, the toast crusts put aside for bread-crumbs and the birds.

She knew in her heart that nothing really mattered, but even now Felix behaved as though she still cared.

'On the other hand, if you have the strength and inclination, there are many families who would appreciate your visits,' he said, his eyes as bright as a suitor's. 'I could make a list. As General and his Lieutenant, we could bring hope and piety back into their lives.'

'Felix. One step at a time. Remember that people are just people. Mostly, they don't have your gifts. I do not have your gifts. Not everything makes sense to me all the time.' It was the closest she had ever got to admitting to him that her faith and their baby-to-be had died together.

His attention had turned away. He tidied his papers, dabbing at his lips and moustache with his napkin. He stood, picking up his papers and books, concentrating on putting them in the right order. The day was no longer their own.

Mrs Dawson loaded the tray; was asked to make up a fire in Felix's study and replied that she had done so already. Ellen crossed that task off her list. Mrs Dawson was on her way out to do the shopping, if Ellen had anything to add to the list.

'You're right of course,' Felix said, when they were on their own again. His face gave nothing away. 'We should not be too ambitious too soon.'

'I don't know what got into me,' she tried to say, 'I was only teasing about the girl,' but he was already opening the door and gave no sign he heard.

The door of his study clicked shut. Outside, the morning sky was overcast again, the daylight obscure and dull. The study door opened again.

The front door closed after him.

BANTLING

The clock made the sound of time passing. Ellen and Colbert were the only tiny flickers of life in the house.

Ellen rubbed her hands together so hard they seemed to burn. It had the benefit of restoring circulation. Her fingers had gone quite white. She squeezed her breast hard through her clothing until she felt herself dissolve into the pain and grow sturdy again. And now she must get going, she had a full day ahead of her. She picked up her list.

Write letters. Sort jumble. Coal.

Thin pickings.

BANTLING

6 Violet. Southampton. 1923.

~~The Mainland, 25 January 1923 Dear Stan, I am sorry if you had a sudden worry or shock when I went off like that. I didn't mean to cause you any bother, but this is my business not yours. You are a kind man, but we neither of us are what the other needs. I have gone away. I could not face you. Please do not ask Mim and Da where I am. I have asked them not to tell you Oh heavens, Violet, pull yourself together. Either say what you have to say or put a sock in it.~~

BANTLING

7 Ellen. Stockwell. 1923.

The door-bell jangled again and again, loud and long. Somebody was tugging and tugging on the bell-pull. The door-knocker banged again and again. It was all a terrible racket, filling up the hallway, filling the empty house, filling her head to bursting.

Bother and blast. Everyone was still out. Ellen would have to get the door herself. She would tell whoever it was they would have to wait until Felix returned or they could come back again once he was home.

'I'm looking for the vicar's wife,' said the man on the doorstep. He was tall and she had to tilt back her head to look him in the eye. She noticed dirt in all the tiny lines of his face, like a fine black net.

'I'm Mrs Holcroft. How can I help you?'

He held his hat in his grimy hands. She'd couldn't remember seeing him before, so perhaps he wasn't a regular church-goer. Perhaps he was one of Felix's former men. It was hard to keep them all in mind.

"Henry Wingrove. We're new to the area. It's my own wife needs you. Things are going bad with her. It's the baby. Midwife's on her way. You best come with me now.'

She thought, why me? What's any of that got to do with me? One can't say that, of course, not out loud.

BANTLING

'Perhaps it would be better to wait for Reverend Holcroft,' she suggested.

The man was most insistent, most urgent. His sister-in-law had sent him, told him the vicar's wife would see them through. They couldn't afford to waste no time.

His husbandly concern overwhelmed her. She had no choice, no choice at all. Duty, duty. One rose to life's challenges as best one could. She pinned on a hat and set forth.

At the top of the rickety stairs, Wingrove opened a door and gestured her through. She heard a low keening; perhaps the wind, perhaps a child.

The open door screened whatever was just inside the room, but it was the awful smell that stopped Ellen in her tracks. Medieval. That was the politest word for it. A stench – one had to be honest – of unwashed people living on top of each other, old sweat and decaying vegetables. Also –there were no two ways around it – of unlidded chamber pots left standing. The tail end of January with nothing to take the chill off the room and still the stink was high.

The puling sound in the room seemed full of meaning, but had no real words in it. It was a sound to raise the hairs on your neck.

So dull and gloomy in here too, no glowing gas mantle, no electric bulb hanging from the ceiling as far as she could see, and precious little daylight either. She made out the two children jumbled up together on the small bed in front of her, jammed under the window, she stepped forward and stooped down to smile at them.

The boy looked scared out of his wits, poor thing, cuddling a little girl who could not have been more than a year and a half old.

Heavens knows what the smell would be like if it was not so cold.

Bare floorboards. The dead remains of a tiny fire in the small grate.

The girl was wearing no more than a short grubby cardigan, with not even a rag on her lower half. Never mind decency, she must be about to catch her death of cold. And as for hygiene ... The room was likely to be rife with germs, a breeding ground for cholera, typhoid, Spanish influenza.

Stop it, Ellen. Pull yourself together.

There was no point getting stirred up about germs at this moment.

Wingrove squeezed behind and past her.

Chin up and best foot forward. No use coming over all namby-pamby or wondering what on earth had possessed her to rush over here.

Something reeked strongly, sickly, sweet and familiar, like discarded uncooked offal. The atmosphere of the room was closing in on her, making it almost impossible to breath. She tried not to think what the sound was. A broken sound, stopping, starting, closer, more and more insistent. It was in the room with them, it was slicing into her head.

She busied herself with what was in front of her.

'Hello, children. You look like a very grown-up little boy looking after your sister. Can you tell me your names? Or has that greedy old cat got your tongue?'

From the blank way they looked at her, there was a chance both children were deaf. Or mute. Or even a little simple. That was quite usual, so she understood, amongst this class of people. It was a deficiency in their diet, supposedly. Or lack of air.

Ah well, onwards and upwards.

She would open the window for a start, this minute, before she so much as looked behind her. When it was open, she might be able to breathe again.

Ellen removed her gloves and tucked them into her handbag. There was nowhere prudent to put her hat, so it stayed on her head.

Black mould speckled the wall below the window. The curtains had no lining and the hems were dark with dirt and grease, the window frame crumbling in places and the sash cord gone the way of all flesh. She put her gloves back on and pushed and jiggled at the frame for all she was worth. The window was smeary and filthy. Her nose was beginning to itch already.

'Do you know how to open the window, dear?' Her throat was ticklish and when she swallowed, she tasted dust.

The boy shook his head. 'Can't. S'nailed.'

So much for that. At least the boy was no mute.

'Mrs Holcroft, ma'am. Please, my wife.'

She turned towards Wingrove crouching in the cleft between two beds that took up most of the room. There was not space enough to swing a cat. A woman – she must be the wife – sprawled on the far bed, leaning against the wall in the semi-darkness and bundled up in a none-too-clean eiderdown. Those thwarted sobbing, gasping sounds were coming from her. Of course.

She looked up at Ellen. Ellen did not look away, did not let herself flinch.

'It's no good, no good at all this time,' the woman whispered to her. All of a sudden, her skinny face glistened with sweat and turned from far too pale to blotchy, like meat left out on the counter. Nobody healthy could be hot in that room, but this woman flapped away the eiderdown and began to fan herself with one hand. The shoulders of her dress drooped down her arms and her wrists stuck out from her sleeves like candlesticks, but her swollen belly strained against her flimsy skirt.

I am out of my depth, thought Ellen.

The toddler started to wail. A thin, shrill noise, enough to set everyone's teeth on edge. The boy fetched her onto his lap, jiggling her, trying to shush her, getting nowhere. She needed a good deal more than that. Their mother – Ellen assumed she was their mother – turned towards them.

BANTLING

'Shush-shush. Dorrie.'

It looked for one awful moment as though she was getting up to deal with them herself. Wingrove held her by shoulders and she slumped back, her face contorted.

She put down her handbag and her eye caught a postcard pinned to the wall, a young woman with loose hair and flowing draperies. Hard to see more in the dingy gloom.

Ellen picked up the girl, bare as she was, and rubbed her back. Her little behind was as cold as a dead fish and her feet like chips of ice.

'Your sister needs a nappy, dear, and something to keep her warm,' she said. 'Do you think you can find something? An old sheet or towel would do very well.' It was worth a try, through frankly, she had no hopes that anything suitable could be produced. If only she'd thought, if only she'd known, she'd have brought that sort of thing with her. She eyes flicked around, hoping to see something she could use, but got no further than the couple.

The wife clutched at Wingrove so tightly his fingers were white. With his free hand, he stroked her face and hair as she sank against him, and he held her. Neither of them spared her so much as a glance. Wingrove held his wife as though there was nobody else in the same room, nobody else in the whole wide world.

That lucky woman. That poor lucky woman.

'My dear,' she said, intruding upon them.

Her head was beginning to ache awfully. She could imagine the fuss Felix would make about her being here. Ellen, he would say, this is the sort of visit best left to me, and he'd tell her she should stick to supervising the ladies' Mission teas. Many apologies, Felix, but it was too late for that now. It stood to reason there were times when only a woman's presence would do.

'My name is Mrs Holcroft, from the Vicarage. You must be in some considerable discomfort. Let's make you more comfortable, Mrs … Mrs …'

'Wingrove,' said Wingrove. 'Mrs Alice Wingrove.'

'Of course.' How silly she must sound. 'Mrs Wingrove, let's put your feet up on the bed, keep you flat for the moment.'

Everywhere that sickly awful smell. It was sitting in the back of her nose, had been there for years, ever since Ellen's own dreadful time, waiting to clutch at her and rip the heart from her all over again.

Alice Wingrove whimpered. She was surely not intending to give birth here with only Ellen to help?

Wingrove lifted his wife's legs, so that she sat propped against the bedstead bars, gasping for breath, while he settled her skirt around her legs.

A man who could comfort his wife no matter what, that was a rare man.

He seemed to run out of steam; he stood there like a post, holding her hand. That was all very well and good, as far as it went.

BANTLING

But.

But.

Alice Wingrove was a terrible colour, not so different from the dingy yellow pattern – probably roses once upon a time, it was almost impossible to tell – behind her head. It was very clear that her pain was not of the usual sort. And she was far, far too quiet for a woman about to give birth.

It was the Wingroves' bad luck to find her at home and not Felix. He always had the right words.

This would not do. This self-pitying sort of nonsense would do nobody any good at all. She must pull herself together; stop feeling sorry for herself for a start. All that had happened to her was back then and all this happening to Mrs Wingrove was here and now. It was only that the conversation with Felix this morning had brought everything to mind again. That and the smell.

'Mr Wingrove. It's probably best if I take over for a little while. Perhaps you could see to the children?'

To her surprise, he did as she suggested, taking the infant from her, though he started going on at the boy – he called him Bertie – about Doris's caterwauling doing their ma no good at all, and where was Doris's clothes? and was there any sign of their Aunt Flo yet? and Bertie answered that Doris had wet herself so he'd taken her things off her. He sounded close to tears himself, and who could blame him?

BANTLING

The counterpane was dark and sticky where Alice Wingrove had been sitting.

Don't think about it. Do what you can.

The unhappy woman's eyes flicked here and there, back and forth, around and about. Sometimes they settled for a moment on her husband, then off and away they went again. She was paler than anybody had a right to be and was shivering so much Ellen could swear she heard the bed-frame rattling. Alice Wingrove wrapped her skinny arms around her distended body and rolled onto her side. Something was staining the back of her skirt. She was making the sorts of sounds that Ellen herself had made a lifetime ago.

'Is there any hot water? More blankets, if you have them? Even towels will do. Your wife should be kept warm.'

Wingrove frowned. 'I could do her a hot-water bottle, except that there's probably not enough left on the meter.'

Ellen could manage a shilling for the gas. This was no time for false pride, for pride of any sort, she would have said if he'd refused it, but he took the silver quick enough and went to feed the meter on the landing, ordering Bertie to fill the kettle from the bucket, not too much, mind you.

Ellen eased the eiderdown under Alice Wingrove. It was pretty much ruined already. There was no justice in whether you had it hard or easy. Just look at some of those who sailed through it when they'd done nothing to deserve it. She folded the eiderdown over the woman's legs, tucked her own scarf around Alice Wingrove's neck and shoulders, and pretended to herself that her own hands were quite steady, thank you. It would have been a good time to pray, if she'd thought it would do any good. Instead, she took off her coat and tucked it around the shivering woman. Desperate times, desperate measures. With any luck, any mark could be sponged off, would not show up too badly.

Wingrove was back in the room by that time. He dumped Doris on the other bed and ordered Bert to keep a good eye on her this time. At least the girl was a bit more decent now, with less chance of having an accident over the bedclothes.

Wingrove lifted the mantle off the gas jet on the wall and set it aside as carefully as if it might have to last for ever. It was not until he had picked up a length of rubber tubing, fitted one end of it over the gas pipe, and jammed the other end onto a gas ring standing on a tiny rickety table that Ellen grasped what he was doing. Only one gas jet – better than none at all – but nevertheless ... He lit the gas under the kettle. The flames hissed and flickered bright yellow. There appeared to be an asbestos mat between the ring and the table – a folding one from the flimsy look of its legs – but the whole caboodle could go up in flames or down in scalding water at any minute. If one of the children fell over or moved out of turn ...

Leave worrying to Wingrove and keep her own mind on what she must do.

'You must be brave Mrs Wingrove. For them ...' Ellen nodded towards the children. Bertie was standing holding the metal bars at the foot of the bed, staring at his mother, great big eyes in that peaky little face. 'For them as well as for yourself. You will bear it, because you have to, though it does not seem at this moment that you can.'

Out of nowhere, Ellen knew that she would breathe the necessary strength into Alice Wingrove, would walk through this dark valley with her and out the other side. She was not sure what had come over her. A minor sort of miracle, some might say. She might even give Him the benefit of the doubt if today ended well.

She took Alice's hand. Clammy. Cold.

The woman was nodding. Her head was jerking too fast, too hard. She was thrashing about, banging her head against the bed rods, fighting to get to her feet.

'Shush-shush, dear. There, there. Lie back. I'll help you.' She tried to press Alice back onto the bed.

They were dreadful, the noises Alice was making, like some sort of a wounded animal, as if she'd lost all sense of herself.

Doris started wailing all over again. Bertie was sniffing and looked as though he would start blubbing any moment. It was hardly their fault, but one thing was certain, the children were not helping the situation one jot. She herself was having enough trouble thinking in all this brouhaha. The smell in the room, the closeness of the air, made a pain that sliced across her eyes and through the bones of her head.

'The children should go into another room,' said Ellen. 'Or rather, Bertie can run for the doctor. I'll give him a note to take. Your wife needs proper medical attention.'

It was a harsh look Wingrove gave her. Harsh, exasperated, unfair. She really did not understand it at all. Ellen was doing her best. Her eyes began to water. There was no need at all to look at her as though she were somehow in the wrong. He could not surely expect her to deliver the child by herself.

'The other room's Flo's and her lot's, like the shop downstairs, not for us to use, not until she gets back. Like I said, Flo's out fetching someone from the hospital,' said Wingrove.

For small mercies, give thanks. But why was it taking so long?

'For pity's sake, you kids, give it a rest. Go sit on the landing if you can't shut up. Just clear off.'

He lifted his arm and she got the impression he might actually strike one or both of the children.

'Has that kettle boiled yet? You say the doctor is on his way? Does he know your wife well?' she asked.

He licked a finger and touched it to the kettle.

'Give it another minute.'

Alice had quietened again, thank heavens. Ellen tucked all the coverings around her yet again.

It was then that Wingrove told her, or perhaps he'd said it earlier, that they'd only been staying here with Flo the past month or so, didn't know the first thing about the hospitals and doctors around here. Ellen would see to getting Alice into the hospital, deal with all the formalities, like, wouldn't she? He'd pay her back anything it cost, however long it took; he swore it on a stack of Bibles. Just make sure Alice was looked after proper.

'I'll do my best, of course,' she said, and rubbed the floor with her foot to serve as touching wood.

People usually listened to a vicar's wife, but nothing was guaranteed these days. And she couldn't bear the cost. A shilling for the gas meter was one thing, paying for hospital treatment quite another. She had no idea how many charity cases might be admitted at any one time. What if the maternity hospital wanted money in their hand before they would admit Mrs Wingrove? She'd heard of more than one doctor playing that game.

Let them try. Let them just try. They would learn how fierce Ellen could be.

Wingrove thrust a hot-water bottle at her, wrapped up in a piece of greasy flannel. She pressed it against Alice's back.

'The doctor will be here soon,' she assured the woman.

'Won't make no difference. I'm losing this one.'

If faces were a mirror of people's lives, the streets would look as though the dead had risen from the trenches. Still, one came through it, one had to, one way or another.

'If that is so, and I pray it is not, others have been here before you,' Ellen comforted, doing a vicar's wife's heartening duty. 'Don't give up yet, it might not be as hopeless as you think.'

Alice clutched her hand so hard the bones scraped against each other.

In point of fact, it was clear these people could not afford another child. Another infant would not add so very much to the sum of human happiness, its loss not be such a tragedy. 'Besides, there is every chance that this one may yet be safely delivered.'

Alice did not respond. Served Ellen right for spouting nonsense.

'But if your worst fears come true, it will test you in ways you cannot imagine,' she continued. 'But life will one day be bearable again, perhaps sooner than you think.'

It was all platitudes in any case, the sorts of things Felix might say, but without his reassuring conviction. Alice had stopped listening, if she ever had been. Her eyes slipped sideways. It was hard to tell if she was still breathing.

BANTLING

Ellen patted the inert cheek. She was at her wits' end now, had no idea what she could do to bring the woman back. Her head felt as though it were being squeezed in some sort of fiendish contraption. Panic rose like silt inside her, so her breath came short and desperate.

'Look at me, Mrs Wingrove. Look at me. Open your eyes. Please.'

There were the sounds of a door opening somewhere downstairs, footsteps running heavily up the stairs, a woman's strident voice.

'Alice! Alice! I've brung back the nurse.'

Not before time.

Nurse Henderson looked scarcely old enough to have left school, but she had a bossy manner and a torch to support her claim to be a midwife. She set Bertie to bringing his mother some tea.

'Plenty of sugar, mind, dear. I've some extra in my case if you've none.'

She handed Doris over to Flo to sort out in the other room. Wingrove she dispatched with instructions to find a conveyance of some kind, any kind, for his wife.

'Spit in your hand, Alice, and hold tight,' he said before he went downstairs and there was some sort of sound from his wife that might have been both laugh and whimper. After that, she seemed to more or less give up on speech, just wincing, biting her lips, mewling with pain from time to time.

BANTLING

The baby was in quite the wrong position, it turned out. Nurse Henderson would not say what the chances were for mother or child, just that Doctor, her midwives and the hospital had never lost either as yet and she did not intend to be the one to break that record. All the same, she thought it was touch and go. It was a crying shame they had not seen Mrs Wingrove weeks earlier. If she was to have any chance at all now, it would be at the hospital.

'How much is it likely to cost?' whispered Ellen. 'They can't afford much. They seem to have no money at all.'

Nurse Henderson answered that it was the cornerstone of the hospital that all women should have the best possible maternity service. It did not come cheap, but women like Mrs Wingrove did not pay.

Wingrove carried his swollen wife down the narrow stairs and onto the street. Below the rooms was a seedy-looking green-grocer's shop. Alice was lowered into a vegetable barrow that Flo dragged out, all dusty and grubby. Ellen had never imagined such a thing, but it was better than nothing. Beggars can't be choosers, after all, though Ellen would not have put it past Wingrove to have carried his wife in his bare arms wherever she had to go, however far that might be.

Nurse Henderson pushed the smelling salts at Ellen and took off on her bicycle to get everything in order at the hospital.

Wingrove pushed for all he was worth, the barrow

jolting and tilting. Alice Wingrove groaned ever more quietly after each lurch,

When she stopped making any sound other than some harsh, rattling breaths, they stopped and Ellen waved the smelling salts under her nose. Alice started to choke and cough. She came round. The ammonia caught in Ellen's throat and eyes as well, but it cleared her head a little. She was almost running, her breath coming in gulps, her throat burning, her bruised breast hurting to high heaven.

Wingrove touched his wife's hand. 'Be there in half a jiffy, Alice.'

On Alice's face all the lines of pain fell away, just for a moment. For that instant, her skin seemed smooth, her mouth relaxing into the tiniest of smiles.

The peace had lasted no time at all, but it was long enough for Ellen to know that everything would work out for the best. The baby would be born whole and healthy and Alice herself would be well. Suddenly Ellen was filled with a sense of grace and airiness. She put her hand on Alice's shoulder as they rushed on. Reassurance and conviction poured through her touch. Women have a secret language, a strength that they lend each other, invisible to men. It had taken her until now to learn this. Better late than never.

Through high wrought-iron gates and into the forecourt. Later she recalled porticoes and architraves and Doric columns framing the doorway, a stack of bricks, a pile of sand, lengths of scaffolding and timber. She saw

BANTLING

a stretcher on wheels coming towards them, Henry Wingrove scooping Alice off the vegetable barrow, blankets, coat and all, and arranging her gently on the stretched canvas, porters wheeling her into the building. They all followed, Ellen still hurrying to keep up.

Parquet and linoleum flooring. Lysol, floor polish and bright lights. Swift, purposeful, rubber-soled footfalls on the floors and stone stairs. The cries of babies somewhere in the distance. Ellen had the impression that there were no dark corners here, that everything was in the open, scrubbed and illuminated. No place for sprites and imps to make mischief.

The stretcher stopped by a part-open doorway. A glimpse, nothing more, of the room beyond. Cream tiles and surgical lights and enamel trolleys holding those hard cold tools that made her flinch.

Wingrove stepped forward to touch Alice's face and murmur something to her and hold her hand before she was wheeled into the theatre. When Ellen had faced such a moment, she had been alone, Felix busy elsewhere. It was not fair. Life was not fair. Let it be fair this time.

Somebody touched her arm.

'Thank you so much, Mrs Holcroft. You've been a great help.'

Ellen hoped that was true. She could not tell how much she had done or not.

'We won't hold you up any longer,' said Nurse Henderson. She handed Ellen's coat to her. 'It's in a bit of a state, I'm afraid. I do hope it cleans up. Excuse me now. I must go back to my patient.'

Ellen stood her ground. 'I promised I'd stay with her,' she said.

'And so you have,' said Nurse Henderson. 'But now we take over. It does not look so good for her, and every moment counts. Doctor is on her way down. Mr Wingrove, a word before you go.'

Ellen walked back along the corridor. A short plain woman wearing a spotless white linen coat over a tweed skirt and with a stethoscope around her neck moved swiftly down the stairs and along the corridor. Nurses stood aside to let her past. One or two almost curtsied. This must be Doctor, Ellen realised as they passed each other. A woman and a doctor, one and the same. Purposeful. Respected. The times were certainly changing. A shock of emotion arrived so clearly and so suddenly it had no time to disguise itself. Envy.

The heavy doors closed behind her. Ellen stood in the courtyard and gulped in air. She had been living on her nerves for hours, but all things considered, she had not conducted herself too badly in all that excitement. She had stayed calm, on the outside at least, and had been, in some modest way, a soothing presence. To tell the truth, she felt marvellous, uplifted, better than she had for months. Perhaps years.

Clouds darkened the day. She had lost track of time. Windows around the courtyard began to glow here and there as lights were switched on around her. Then the blinds were drawn down, the building turning inwards.

Now that she had come to a halt, Ellen felt the nip in the air, the cold clamminess between her skin and her clothes. She could not bring herself to put on the soiled coat. She had forgotten all about lunch until this minute. Poor Felix. Mrs Dawson would have fixed him something, surely.

She knew that it took Felix no more than a quarter of an hour to walk here from their house, but it was so out of her usual way. She didn't know if she was topsy or versy. Her jubilant mood was sliding away. She was cold, hungry, and, she might as well admit it, a little bit upset and trembly all of a sudden. It was a reaction to everything that had happened. That, and missing lunch. She should have had the sense to ask directions home before the doors had closed.

The sounds of heavy footsteps and wooden creaking. Henry Wingrove reached the gate just before her and opened it to let her through. She held it for him as he manoeuvred the barrow into the street.

'You must be relieved your wife is in such capable hands,' she said.

He shrugged. 'Good news never came out of a hospital. It won't be no different this time, I expect. Anyhow, Alice is too quiet and too greasy-looking. I reckon the kid's a goner.'

'She might need all her strength for herself,' she agreed. 'But let's hope it's a happy outcome all round.'

'Just so long as she pulls through, the rest don't matter.'

She looked around her again, wondering where to go. She felt awfully lost.

He must have read her mind, because he offered to set her on her road, seeing as how it was all a bit unfamiliar to her. It wasn't that much out of his way.

He was a good man, she thought, one who took the best care he could of his wife and his family, and with better manners than one might have expected. She felt safe walking next to him. As she told him, it was being unfamiliar with the area that made her nervous and it all being new and so different to the small town where they had last lived. And the light was failing, too. One never knew what lay in wait in the dark nooks and crannies of the street, did one? Without a doubt, she would get used to it before long and soon she would laugh about getting lost so close to home, but for the moment she very much appreciated his courtesy, especially given he had such a lot on his mind.

He hardly said a thing.

'Are you a military man, Mr Wingrove?' She'd noticed the set of his shoulders earlier, his way of walking, straight-backed and precise, like some of the men who came to Felix. Pushing the barrow, she saw he had a limp, one foot turning in at an angle.

'Was once,' he said.

BANTLING

'My husband, too, before we married. He was a chaplain in Flanders, and before that with the troops that relieved Ladysmith.'

Even now, all these years later, she could hardly speak the name of the cursed place. He did not seem to notice that her voice had thickened. She blinked hard. My, she really did need a little pick-me-up.

'She'll pull through, won't she?'

Now he was looking at her as though she held all the answers.

'Your wife is in the best of hands, I'm sure,' she said.

He turned away. She should be able to find her way from here. He had to get the barrow back to the shop, then front up at the coal-merchants to see if he still had a job. His black-lined hands made sense then, and all at once she knew she'd seen him before, leading the horse and unloading sacks from the cart.

'I'll pop into the hospital tomorrow and see how she's faring,' she said. 'Would that set your mind at rest?'

'You could make sure they're doing everything proper.' he said. 'For herself, I can't see as she'd notice one way or another, not the way she is. Otherwise, it's all down to what the hospital says. If you can trust a word they say.'

8 Ellen. Stockwell. 1923.

The vicarage was orderly, gleaming, spacious when Ellen opened the front door. Smells of coal-smoke and polish lingered in the hallway, wafts of tonight's dinner. Mrs Dawson had been busy while Ellen was out. And made a pretty fair job of it, too, it had to be admitted.

In that other room today, Ellen had not wanted to put her hand on a single thing. But she had overcome her squeamishness, had handled bedding, clothes, children, cups, bowls. She had breathed that fetid air. She had done her duty as best she could. She could be proud of herself.

She hurried to the bathroom. The soiled coat went into the laundry basket. Mrs Dawson could deal with it tomorrow. She scrubbed and scrubbed at her hands and fingernails. The angry geyser in the bathroom spitting out its scalding stream was never to be taken for granted again.

Felix was not in his study, but it smelt of other people's cigarettes. She opened the window wide for five minutes and then added another few coals to the fire. Felix would work in there later as he did every evening. She stood in front of its warmth for a few minutes.

As it turned out, Felix and Mrs Dawson had managed quite nicely without her. As Mrs Dawson put it, these things can't be helped from time to time. The Vicar had had an unexpected visitor, who'd been given a meal of sorts that Mrs Dawson had cobbled together with no notice, and now they'd gone off together. She'd got on with dinner off her own bat and put a sheep's heart stew with dumplings into the oven. Ellen could dish up later when the Vicar got back. There were some prunes soaking in a bowl in the pantry, for afters, and a baked custard to go with. Seeing as how Ellen had missed lunch, Mrs Dawson could fix her some tea and toast. Perhaps a scrap of cheese and all?

Afterwards, Ellen gave Mrs Dawson a hand folding all the sheets for ironing so she could get off on time. It seemed only fair. The linen was white, stain-free, an advertisement for Sunlight soap, drawn thread-work along one edge, a delight to fold and smooth.

The smell from the other room was still in her mouth and nose. To live like that ...

She lit a gas lamp in the hall and one on the upstairs landing, and thought about the rubber tubing Wingrove had used.

She fed the budgie, changed his water and cleaned out the bottom of his cage.

'There's a lovely boy,' she said. 'Pretty Colbert.'

He gurgled back at her and rubbed his head against her finger. He lived better than some families.

There were letters to reply to, her day's to-do list, the sorting out of the remnants from the church's Christmas bazaar. Porcelain and glass and stained doilies. Inlaid boxes with chipped veneers. Unfashionable brooches. The cartons cluttered up the front parlour.

She opened one box to find cushion covers and antimacassars. She checked for signs of moth and put them aside for washing and another bazaar.

Mrs Dawson offered to help shift the parcels into the conservatory before she went off for the day. All the room in the world to lay them out there for sorting, she pointed out. It was the thought of the hungry dark pressing in on the glass even more than the cold that made Ellen say no, not now, perhaps in the morning.

In the empty house, she couldn't settle to anything anymore than she could sit and rest. Having the jitters, her mother used to call it. She would also have said it was no excuse for wasting time. Mother would have been right.

Ellen unwrapped three vases and inspected them for cracks and chips, her hands blackening with newsprint. She thrust the vases back into their box and went upstairs to wash again.

She waited for Felix. The house stretched around her. Had she made any difference at all today? Perhaps with words of comfort, but as far as practicalities went, almost none. A shilling for the meter was about the sum of it. She plumped a few cushions in the chilly front parlour, no point in lighting a fire in there this evening; she straightened a crooked print above the fireplace. Her mind was on Alice, trundled through the streets, more distended than ripe. The midwife's comments had sunk in by now, and Wingrove's grim opinion. Ellen's earlier optimism seemed like a delusion.

In the dragging time before dinner, she pushed herself through the rooms. The gas light cast shadowing flickers over the walls and in the corners of the room and all around and about the furniture, and she tried not to think of the sprites and spirits that made their homes within.

Unballasted and untethered, Alice Wingrove floated on a bed in darkness.

In the back parlour where she and Felix would eat and sit alone together, Ellen poked the fire and laid the table for dinner. There were interminable, never-ending tasks in her life, some laborious, some worthy, some just tedious, but none of them counted in the final balance. Today, she had had a taste of what it was to get her teeth into something. Had Nurse Henderson meant that things might well have turned out differently if Alice had sought help sooner? She shuffled the pile of letters, reread the one from the Fellowship, put it down again. If the hospital cost her nothing, why had Alice not gone there earlier?

Her breast throbbed. The pain was always stronger at night.

She ran her finger across the books in the case, not at all sure what she was looking for. She pulled out the heavy album that came from Mother's house. Names and dates had been written here and there; some matched a few anecdotes that she had once been told. Inside the thick, embossed covers, the handwriting and photographs were fading to brown and beige. The clothes and hats and beards might look heavy and solid enough, but they were only fancy dress nowadays. She turned more pages, recognised groups that were her mother's parents with their children and her own parents with theirs. They were all witnesses from before the war and the war before that one, revenants from the other side of history and the other side of the world. The older war in Africa, half-forgotten now, had been so far away, the way people in general preferred their wars, and somehow shameful, sickness carrying off more men than all the bullets and sabres and cannons put together.

Alice again, in Ellen's mind's eye, lost in the gloom.

Towards the back of the album, there were pictures of an infant, Ellen's name written underneath, beribboned layers making her as stiffly wide as she was tall. Hard enough to believe that frothy child was her, but even more remote was the later delighted proud miss, posing with her true love. Ellen stared into those faraway, long-gone faces.

The front door opened. She heard voices, the rustles and noises of Felix putting away his umbrella, adding his coat to the rack, footsteps from the front door to his study. He'd found another lame duck to bring back home, one of his army lads, no doubt.

BANTLING

She touched her young love's face with her middle-aged finger. Arthur. They had had to stand still for ages while the photographer fussed about. Staying as unmoving as instructed, she had been in a state of joy, her whole body humming as if made of thousands of vibrating wires. She had felt the warmth of his body beside her, their spirits as united as any that Plato described. Amid the squalor and fear of today, she had recognised the same charge passing between the Wingroves, and recalled what she had lost.

By the time Felix entered the room with his shabby guest, she was standing by the book-case, nothing worse than Kipling's poetry to hand.

'Shall I put out another setting for supper?' she asked.

Felix ate well, as did Sergeant Wilson, down on his luck more or less since his army days. Over the stew, the dumplings, the carrots, the bread and the butter, all through the prunes and custard, Felix talked about his day. On and on, about planning a funeral, of helping to repaint a room to be used as a nursery, of visiting somebody or other, of encouraging a couple of lads back to school. He talked to Sergeant Wilson about the old days, of Sergeant Wilson's planned journey on foot to his sister's place in the Midlands somewhere and his chances of a job up there. She was quiet, hardly listening. The smell of the stewed hearts caught in her throat along with glimpses of Alice, suffering, lying on the sticky bedding, rocking on the handcart. She put down her fork, nauseated.

Felix was full of the joys of his good works. He never stopped talking, not once. Sergeant Wilson hardly spoke. He was busy eating everything put in front of him.

Ellen thought of her day. For all his love, even Wingrove was not able to protect his wife from the risks she faced.

The letters sat on the sideboard. In the corner of her eye, one seemed to gleam out at her, an insistent call from a girl she did not know. Ellen told herself not to be silly, that Felix did not favour it. Her sensible lecture did not work. Leaving the reproachful letter unanswered would be too callous, would throw away a chance to do some good. She could not let another woman lose another child. That would not do, that would not do at all.

'Sergeant Wilson is staying the night,' announced Felix. 'Is the spare bed made up? He'll need a fire it there, I expect.'

'I'll see to it now, dear.'

It wasn't the first time Felix sprung this sort of thing on her. Two could play at that. She smiled kindly at Sergeant Wilson.

'I'll find a pair of pyjamas for you, and show you the facilities when you're ready.'

'And he'll need some rations for his journey tomorrow.'

BANTLING

She dug her nails into her wrist and as she released them felt herself come back to herself.

'Felix,' she said.

They lay side by side on the island bed in the dark, among the faint odour of lavender and a stronger one of mothballs. Mrs Dawson had found a second quilt after all.

'I believe it would be a good idea, in the end, to do what we can for the young woman from the Fellowship that we discussed at breakfast the other morning. Much in the same way as you giving Sergeant Wilson a helping hand.'

'Really, my dear?' asked Felix mildly. 'It's a fine sentiment, but what can you offer her that she would not find in the Fellowship's Home? One night's shelter is nothing compared to all those months. Remember that the parishioners have a prior call on your time and attention also.'

She knew that deceptive tone, would not be turned aside.

'Of course, Felix. That won't change.' She started to tell him about her day, about the conditions in which Alice was expecting her baby, the hardships and dangers she faced. He had seen it all before, of course. Moreover, he'd seen worse, much worse, let him tell her.

'I said this morning and now you have seen for

yourself, how much there is to do. Throwing yourself into my work would be an excellent use of your time.'

'Possibly,' she said. 'He was a soldier too, her husband, but they have nothing.'

He nodded. 'A lot of people are like that around here. It makes me sad, the way so many have come back to so little. That's why my pastoral work is so important, looking after the many rather than the few. A meal here and there, a roof over his head for one night for a man trying to help himself. These are realistic kindnesses for us. The Fellowship can take care of its girls.'

'One charitable act need not exclude the other,' she replied. 'It strikes me that if the girl does not fit in at the Home or feels out of her depth, she might not be able to stay there. Besides, I am sure she could lend me hand. Bits of sewing, sorting jumble, perhaps some paper-work. She has book-keeping skills that might be useful.'

'You must not test your own strength too far.'

The image of Alice Wingrove clinging to Henry as though he were her life-preserver came back to Ellen. Ellen, too, wanted, needed, something akin to that.

'We've talked before of having a common purpose. What better thing could we do than mend a broken life? It's harder than you can imagine for girls like that to keep their babies. Surely you would like to prevent at least one unnecessary separation or loss?'

BANTLING

She felt his muscles become rigid and sensed him draw away as he patted her shoulder through the eiderdowns. He used the muffled touch to make distance between them. She pressed on. All wounds could heal, she was certain of that now. Mothering was more than a matter of merely giving birth.

Ellen would be a fairy godmother to the young woman and her child.

'This girl needs us. Her child, too. To nurture and even love them.'

Her words, the spoken and the unspoken, hung in the air.

'Love, love. You're a kind creature, Ellen, but you mustn't be sentimental. Compassion for all God's creatures is one's Christian duty.'

'Yes, yes, of course. But take your army men, like Sergeant Wilson tonight. You have a particular affinity with him because you have witnessed and shared his experience. I feel a similar kinship with this young woman.'

'You're being silly now. You cannot compare yourself, a married woman struck by misfortune with someone like her, an unmarried girl who has let herself and her family down. You have no idea what sort of person she would prove to be, but I can imagine.'

He was such a peevish, pickish sort of chap when it came to anything except what he knew.

'Loss is loss, whoever and however it is suffered. I don't need to tell you that,' she said. 'As for practicalities, the Fellowship draws up a contract of sorts with its girls, and so will we. Any important matters we will consider together. If we find she is not suitable after a while, we can ask her to leave,' she explained, though she knew in her heart that would never be the case. The girl and Ellen could be, must prove to be, the moorings of each other's lives.

She fumbled for the matches and lit the candle by her bedside. She sat with her face in its light, hoping it gave her a pleading, vulnerable expression. Her eyes filled with tears.

'Please.' She tentatively squeezed his hand.

He could hardly accuse her of being selfish.

'The Fellowship's letter comes with the bishop's approval. It seems he has endorsed their pioneering work,' she added.

His shadowy face was turned towards her. He seemed to pause.

'I will pray on it, my dear, but if you feel so deeply about it, perhaps you might try it for a month or two. Not at the cost of your health, however, nor if it interferes with my own work. It is, for example, inconvenient if you are unexpectedly absent at mealtimes, as it was today.'

'I will deal with all the day-to-day things. You'll hardly notice she's here. I'll ask Mrs Dawson to do a few more hours around the house.'

'Let's not be too hasty,' he interrupted. Onto the shadowy flickers she imposed the worried expression he adopted whenever the spending of money was implied. 'I don't have to remind you how much everything costs.'

She had kept the best for last.

'There's a monthly payment offered for accommodation and board,' she said, and saw his shadows adopt a more cheerful deportment. 'I'll make sure your routine is not disrupted,' she promised. 'It won't make me ill, Felix. On the contrary, the mere idea fills me with hope and energy. After all, I will have you by my side for any big decisions.'

'I suppose so.'

'There is one more thing,' she confided. 'I am putting myself forward to join the Hospital Committee, if they will have me. They were so kind to Mrs Wingrove today.'

She felt him sigh.

'If you must, you must,' he said.

'Thank you, Felix.'

He had no faith in her, but he would change his mind. She thought about going every day into rooms like the Wingrove's one, seeking out women like Alice Wingrove. Not only Ellen by herself, but a whole band of women, not trained nurses or midwives, but good, sensible women like herself, bringing succour as Felix might say, making sure those who needed it found their way to the hospital.

'Put out the candle if you would, dear.'

BANTLING

9 Violet. Southampton. 1923.

Southampton 27 January, Dear Stel, You must be sick of me being down in the dumps. I'm sick of me. Mim & Da are on at me to tell them who sired the Wriggler. They say I owe them that much. Perhaps they are right, but what good would it do? I think at least they believe it wasn't Stan, not that he wouldn't have leapt at the chance. I've little enough left that's private & it isn't their business, never mind how good they are to me & the money they have loaned. They never even met him & he's not from the island so there's no family to chase. There again, what do I really know? Except the blighter's scarpered & left me in a mess & I've just got to get on with everything now. You know he never forced me, though I think they'd prefer he had, so I'd be their innocent daughter, ravished against her will. I might have had stars in my eyes, but I can't say I didn't want what he was offering & to be fair, he never promised me much when I think about it, though if I could find him, he might do the right thing by me. I wouldn't turn him down, not by a long shot. But when it comes down to it, I'm a grown woman & I should have known better & I did know better, but went ahead in any case & never thought about the cost. I can't say that to Mim & Da, of course. They'd hold themselves worse parents than they do already & Mim's tears & Da's silence are hard enough to swallow as it is. No more news about London yet. The other girls who came at the same time have all gone off now. I would feel better not hanging about waiting, but otherwise am keeping fine. Tell me news about you. My best to you, Violet.

BANTLING

10 Ellen. Stockwell. 1923.

Alice Wingrove was hardly ever out of Ellen's thoughts, but even so, more days than she noticed had passed before she walked back to the hospital. It was true that Ellen had had other things on her mind, serious matters to which she had been giving serious consideration, so there were good reasons for her delay and now good reasons for her to go there. But if she was honest, deep down, it was the thought of going into the wards that kept her away. Well, the dread of seeing Alice, at least. Grief, whether one's own or other people's, was never a pretty sight.

The hospital forecourt was as frantic as a marketplace today, workmen shouting from scaffolding and ladders and striding around with hods of bricks and mortar. From the height and extent of the scaffolding, it looked like a whole new wing was being added. The place was loud with banging and clanking, lengths of timber and window frames being stacked against walls. Inside the building, it smelt as reassuringly hygienic as she remembered. All was calm and orderly here. Even so, nobody was sure if Alice was up to visitors or not. Losing the baby was bad enough, but it had been touch and go for her as well.

Matron shook her head. 'A terrible business. The poor woman has turned inside herself. What can you do? Some of these women, they seem to live on air alone. They feed and bathe their children, and forget to do the same for themselves.'

'Could I pop my head around the door to see if Mrs Wingrove will see me?'

'The husband's with her now. I dare say he won't mind.'

Sometimes being the wife of a vicar paid some sort of dividend.

It was a kindness, Ellen thought, to have put Alice in a small room on her own. The builders' noise was audible, but the babies' hardly at all. Dark blinds were drawn down over the long windows, edged with a thin grey frill of light that shifted with the draught. Alice lay in the half-gloom, neatly packaged in the white sheets and blue-hemmed grey blanket. Her eyes were shut.

Wingrove sat next to his wife, holding her limp hand. Ellen touched his shoulder, murmured sorry, so sorry. He hardly even glanced her way, but pointed his chin towards his wife.

'Look at her. Picking up, my foot. She's as pale as milk on the turn and about as sour.'

'It's early days yet,' Ellen said, though it was more than a week.

He stood up to give Ellen the chair, but did not let go of Alice's hand.

There was a posy, if you could call it that, in a vase by the bed. A few almost bare twigs with buds hardly even green, a bedraggled hellebore and a frond or two of fern. A random gathering from several front gardens. Alice deserved to be given better, Wingrove to give it.

There was nothing to say that would make any difference whatsoever, but she told Alice how very sorry she was, how very, very sorry indeed. After that, there was nothing but to sit in silence, because Ellen would have liked that herself, during her dreadful time. There was a certain peacefulness in the quiet, dim room. Time as measured on a clockface seemed a long way away. Beyond the closed door, the building hummed gently, footsteps coming closer, fading away, voices too, and the muffled sounds of babies behind distant doors.

'You'll never guess what Doris did yesterday.' Wingrove's voice broke up whatever peace there had been. 'Only go and eat the soap. Try to, anyhow. You know how Flo is, saving all those scraps and ends of soap. Well, she'd had all them bits soaking in a pot for a fair while and ended up with this load of soft goo. She was just about to start mashing it up into balls when Doris, she only went and stuffed her mouth with some of the mess. To listen to her yell, it would have made you laugh out loud, girl.'

Alice turned herself over, and her hand went with her and the covers over her head, and they were left looking at the long lump of her.

His face closed down, and she saw his arms and

shoulders stiffen, his fists tighten. He walked out with hardly a nod to Ellen.

Temper, temper. Not that she could completely blame him. It would be discouraging that Alice seemed to be making no effort at all. Her heart went to both of them.

'Don't you worry about him, my dear. I'll have a quick word with him,' said Ellen.

In the corridor, she told him what Matron had told her, about the child being damaged in some way. Its life would have been a hard one in the best of circumstances. Perhaps he and his wife would take some comfort from that one day.

He nodded and walked off without a word

Back in the room, she sat by the bed again, touched that unresponsive shoulder. 'How are your children? Bertie and Doris, isn't it? Such dears, they are. I know it's hard to see it now, but you are a fortunate woman.'

The blankets shook slightly. A response of a sort to her children's names. It was a start.

Ellen sat a few minutes longer. She could hardly do less, though by now, she was eager to see Doctor, or her deputy, whoever it was that oversaw the hospital's welfare activities. She had never been this fired up before, this sure of her ground, not for years and years. Finally, her life was about to start, or to start again. It was like waking up after the sleep of ages. And to think it was all because of Alice and her sad loss. It was truly an ill wind ... For women like Alice the hospital was a lifeline, or could be, given half a chance. Whoever was in charge would surely jump at Ellen's proposal to make sure women received that chance.

She felt radiant. Her whole body felt so different, so charged and energetic, so youthful, that was almost a shock to look at her hands and see their usual pale, slightly rough skin. She turned over her hands. The insides of her wrists were pale pink, blue-veined, the scratches and bruises almost faded to nothing. She felt solid, intact, one and indivisible. It passed through her mind that it was more than possible she might never have to hurt herself again.

BANTLING

11 Violet. Southampton. 1923.

Southampton, 29 January 1923, Dear Mim, It was lovely of you to come & see me at the weekend. I am sorry it was not more cheerful for you, but I have had some good news today. But first, please tell Da thanks again & again for the money. I will repay it all as soon as I can, I promise. I wish I could tell him myself. Perhaps he will come round someday & talk to me again, do you think? I will be careful with the extra money & only use it for emergencies. I am sorry I am so much bother to you all & make you cry. Perhaps things are looking up now. I heard today that the Fellowship has found me a place with a vicar & his wife, or otherwise I would be with other girls in a Home. So I am heading towards London very soon. There won't be any extra expenses. I asked three times to make sure. Fingers crossed that they are nice people. I expect they are to take me in. If all goes well, I have been told I might stay there about a year to get over things & find a job, so I hope I get on well & do not disappoint again. Even if I go to the Home in the end, it will not be too bad because there would be other ones like me there. You might be right that Stan would forgive me if I could make arrangements for the baby, but even if Stan was the best I was to find & likely he is, even if things were different & all this had not happened, I do not think I could have settled with him & now it is too late to find out. Plus, I am set on keeping the baby if I can. That is why London seems like the best place. I will not stick out quite so much there, I think & my chances of supporting us both will be better. I know you & Da think that I am in cloud cuckoo land & maybe you are right, but I feel I owe it to the little one to give it my best shot. Why should a baby suffer more than he already has to? Who is to say he would be worse off with me than a stranger? The Fellowship letter told me they were set up to help girls who feel like me and that more girls are managing it these days. Time enough for adoption or a Home later if it comes to it. I am wearing your ring & I feel better when I am with strangers now. Giving me your wedding band is the kindest, most generous thing I could imagine. I will keep it safe. Thanks everso for making the dress too. You know how much I like green. It's so jaunty & it makes a big difference to wear something that fits. I will wear it on the train to cheer me up. As you said, it will be a fair while before we clap eyes on each other again. I don't expect you will be able to make the journey to see me up there, though I wish I could have my Mim with me when my time comes. There was the full moon last night. It was small & far away & I felt sorry for it being so distant & lonely in the clouds. You are the best of mothers & I could not wish for a better example. Give Da my love & tell him what you think best. With love from your Violet.

BANTLING

12 Ellen. Stockwell. 1923.

Dawn had broken, the great day had finally arrived, and so far, Ellen had done nothing but fidget about the house. Flitter-flutter, flitter-flutter. She checked on Mrs Dawson, making up the bed in the spare room. Violet's room. The sheets were well-aired, Mrs Dawson informed her, but Ellen fretted they might not be absolutely dry, or that the air might be damp since the room had not been used for such a while. It would not do for their guest to catch cold her first night in their house. Not with a baby at stake. Mrs Dawson laid a fire and Ellen wondered about lighting it before Felix headed to Waterloo to meet the train. She decided it was more sensible to wait until he got back with the girl. Then she lit it in any case. Better safe than sorry. The room was small enough to warm up quickly, but she wanted to make sure the air was nice and dry.

She couldn't put her mind to the thousand and one other things she had to do, not even the letter-writing to get her scheme off the ground. Her scheme! Her scheme that the Hospital received with such enthusiasm. She rearranged the cushions in the front parlour, and moved Colbert's cage so he had more afternoon light.

She went back upstairs and sorted her dressing table, not that there was much on it, but she washed her hairbrush again, cleared out the tiny bits of fluff gathered in the corners of the glass dish in which she put her hair pins at night, and though there was no need for it, carefully rinsed and dried the coral necklace that had been a gift from her true love on her sixteenth birthday, held it against her throat. It was too short to clasp about her neck these days. She sat and held it for a while, holding it against her throat, looking from the mirror to the irregular pink beads and back at herself.

She went back to the guest room and plumped the pillows again and shook the quilt and tweaked and smoothed the cover and poked the fire and fed it a few more coals.

The parlour was in order, her desk neatly laid out. The clock showed she had at least an hour before Felix would be back with their visitor. To work, to work, after all. It would calm her nerves if nothing else.

Dear Madam,

You are doubtless already familiar with the work my husband, the Reverend Holcroft, has undertaken in the parish, especially amongst returned soldiers and young men with no employment and few skills to help them secure it. I have recently become acutely aware of the effects of poverty and deprivation on the impoverished women of the area, especially regarding their health as mothers and mothers-to-be.

Ellen took a break while she pushed back her cuticles and thought a little. Grace and elegance of the begging words were hard to come by today.

BANTLING

My aim in writing to you, and other similar ladies of the parish, is to interest you in a new charitable activity that will improve the situation of these women and complement the work of my husband, especially in his capacity as the Chaplain of the Maternity Hospital.

Her eye was caught by a thread hanging from the braid of the table-cloth. Any excuse. By the time she had extracted a suitable needle from its case, hunted down the thread and made it fast, she was ready to continue.

Doctor McCall, herself no stranger to the hurdles that females face in our efforts to contribute as much as possible to society, spearheads our commitment to serve all expectant and nursing women of the area, the poorest as well as the more fortunate.

Outside, there was the clank of the coal-hole cover and the tumbling clatter of nuggets.

You may already be familiar with the conditions that some families live in, conditions which defy belief or imagination and which promote rather than prevent the spread of disease and infection. Consequently, impoverished expectant women's so-called health, and that of their children, both before and after birth, is often heart-breaking. Being a relative newcomer to the city, I had long been sheltered from much distressing knowledge, but I have recently seen for myself the tragic consequences of self-neglect caused by lack of basic food, hygiene and medical attention.

She got up and stood sideways to the window,

watching, unseen. Henry Wingrove heaved a sack almost as large as himself onto his back. His clothes were as black and shiny as coal dust and his face and hands much the same. Bent almost double, he came back up the path like a great black two-legged beetle, swung the load with a grunt and emptied it into the cellar. He strolled with back to the cart, tossed the sack onto the back and took the horse's reins. Before Ellen sat down again, she saw the son high up on the seat, holding onto his sister. The children were nearly as sooty-faced as the father.

In order to alleviate this situation, we are ... (How utterly delightful it was to be a – perhaps even the most – significant part of that 'we') ... *establishing a Helpful Visitor Scheme. It is my pleasure and my privilege to assist the Hospital by encouraging ladies – some are committee members; others are supporters of our work – to visit families' homes and make certain that mothers-to-be understand what they and the Hospital can do together to ensure a healthy confinement.*

She stroked her breast softly. Sweet, soft thing that it was, it hardly ached any more. That brittle, bruising night seemed long ago, belonging to a different life. She could not remember why it had seemed there was no way around hurting herself.

At a practical level, volunteers will demonstrate easy steps to improve expectant mothers' health and that of their unborn children, and encourage them to attend our Free Clinic from an early stage of pregnancy. This is by far the best way of promoting the well-being of mother and child throughout her term.

If the children were with their father, Alice Wingrove was perhaps still unwell. Or, busy elsewhere and glad to have the children out from under her feet for a few hours.

At Wingrove's instruction, the horse walked on a few yards. She listened to the clop of hooves, the drag and creak of the cart, and after a while, faintly, more coals falling into the cellar of the next house along.

Our ladies extend a helping hand from the goodness of their hearts and even in the few weeks since we commenced in a very modest manner, the results have been gratifying.

Speaking of which, Ellen had meant to visit Alice Wingrove again these past few weeks, but there really was so little time nowadays, so much pressing work. And what with this girl arriving any minute ... Next week, she promised herself. Next week she would make sure she called in.

I am appealing for more women to join us in this enterprise.

Or sometime soon, certainly.

Our budget is most limited and we are seeking to establish a fund to enable this work to flourish. Any contribution would be most appreciated.

She would take something tasty and sustaining to tempt Mrs Wingrove's appetite. Ellen had been remiss in her duty; there were no two ways about it. Still, one could only do what one could do.

I sincerely hope that, having considered the Helpful Visitors' Scheme, you will want to share in this endeavour, either as a volunteer if time permits, or with such donations as you are able to offer.

It goes almost without saying that I will continue to make myself available to my husband's parishioners, to attend choir practice and to play my part in the life and decoration of the church. Reverend Holcroft is most enthusiastic about this new scheme, and intends to make it the beneficiary of some of his special appeals.

For your interest, I enclose a copy of the most recent Annual Report, which better describes the work of the Hospital than I can.

I remain in happy expectation of your swift and amiable response.

Yours most cordially,

Mrs Felix Holcroft, Hospital Committee Member (pending)

She looked back at the clock. She addressed an envelope. She looked again at the clock.

If it was on time, the train should be arriving at Waterloo any minute now. Felix had thought it would take them about half an hour to reach the Vicarage if they took the tram. A cab would be quicker, but an unnecessary extravagance. She blew on the letter to make sure the ink was dry, folded it, put it in the envelope and sealed it. It was time to check again on the fire in the guest room, to start heating the kettle and to freshen up a little.

In front of the bathroom mirror, Ellen licked her finger and tried to smooth down a few hairs that sprang and twisted away from her scalp. She'd kept her hair long as others, more swayed by fickle fashion, had cut off theirs. She favoured the classic look herself, hair smoothly parted, drawn back and pinned, and for the most part it still curved darkly around her scalp as smoothly as the carving on a Grecian statue. Those new disobedient hairs of hers, like little wires poking from her scalp, they were annoying. Mother had complained of them too, if Ellen remembered right. They must run in the family, another unwelcome club one joined as one aged. The lines on the face one expected, though the ones round her mouth made her look sterner than she knew she was. How ironic that it was smiling that lined one's face and seemed to harden it.

'Ellen, dear, come and meet our young guest.'

Felix's voice, following the hall, up the stairs and around its curve, along the corridor and into the bathroom.

They were back so soon, before she was fully ready.

She fingered the wiry hairs again, jerked them, one by one, as close to the root as possible. She looked at them more closely in her hand. Dark at one end, they became almost colourless, what was called grey. No doubt she would get used to them in time. She felt a little breathless, and pulled at the neck of her blouse. It must have shrunk a little. Perhaps Mrs Dawson was being too enthusiastic about boil washes.

'Ellen!'

She prinked the lace of her collar and made sure that all her buttons were still in a straight line down her front, checking for stray crumbs and patting her skirt smooth at the same time. Her outfit might doubtless be considered a bit old-fashioned these days, but the Vicarage was not a couturier's salon, and all the better for that. It did not do to overawe people. It was better to seem to be what one was. Kind. Trustworthy. She practised a welcoming smile. Again. Better. Breathe out. Smile again. She would do.

'Ellen, come out, come out wherever you are,' called Felix. He could be a nagging fusspot when he put his mind to it. 'We are standing waiting in the hall.'

My oh my. Here we go.

She wiped down the basin again and straightened the towels on her way out of the room. From the top of the stairs, she saw the back of the girl, slender across the shoulders and backside, and with a funny little fur tippet around her neck. It was sweet, really. Felix was taking off his outerwear, his shoulders slightly stooped. From above him, she could make out the balding patch on the top of his head. He was getting old, and he didn't even notice, but the girl would rejuvenate them both.

'Hello, hello! It's Violet, isn't it? I'm Mrs Holcroft. I do hope you will feel at home with us. We both think of you as one of the family already.'

The girl turned towards Ellen and gave a perfectly proper little bob. Her coat strained at the few buttons that met across her chest. From front on, she looked further gone than Ellen had imagined. Her colour was good, her skin clear and rosy, her face slim.

'Pleased to meet you, Mrs Holcroft. I'm everso grateful to you and the Reverend.'

Her voice was low, soft round the edges and full of the countryside.

Her eyes were the clearest grey. It was the luck of the draw, how some women suffered so much and others thrived while they were expecting.

'I expect your family call you Vi. Would you be happier as Vi with us too?'

'I'm called Violet at home, if you don't mind. I never got on with Vi myself.'

Those clear eyes did not leave Ellen's face

Ellen felt herself judged and, ridiculously in the circumstances, was not at all sure she passed muster.

'Of course,' she said, still smiling. Young women can be so uppity, so silly. Bless them. Nothing Ellen couldn't smooth out. 'Whatever you prefer.' It was probably exactly that sort of attitude that had got Violet into trouble in the first place.

'Right then, Violet it is,' said Felix. 'Coat?'

Underneath the coat she was wearing a dress that looked as though it might have had a place on the amateur stage. Even the girl's excellent complexion was not flattered by the harsh, bright green and its white collar and cuffs. It was the sort of colour permissible in spring – as summerhouse cushions, perhaps. In this sort of weather, it would show every smoke smut and streak of London dirt. Indeed, the collar and cuffs were noticeably grubby already. Not the most sensible thing to wear on a long train journey. Not even the way she held herself, surprisingly good for a country girl, could carry it off.

Ellen reminded herself the chances were that the girl probably did not have a great deal of choice. Ellen would set that right before the week was out. She and Violet would go together to select some fabric and dress patterns, something pretty. Arding and Hobbs in Clapham Junction always had a good range, and Miss Grinston there was always helpful.

Once she had removed her hat and thanked Felix politely enough, the girl put her fingers to her head, fluffing up her dark curls. Preening. Her hair was short, not quite as short as Ellen had seen in a magazine not so long ago, but short enough to be aiming for modernity, much too short to tie back or put up with pins.

Vanity, vanity.

Ellen looked towards Felix. He held decided views

about stiff-necked pride, but he seemed to have not noticed this example of it. Men were not always the most observant of creatures. Probably all for the best in this instance.

'Oh my. What a very interesting haircut.'

Nobody could accuse her of not trying.

'Do you think so? I cut it myself,' said the girl, in her low, slow voice that brought to mind hayfields and broad skies. 'I was that fed up with washing it and getting it dry.'

'You've done a very good job,' said Ellen. There was nothing much else she could say, but her voice sounded too bright. 'You'll want to rinse your hands and face straight away, I expect. The bathroom's just along the landing at the top of the stairs. You can put your bag down here for the moment.'

The girl nodded.

'After that, I've laid out some tea in the front room,' Ellen said. 'I'll show you your room when you've caught your breath. We'll get to know each other a little bit before you start unpacking.'

Ellen had her heart set on cheerfulness and on putting their young visitor at ease. She had thought to make the tea informal, all three of them sitting on settees and comfortable chairs with tea and biscuits beside them. Ellen's own heart was beating high up under her breast-bone, so she felt for this young woman, newly arrived amongst strangers, was determined to give her everything she needed, to make a fuss of her.

Violet was not as sad and sorry a creature as Alice Wingrove, but, then again, it did not do to make comparisons.

'I've made up a fire in here. And one in your room too. It's very chilly today, don't you think? Even though spring must be just around the corner by now. You must be tired after your journey. Not too many delays, I hope. Oh, of course not. Silly me.' If only she could stop blathering. 'The train must have arrived on time or Felix would still be kicking his heels at Waterloo Station. Come in, come in, make yourself comfortable. Oh, not there, if you don't mind, that's usually where Felix sits. Come and sit by me on the sofa.'

She patted the upholstery next to her.

The girl hesitated.

'A hard chair suits me best, if you don't mind, Mrs Holcroft. With arms. It's the getting up again, see.'

Ellen should have thought of that before.

'Of course, dear. Felix will fetch the dining room carver.'

As well as all the fetching and carrying, they had to move Felix's chair to one side, and Colbert's cage too, which caused a bit of an upset in the feathers department, before she could be seated. That was not quite the end of it.

'Your poor swollen ankles,' said Ellen. 'Would

you like the footstool as well? Felix, perhaps you could...? That's comfier, I think. Help yourself to a biscuit while I pour. Ah, I see Mrs Dawson has made us some scones. I do recommend them.'

The girl glanced around the parlour, and as she did, the room suddenly appeared to Ellen as stuffier and more overcrowded. Probably that was only to be expected with a whole extra chair and a very expectant young woman squeezed in. Even so, Ellen found herself wanting to tug at occasional tables and push plant pots back towards the walls, to clear away some of the keepsakes and books. To apologise, for heaven's sake, to this girl and make excuses, to say it always astounded her how Felix could work in every room of the house, even though he had a perfectly decent study of his own, leaving a trail of paper, pamphlets and pens everywhere. She had an urge to insist that she kept this room as clear as possible, that she had moved all the boxes of jumble.

Oh dear. Sitting around the table in the back parlour might have been better.

Ellen must not be too hard on herself. Just remember, she was not the one who had ended up in a predicament. She poured out cups of tea.

'Sugar?' She dropped lumps carefully into the hot liquid.

Everything in here was cleaned and polished; she and Mrs Dawson made sure of that, even if all the furniture was serviceable rather than spanking new. It would be surprising in the extreme if the girl was used to better. All the same, Violet would do herself a favour if she learnt to look a little less sulky, a little more grateful.

Ellen passed around the cups and saucers. Not a drop spilt.

Violet put hers down on a nearby table.

Ellen stretched across and patted the girl's hand. Smiled yet again.

'No need to fret, dear. We'll do our best to take care of you while you're here. I'm sure you have a lovely smile when you let yourself.'

'We are glad to offer you shelter from the storm, Violet,' said Felix.

'Butter with your scone? Jam?' asked Ellen.

The girl stared at her hands and shook her head.

'It must be a very worrying time for you. Mr Holcroft and I understand that very well,' continued Ellen.

She glanced up at Felix, but he had his head down, buttering a scone, crumbs everywhere. Of course, this was not the moment for Ellen's own confidences. There would be opportunities for such intimacies later. She reached again for the teapot.

'Your family, they live in Hampshire, I believe? Lovely county.'

'Isle of Wight, Mrs Holcroft. Cowes is where my people are.'

'Can I freshen up your cup? Felix, more for you?'

BANTLING

Felix nodded his head. The girl shook hers.

'Nonsense,' said Ellen. 'No need to stand on ceremony. You must be chilly. The tea will warm you up. So, you live in Cowes?'

'Not any more. I've been working in Shanklin for a few years, doing the books for a grocer.'

Living away from home. That would explain a few things. There was more and more of it happening these days, but parents did not seem to learn that they should keep their daughters close by.

'Did you live-in at the grocer's premises?' Ellen was fishing now.

The girl looked at her hands.

'I shared a room with my friend Estelle. She does clerical work for the Parish Council.'

Ellen poured and handed around biscuits, more scones. It filled the gaps in the conversation. Her hands were busy, busy. It was strange to think this quiet lumpish girl would be here every day, sitting on the other side of the table, sharing the bathroom. What on earth would they find in common? Still, it could be worse. She might have been raucous.

'Mim – my mother – and my Da say to tell you thank-you for taking me in.'

'You're welcome,' said Ellen, putting down the teapot for a moment. 'Milk? Sugar? Scone? More jam?'

You could never tell with families. Some of the homes these girls came from were the cause of their daughter's downfall. Drunkenness and worse. She would have to keep an eye on any communication between Cowes and here.

'They say I'm to do my best to make myself useful to you.'

'I'm sure we'll find enough to keep you from being bored.'

She wondered when Felix would do his bit to break the ice. The girl was not the most talkative she'd ever met. In the meanwhile, Ellen soldiered on. Her cup rattled slightly as she put it down.

'It sounds as though your parents are sympathetic towards your situation.' she said.

The girl nodded. 'They've been …'

She seemed to searching for the right word. Ellen leant forward.

'… very good. It's not been easy for them.'

'That's lovely. Quite unusual, wouldn't you think, Felix?'

'Most commendable,' said Felix.

There seemed to be no more small talk that came to mind, nothing that made sense when the fact of the matter was that they were dancing around the only reason the girl was with them.

'Now, as you can probably guess, there are a few matters we should talk about. Let's get them out of the way. Reverend Holcroft might have mentioned one or two of them already,' she said.

Felix shook his head. 'I'll leave that to you, my dear,'

he said. 'If you don't mind, I'll leave you young ladies to chat together. I have a few things to get on with.'

It was so like him to slide out of matters that concerned her. On the other hand, the girl would probably feel more at ease, speaking woman to woman, so Ellen did not press him to stay.

'Let's get the, you know, finances sorted and out of the way,' said Ellen. It was always such a touchy subject.

'I've got some pound notes here,' interrupted the girl. 'Shall I give you a month now? I was told it includes all my meals. I'm not a big eater, but I don't think I should skip meals, do you? Will there be anything on top for bed-linen or washing or anything?'

Ellen held up her hands.

'I think we agreed ten shillings a week for everything,' she said. 'You must wash your own smalls and light things, the rest is done weekly, and we change one sheet and the towel every fortnight, once a week in the summer. I might ask you to help me out every now and then, if you feel up to it.'

'I'm more than glad to do my bit. Ten shillings? That covers gas and coal and baths and the like?'

She seemed on edge, needing to pin down the cost of her room, as though Ellen would spring extra charges on her out of the blue.

'Yes, yes, of course. It covers everything I can think of.'

The girl sat quiet for a moment, then she asked, 'Is that ten shillings a week or two pounds a month? Months is easier, don't you think? I can give you a pound and ten shillings now to the end of the month, and after that, two pounds at the beginning of each month. That's best, isn't it? We both know where we stand then. Only if that suits you, of course, Mrs Holcroft.'

Ellen blinked in surprise. 'I suppose that's all right.'

From one of her big pockets, Violet pulled a purse. She hunched over the contents while she counted out the notes. Ellen got up and chatted to Colbert and watched him fluff up his feathers, giving the girl a little privacy. She was not used to this sort of transaction in her own home and felt more awkward than she liked, though Violet did not seem bothered.

'There you go, Mrs Holcroft. Three ten-shilling notes.'

'Thank you, Violet.'

She pushed the notes into her pocket, where she could hear them crackling as she sat down again. She would feed Violet properly of course, and not stint her with coal, but all the same there would be a little extra left over every week. She added some hot water to the pot and poured again, but the tea tasted stewed and not much better than lukewarm all the same. She put it down and wondered about making another pot.

'Would you tell me how far along are you now?' asked Ellen.

'It's something over six months, I suppose,' said the girl. Her voice was quieter than ever. She had gone bright red and sounded diffident. 'They tell me I'm due sometime late April.'

'And everything is going smoothly?'

'As far as I know. I feel very well in myself.'

'We've arranged for you to see Doctor herself at the hospital. My husband is chaplain there and I serve on the committee, so you will be well taken care of. They are proud of their facilities and Doctor has an excellent reputation. You will need to abide by her programme regarding exercise, diet and the rest of it. Some of her ideas are a little unusual, but one presumes she knows what she is about.'

Violet inclined her head.

'Now, I see you're already wearing a wedding ring. Sensible, of course, but I hope you didn't spend a lot on it.'

'Mim gave it to me,' said Violet. 'It's her very own.'

She sounded as though she had taken offence, silly girl.

'Well, that's quite exceptional, I must say. Lovely. Now, while you are here at the vicarage in our care, we have to keep an eye on all your visitors, especially any men. To avoid any hint of impropriety, I'm sure you'll agree it's only sensible to get Reverend Holcroft's or my permission for any visits or meetings.'

Violet nodded silently. She still had not touched her tea.

'Do you know anybody else in London? Do you have any friends or relatives?'

The girl shook her head.

'Is there anybody else likely to want to see you? Or who you might want to see?'

Ellen was being nosy now.

Another shake of the head, short and subdued.

'In the same vein, and I hope this does not sound too old-fashioned and fussy, please show me any letters before you send them and any you get.'

It could be a thankless job keeping girls away from unsuitable men if they had set their minds to it, but she would have to try. Romantic illusions and carnal feelings had a lot to answer for, and it was always the women who suffered.

On the other hand, if she thought of Felix and her own marriage, self-denying so-called gallantry took its toll too.

'I don't have hardly anyone to write to. We're not big letter-writers in our family.'

A greasy film had settled over the surface of Violet's tea.

'Shall I pour you a fresh cup? Would you prefer a glass of milk? Perhaps you're feeling queasy? That can be so horrid. I have some ginger in the kitchen. Many people find chewing a little root helps the sickness. No? Are you sure?'

How best to ask Violet about the father, and to make sure the girl had put out of her mind any ideas about getting in touch with him? Would she take offence? Would she tell?

BANTLING

Violet turned to look at Ellen, put her feet back on the floor and calmly asked to use the facilities again. Why Ellen felt wrong-footed, she could not have said, but when Violet added that she had her mother's bladder, Ellen knew she had a task on her hands.

She cleared away the tea-things. The girl came back and made it known she was overdue her afternoon lie-down. All done in, was what she said, and she did look rather pale and peaky all of a sudden, so there was nothing for it but to show her upstairs.

Ellen had prettied up the spare room. Even though there was nothing flowering in the garden as yet, she had brought in a few twigs of forsythia last week in readiness and put them on the washstand. Behold! The buds had swelled and yellow tips were already showing.

'A touch of spring in mid-winter,' she said. 'Flowers do cheer up a place so.'

Violet did not comment, but in the mirror, Ellen saw her press the mattress with her hand.

What did the girl expect? This was not the Ritz and in her present mess she should be grateful for whatever she was given. Oh my. That was not a kindly thought.

'You should have everything here, but just tell me if there is anything else you need,' she said. 'Let me give you a hand with your shoes and then you can have a proper nap before supper. It will do you and Baby the world of good.'

BANTLING

She was nothing if not forgiving, courteous to a fault, even when, especially when, it was a strain. Sharing one's home with a stranger might not to be so easy after all. Her fingernails scraped the insides of her wrists, oh lightly, lightly, where the veins shadowed them blue and the skin was slightly raw, just to remind herself she was anchored and not floating free.

Violet sat full-length on the bed and lent against the head of it.

'It's all so cosy,' she said. And she smiled. She actually smiled, and properly too, not dutifully. 'Thank you everso much, Mrs Holcroft. There's not many would have the kindness to do the same. I want to do my best by the, you know, little one. None of this is his fault.'

Ellen stood, silent with surprise. Perhaps it was just a matter of getting used to each other.

Violet placed her hands on her stomach.

'Oops, there he goes again. Quick, give me your hand. Don't worry, you won't do him or me any harm.'

Startled, Ellen found her hand pressed to Violet's stomach.

There was movement, a strong rippling, under her fingers.

'Meet the Wriggler, Mrs Holcroft. Wriggler, this here's our benefactor.'

All was forgiven. All would be well.

BANTLING

13 Violet. Stockwell. 1923.

Stockwell, London SW9, 9 February, Dear Mim & Da, Just a note to tell you that I am safely arrived as you probably guessed from the envelope & have been made very comfortable here with Reverend & Mrs Holcroft who are most kind & welcoming. I made the arrangements about the board & lodgings right at the start, just as you said & Mrs Holcroft & me came to an agreement. Mrs Holcroft has set me at ease like one of the family, with my own room & sitting down to meals at table with them. You will be glad to know that Mrs Holcroft feels as responsible for me as you would yourselves. She has asked me to reassure you that she wishes to safeguard me against any hint of impropriety & that she will keep an eye on all my correspondence & any visitors, though I don't expect to have much of the first & none of the second. I have not been out & about much or not far at least. I'm a bit scared to go on my own as yet. We are just off the main road, though you can still hear the trams rumbling & the boys shouting, but there again there's nowhere you can't hear boys shouting, but none of the houses nearby are cottages, they are all like villas & the streets around here are paved & wide enough for delivery carts to pass in opposite directions. No muddy paths to pick along as they all have pavements, though not golden. The vicarage is behind Reverend Holcroft's church & the house looks out onto a small circus, which has flowers in the right season, but is not too bright now, but there again nothing is. Mrs Holcroft has said that I should finish now if I am to catch the post, so I send my loving greetings to you both, Violet.

BANTLING

14 Ellen. Stockwell. 1923.

There is never enough time to fit in everything. Between what one chooses and what one is given to do, the days are never long enough. All the same, Ellen was as good as her word, though it was a promise she had made only to herself. She took young Violet off to find some suitable dress materials. It meant her correspondence would pile up, but never mind; the girl was virtually living in that one hideous green dress.

'Can we sit upstairs, oh please, Mrs Holcroft,' pleaded Violet. 'I've never been on a top deck.'

It was silly and a bit risky. What if Violet stumbled or the bus jolted before they'd sat down? But Violet called out to the conductor as breezy as anything to mind how he went and not ring the bell for the driver to start until they were well and truly sat down.

They clambered up the stairs clutching their skirts tightly with one hand and the handrail with the other. It was all a bit of a palaver. At least it was not raining and the seats were almost dry. Violet was just like a little girl, pink with excitement and the nippy wind, peering into the upper stories of the buildings and down onto people walking or on bicycles. Quite an adventure, all in all.

Miss Grinston was on duty behind the haberdasher's

counter. All of a sudden, Ellen was not sure how she should introduce Violet. There'd been no call so far. At church on Sundays Violet had slipped discretely in and out of the service – her own choice – and at home kept largely to her room if she wasn't lending a hand to Ellen or Mrs Dawson. She'd met nobody as yet. Mrs Dawson didn't count, of course, though one never knew what the help might say or had said, outside the vicarage. There again, Violet's presence was not a secret, nothing about which she and Felix were ashamed. Ellen would prefer not to lie, did not want to actually hear herself introducing Violet as Mrs This or Mrs That.

Violet was already fingering some of the fabrics, touching them gently with her fingertips. Rolls of fine, delicate florals, subtle, flat-stacked tweeds and gabardines, glistening brocades. Drapery promised so many possibilities. One fabric against another, a flamboyant silk instead of a modest lawn, for example, could turn an individual into quite another person altogether.

'How can I help you today, Mrs Holcroft?'

'Something for a couple of dresses, Miss Grinston. And how is your mother these days?'

'Fair to middling, thank-you for asking, Mrs Holcroft.'

Was Ellen imagining it, or was there some trace of disdain in Miss Grinston's voice?

'Do please pass my best wishes to her.'

'Are you looking for yourself or the young lady?'

The sale clerk's expression was perfectly bland.

Violet turned towards the counter. 'I was thinking perhaps of a dress and a skirt and blouse. That might be more versatile,' she said.

She asked about light wools, whether Miss Grinston could suggest something suitable? She stood so straight and so prickly, so young and in need of protection.

'Violet is staying with the vicar and me for a while,' said Ellen. 'I do hope you have something suitable to her taste here.'

'From out of town, are you, Mrs ... ? Family of the vicar, I suppose? Staying long?'

'Violet Bantling.'

'Family friend, Miss Grinston,' said Ellen.

There. Another lie. Or rather, a truth in the making.

Why had she never noticed before now how nosy Miss Grinston was? She should have expected it, been better prepared.

'The hospital is much recommended for laying-in,' added Violet. 'We all felt it best I be here.'

'I don't mean to rush you, Miss Grinston, but I promised the vicar I'd only be gone an hour,' said Ellen.

Violet kept her eyes straight ahead. She patted her hair and her mother's ring caught the light. It had to be a good sign. Miss Grinston nodded as though she had made a decision.

'Over this way, please, Mrs Bantling. Is for a dress or a skirt?'

BANTLING

'A loose shift to start with,' said Violet, and flashed a sweet, sweet smile towards Ellen.

'That's all the fashion now, of course,' said Miss Grinston. 'Straight up and down and a bit of detail on the hips. Covers a multitude of sins, I always say. Not that I mean to suggest that there are any sins to hide.'

Violet said easily, 'Sin or no, you can probably tell I'm fast growing out of the clothes I'm standing in. I'll take a look at those worsteds first.'

Miss Grinston said very little after that. There and then, Ellen decided on making one smock-dress with sleeves, one sleeveless shift, one skirt and two blouses.

She had clear ideas about what was right for an expectant mother. Who could blame her for wanting to steer Violet away from anything remotely like the green outfit she'd been wearing almost non-stop since she arrived? Miss Grinston had a fair choice to put before them, and she swathed and draped the counter with her offerings.

Violet oohed and aaahed, stroked and rubbed. 'Perhaps another time,' she said about the cashmere and silks. Gradually they narrowed the selection.

'You can't go wrong with a nice stripe,' said Ellen. 'They're always flattering'.

Violet seemed to listen to Ellen's advice, to appreciate it, but just when Ellen thought they'd settled on a lovely fresh stripe, a pretty floral and a classic houndstooth for the main articles and some soft flowery lawns for the blouses, Violet dug in her heels for a rather drab gun-metal grey wool. Even with a lacy collar and cuffs, it would look rather severe, as Ellen tried tactfully to point out, but Violet would not be swayed.

'The hounds-tooth is lovely, so is everything you've picked out, but they're like something I might wear for best, especially the flowery one. Smart suits me better than dainty. This will be good for every day, won't show the dirt and it's so cosy,' she told Ellen and whispered that she could pay for it herself, pay for everything, come to that, and pulled out her purse.

'Don't be silly, dear,' said Ellen. 'There's no need for that. It's my pleasure.' She put her hand across the purse so Violet could not open it.

Miss Grinston was putting away some of the rolls, but Ellen could tell from the set of her back that she was listening, or trying to listen, to everything they said.

'But I should pay,' said Violet. 'I can't accept all this, it's too much. I've got my savings and I'd have had to splash out on some outfits sooner or later. I only want what I can afford.'

'I'll buy all the material,' said Ellen quietly, but very firmly. Her voice brooked no argument, as they said, whatever that meant. 'It's not a lot compared to what Felix hands out in so-called loans.' She had not meant to say anything like that. Perhaps she was being disloyal, though she only meant to put Violet back at ease. 'You get the thread and trims and anything else you need. Go all ritzy on the buttons.'

Violet said, 'Not the floral then, nor the black and white check, just the stripe and the grey, those'll do me very well. I'm not being ungrateful, but also, I'd prefer plain voile or muslin for the blouses rather than patterned or loud.'

It crossed Ellen's mind that the green might not have been entirely of Violet's choosing.

'You'll need something a bit lighter and prettier, come the spring,' she argued. 'We'll get one floral too, and the plain colours for the blouses.'

'Only if you're sure.'

Miss Grinston measured off the material with her arm outstretched, holding one end of the material, bending her elbow to pull out more material.

'If you don't mind, I'll take half a yard extra of each,' said Violet. 'If I make the seams nice and generous, I can let them out when I need to.

It was a sensible thought and Ellen wished she'd had it first, and said so.

There was underwear flannel to be bought as well, and some lining silk; elastic and trims and thread and buttons and bias binding and needles for the Singer and other bits and pieces.

'Would you like to look at some collars?' asked Miss Grinston.

Ellen said that was probably a good idea, but Violet thought she could make do with the ones she had.

'That's everything now? Nothing else?' Miss Grinston asked, and started to tot up the figures, her lips moving as her pencil slid from one figure to the next.

'Nine and tenpence half-penny,' said Violet.

Miss Grinston smiled, a tight polite little twitch of her lips, and moved her pencil back to the start of her numbers. Violet raised her eyebrows at Ellen, but didn't say anything.

'That'll be nine and tenpence half-penny,' she said eventually.

'I'll put in four shillings,' said Violet and counted it out.

'What a good head for figures you've got, Violet.'

It did no harm to compliment people from time to time.

'I'm used to it, see, like Miss Grinston. I've had no complaints from my employers so far.'

There was Violet's vain streak coming through again.

'Do you want these delivered to the vicarage?'

'We'll take them with us,' Ellen and Violet said at the same time.

It was only a little thing, but it had been such an age since Ellen had felt so in tune with another person. They made their way to the bus-stop, the sun low in their faces. They walked together into the glorious radiance.

The rest of the afternoon they cut and pinned, and as Mrs Dawson cleared away to set the table for dinner, Violet tried on one of the new smocks. It was only tacked together, but it was touching to see how pleased she was, twisting in front of the mirror to see as much of herself as possible, stroking the fabric, smoothing the neckline, checking the length of the sleeves. Her eyes were very shiny, as though she might cry. Cumbersome as she was, the blue-grey material they had chosen for her dress suited her well. On the roll it had looked military drab, but made up, it had a lilac sheen that brought out the colour of those watery eyes.

Ellen had been right, as well – the stripes were as flattering as she'd hoped. They would lift anybody's spirits to look at.

Meals were a much more pleasant affair nowadays. Violet was a delightfully neat eater. And there was generally more conversation to be had. This evening, they were both of them quite chatty over dinner. Felix hardly got a word in for once. He chewed steadily and read the paper, as his young ladies, as he called them, talked about one thing and another. In the end, and rather naughtily, Violet hoped that the Reverend had had a good day too.

Felix sighed and muttered, and put down his paper with not a lot of grace. He muttered something about shelling out again and not being sure if he's already loaned these people a sum for the same reason before. Ellen could have tutted with irritation, but kept her mouth shut. A husband and wife should never argue in public. If at all.

BANTLING

Violet said that his receipt book should tell him, and he looked shame-faced, muttered about bits of paper littering his pockets and study. Violet's face was a picture too. She was taken aback, trying not to show it, not very successfully. She asked what system he had for keeping tabs on who had repaid how much.

Quite.

It was the question Ellen often asked herself, though she knew the answer full well. Simply put, if Felix ever got any of his loans back, it would almost make her believe in miracles again.

'Do you have a special fund from the Church?' Violet asked.

He shook his head.

'That's the kindest thing I've heard of,' exclaimed Violet. 'Between the two of you, you're almost saints. But it's got to run out sooner or later, hasn't it? I mean, if the money doesn't come in, it can't go round again, can it?'

'That's true, but the Lord provides, and I don't like to press people. They have so many worries.'

'Don't I know it, and of course, I've got no right to say anything, not after Mrs Holcroft was so kind to me today, too kind most likely, but all the same most working folk, and I mean even them that don't have jobs at the moment too, they don't expect something for nothing. Not most of the time. Sometimes it can't be helped, that just how things are, you have to make allowances, but mostly people want to be honest and not feel they're taking advantage. I know that's how I feel.'

'Oh, they always say they'll repay it, don't they, Felix, but when it comes to the crunch it's a different story. One can't blame them, I suppose.'

'Nobody likes to be beholden,' said Violet.

Ellen could not judge whether or not she was talking about herself and the dress materials.

Felix stopped chewing, swallowed, put down his fork and knife. He looked very fixedly at Violet.

'I suppose you would do it differently,' he said. It was the same mild tone he always used when he disagreed with someone. Ellen sometimes thought he did it on purpose to wrong-foot a person, to make them feel uncomfortably belligerent and ashamed of themselves. How could you argue with somebody so gentle?

'I could give you a hand, if you like, try and sort out what's what, how much you've given this person and that one.'

'That's kind of you, Violet, but I'm sure there's no need,' said Ellen. 'I've seen how good you are at mental arithmetic, but Reverend Holcroft knows what he is doing too.'

There was one of those awkward pauses, where the longer nobody says anything, the less there is for anybody to say.

Felix lifted more mashed potatoes and gravy to his mouth. Violet played with the food on her plate. When she looked up again, her expression was obstinate.

BANTLING

'We could work out a system so people could afford to repay you bit by bit. That way, the money keeps going round, does good more than once. It's just a matter of keeping track,' she said. 'It's not that hard,' and pushed a forkful of cabbage into her mouth.

Ellen leaned back in her chair to watch her husband be challenged.

BANTLING

15 Violet. Stockwell. 1923.

Stockwell, London SW9, ~~7 Feb 15 February~~, 3 March 1923, Dear Stel, If you could see me, you'd say I was like a pig in clover, what with my own room & a bathroom down the hall with cold water from the taps & hot water from the geyser straight into the bath. Beats a lick & a promise in the kitchen with pump water any day. Still, everything has its price. Reverend & Mrs H are kind enough, but she is always on to me about one thing or another. She's had me earning my keep, ripping up sheets for bandages & putting pen to paper for her, says I have a neat hand. So I am kept busy. Mostly I don't mind, but she sometimes forgets my feet swell up like Bath buns. I got out of washing a barrow-load of bottles (for the free dispensary since you ask) by saying I would take a look at the Reverend's books for him. They're a bit of a mess & no wonder as he never gets anyone to sign for any of the hand-outs or asks them for receipts. Still, you know yours truly, I can get most things untangled. He hardly said a word to me when I got here, but me getting his figures more or less balanced has softened him up no end & now he always has a kind word for me. I make him carry a receipt book with him & account to me every night. She says I'm being cheeky, but I don't think she minds too much. I've been chasing up who owes him for what as well, so you might say I am working my passage. If I keep this up, but don't hold your breath, he

BANTLING

might give me a reference afterwards. She is a bit of an odd one. I hear her around the house in the early hours sometimes. Some of the floorboards & doors creak & scroop, so I can tell when she is wandering about. I am not a good sleeper at the moment either, can you believe it, me, who can nod off under the dentist's drill. Your stamps are a lifeline, bless you, but best not to send any more for the moment & for pity's sake don't write back as I don't want Mrs H intercepting them, even though I miss hearing what you are up to. She keeps trying to trick me into letting slip about Wriggler's father, but she doesn't get a scuddick out of me. I have my mind set that his name will never soil my lips again. She watches the letters I get & makes sure they are from Mim & Da & doles out stamps & envelopes to send back as though they are licensed goods. All for my own good, ha-ha. She fitted me out with material for three smocks & the underwear to go with them, though I said I had the money. Mrs H's taste is not mine, but she was paying & as I look like a sofa whatever I wear it hardly matters, though I did hold out for a nice plain blue. I will be able to cut it down later & turn it into something I can wear for working & she has found me a thick old cape for outdoors, a real mildew Mildred outfit. I saw Doctor, a lady one no less. I'm coming round to the idea bit by bit. Very neat & clean she is, a Temperancer. I think she knows what she's about. She does not believe in eating for two. Turns out that too much food makes Wrigglers too big & gives us poor women a harder time. She's only little herself, but

BANTLING

with hands like a baker, nice & strong & very reassuring, though I don't know she will deliver the Wriggler herself unless I am an emergency. She tells me I have to take warm baths & walk 3 miles every day, come rain or shine, so it gets me out of the house, though Mrs H often comes too & I'm only by myself every now & then, which is why this letter is so late again. I don't go off with her on her Lady Bountiful visits because there might be something that would be bad for the Wriggler. I don't want her to catch me posting anything, she'd only want to scrutinise it first for loose morals & secret assignations. You know how nearly all the pictures you ever see of London show the river so you think you can see it from anywhere you might happen to be? Not true. Round here is not exactly the same all over & true there is a big flat piece of green common with ponds not so far away that they are all very proud of, but mostly London is paved roads, houses, street lamps, trams & air full of gritty bits so that when you blow your nose your hankie is a sorry sight & the river might as well be a hundred miles away. I wish you were with me. Mim too, though she would fuss more than you, but I wouldn't care. Mim says Stan still asks after me, but she doesn't think he's got a clue. I suppose I should drop him a line, but what to say? I don't suppose you've run into the other one? Whatever happened to him? I thought he'd come good for me, I really did, though I know I said different. Just goes to show, never a penny's worth of pleasure without a pound's worth of pain. Hey nonny nonny, what a pickle. Violet.

BANTLING

16 Ellen. Stockwell. 1923.

A good stock takes time, but it's well worth it. Ellen got going early, ages before Violet was likely to rouse herself. All that toing and froing during the night twixt bed and bath, it was a wonder if the girl shut her eyes at all. If she was sleeping now, Ellen did not want to wake her. Ellen herself was not sleeping much these days; found she did not need much rest. It was true that the more one did, the more one was capable of doing. Besides, it was easier to get on without having to worry about anybody else. Even Mrs Dawson hadn't arrived yet.

She started the broth for unfortunate Alice Wingrove, still very much under the weather, even after all this time. She filled the big pot with water and heaved it onto the stove. Then she found she had to get the range going again, raking out the ashes and feeding the embers still glowing inside the stove. Happily, Mrs Dawson had set everything to hand before she'd left the night before.

Perhaps it was the clatter, perhaps it was just how it was, but Violet was soon up and about after all.

'Shall I make us a pot of tea and give you a hand? As long as I can sit down while I chop.'

By the time Mrs Dawson arrived, the kitchen had become a warm savoury fug of chicken and pigs' trotters, vegetable parings and bay leaves. It was such a nice change to work side-by-side in harmony with somebody else.

Every now and then she or Violet stirred the pot, or pushed it further to the side of the range to bring it down to a gentler simmer. It was possible they got under Mrs Dawson's feet, but never mind, tra-la. She made it clear that Mrs Dawson in no way fell short, that her soups and stocks were more than adequate. This time, however, with a little help from Violet, Ellen was preparing a tasty little something for a parishioner who was poorly.

'She's taking her time getting better, that woman of yours,' said Mrs Dawson.

'At least she's up on her feet again,' replied Ellen. 'She seemed so partial to the broth last time, and she's eating so little else. I can't expect you to take on my duties, especially such a time-consuming one.'

'You can leave the pot to simmer. It will look after itself,' said Mrs Dawson. 'Go and have your breakfast, you two. The Reverend is waiting.'

When Ellen started to say that she wasn't hungry, Mrs Dawson put her foot down. 'You'll make yourself ill if you go on like this,' she said, funny old fusspot that she was.

After breakfast, they confronted the boxes and bags of goods for the Sale.

'Honestly, Mrs Holcroft, I don't mind what I do as

long as I can do it sitting down,' said the dear girl, and she was as good as her word.

Together they sat and mended doilies and antimacassars, cushion covers, beadwork, shawls, tablecloths and dolls' clothes. They darned woollen jumpers, scarves, gloves and the odd jacket and coat. Then for a bit of a change, as Violet put it, they tackled the polishing of silver-plate and costume jewellery until their fingers were black, their faces smeary and their noses itching. Just before lunch, Violet and Ellen strained the stock through the colander, pressing the bones and soft flesh to extract all the goodness. Violet pulled out the pieces of sweet meat from the mess of vegetables, skin and gristle and put them aside for later. Mrs Dawson could make a pie from them. Ellen finally asked the question that had been on her mind since Violet arrived.

'With all due respect, I've not told Mim and Da who the father is and I'll keep to it myself, if you don't mind. Thanks to you and the Vicar, the Wriggler and me have got a chance to make a go of it on our own, so what does he matter? You two have done more for us already that he's ever likely to.'

So, no answer, but the appreciation was touching.

Ellen covered the bowl of broth and set it in the larder to cool.

Later, she scraped off every last bit of the fat and set the jellied stock by the stove so that it became liquid again. As she lathered up some hot water, Mrs Dawson said rather pointedly that the bowl and saucepan were already perfectly clean, not a scrape of grease left on them. Rinsed to boot. Ah well. It was best to make sure.

Now to put most of the stock into the spotless pan to heat up.

Separate two eggs; put the whites into the sparkling bowl. They could use the yolks for an omelette or custard later. My oh my, if only she'd thought of that earlier. An egg custard would be easy for Mrs Wingrove to digest. Nutritious as well. On the other hand, it would be heavy to carry both broth and custard.

'Mrs Dawson, I'd like you to use these egg yolks in a custard for tonight. It will be nutritious for Violet.'

'I'll put them in the larder for tomorrow, Mrs Holcroft. I'm about to go home. Your dinner's done for when you want it. You just need to do some toast.

Beat the egg whites with half a pint of cold stock.

Violet poured the hot stock into the egg white mixture, Ellen beating all the time. Onto the stove with it, stirring carefully. Ellen did not take her eyes off it for a moment.

The liquid began to heat up. The egg whites appeared as white threads and speckles at first, whirling like snow, before rising to the surface. Already they were catching the bits and pieces of matter floating in the stock. She stirred smoothly until the surface began to shudder, then moved the pan to the side of the stove so only one edge caught the heat. Her face was moist with steam and her hair stuck to her forehead. The white foam thickened. From time to time, Violet took a hand with the stirring, but not for very long. It was difficult for her to stand on the stone floor for more than a few minutes. After ten minutes, Ellen gave the pot a quarter-turn. Felix poked in his head and muttered something about lost papers and clean collars. She waved him away. Let him fend for himself for once. A second turn, after ten more minutes, then a third. Violet heaved herself up, saying she'd give the Vicar a hand finding whatever it was he'd lost.

The surface of the stock had become a solid layer of brown and grey-flecked foam. This stock would be less like gruel and more like the sort of thing Mother used to serve at supper parties, a real treat for Alice Wingrove. It might even make up for Ellen not being as attentive of late as she might have been if she'd not had so much on her plate.

Five layers of butter muslin in the sieve, and Ellen was ready to ladle the hot stock into a deep jar.

She called out into the hallway, 'I need the bottle of port, Violet. You'll find it in the sideboard. Then, please come and hold the jar steady.'

Felix could be so selfish sometimes, keeping the girl busy when she clearly needed to take it easy.

A deep golden liquid cascaded down, glinting in the light, as transparent as glass, as rich as amber, as tasty as could be. A tablespoon of the port. There. It was done. Let it cool. Tomorrow, she would take it to Alice.

They feasted for supper on the marrow from the trotter, spread onto hot buttery toast, the three of them together, Violet quizzing and teasing Felix about loans and his receipt book, Felix looking positively merry. It struck Ellen how quickly and naturally they had all settled down together. Even when Felix tutted about the amount of time Ellen had spent on her feet in the kitchen and how she mustn't let things pile up, as much for her own sake as that of the parishioners, she still felt more kindly towards him than she had for years. Extraordinary to think she and Felix had not even known of Violet's existence until two months or so ago, nor she of theirs, and here they were today, chatting and at ease with one another. Just like a real family.

BANTLING

17 Violet. Stockwell. 1923.

London, 28th March, Dear Stanley, I have put off & put off writing this letter or actually I have written a deskful of letters & not posted any of them. This time, I have promised myself that I will finish it come what may & send it. I don't know if it was the thought of upsetting you more than you most likely already are or the shame of showing myself up for an ordinary fool that held me back. Anyway, I should not leave you in limbo any longer just because of my needless pride. You are no fool yourself & you always notice more than you let on & you'll have most probably guessed something of what I shall tell you from when you saw Mim & Da. Do not blame them if they were secretish. I asked them not to let on what has happened & said I would tell you myself. Perhaps I have taken comfort, false or not, that you might have an inkling of why I went off like I did & so will not be taken unawares. Even so, you must be puzzled & miffed, especially as we had some sort of understanding between us. I have so many things to say sorry to you for that you will have to take it as given, or I shall spend the whole letter apologising & none of it explaining. Yet what can I explain? I met someone who made me laugh & I made him laugh & I felt like a different person to the one that everyone else knew, more like the person I was inside. He didn't force me to do anything, I fell for his patter & the inevitable happened. He went away, of course, before

BANTLING

I even knew I was expecting & so here I am. Mim & Da were champion, clubbed together and with that plus my savings here I am now in London staying with a vicar & his wife. The plan is that I will stay in London & keep ~~the Wriggler~~ my baby though Mim & Da think this shows how much more of a fool I choose to be than I need be & that I am hell-bent on destroying not only my own life but theirs too. Perhaps they are right. I suppose I might have spun you some tale, or even told you the truth if I gave up my baby & you might still have given me another chance. But you deserve better & I can't abandon a kiddie through no fault of its own. This baby & me will love each other just because we have each other & we will start with a clean slate & he will need me. It is probably no comfort to you, but even though I had feelings for you & even if I was not in this mess, I was not ready to settle down. I should have told you that earlier & not kept you hanging on. The last time I saw Mim & Da they were thinking that if I had to make a show of myself with anyone, I should have picked you, that you would have stood by me & made everything alright. Most likely you would have, I know that as well, but it was not what I wanted. I have set my course & must steer the best I can & keep my baby safe however I can.

Now I have told you more than I have told Mim & Da or even my friend Estelle. I was always mostly open with you, more than with nearly everyone else. All this business aside, I hope you are well & your parents too. You must tell them what you think fit. I wish you only the best for the future, yours, Violet Bantling.

BANTLING

18 Ellen. Stockwell. 1923.

Ellen made her way in the direction of the coal yard. If she could catch Wingrove before she paid a visit to his wife, so much the better. She could use the excuse of ordering more coal for the vicarage, if it came to that. It was quite unfair of Felix, but so like him, to accuse her of neglecting her household and parochial responsibilities. That was what he thought, however much he smothered it in honey words about his concerns for her health. It was almost enough to make one sympathise with those more extreme advocates of women's rights, the way Felix plotted and schemed to put her back into his shadow. She wouldn't be surprised if he were jealous of everything she was achieving, befriending Violet, devising the home-visiting scheme and raising funds for it. No, on second thoughts, she would be surprised. He did not have enough inner fire for jealousy. His grumbling was because he felt himself being inconvenienced if she was not around whenever he looked up from his own tasks. And this in spite of all the benefits he had from Violet's presence. He had said himself only yesterday that it was much, much easier to manage his purse-strings now that Violet had devised a few simple rules for him. And as for Ellen's own health – just look at her. Bursting with vim. She had never felt better, never been better.

Wingrove was out on his rounds, she was told, due back sometime in the next hour. One of the men, the foreman perhaps, wanted to know if Harry was in some sort of bother or causing her any trouble, and she told them of course not, she just wanted to ask him about Mrs Wingrove. She wouldn't wait, thank-you and she'd leave no message.

Not far away she came across him unloading his children from the coal cart and telling them to scoot off home before anyone caught him. The boy put his arms around his sister and picked her up.

'I'll see them home,' she offered. 'I'm on my way to see your wife, as it happens.'

She pulled out one of the chocolate bars she had in her bag, and carefully broke it into pieces. Bertie put Doris back down on her feet.

'Just as long as you don't mind, Mr Wingrove. They say chocolate is very nutritious. And it's always a bit of a treat, isn't it?'

'Feel free if you can spare it.'

She handed each child a decent portion of chocolate. It sat, rich and glossy, in the palms of their grubby paws. She looked away. Dirt upset the heart of her.

'How is Mrs Wingrove these days?'

He pushed out his lower lip. 'Much the same.'

The children stared at the chocolate, then sniffed it. It must be the first time they had seen it, the first time they had it in their hands. Bertie risked a lick. Very serious, as cautious as a man experimenting with dynamite.

'It's been weeks,' she said. 'Months, even. She must surely have picked up since then.'

Bertie was grinning. He licked again. He nudged Doris, who still looked suspicious.

'Not so's you'd notice,' said Wingrove. 'She just lies there all day staring at whatever it is or nothing. Can just about get herself up and dressed, does a bit of the domestics, but leaves the kids and me to fend for ourselves more often than not. If it weren't for Flo, I don't know where we'd be. I told Alice what you thought, that the poor little blighter is probably best out of it.'

She stooped down to encourage Doris's hand towards her mouth.

'I did not say that, Mr Wingrove. I would never say that.'

'It's what you meant, what you all meant.'

She stared down at the pavement, did not deny it.

'No matter. I wouldn't say different myself. There's more where that one came from, I tell her, but it cuts no ice with her.'

'Give her time,' said Ellen. Her own eyes prickled, she felt so sorry for the woman, grieving not only the loss of one child, but the emptiness of hope. Men always assumed there would be another chance, another time. Women knew one could not assume anything but the worst. All the same, Mrs

BANTLING

Wingrove had other responsibilities. She should not let herself succumb.

Wingrove shook his head. 'We've seen hard times before, but Alice, she's never turned her face away from me before, not once.'

She wondered what it might be like to share your life with somebody whose gaze you always relied on, come good times or bad.

Doris took a little bite of chocolate. Ellen nodded and smiled encouragement. Doris nibbled again.

What a marvellous mother Ellen would have made.

Bertie's method was to suck at the chocolate. It became thinner and thinner, more elongated and pointed, until it had more than a passing resemblance to a tongue itself. When it was finished, he licked his fingers and around his lips, trying to get every last skerrick. He looked at Doris's portion with a calculating eye.

'See what happens when you gobble it all down at once, soft-brain,' said Wingrove. 'You should have made it last longer.'

'There's more where that came from,' said Ellen, 'once they get home.' She gave Bertie another piece in the meanwhile.

'I best get on,' said Wingrove. 'They'll be missing me at the yard.'

Doris tugged at Ellen's hand, angling for another treat. She got it.

Bertie picked up Doris again, and started to stagger

down the street with her. Ellen walked with the children, and after a while took a turn to carry Doris. The chocolate she kept in her pocket, dishing out a morsel every now and then.

BANTLING

19 Violet. Stockwell. 1923.

Stockwell, London SW9, March 28th, Dear Stel, I'm making hay while Lady Bountiful goes off on one of her mercy missions. I shouldn't mock, the poor woman she has gone to visit sounds in an awful sorry state & it could be me next month, but oh the fuss about making her some soup & getting it just so. I am miserable fed up with London, Stel. That makes me sound ungrateful & perhaps I am, though not really. I'm just that tired with being so grateful all the time to everyone. Yesterday I was out walking & went by a fruit shop, very fancy with greenhouse fruits displayed like jewels. I trod on a grape that had fallen on the pavement. As I felt it squish, it so reminded me of us walking on the beach, jumping & stamping on the bladderwrack like a couple of scallywags to make it pop. I tell you Stel, I had a month's mind to catch the train there & then & not give a fig for anything, just to see rocks & waves & boats at work again. I want to see big skies & clouds piled high one above the other & the sea stretching out from the cliffs, all those greys that make me think of pearls & silver & shot silk & sometimes the sea is blue or green or so dark I haven't got a word for it, but it is always huge & alive, making you feel as vast as it is & smaller than a speck of sand, all at the same time. Sometimes, standing on a rock, hair lashing & spray dinning all around me, I used to feel as though I was part of it, like the little mermaid turning into foam

& light & air. Other times, the sea's out to get anybody proud enough to think they can sail upon it & come home safe & sound. They say we all come from the sea once upon a time, Stel, but I reckon Londoners never did. They stumbled out of mud. I trust you are cheerier than me, your home-sick, soul-sick friend, Violet. P.S. I think you might write back, so long as you make it seem as though you haven't heard from me. Tell me where you are going, what fun you are having & if you are reading anything I would like too. P.P.S. I have written to Stan & burnt those bridges.

20 Ellen. Stockwell. 1923.

Flo was hard at it in the green-grocer's shop, shifting sacks of potatoes and such. She opened the door from the street and pointed Ellen up the stairs.

'Look smart, Alice. Visitor!' she shouted.

Doris ran up to one of the doors on the landing. The handle was too high for her, so she banged her hand against it.

'Ma! Ma!'

Bertie dragged his feet, Ellen thought. Perhaps, like her, he wasn't sure what he'd find on the other side. Chin up, Ellen. Deep breath. There's probably nothing you won't have seen before.

Bertie pushed open the door and grabbed hold of his sister.

The room was nowhere as bad as she remembered. There were faintish traces of ammonia and sour milk in the air, more or less hidden by the savoury wafts of meat essence, the sulphurous lingering of cabbage and the smell of damp clothes trying to dry, but the reek of blood and human waste had gone. The light in the room was brighter. The windows had been cleaned, she thought, and the curtains washed. Good signs.

Alice had her back to the door as they came in. The wall around her glistened with condensation.

'Mind how you go. There's boiling water here', she

said. 'I've made some potato stew for your tea. What do you think to that?'

'Ma,' said Bertie. 'Ma. There's a lady here.'

'What lady is that, Bert,' she said and looked around. She was as pale as salt, her face darkly shadowed, but her hair was neat and her clothes clean. Alice Wingrove beckoned and pulled her children close.

'Lady gave us chocolate,' said Doris.

That's nice,' said Alice.

'Hello again, Mrs Wingrove,' said Ellen, as brightly as she could muster. She took the jar of consommé from her basket and held it out. 'Just a little something to build you up a bit. Freshly made yesterday.'

It would take more than even Mother's recipe to get rid of the dazed look in Alice's eyes and the hunch of her shoulders.

'Very thoughtful, Mrs Holroyd,' she said. She took the jar and stood it under the little table. 'You two, wash your hands. Bertie, make sure Doris gets all that coal muck off herself. There's some clean water in the pail. I'll dish up while it's still hot.'

She seemed distant, cut off, but it might do Alice Wingrove good to talk to somebody. To Ellen, for instance, who had seen so much of what she had been through, had been through it herself.

'Would you mind if I stayed for a cup of tea? I don't need to be at the hospital for the best part of an hour.'

Alice gave a defeated shrug. 'As you please. If you

don't mind the mess. There's nowhere to dry things except over the bedsteads. Sit over there, if you want.'

Alice gestured towards the bigger bed, but all things considered, Ellen preferred to stand. The bed was neat enough and seem clean, but Ellen had too vivid a picture of what had, or might have happened, in it and on it. All that blood and agony and loss of hope. All that intimacy and touching. The smalls and bodices draped over the head and footboards didn't help. Still, at least and with a bit of luck, it meant Alice was up to doing the washing.

She looked around the room. The walls were dotted every now and then with postcards, five or six in all. She looked more closely. Only black and white, and tiny reproductions of course, one or two of young women not quite on the right side of decency, covered in drapery and sporting long, unbound hair. Others were of country and seaside views.

Them's ma's,' said Bertie. 'She likes pictures.'

He scrabbled under the children's bed and produced two orange crates.

Out of curiosity – the pictures seemed so out of character for the rest of the room – and with a quick 'I hope you don't mind?' she unpinned a picture of cliffs and women in old-fashioned dresses on a rocky foreshore and read the back. William Dyce, Pegwell Bay, 1858. From the Tate Gallery, of all places. Who would have thought it?

'Is this your part of the country?' she asked

BANTLING

Alice was ladling something steamy into bowls. The potato stew, Ellen surmised. Potatoes, cabbage and bottled meat essence from the smell of it. It didn't smell too bad.

'Me? I'm from Battersea. I used to go across the river to look at the paintings from time to time when I was young. It's free to look if a person's got the time. And it's warm.'

The children sat on the crates and Alice handed them each a dish.

'Careful now. It's hot.'

'You're still young, time enough to do anything you want,' encouraged Ellen, but it was hard to believe, looking at the demoralised, exhausted woman in front of her.

Alice sighed.

'The gas's run out before the kettle's boiled. At least you two got your tea. That's it until our lord and master gets back.'

She sat down heavily on the bed. Her eyes were raw and red-rimmed as she looked up at Ellen, tears tricking down her face.

'Sorry, Mrs Holcroft. I'm all done in.'

Ellen said, 'I'm sure I have a shilling for the meter,' and started to rootle in her bag. 'I could make the tea. Where do you keep the tea leaves? And the pot? Or I could heat up some broth.'

Alice shook her head. 'Once I start crying, it doesn't

stop until it stops. I could be made of salt water. Only thing to do is sleep my way through it.'

She lifted her feet onto the covers, moving slowly and heavily. Even Felix was sprightlier.

'Bertie love, keep an eye on your sister for us.'

She rolled on her side and was immediately still.

Ellen understood, she really did, how grief can take you up and shake you ragged, how hard it is to set your feet on anything like firm ground again.

BANTLING

21 Violet. Stockwell. 1923.

Stockwell, London SW9, 3 April, Dearest Mim, Your letter was such a shock. How is Da? Is he getting better? I wish I was there with you all, though much good I would be in my present state & you don't need anything else on your plate. I am so far along, only another couple of weeks or so to go, that Mrs Holcroft will not let me risk the journey down & then even if she did what happens when the baby comes? You'd have two more of us on your hands. Besides the sight of me might upset Da & do more harm than good. Now more than ever I wish I had not got myself in this predicament. I know you will be run off your feet, but please if you have a crack of time tell me how Da is doing when you can. I don't suppose Collin's are giving him anything for compensation even though he got hurt at work. Here is £9 of the money you lent me, which will help with doctors. I will send a bit more as soon as I can. Poor Mim, I am crying for you both, please make sure you eat & sleep too. I send a kiss from me to you & to Da as well. I hope he likes the Turkish Delight. I made it myself as it will not break like lemon curd if the postman drops it. Oh Mim, you are in my thoughts all the time. Love from Violet.

BANTLING

22 Ellen. Stockwell. 1923.

'Some bacon, my dear?'

Violet looked at the rashers. She put down her knife and fork very neatly across her plate.

'Actually, I won't, thank you, Mrs Holcroft. Though it smells lovely.'

'Come, come, Violet. I know Doctor McCall has taken you off meats for the rest of your term, but you have to eat something. Bacon's tasty and nutritious. It won't help your father if you don't eat. You mustn't give them anything else to worry about.'

Violet shook her head.

Felix said he wouldn't mind a bit more bacon himself in that case, if it was going begging.

Beyond the window, the greens of the garden were so vivid she could hardly look away. The daffodils were dying off, but tulips still gleamed like fresh paint.

Ellen passed him the dish and picked up the toast rack.

'Have some more toast and marmalade, at least. You're eating for two, after all.'

Violet shook her head and dabbed at her lips. 'I've had quite enough, thank-you.'

'If you feel up to it, Violet, I thought we would take the tram to the Common. It's so pretty up there at this time of year. We might walk to the Junction for a cup of tea. Then perhaps we can see if we can't find some nice material for a christening dress,' said Ellen.

That should cheer the girl up a little, take her mind off her father. It was not good for her to fret so, not so close to her delivery time. In Ellen's opinion, the parents had been reckless telling Violet about the accident at this stage. It was not as though she could be of much help.

Ellen had in mind a fine lawn, something soft, that she could trim with a little lace and a narrow pink satin ribbon.

Outside, the blue-tits scrabbled at the bird table alongside a robin and a blackbird. Ellen started to collect together the left-over bacon rinds for the birds.

'That's everso so thoughtful, Mrs Holcroft, but I can't have you paying for anything else, and with Da off work like he is, I've got to watch every penny now, even more than before. I don't want to be a burden.'

'It was kind, but possibly a little hasty to send off that large postal order to your parents. You'll have enough expenses of your own soon enough.'

'Besides, they're expecting me at the hospital before lunch.'

Ellen had received no notice of this new appointment. 'Is everything alright? There's nothing wrong with you or Baby, I hope. What time do we have to leave?'

Violet looked startled, turned to Felix, looked back again at Ellen.

'What? What?' asked Ellen. 'What's going on?'

'It's not an appointment,' said Violet. 'There's no need for you put yourself out. The Reverend has arranged for me to look over their books. It just came up yesterday.'

'Felix?'

He looked up, egg and toast crumbs in his moustache. You would think a grown man could at least keep his own mouth clean.

'I mentioned to Miss Barnabas and Doctor what a grand job Violet did getting us ship-shape here at the Vicarage, and as the girl that did the books has gone off sick, it seemed like the perfect solution,' he said.

It was not up to him. They'd agreed. They had an understanding, right from the start. Ellen would concern herself about all the day-to-day matters regarding Violet, but any important decisions would be made by both of them, him and her together, hand-in-hand.

'She's about to have a baby. She shouldn't be worrying about that sort of thing at this stage. Honestly Felix, sometimes I think men have no sense at all.'

Violet looked dismayed.

Felix said, 'But dear ...'

'But nothing,' said Ellen. She had to be firm. It was all for the best. It was not pleasant to be cast in the role of kill-joy, but somebody had to behave responsibly.

Felix and Violet looked at each other in that way she'd begun to notice.

BANTLING

She scraped her fingers lightly inside her wrists.

'I promised I'd do what I can before the Wriggler arrives,' said Violet. 'It'll take my mind off Da, perhaps.'

Felix added in a low voice, as though Violet could not hear him, that there would be a little payment for Violet's time. It would be a small help for her, and once she had recovered after the baby, there might be a few more opportunities.

'I suppose if you've promised, you've promised. I don't know why nobody thought to mention it to me.'

'Sorry to inconvenience you, Mrs Holcroft.'

'My apologies, my dear. It was all rather last minute and it slipped my mind.'

She rang the bell. There would be no time for another cup of coffee.

'It's just that I have so much to do this morning, so much, but I suppose I must just rearrange everything. I have obligations as well, you know.'

Felix piped up. He would go with Violet to the hospital; he had business there this morning in any case. Ellen should do whatever it was she needed to. He would make sure Violet did not overdo it. In the end, Ellen had to be content with that.

BANTLING

23 Violet. Stockwell. 1923.

Stockwell, London SW9, 15th April, Dear Stel, I am in such a state, such a frenzy. Did I write to you last week or not? Between the Wriggler almost here & Da being so poorly, my mind's not my own. I churn through days like old ships' timbers afloat & fidget & heave-ho in my bed & wait & worry. Only another week to or so to go. Golly. The Wriggler was like a Jack-in-the-box for centuries, though he's got quieter as he fills the space more closely & now seems quite settled, his little backside riding up so high I can almost touch it with my nose. I pat & rub him & hope he cannot tell what sort of state I am in. Though of course the Wriggler might not be a he at all. I am fair scared, though I can't tell anyone of course. I think Mrs H is worried sick about the delivery, which is not a great help. She hovers over me & is even more solicitous than I think Mim would be if she was here & did not have other things on her mind. I fret & miz about Da the whole time. Mim has gone all quiet on me. Mrs H says that is probably a good sign, but I have the feeling that Mim means not to worry me with more bad news. There's nothing I can do, not presently, there's no going back now. I tell you, don't fall for a baby if you can help it. Rev H has given me a bit of book-keeping to do to take my mind off things, but it is not working & seems to have put Mrs H's nose out of joint as well, though why it should, who knows. My brain limps around &

pretends it never knew anything & double entry least of all. For the most part, everything seems mostly in order, but there is one thing I cannot get straight & the girl is off sick & nobody else knows, so it niggles at me. I have asked some tradesmen for statements. It would be nice to have it clear in my mind before the end of the world arrives, but I care less & less. I want my Mim here & I want Da recovered. How will I manage once the Wriggler is in the open? Yours in a state, Violet. P.S. I want to know how things are with you too, but if you told me, I'd probably forget. Oh, that's right, you've been off shimmying on a Saturday. I bet you're a lovely sight. Will you teach me one day too?

BANTLING

24 Ellen. Stockwell. 1923.

It would not do to be caught unawares. She closed the door of the box room and pushed a broken chair under the handle. No doubt Felix thought a chair with a splintered leg might yet be mended – though who was to organise that, she'd like to know – or be useful in some other way – and lo! so it was.

Mostly the view from the room was of the church's stucco wall, but she caught glimpses of traffic beyond the greening trees. People were busy about their business. She stood still, taking her time for once, stretching out the moments of longing. Her breath misted the window. When she couldn't bear to delay a moment longer, she drew an open eye on the fogged glass and left it there to stare out in her place.

The small room was stacked with cases and boxes, with odds and ends that Felix was sure could be useful again or that he was keeping safe for those shadowy ageing lads who passed through. Beyond the room, the house was almost silent, Mrs Dawson safely in her kitchen, Felix and Violet out and about, even lumbering as Violet was, and complaining about her back and legs. They'd said they didn't expect to be back for at least an hour. What exactly was it that Felix had insisted Violet do at this time? They'd rushed off in a panic together to the hospital after some tradesman or other had turned up at the door in a bit of a mood. What hope was there if tradesmen could not even keep an account of what they had sold to whom? Violet should be thinking only of the baby, keeping calm, not allowing her nerves to have the better of her. Such a silly tizz about some records not matching. What did it matter in the end? Not that Violet saw it like that. Such a conscientious young woman. She'd even shaken off Ellen trying to soothe her. She was doing Baby no good. Felix should have known better than to have got her started on more columns of figures just when she needed to be placidly waiting for her time. And he should have known it was typical of Violet to feel she had to earn the charity the hospital was offering.

But every cloud, as they say, has a silver living. Here she was, by herself. An hour was not a very long time, but an hour alone was certainly not to be sneezed at. She had to move a hat box or two, and balance them on the chair against the door, and push a box of jumble against it too. Anybody trying to get in now would find it awkward. They would have to push and make a noise and could not take her by surprise.

The case was hidden well enough, but with a little squeezing and stretching it was within her reach. Old and worn as the red leather was, and with her girlhood initials on the lid, the case would not tempt Felix to open it, not even in his most distracted moods. Even so, better safe than sorry. She untangled the key from beneath her dress. Drat her fingers, coming over so thick and stiff. More haste, less speed. There we go. Open now.

Arthur's jacket. The one he wore when they walked together. The touch of it still reassured and calmed her. Shaking out the creases, putting it on, was like climbing onto a life-raft, with fathoms still below her and wild waters all around, something buoyant now between her and the raging current, keeping her afloat, at least for the moment. She hugged herself into the lining, rubbed her chin against the rough material of the revers, swaying into the embrace, the collar sheltering her neck. She breathed in and smelled only naphthalene. Any scent of Arthur was long gone.

She stroked the fabric, looking for a message in the fine herringbone of the pattern, in the light and dark of the browns and flecks of red, even though that was nonsense and she should pull herself together and get on with her never-ending list of tasks.

The sound of the front door opening and shutting. Some clattering in the downstairs hall. Voices, a world away.

The lining of the jacket was smooth and icy and slightly musty when she pulled it up against her cheeks, and the sleeves hung down past her fingertips. It was so bulky that it sat as comforting as an overcoat. Mothballs or not, now, when she breathed in, a sunny afternoon in a garden flickered in her mind's eye, smooth lush greens, dark hedges and a sky the colour of forget-me-nots. They must have walked, she and Arthur, young sweethearts that they were, towards the river or across the golf-course, passing picnics and ramblers, with views and perspectives changing all the while. All that had disappeared without a trace. It was a thousand years ago.

A car's motor outside, doors opening and slamming, both metal and wood.

Mrs Dawson's voice, Felix's, Violet's, one on top of the other.

Another minute or two more to herself would make no difference one way or another.

She wrapped her arms around her shoulders and could feel the texture of the jacket through the fabric of her dress, and the weight of her young love's arm, briefly, guiltily around her shoulders. It was not disloyal to the life she actually had, surely, to honour the one that never was?

Somebody called her name, and for a moment she was caught between then and now.

'Ellen! Where are you? Ellen?'

It was a man's voice, heavier and older than the one she still missed.

'Ellen!'

More doors opening and shutting downstairs, footsteps heavy through the hallway. He was looking for her.

She looked towards the door. If it came to it, perhaps it would all be so much easier if Felix were to find her like this, wrapped in the past. It was her other life, the life she would have had, her if-only life.

'Ellen!'

The hodgepodge of noise started to separate. There was Mrs Dawson's voice, slow and even, as though instructing a simple person, the odd inaudible response from Violet, Felix's loudness.

'Ellen! Are you here?'

There were other bits and pieces in the red case, carefully wrapped in tissue. Little knitted bootees, so soft. The tiny bonnet. She would knit something charming for Violet and her child, surely, but she would not give up these treasures. No time today to do more than stroke the relics. She had been a different woman when she knitted them. The might-have-been, the if-only woman.

'Ellen!'

'Mrs Holcroft!'

'She can't have gone out. Ellen!'

She'd tell Felix if he asked, which he won't if she knows the first thing about him, she'd tell him the vanity case was sentimental, a gift to a girl from her parents, which was true. Naturally, one did not lie unless to spare another's feelings. She would tell Felix that it only contained a few mementos, which was also true - not quite the full truth, but one didn't like to cause unnecessary hurt any more than one liked to tell untruths. Felix had first met Ellen in tears and sorrow when he brought her the news about her Arthur's senseless death in the camp outside Ladysmith. Her grief had won his sympathy in the first place, but he had married her for her fortitude. If this little case, with its padded satin lining kept her strong, that was all for the good. The jacket and baby clothes might unsettle him, but only because he'd worry about her fragility. The greater danger was he'd think they were intended for Violet and she would lose them.

'Ellen? Please, dear. Come quickly! For Heaven's sake, where is she?'

He was a good-enough man and she had accepted his limitations the day she'd agree to marry him.

She heard or felt his heavy footfalls on the wooden floor of the landing. Running, at his age.

Quick, quick. Tissue around the knitting. Fold the jacket, sleeves to the inside, lining out, roll it and fit it inside the case. Turn the key. Thrust the case away. Free the door.

'Really, Felix. What on earth is all this hullaballoo? I'm just sorting out the rubbish up here. Look at what you've gone and done, knocking things about pushing at the door like that.'

Felix was trying to say something, flapping his hands, opening and closing his mouth like a goldfish. Whatever it was, it could wait until she had given enough reason and indignation for her to be in the trunk-room.

At the far end of the corridor, Mrs Dawson came out of Violet's room and started back down the stairs.

'Do you want this broken chair, or can we consign it for firewood? Never mind. I am going now to the kitchen to discuss with Mrs Dawson what there is for lunch.'

Felix stopped her. He stood in front and blocked her way and put his hand on her arm. Not so gently either. With purpose.

'Ellen. Forget about lunch. Quickly, prepare yourself. It's Violet. It seems her baby is on the way. Pains, you know, very sudden, - on the way back. I had to flag down a cab. Mrs Dawson's running for the midwife.'

BANTLING

25 Ellen. Stockwell. 1923.

As Felix was prattling, the front door banged shut. A picture came to Ellen's mind of Mrs Dawson scurrying away down the path to fetch the midwife while Ellen walked swiftly and calmly towards Violet's room. For some reason it made her smile, one person going away, the other coming closer, her Violet at the centre of it all. Perhaps she would consider passing on the bootees, after all.

She sent Felix to fetch the stack of old clean towels and sheets she'd had the sense to put aside, and to put saucepans of water on to boil and make sure the copper was stoked up. He grumbled about where to find the right pans and the matches, so she ended up more or less doing it herself; it was so much quicker. It just showed how much she could do, how much the smooth running of their lives, all their lives, rested on her. Thankfully, after the initial flurry, and a bit of fuss and moaning from Violet about her aching back, everything quietened down again. It seemed her waters had not yet broken. They had some time ahead of them still.

Felix was put to drag rugs and the chair out of Violet's bedroom, and when Mrs Dawson made it back with the news that a midwife would be there soon, the two of them tackled the dressing table, the chest of drawers, and even manoeuvred the small wardrobe out into the hall.

They call it the calm before the storm and no wonder. Still, it gave Ellen time to help Violet get ready. First a good dose of castor oil, and then a warm bath. Violet insisted on having this by herself. She had managed up to now, she said, though Ellen would have been perfectly happy to lend a hand today of all days. They were both women, after all, and this was no time for prudish modesty. What if Violet slipped on the soap and could not get up again and they could not get in to help her? What then? Eventually Violet agreed, or was persuaded, to leave the bathroom door unlocked, just in case. Ellen hurried downstairs to hang out a fresh nightdress to air in the kitchen. The girl spent so long in the bath that Ellen had to knock once or twice, just to check she was alright. Violet kept saying she was very comfortable, it was lovely just lying there, her back was hardly aching at all.

How would she tell if her waters broke?

Under Ellen's instructions, Mrs Dawson mopped down the floor with hot water and disinfectant, wiped over the skirting boards and windowsills, opened the window top and bottom, laid a new fire. The housekeeper had already had the curtains down a week or two before for washing, which Ellen thanked her for. What with everything else that had been going on, she'd not thought of it herself. Mrs Dawson and Ellen got the sheets off the bed and replaced them with several layers of older ones, boil-washed and properly aired.

They ate a make-shift lunch as they worked.

More than once, Ellen heard gurgling water from the bathroom and then the roar and swoosh of the geyser as the hot tap was turned on again. For heaven's sake, if Violet didn't get herself out soon the baby would be born in the bathroom.

They swilled bowls and basins and a chamber pot with more boiling water and Lysol. They hung up Baby's delightful first clothes to air, the sweet little pale-yellow bonnet and bootees, the soft gown. They made up the crib. The nappies and safety pins, water-softening powder, fine talc, Vaseline, lanolin, Hazeline and small soft sponges were all placed close to hand.

By the time Violet had heaved herself out of the bath, put on a clean nightdress, and opened the bathroom door, everything in her room was as hygienic as they could make it. Ellen had changed too, and put on a spotless apron. She had washed her hands with carbolic soap several times, Mrs Dawson as well, though by now it was almost time for her to go. Of all the days for it to be her half-day.

'I'm sorry, Mrs Holcroft. I'd stay if I could. You're as ready as can be. I'll get here early in the morning if I can.'

Felix had taken himself off a while ago, of course. Getting out from under their feet he called it.

'Nobody told me it would be like this.'

It came out as a sort of yelp. Violet had one hand pressed to her back, another to her abdomen, rocking where she stood. She hadn't made it back to the bedroom yet, seemed marooned in the hall.

'Oh, dear,' said Ellen. She found herself pressing her nails into her palms. 'I do hope everything's going to go smoothly. What if ... ?'

'You're doing everything just fine,' Mrs Dawson interrupted. 'A nice blooming strong girl like you, properly fed and fit as a fiddle, everything that happens will be par for the course. Not easy, mind, but just you keep breathing. You take my word for it. By the time I come back tomorrow, you'll have a healthy good-looking baby and you'll have forgotten what all the fuss was about. Just be prepared to put your back into it when the time comes. Now, you lean on me. I'll get you settled into bed before I take off. If you're a good girl, Mrs Holcroft will make you some nice sweet tea, isn't that right Mrs Holcroft, and perhaps a piece of toast. There, there. Mrs Holcroft and the midwife will take good care of you.'

She rubbed Violet's back for few moments and it seemed to calm the girl down a little. Watching the house-keeper leave fifteen minutes later, Ellen felt her singularity, her loneliness, her loss. Panic eddied just below her calm. She dug her nails into her wrists and picked up the tea tray.

BANTLING

Let the midwife arrive soon. Please. Let it better than the last time.

A midwife called in when the sun was already noticeably lower. She examined Violet and set off again on her bicycle, deciding for some inexplicable reason that Violet would be perfectly fine for another few hours, saying that there was a more urgent case elsewhere. She, or someone else, would be back soon to check on the situation. In the meanwhile, Violet and Ellen were to carry on just as they were, but to light the fire before long if it started to get chilly and to close the windows a bit.

Violet could not keep still, wanted to roam the house, but Ellen managed to keep her to her room most of the time. There was a lot of waiting around, when Ellen would fill the hot-water bottle, make some more tea or pour lemonade. Violet would pace around the room, then cling to the bedstead panting and huffing, clutching and rubbing her abdomen. She was much noisier than Alice Wingrove and much less well-behaved.

Perhaps that was all for the best.

My oh my.

Time dragged. Violet dozed and woke yelping or wincing or smiling dreamily, secretively.

Time rushed by, clouds floating across the sky, tinged rosy-pink along one fluffy side.

Violet became very grumpy, verging on rude. One must not take it personally.

BANTLING

Ellen noticed the trees, dark against the pale green sky. It was so late, already.

Felix came home and wanted something to eat. There were sandwiches left from lunch under a damp tea-towel downstairs, and Ellen told him to fend for himself and bring up some tea for them both while he was at it.

Her hair was sticky across her forehead.

The moon was just visible behind the trees, had hardly risen at all and the sky still had lightness in it, was nearly as pale as the moon itself.

She heaped up the fire, lit the gas lamp and wished there was an electric light in Violet's room. No tea arrived. Violet was on her feet whimpering again, water on the floor beneath her.

'I'm so sorry. Look what I've gone and done.'

'Don't worry,' said Ellen. 'It's perfectly normal. You had better lie down again. It won't be so long now.'

'I CAN'T MOVE, YOU … YOU … SILLY WOMAN AND I DON'T WANT TO LIE DOWN. I just want this over and done with.'

She started crying.

Ellen ignored Violet's rudeness. She let Violet lean on her as she waddled back to bed. Her nightdress was soaked, so Ellen helped her off with it. Unclothed, Violet seemed huge. Blue and purple veins threaded her stretch-striped rosy-cream body. Her swollen dark-pointed breasts rested against her high abdomen. Hastily, Ellen gave her a towel and clean nightie and looked away as Violet tidied herself up.

There was darkness outside the window and inside the room, and the moon was a little higher.

'I'm so tired already,' sobbed Violet. 'How much longer will this go on for? What happens if my baby comes and the midwife is still messing around somewhere else? Why doesn't she come?'

Ellen's thoughts exactly.

'It's never easy. You're doing well. I'm sure she won't be long now.'

She took away the wet nightdress and fetched a mop.

In the gap between the curtains, the moon had risen well above the trees. They had been in this room their whole lives.

It was as she was wringing out a Lysol-soaked cloth to wipe the floor that she heard the doorbell at last, and Felix going to answer it. When she saw Nurse Henderson appear with her case at the top of the stairs, Ellen could have hugged her.

Time twisted and curled up on itself, then stretched and stretched. She forgot there ever had been a moon or a sun. There was nothing except Violet's pain and exhaustion, the smells and noises.

She wondered aloud if a little alcohol might help poor Violet, take the edge off the pain; she was sure Mrs Dawson had some brandy or sherry put by.

'No,' said Nurse Henderson, a little sharply. 'It

gives false comfort, clouds the patient's mind when she needs it most, and does the child no good whatsoever. Doctor McCall never uses it and has never lost a mother. Don't fret. Violet is doing well.'

Well might be good enough, but Ellen herself was all of a jitter, what with all the grunting and wailing, and watching Violet suffering and the lack of sleep and the not-knowing. It was more than a person could stand. A sip, just one, would steady her, set her up for whatever was coming. Doctor might advocate temperance, and so did Ellen for the most part – she'd had no medicine for months – but this would do no harm. On the contrary.

'I'll fetch some more coal,' she offered, and added in a whisper, so as not to discourage Violet, 'It's going to be a while yet, isn't it?'

'Don't talk about me as though I'm not here,' shouted Violet. 'I'm not deaf.'

Ellen picked up the coal scuttle. She did not have much time, but she had enough, as long as Felix was not wandering around. Usually, he would have gone to bed by now, but usually there was not all this hullabaloo going on. Sure enough, as the stairs creaked, he emerged from his study. He asked the obvious questions, and she answered best she could.

She was suddenly weary to her bones.

She handed him the scuttle. 'Would you mind filling this for me?'

She turned on the light at the top of the cellar stairs

for him, and commented, as one or other of them always did, on the generosity of the diocese in agreeing to the installation of an electric light down there as well as throughout the ground floor.

'Easier to replace a bulb than a vicar.'

'And even cheaper.'

She left him to it.

Tucked away in the back of the larder was the sherry Mrs Dawson used in trifles on high-days and holidays. It would have to do. She would prefer the comfort of the medicinal draught in the linen cupboard upstairs, but it was too risky with Felix on the prowl. She uncorked the bottle, no time for a glass, and took a decent sip. Another smaller one, just a pick-me-up to see her through the night.

The clatter of coal against metal stopped. Another little sip, her lips wiped with the back of her hand, the bottle recorked and pushed back in place. Mrs Dawson would never notice.

'Be a dear and carry that up for me.' She smiled at him. 'Just leave it outside Violet's room. I'll rinse out these cups and make up another hot water bottle. I'll be up in a jiffy. You'd best get to bed. No point in all of us losing our beauty sleep.'

Did Felix look at her strangely? She turned to the sink, ran herself a glass of water. If she was not mistaken, she still had some cachous in her pocket. Probably best to chew on a couple. Nurse Henderson was not the understanding sort.

BANTLING

'You will let me know when anything happens, won't you? Wake me up if necessary.'

His voice startled her. She had no idea he was still standing there, coal scuttle in hand, black dust smearing his hands and forehead. It took a moment to catch what he meant.

'Yes, yes, of course.'

Nurse Henderson sent Ellen to rest for an hour or two. Obedient, warmed by the sherry, not sleepy in the slightest, she sat, fully clothed, on the sofa, and thought of this and that. She opened her eyes again, barely moments later, surely, and found the grey pre-dawn already in the room and a rug tucked around her. Felix was up too, already or still, it was hard to tell, loitering in the doorway, fidgeting up and down the corridor and stairs. He looked as though he had slept even less than Ellen. She called out to him in alarm, pushing away the rug, finding her feet. He came over.

'Best to let you sleep a little, I thought. I would have woken you if ... but nothing ...'

He squeezed her hands, which brought tears to her eyes.

'Well then, well then,' he said.

She sniffed and nodded and went back upstairs into the fray.

The room was close, the windows long shut against the night chills, Violet still sweating like a horse, red-faced and lank-haired. Ellen wiped her face, neck and throat with a damp flannel, gave her sips of water, tried to hold her hands, those slippery hands with the finger-wrenching grips at the end of flailing arms. Sobs and wails and great heaving gasps, Violet shouting for Nurse Henderson to get it out, just get it out, she knew she could, she'd pay anything they wanted, she had money, she'd get hold of more, just get it out of her. Noise and smells and the juddering light. Nurse Henderson, calm as anything, covered to her elbows in blood and worse, instructing Ellen to hold the torch steady.

Violet's private parts stretched huge, the creature came slithering from the maw, head as hairy as a coconut, the whole unearthly horror of pale translucency and glistening purple-red jumbled together. Blood, slime as thick as membrane, vivid green-yellow streaks all mixed and muddled as flesh yielded to flesh, one being thrusting forth another. She turned her head and backed away, but not before she had seen the pointed head and the sodden hair of what, after all, was only a miserable boy. She had not thought, did not know beforehand, that she cared one way or the other. But care she did. It should have been a girl. This creature that Nurse Henderson held aloft, the twisted marbled cord for all to see, this creature whose mouth was carefully cleared of slime, whose limbs and dark crumpled face were sponged clean, this gape-jawed stranger, this thinly-crying whelp, would spoil everything.

BANTLING

26 Violet. Stockwell. 1923.

London SW9, 23rd April, Dearest Mim & Da, Your grandson, Samuel, was born three days ago, all his limbs & other parts present & correct. I am managing to feed him & he is taking it well enough. Reverend Holcroft tells me him and Mrs Holcroft could not be better pleased with him if he was their own, which is most touching. I do wish you could see him for yourselves, you might even begin to forgive me. The hard part is just beginning, everyone tells me & I know it myself & wish his start were different, even knowing how lucky I am in so many regards, not least in my own parents. I am recovering well in myself, though naturally not out of bed yet & Mrs Holcroft is waiting on this note to go out, because she will post it for me. I am so pleased to hear that Da is on the mend also, With love from Violet. PS Thank-you for passing on the gift from Estelle. Mrs Holcroft & I admired her needlework. I will send her a note when I am on my feet again.

BANTLING

27 Ellen. Stockwell. 1923.

She studied the vicarage as she walked towards it, windows reflecting the sunshine back to her in rainbow flashes, the tiles of the front path clean and shiny. She must remember to compliment Mrs Dawson on her efficient house-keeping when she discussed tomorrow's shopping with her.

Yes, the house looked well-tended, but today, standing in the new warmth of the sun, thoughts of summer hats coming to mind, it seemed to her that its symmetry lacked something. Come May or June, the house would need a rose. A delicate fresh rose, not a cold white one, nor anything so harshly-coloured that jangled the eyes or so intensely velvety deep it seemed improper. Something with a touch of pink. Or a hint of gold, the colour of cream on the top of the milk. It might arch across the path or it could clamber beside the portico. A tender-coloured rose would soften and beautify the house that supported it. Not unlike Felix and Ellen these days, if she might be permitted the poetic comparison.

Post was sitting in a little pile on the hall table. One for Violet, several for Ellen, tedious and routine. A request from the Fellowship for a short report about Violet. She would be able to give them only good news. The final envelope did not give itself away. When she opened it, she had to read it twice, thrice, the brief words twirling on the page. Truly, this was Ellen's moment, a prize to be announced to Felix. She would not wait until they were seated at lunch together. He did not like to be disturbed in his study, but this time, she was sure, he would not mind in the slightest. She held her letter carefully in case she creased it from excitement, knocked and opened the door. She noticed her hand was shaking just a little from exhilaration.

'Back from your rounds?' he asked. 'Is it lunchtime already?'

She took his enquiry as a good sign and smiled from her heart.

'We still have quarter of an hour. Felix, I've had the kindest letter.' She held the headed paper out towards him. 'Have a look at this. I've not been wasting my time these past months.'

'It never occurred to me that you were,' he said, but he was looking back at his desk already. He did not take the letter.

'Please read it,' she said, putting in his desk. 'It's addressed to me, but reflects on us both equally. Without your patience and faith in me, I could never have done any of it.'

He was busy opening drawers.

'Perhaps you'd rather I read it out to you?'

The words held their magic even spoken aloud.

'*Stockwell, 24th April, Dear Mrs Holcroft, just a little*

note to thank you personally for all of your efforts on the hospital's behalf. The success of your Helpful Visitor scheme in such a short space of time has surprised and delighted us all, and all credit is due to you for your good organisation and dedication'.

'Doctor McCall has not only signed it herself, she has taken the time to pen it all in her own hand. What do you think of that?'

Ellen held the letter tenderly; she would most certainly treasure it. She knew the words were not mere flattery. Doctor had hit the nail on the head. Ellen had done very well indeed, and in only three months. It just went to show what could be achieved when a woman, when *Ellen*, set her mind to a task and was given the license and latitude she needed. Doctor McCall understood what was involved.

'There are ten regular lady visitors on my roster now,' she added, 'One or two occasionals, plus several more on the verge of pledging themselves. Very soon, if all goes to plan, some of my regulars will start showing the ropes to new volunteers.'

She felt she should share the credit and praise with him, she wanted to share it, even though a nagging voice asked her if gratitude didn't go against the grain, gratitude that he allowed her to do work she was so clearly suited to. Felix, like most men, never thought to seek such permission for themselves or their life's works. But still, things were as they were, and if she had not been able to bring Felix around to agreement, she would be howling in that freezing bathroom to this day.

'I am glad they appreciate your efforts,' he said. 'Don't let them drain you to the last drop, however. There's your own health to consider, and your work for the Church and parish generally. I have heard one or two comments in recent days about you missing choir practice ...'

She started to speak, but he held up his hand.

'... I'm not judging you – or criticising - you also have your hands full here in the house – and I have said as much to the grumblers whenever I have the chance. All the same ... if we are to present a united front ...'

She felt as though she were a naughty child in school, standing in front of the seated stern teacher. She flushed and pressed her lips together, the air dragged hard through her nostrils and forced out again. She made herself count slowly.

'Choir practice? Choir practice? I was a little late, hardly at all. Who do they think will do the work for the Bring-and-Buy sale, if not me? The choir can manage perfectly well without me for a few minutes, whereas...'

He interrupted her. 'Yes, yes, I know. You have your hands full. And with Violet still not up and about ...'

'But almost. She's on her feet more and more each day. There's nothing wrong with her, she's recovered exceptionally well, but you know that she was advised to spend over a week in bed resting. That's the way it always is. It's more a matter of making sure she does not overdo it than anything else.'

Felix mimed weighing scales, one hand moving up as the other came down.

Up.

Down.

Up.

Down.

'As you say, the Bring-and-Buy sale is coming up. It won't organise itself. And then, of course, there's Baby Samuel,' he said.

Of course. There was always Baby Samuel. Ellen was still not easy with him. He squirmed when she picked him up and she felt herself do likewise, though she was quite sure she hid it from the others. She could almost look at Violet and almost not remember every detail of what she had seen as Samuel was born. And yet ... and yet she had been cheated. There was something about this Baby Samuel that upset some fundamental law of what was right and proper, that provoked unnatural feelings in her. He cried such a lot and hardly slept. Most babies brought forth only the finest and most tender of feelings from those around them. She had expected to feel much affection for Violet's child, not this irritation that her good manners barely concealed. It was that he demanded everything of Violet.

The clock chimed them to lunch. Felix held her

chair as she sat down and she thanked him, though her mouth was stiff with disappointment. Of late, she had found she enjoyed the two of them eating together more than she had for ... for longer than she could put her finger on. Today, all that was upset, but she must do her best.

'Mrs Dawson has made shepherd's pie. How very nourishing,' she remarked.

Across the table, Felix seemed intent on his lunch, but he looked up.

'Very tasty,' he said. 'We're lucky to have her. Between you both, the house is run very well, my dear.'

He had declared a truce.

Back bacon, she wrote.

'A well-ordered home is a man's anchor,' he said.

Salt.

'Or perhaps, it is rather his ballast, steadying him as makes his way across the choppy waves of an uncertain world,' he continued.

Toilet soap.

'I think I might have the beginnings of a sermon here. What do you think, my dear?'

Which lady to which stall? Draw lots?

'Just so, my dear, just so.'

Naturally, with all the attention Baby Samuel demanded, not to mention Ellen's own load, there was not quite the same intimacy between Ellen and Violet as there had been. Ellen missed it and was sure Violet did as well, though it was not Violet's way to grumble.

BANTLING

Mrs Dawson would scrub the trestle tables.
Household soap.

'I'll take Violet's post up after lunch and have a cup of tea with her,' she said. 'It's nice for her to have a little break.'

'Of course, I don't know about these things,' said Felix, 'And it's early days as yet, but Baby Samuel seems like a very good little chap, doesn't he? Coming on nicely.'

He wiped his plate with a piece of bread and butter and popped the mass into his mouth, scattering crumbs over his moustache. It was a marvel he'd seen the baby at all, with Violet still hardly out of bed.

Grate blacking. Mrs Dawson had mentioned it was running low.

'I'm most impressed by how Violet has put her mind to motherhood,' Felix continued. 'A married woman couldn't be more devoted or attentive. It was a good decision to offer her your kindness.'

The compliment took her breath away, dizzied her so that she could not reply at once. She had dreamed of this, but hardly dared hope.

Sugar, she wrote, her hand shaking. *Honey. Vanilla pod.*

'And you were right about the benefits of having someone lively about the place. She is a breath of fresh air.'

She placed his plate on top of hers and set them both on the sideboard.

'And now we must make sure she does not run herself ragged spoiling the baby,' she confided. She was careful always to call him *the baby* out loud, cutting off the other words that leapt to her mind.

Mrs Dawson had left them a custard tart for pudding, nicely browned in patches on the surface and giving off a faint scent of nutmeg and vanilla.

Should jams and cakes go on separate stalls? Would there be enough of each?

'I worry for Violet,' she continued. 'She is transfixed by him. She wants to cuddle him or feed him or change him whenever he so much blinks or waggles his little finger. She never puts him down. It can't be good for either of them.'

She cut them each a slice.

Should they serve teas at the sale? There wouldn't be room to sit down, not with the stalls. Perhaps best not. Unless the vestry could be used.

Look over vestry for suitability. Cleaning. Clearing. Storage?

'I bumped into the daily nurse. She seems happy enough with how things are going at the moment,' he said. 'Though I dare say you are right in the longer term.'

Tables & chairs. Urn.

'It's a mistake not to start as you mean to go on,' she continued.

Crockery

There was a little cough from him, a clearing of

the throat, and a comment that it would all turn out for the best.

'He has the rest of his life to learn that most times he won't get his own way.' It was Violet's voice taking her by surprise. 'And he likes to go to sleep when I'm holding him.'

'What are you doing up and about?' cried Ellen. 'You know what the nurse said about staying off your feet. Come and sit down at once.'

Felix was already standing up, pulling out a chair, helping Violet into it, smiling down at the quiet baby. He was an oddly blotchy creature.

'We just wanted a little walk and change of scene, didn't we my little lovely?' said Violet. 'Say hello to Uncle Felix, sweetest.'

It was strange to see Felix look down into the bundle and extend one uncertain hand to pat it. She had certainly not expected him to be so taken with the child, or so taken in. He might not feel the same if he had watched Violet's agony.

'Custard tart?' she asked.

'Lovely, thanks, Mrs Holcroft.'

Eggs. Violet need building up again

Violet sat, holding the baby on her lap with one hand, grappling with her tart with the other. There, that was the sort of thing Ellen meant. The girl could not even eat a meal in peace. She probably did exactly the same when she had her meals upstairs in bed.

Ellen was doing her best to teach Violet some good

habits, to make sure Samuel knew who was in charge right from the start. Violet seemed amenable enough to her face, but Ellen suspected it all went out the window the minute her back was turned. And so it was proving.

'I'm only worried for you, my dear, worried that he'll just learn to cry and stamp his feet to get what he wants,' she warned Violet.

'He's too little to know what he wants,' Violet replied. 'He's only a week old. He cries when he needs something, that's all.'

Her voice was polite and subdued, but face was set and determined. When she and Baby Samuel looked at each other, it sometimes made Ellen think of people she had seen reunited when the troops came home. There was a glow about them, a fixity in their regard as they soaked each other in, a recognition that pushed everyone else to one side.

Ellen's point – she kept it to herself this time for the sake of harmony – was that he seemed to need something every second of every minute. Violet got not a moment's peace.

Vinegar. Carbolic.

'Yes, yes, time enough for everything when he starts to settle down,' said Felix, as though anyone had asked for his opinion.

'Well, she doesn't want to make a rod for her own back, that's all I'm saying.'

Violet sniffed. Felix made a warning noise at the

back of his throat. Ellen looked up. Under the guise of canoodling her child, Violet was trying not to cry.

'There, there, don't take on, I meant no harm. More tart, anyone?'

'Did you see there was a letter for you in the hall?' Felix asked Violet. 'Let me fetch it for you.'

'I know you only mean the best for us both, of course I do. I'm not myself yet,' said Violet. 'And I will get Sammy into a routine, I will, but Nurse says the most important thing for now is to make sure he has enough milk. But once I'm up and about properly I'll put my mind to training him. This custard tart is lovely. Is it your recipe, Mrs Holcroft?'

'Mrs Dawson's,' said Ellen.

'There you go,' said Felix, handing over the envelope to Violet. 'I could manage another slice, if there's one going spare.'

Violet fumbled with the envelope, hampered by the baby in her arms.

'Would you like me to do that?' offered Ellen.

Violet shook head and shook out the folded sheet. A separate sheet floated out.

Pen-nibs and ink.

'Oh gosh. Isn't that sweet of them? And generous too. I never expected that.' She held the letter in one hand, a postal order in the other.

'Five pounds!'

Felix took the paper from her.

'It's well-deserved,' he said. 'The very least they

could do. Ellen, see what our young protégée has received. The hospital treasurer is very grateful to her.'

The letter was brief, congratulations on Samuel's birth and a thank-you note with an offer to supply character references if needed. Not to mention the postal order.

'What does it all mean?' she asked.

'Violet uncovered some monkey business to do with the building works at the hospital,' said Felix.

'It all seems ages ago,' said Violet. 'There was one supplier where I couldn't match payments up with invoices,' said Violet. 'I thought it was my porridge-brain not making sense of what was in front of my eyes, but I wanted to make sure, get it all neat and tidy. So I asked to see statements. The tradesman was a bit cagey and kept putting me off.'

Felix added, 'When she couldn't get a straight answer out of him, she got more suspicious ...'

'I kept thinking it was just a mix-up.'

'... but then he suggested he and Violet come to some arrangement to overlook his 'little confusion'. When she said no, he came here and caused a scene.'

'So, then I knew for certain. That's why we set off for the hospital that day. I can't believe it all happened only a week ago. Come to think of it, it was probably all the brou-ha-ha that brought me on so sudden. Turned out he was really a paper supplier, but had been putting in for wooden joists and frames.'

BANTLING

Ellen felt proud of her, naturally. The temptation must have been real, to take the money and say nothing. Heaven knows, Violet could use some extra cash. It reflected well on Ellen, too.

'We still don't know if the last girl – Liza – was just careless – or naïve, as Violet likes to think – or whether she had some similar arrangement with the builder,' said Felix.

'Either way, she was paying him from the cash donations and not keeping proper records of anything,' said Violet, taking another piece of tart.

'Such a shame. She was a dab hand selling raffle tickets.'

'I feel sorry for her,' said Violet. 'I expect she might lose her place. I don't suppose they'll give her much of a reference either. Poor thing.'

Any moment now, Felix would mention Ellen's own letter from the hospital, Ellen's contribution, Ellen's achievements.

'And it's all so very inconvenient.' said Felix. 'The building works have had to be put on hold while the hospital ascertains whether or not they received the goods in question. If they have, they need then to find out if they are sub-standard or not. It is all a bit of a botch at the moment. At the very least the girl has been irresponsible and caused a lot of bother,'

'All the same,' said Violet, 'you never know what happens in people's lives, what makes them do something they'd never normally think of. I'm not saying she should keep her job come-what-may, just that I feel sorry for her.'

'As Ellen so wisely said some months ago, we should not judge a person by a single mistake.'

'All the same, if she's at fault, she must take the consequences,' said Ellen. 'There's nothing about all this in the letter.'

She looked at Felix. How did he know so much?

'Miss Barnabas, you know, the hospital Treasurer, told us should keep it to ourselves until they knew for certain,' said Felix.

'It all happened on the day Samuel was born, so it went clean out of my thoughts,' added Violet.

Was it so very churlish of Ellen to feel her thunder had been stolen?

'Well done again, Violet. You're a credit to us and yourself. I need to get going now. As Felix has kindly pointed out, the Bring-and-Buy Sale won't organise itself. Can you give Mrs Dawson this shopping list, please? And then back to bed.'

Violet gave her a dreamy look and nodded. A sweetish, milky, slightly feral scent hung around her. She had dark smudges under her eyes, her skin was puffy and blotchy and her hair hanging lank.

The baby was wearing her out and she could not see it.

'You might think about a little rest as well, my dear,' said Felix to Ellen.

BANTLING

Baby Samuel opened his eyes and shuddered. His whole head darkened as he screwed up his face.

Violet's arms twitched and she grimaced.

'Already! He needs changing again already.'

One might almost say she wailed the words. Poor girl. Still, one makes one's bed and in it one must lie.

BANTLING

28 Violet. Brixton. 1923.

London SW9, 5th May, Dearest Stel, my 1st proper day out of doors for almost 2 weeks & I sped down to the Town Hall while Mrs H is off doing her good deeds. Today was the first time I had taken Sammy out & I registered his being on this earth. I wore Mim's ring, like I do nearly all the time for fear I'll lose it if I leave it lying about, but of course I did not, could not, would not, give them the name of you-know-who. What would be the point? Anyway, it seemed to me the registrar must be used to girls like me & babies like Sammy. I imagined there might be a bit of a scene, but he never even blinked, just wrote down what I said & stamped the form & gave me a copy. I wish the rest of life & motherhood was going to be that simple. Now the Wriggler is officially Samuel Bantling. He & I will need all the bravery we can muster. I hope he will be kind, & not just to his mum. What goes around comes around. Sorry for the previous stiff scrawl. Mrs H watched while I wrote it. I trusted you'd understand, your own missive being my model for discretion. I knew you were a fine seamstress & embroiderer from all your pretty frocks & unmentionables, but to take the time to make those little smocks is a thing apart. They passed even Mrs H's jealous inspection. Sammy will wear them as often as possible. It makes me feel he & I are less alone if I see him in the clothes you sewed for him. Sammy is a darling, so beautiful with subtle eyes, the colours of light caught on the sea on an overcast summer's day, always changing & delicate. He has a glossy fluff of hedgehog hair, the softest of spikelets that are already beginning to curl after only fifteen days. His head is a little pointed, like a pixie. Mrs H assures me over & over I must not fret (why would I fret?), that in a few weeks' more he will be good as new, but he is so already to his love-blind mother. All his fingers & toes have tiny nails like dewdrops on a spider's web & his skin shimmers too as though there is a lamp lit inside him. At least, it does where is not scabby or full of rash. Please allow a doting mother her silly fancies. His face is never still, his mouth & eyes always on the move except when he gazes at me & hardly so much as blinks while he feeds. As soon as I can I will arrange for a photograph if it does not cost too much & send it to you. I am quite well, though still very tired from the delivery & every night broken for feeding. Mrs H thinks I should follow the times she has set down for him to feed & sleep, but I cannot bear to hear him wail & particularly at night, it's not just me he disturbs. She does not feel very fondly towards him in any case, but is such a busy bee with her good works & bring-&-buy sale that she does not have to see so very much of him. I never knew it was such hard work to stay awake around the clock & keep pace with so tiny a being. He doesn't hardly sleep. I have never been so tired and it is only 2 weeks. I am glad to be up & about again & in some proper clothes, but it's not easy & I am fearful about how I will manage to have a job & care for him too. Did I tell you that the Fellowship that sent me here has some nurseries not too far away for the girls in their Home & perhaps Sammy can go there once I find a position or even while I am looking? But it will not be so easy to take him there & still make my way to work & then bring him home every evening, but it may be the only solution. The best thing would be to get employment near the nursery & the Fellowship will use their influence to that end as well, such as it is, which may not be that much. Everything at the Fellowship seems done on a wing & a prayer, so there are no guarantees & doubtless I would better do as Mim suggests & not get too fond of him. Too late for that. My worries crowd in, though I have some time as yet & am not abandoned entirely to my own resources. I am fortunately in the hospital's good books & I have my lovely Sammy, for the moment at least. But in all this daze of sleeplessness & my concerns for the future, for the first time in months my feet do not puff over my shoes, even with them properly laced & I am still vain enough to be thankful. Every cloud & so on. Much love & many thanks again to the best friend I could have, Violet. PS Opposite the Town Hall there is a theatre & a cinema & others nearby, so a girl would be spoilt for entertainment if she had a mind for it. A carefree unencumbered girl like you could kick up her heels & shimmy as much as she liked here amongst the dance palaces of Brixton. If it were not for the leaking of milk, I might have shifted myself onto one of the seats in the garden outside to eat my apple in the sunshine. But it was back to the vicarage for me for another feed. Now I have wittered on enough so I must dash to the postbox. Hattie Dawson has said she will keep an eye on Sammy for a few minutes. She has been the proverbial tower for me. As ever, Violet

29 Ellen. Stockwell. 1923.

At night, the house belonged to Ellen. She and it breathed the same rhythm. Streetlight rippled on walls like water through sand and when the moon was full, its light fell through the skylight into a blue pool high up on the landing wall. Standing on the landing or moving along the hallway, she heard in mysterious rustlings and whisperings the sleeping lives around her. She heard Violet pacing her room and murmuring, Sam's cries gathering strength and petering out. She heard the mattress's faint twang and sigh as Violet got back into bed.

She was the protective angel of the household, the good, invisible, fairy who had made all this possible and on whom it all rested. Her will and love flowed like a river through the rooms.

There were times when Baby Samuel would not settle, when his cries intruded, agitating the house around him. She heard the exhausted sobs and Violet's pleas. When that happened, the full weight pressed down on her and was met by strength of her resolve. You must never let down your guard, Ellen. Never. You must dote even more on Violet in the morning. It is the only way to protect her.

BANTLING

30 Violet. Stockwell. 1923.

Stockwell, London SW9, 19th May, Dearest Mim, poor Da, he must be frantic he is not on his feet yet & the worry cannot help him improve, I am sure. Please find enc. a postal order for £4.18s. I had a bit of unexpected luck the other day. I am sorry I cannot send any more yet. The nurse is still coming & though they have kindly given me a very reduced rate I must pay something & my rent too & of course there are things I have to get for Sam, though I cut as many corners as I can. I don't think it would be right to borrow from Mrs Holcroft or assume more of her charity than I do at present (please don't mention this letter when you write to me as I do not want her fretting for me more than she does). I am putting out the word for a job, but even if I am very lucky that won't come off for a little while, though I am making every effort for it to be as soon as possible & I have some respectable references that should count for something. Mrs Holcroft thinks I should rest up another few months, but she is over-cautious. I have told her that the women in our family are back on their feet & at their duties much more quickly than her London softies. I am telling you this not to worry you, but to show you I am taking everything seriously. I am more likely to get a decent job here, I think, but that's not the be-all & end-all. You must be worn out. Would it be better if I came back home with Sam? At least we would save on the rent here & I could help out & perhaps Da would not mind too much, if you did not mind the gossip. From your Violet.

BANTLING

31 Ellen. Stockwell. 1923.

After the Sunday morning service, Felix busied himself greeting his parishioners, asking them about this and that, reminding them about the coming Bring-and-Buy Sale, mentioning the cause particularly close to his wife's heart. Several ladies stopped to ask her about it, to offer help or find out about her work and if they could be of any use. One of them, Mrs Cartwright perhaps – there were so many, too many, names to keep in mind – promised a pram for which she had no more use.

Standing at Felix's side, Ellen nodded and smiled at the parishioners, her mind busy, busy, busy. With any luck, all the bric-a-brac cluttering up the vicarage for so long would probably sell quite well. Or most of it, at least. It all depended on the weather. Somehow, second-hand plates and vases and discarded jewellery always looked more appealing in summer light, even inside the church hall, than they ever did on an overcast day.

'Reverend Holcroft. Mrs Holcroft,' said Henry Wingrove raising his hat as he passed them in the porch.

With all that had been happening, she had almost forgotten about the family. Nevertheless, it was a good sign, was it not, for him and Alice to be among the congregation?

Alice nodded an acknowledgement, but kept moving when Henry Wingrove looked as though he'd pause for a civil word. Felix failed to notice, of course, already turning towards the next person. It was a shock to realise that her husband did not recognise Alice and Henry Wingrove. But of course, why should he? She had never pointed them out to him. She'd never had cause to.

She followed them onto the pavement.

'How are you feeling now, Mrs Wingrove? I'm delighted to see you up and about again. The children are well?'

'Mustn't grumble,' said Alice, and was silent again.

After all Alice and Ellen had been through together, after all that Ellen had done for her, one might have expected a little more. Mind you, the woman still had a sickly look.

It was Wingrove who covered up the awkwardness, saying that the children were well, thank you, but they had best get back to them now.

'Come along, Alice. Look lively,' he said. 'Flo will be at the end of her rope with the kids by now and the gravy'll need stirring. You're up to that, aren't you?'

Alice started to move slowly down the street.

Wingrove turned to Ellen and shrugged.

'She does her best. This is one of her better days,' he said. 'I can't hardly get her out and about. She wants to. She just can't help it. God knows, Flo's done her best to talk some sense into her.'

'I'll pop along this week, if that would help.'

He raised his hat again.

Ellen watched him guide Alice down the street, moving as someone dazed, as though she could not change direction without his lead. There was tenderness in the way he gave her his arm and how she leant against him, but it was of a weary kind. The man was suffering too, she could see that, though he didn't seem the sort to fuss for himself. She felt sorry for Alice; one could hardly feel otherwise. But there again, Alice had two children who she gave every appearance of having forgotten about, whereas Ellen had none and never would have, not to call her own. And Henry Wingrove had come back whole in mind and body from France and Flanders, which was more than many women could say for their men; more than she could say for her Arthur, dead in the Transvaal under the African sun. Still, when the worst hit you, it hit you however it did, and always for the worst. What others might have suffered had no bearing.

'Ellen!'

She looked across at her husband. He held up his watch.

'I'm on my way, dear,' she assured him.

There was gravy to stir at the vicarage as well, and then she would have to sort and pack boxes for the sale.

To all intents and purposes, Alice Wingrove's sorrow overwhelmed her sense of duty. In their dingy room, Ellen had glimpsed Alice's efforts to be who she had been before, never mind how curtailed. Alice had a blessing in her husband, helping to do a woman's work as well as a man's job, and Flo too, was doing more than her bit. The harsh truth of it was that even losing a baby didn't bring the world to a stop as far as the rest of the family was concerned. If it was, the human race would have died out before it had begun. Take herself, for instance. She'd been back on her feet as soon as the worst of the physical debility had passed, well before the doctor advised. And why? Because Felix needed her and expected it of her. She had expected no less of herself. Surely if she could find it within herself to pull herself together, so could Alice Wingrove. There must be something that would help.

She let herself into the house, smelling the roasting lamb from the doorway. There was no sign of Violet, but from upstairs came the sound of the baby's jerky wail. Glimpsing the dining table as she passed, she saw that Violet had managed to lay three places while they were out at church. Potatoes and onions that Mrs Dawson had par-boiled the day before were ready and waiting in the kitchen to go straight into the oven to crisp up.

Of course – let her be scrupulously honest – Ellen had had help around the house during her dreadful time. Shopping and carrying, even bathing, had been beyond her for much longer than she had foreseen. And lifting the teapot, let alone the kettle, had been almost impossible for weeks. But just look at her now!

Jams. They usually sold well, too, so she must make sure everyone who had offered brought along several jars. And plants would be lovely, of course, just the right time of year for them. Those lovely begonias!

She lit the gas under the saucepans of sliced carrots and chopped greens. The front door opened and closed. She heard the rattle of Felix hanging up his hat and coat in the hall.

What assistance did Alice have other than her husband? Flo was close by, and the Wingrove boy was big enough to be of some help. It was handy, too, that they lived above the green-grocers shop. And – this was honesty speaking again – Alice had only the one room to keep clean and orderly.

'I'm home,' Felix called out.

Whatever the cause, if something did not happen soon to snap Alice Wingrove out of her listlessness, it would go hard on the family.

'The vegetables are almost ready,' she called back.

She manoeuvred the hot, heavy roasting pan out of the oven and put the joint to rest. She drained off some of the fat from the pan and stirred flour into what was left, heating and scraping, adding a few ladles of vegetable water.

"Call Violet, if you will, but only if you can still hear the child. No point in waking him if she's managed to get him off to sleep.'

BANTLING

He was a noisy little brat. Felix had foreseen that correctly enough.

All that rapport, all the spousal tenderness that Ellen had witnessed between Henry and Alice Wingrove seemed to have shrunk in on itself, much as her own feelings for Felix had grown ever more remote since her dreadful time. If a loss like Alice's erased even the fondest and most passionate of affections, Ellen's marriage had been doomed. Felix had been absent even when his physical presence was in the same room with her, just at the time Ellen needed him most. But that was no longer the case, surely. She and Felix had found a way to forge a new and stronger alliance than any based on the happenstance of a child.

She stirred again, added another ladleful of boiling water. She drained the vegetables, the steam blinding her for a moment, and put them into serving dishes. A knob of butter, a sprig of parsley.

Perhaps Alice Wingrove was the sort of woman for whom the loss of one child was akin to the loss of all.

Violet came into the kitchen, carrying bundles of familiar green fabric. She made Ellen swear never to tell her Mim, but she had sewn pot holders from that old smock of hers. Unduly wasteful, perhaps, Ellen suggested. Could the dress not have been refashioned usefully? Violet laughed for the first time in an age and said that she felt like a summer-house settee the whole time she had worn it, and she was glad to see the back of it

BANTLING

Pot-holders. Humble, but always a popular item with those with less to spend. Every penny counts. It was all in aid of such a good cause. She and her ladies would be able to do so much more with a little cash behind them.

When Violet had done laughing, there was a furrow between her eyebrows.

The poor thing looked exhausted, and no wonder.

'Is there anything I can do?' asked Violet. 'The Reverend's got Samuel on his lap. They look so pretty together.'

'Did you have another difficult night?' asked Ellen. 'I heard you up and about a bit.'

'You do think I'm doing the right thing, don't you? Looking after him by myself, I mean? Sometimes I wonder what possessed me to think it was possible.'

Spilt milk, crying, no point.

'One day at a time, Violet. Do you want to start taking the vegetables through, please?'

So, if Alice Wingrove could or would do nothing for herself, she, Ellen, must. Alice's lethargy was probably as much due to neglecting herself, to not eating properly, as it was anything else. Later today, tomorrow at the latest, she'll make time to make some lamb and barley broth. It was unlikely that even the most dedicated of men would go to those lengths. Especially on the apology for a stove that the Wingroves had in their room. In the meanwhile, she must put her mind to ways of lifting Alice's spirits.

There was a clatter and crash. Violet's exclamation, the infant's wail.

'It's only cutlery,' Felix called out. 'Nothing broken.'

BANTLING

32 Violet. Stockwell. 1923.

Stockwell, London SW9, 20th May, Dear Stel, last night the Wriggler & I lay in the not so frail moonlight as it cast stripes & shadows across our bedroom wall & the sky outside darkened from one marvel of blue to another. He is exactly one month old. When he is quiet, I am full of hope & expectation. There was enough light for me to watch the miracle of his breathing & his tiny mouth unclosing & closing like a sea-anemone, as I fretted & worried about his future & mine. I'm won't be fit for work for a bit & there's nothing firmly on the cards as yet, though I did myself a favour at the hospital a little while ago by ferreting out a bit of shenanigans with a couple of the invoices. I didn't want to sneak too badly, but tricks like that give us independent women a bad name, not that some of us have much of a name to lose. But to my mind, having a fatherless baby & stealing from the charitable are two different things & fortunately the powers-that-be think so too. The hospital is not exactly hand-to-mouth, but every penny counts. It's an ill wind etc & the net result is that yours truly is in credit with the hospital management. I intend to keep them onside, so have offered to do their books once a month while I convalesce. You could write & tell me what is happening with you. If you ever run into you-know-who, perhaps you could get his letter to me, in a book or something. Not that there's much chance of him turning up looking for me & I really don't care so much as I used to. It's more of a puzzle than a hurt nowadays, where he vanished off to, though he left me in a pretty fair Wriggler pickle that I will never ever get out of, not properly, not if I hang onto Sammy. When I look only at him, something inside me hums & sings. But when I start thinking I start to understand why Mim & Da thought me mad for thinking I could care for him myself. It is so frightening to know it is up to me & only me to make sure he keeps safe & has a roof over his head & enough to eat. I don't have the foggiest what I am doing & have to make everything up all the time. ALL THE TIME. When I think about everything I must do & so much I don't know, I get a sick feeling. See, he is starting to grizzle now & needs feeding again & then changing again. He is lovely, but it never stops & I have no idea how I will manage & I feel worn down. I thought I was tired before I had him, but that was nothing. I never sleep, I drop things, forget my sentences halfway through. I am so short-tempered, so impatient, not all the time, but at the drop of a hat & I don't even see that hat dropping. I scare myself. Hattie Dawson tells me not to worry, it's just like that, all new mothers feel as I do, things get better with time, or at least you get used to them. She says I won't sleep properly for months yet, so make the most of being awake, babies change so fast, you can sit and watch it happen & they'll never be quite like that again. Thus speaks the voice of experience. Still at this rate, I fear I'll never earn our keep, let alone pay back Mim & Da all their savings. Da is not doing so good. Not worse, touch wood, but that's the best that can be said. Stan has been to see them & is keeping in with them even after my letter.

May 29th & I'm sorry I haven't posted this letter yet. There is never enough time to do the nothing that I do every day. I will make a terrible mother, nothing like Mim. The Reverend keeps telling me to have faith, all will come good in the end. He even talks about me getting more qualifications one day, but that really seems like pie in the sky. What with things the way they are with Da, it all seems hopeless most of the time. I need to be able to do my bit for Mim & Da as well, which means buckling down to earning enough to send them. The hospital still looks like a reasonable bet, at least for a while, as long as I can pull myself together to do more than feed and change Sammy, but even one day a month seems beyond me. I feel I cannot cope. It might be better for everyone if I found a good home for Sammy. From what Mim and Da let drop, I might even be in a position to build bridges with Stan again if I had a mind to. Who says we don't get a second chance? There again, who says we have to take it if we get offered it? I am all in a muddle, Violet.

BANTLING

33 Ellen. Stockwell. 1923.

Mrs Cartwright's promised pram had arrived, lording it over the vicarage hallway, a great deep solid thing of wood, black gabardine, tan leather lining and barely-tarnished moving parts. It would be most useful. Mothers other than Violet could use it too, naturally. It wouldn't do for people to think that Ellen had commandeered it merely for her protégée. That would smack of favouritism. It would be very useful indeed for a great many people. Far better to keep it for general use it than sell it for a few pence.

The kitchen door was open. Behind it, Violet was sobbing, not managing to string a sentence together, the odd consonant and vowel floating down the hallway. She might have done something or other, she was that close to having… Mrs Dawson's answer was too low to make out what she was saying. Her tone was soothing. There was a clink of glass, much sniffing, a nose being blown several times, Violet's murmur, a little calmer now. Thank you. Yes.

Ellen was shut out, passed over, reduced to a shadow in her own home.

A chair scraped across the floor. Violet came out of the kitchen. Her face was pinched and blotchy, as though she'd been crying her heart out.

'Are you alright, my dear?'

The girl nodded.

BANTLING

'Reverend Holcroft has set some chairs up in the garden. Sammy's outside with him.'

She ducked into the back parlour, towards the doors to the garden, not meeting Ellen's eyes.

Be calm, Ellen. Be understanding.

Two walnut cakes and three fruit cakes waited in the larder for the Bring-and-Buy sale. Well done, Mrs Dawson. Perhaps she would also make something lighter, a Victoria sponge or two, nearer the time?

Mrs Dawson nodded. Ellen asked if everything was alright with Violet, but the house-keeper merely nodded again. Clearly, she was holding something back. Why did people feel they must keep things from her?

Keep calm, Ellen. Keep smiling.

Breezes blowing through the house, the French doors open to the garden.

The scent of lilac, the air soft and warm and fragrant on her face.

'Yooohh-hooouu!'

They stiffened or jumped as they heard her, or moved apart in some way. Violet in her slate-blue dress sitting on a rattan chair, Felix bending above her, the picture of Sunday School innocence, were it not for the air of scheming that surrounded them. A fraction of a second, nothing more and then they turned their faces towards her. The wildest thought passed through her mind.

Silly-billy that she was, her eye had been tricked coming from the almost-dark of the house into the green of the garden, lush after all the rain. Or perhaps it was the foolery of the white squares of nappy flapping on the drying rails to one side, making things look other than they were.

She was being ridiculously imaginative again. Like fearing the malice of hobgoblins in the night. Or thinking a bruised breast protected her when everything else had failed. Bright sunshine has its own sleights of hand.

The lilac tree was dropping its purple flowers – too dark and vulgar a colour to her mind, fit only for a brothel. The pale and white-flowered varieties smelt so much sweeter, too.

'Violet dear, do you need a bonnet? You want to avoid freckles.'

Though crying might be even worse than sun for the complexion.

The garden was heady with the scents of lilac and wallflowers, vivid with light. Shadows and brightness skittered and rippled across it with the breeze. The first June day with any sun to speak of. The breeze still had a chill to it and already the clouds were thickening. Felix gestured to the chair next to him. Before she sat, she bent over Baby Samuel, as one should with

BANTLING

babies. He gave her his cold, cold eye. A strange and distant child, but she did her best.

'Is he warm enough, do you think?'

Violet brushed something invisible away from her face and picked at the baby's wrapping.

'You're quite covered in magenta stars, my lilac-blossomed lovely.'

It was quite odd how Violet still looked tearful. There again, motherhood would try any woman. Exhaustion was just one of the prices to pay. And of course, this brat was more trying than most. The nurse had been sensible to start him on the bottle already.

As for Ellen, she was light, she was warmth, hovering, spreading throughout the garden and into air they all breathed. Spinning particles waltzed in the ribbons of light under the tree. Once upon a time, Ellen had believed she had seen fairy gold shimmering in the air and today she almost believed it again.

Violet said, 'I think I'll go and lie down for a little while. I'll leave him here, I think, if you don't mind.'

Felix said the fresh air was probably good for him, he and Mrs Holcroft would keep an eye on him.

34 Violet. Stockwell. 1923.

Stockwell, London, 10 June, Dear Stel, I think it is all over, my own doing & nobody but myself to blame. I did the most awful thing to Sammy or so close to it as makes no difference as to trusting myself with him anymore. I cannot tell even you what I nearly did. I am so so ashamed. It was the tiredness & worry acting, said Hattie, no harm was done & swears it is just between us two. So kind of her, but it makes no difference. The line between doing & not doing is so thin, I did not have the time to form the thought in my head of what I might do before I almost did it. I won't be any be less tired by wishing tiredness away. What if next time I hurt him? I cannot express how ashamed I am now, but I could not face life at all if I did worse. Violet

BANTLING

35 Ellen. Stockwell. 1923.

Felix waited until Violet had moved from the brightness of the garden into the shadows of the back parlour, then cleared his throat to claim Ellen's attention.

'Do you think she is quite well?' he asked. 'I wonder sometimes if it's not all too much for her. She has expressed doubts herself, said that she is scared she might hurt Samuel. I think she must have been crying earlier. What's your impression?'

She was touched he would ask her opinion like this.

She said what she thought, that motherhood was taking a toll on Violet and that she was anxious about the effects on Violet's health. The worry about her father was unfortunately timed as well.

Felix nodded as she spoke.

'It is probably too much for one person', he agreed. 'Even one as caring and practical as Violet. And what do you think of her son's future? I have been asking myself if she can provide as much as he needs.'

She could hardly breathe. It would be so much easier if the suggestion came from Felix, if together they could find a home for Samuel and allow Violet a new start, a chance to regain her health. Go carefully, Ellen.

"Few of us get what we deserve or want in this life,' she said. She might have added, *or in the next* for Felix's benefit. 'We must all play the hand we are dealt, and Violet's is better than some. Samuel is quite lucky, so far, all things considered. She is perhaps narrowing the choices open to them both by insisting on keeping him. The Fellowship is optimistic, but perhaps even they underestimate the burdens some unwed mothers carry. Above all, one who has to support her family rather than be supported by them.'

'I think you will agree that Violet is an exceptional person in her own right. She could study, make something of herself.' His moustache shook with excitement. 'I have such an idea to put to you.' She didn't recognise the expression on his face, could not read it.

'Our dear Lord has given me such a wonderful idea and a way to see it through. I see from your excitement we are thinking and feeling as one.' Close to hand, she heard the baby begin to grizzle.

'I pray that is true,' she said.

'Dear Ellen,' he said. 'Dear modest Ellen.' He took her unwilling hand, pressed it gently with his own. His expression was as eager as a lover's. 'I have talked to Violet. I have listened and thought and prayed about her situation, about what she can do.'

Her mood shifted in that instant, the world swivelling to present its ugly face between one breath and the next. The wildest thought was back, claiming its rightful, painful place. Those looks exchanged between Felix and Violet. Not innocent at all. Conspiracy was in the air.

'Getting Violet settled might be easier than we first

thought,' she said, forcing air in and out, taking charge again. It always came down to her. 'I have just come from the hospital. Perhaps you know already. They are willing to employ Violet as soon as she is fit enough. That will give her a start. A very good start.'

"Yes, working at the hospital would be a start,' said Felix. 'I am taking the longer, wider view. I have been thinking about Samuel's future also. Most of all I have been thinking about my own dear wife and the tearing sadness in her life.'

'I have never been happier,' she said. It had been true ten minutes ago. 'My work at the hospital is all ...'

'Yes, yes,' he said. 'It has been a solace of late.'

He raised her hand to his lips. His lips felt dry, but his tongue left a trace of slime on her skin. Best to pretend it was nothing. She was too ashamed to wipe it off against her skirt. He had gone mad, like a man at sea too long. It was up to her to bring them safely to shore again.

She tried to stand up, muttering something about cold drinks, about seeing to the dinner, about checking the water in the bird-cage, but Felix held onto her hand, tugged her so she swayed back onto the seat. She turned her face away from him.

Felix was talking on, regardless. 'It gives me such joy to see you with Baby Samuel, so tender and delightful a picture. I see all too clearly what you have been robbed of all these years.'

He had no right to talk of her hurt and failure, and

certainly not here in the open where Violet or Mrs Dawson or anyone could overhear.

A shaft of sunshine through the French windows lit up a stripe of wallpaper on the inside. Garish colours and the mocking pattern menaced her even in the garden. Inside the open door, light caught a glass vase holding stems of lilac. They were past their best, already drooping and bruising. She could almost smell the dank water from where she sat. Decay and corruption were everywhere. Once again, she'd allowed herself to be tricked into complacency.

Felix was looking at her. Expressions she hardly recognised, alarm, bewilderment, even tenderness, crossed his face.

The baby was louder by this time, more fretful, sucking up the air in the garden. Ellen took the squirming, fretting bundle from his basket and paced. Her back to her husband, she pinched the child. Not so very hard, not enough to mark his skin. If she was lucky, the baby's crying would block out everything else. She was not going to listen to the madman sitting there.

'I asked myself and God, what would give both Violet and Baby Samuel the greatest opportunities? The hospital's a beginning, but for how long? Violet wants to study and that's nigh impossible while doing the work of two parents. And you surely agree, Ellen, that Baby Samuel deserves the best chance in life. You and I have seen enough of the effects of ignorance and poverty not to want to add to it, surely.' His voice was a thousand years away.

'A new family for Samuel might be the best for both of them,' she agreed. 'There are surely many organisations that can help find a suitable one.'

The baby drew back its lips and she could have sworn that sharp little teeth flashed at her. When she looked again, it was all pink gums and tongue and the dark cavern of his throat.

Felix stroked his moustache, played with it for a few moments. 'I have deliberated and prayed,' he said. 'The answer I have been given is that it would be best all round if we brought up Samuel as our own.'

He was babbling, she thought. He was red-faced and bloated, had succumbed feverishly to a dratted summer cold. Or sunstroke? Perhaps she should ring for Mrs Dawson to bring out cool drinks. Was he showing the first sudden signs of senility?

'What do you mean?' Her throat was tight, her voice a whisper. No wonder the girl had had such a sly look on her face. It hadn't been Ellen's mischievous imagination at all.

She stood up.

'We could have the family you have always dreamed about.' He paused. 'That we both hoped for.'

Babbling. She reached down to touch his forehead, to check his fever. He caught her hand in his own, and pulled her back down next to him.

He tucked some stray hairs behind her ear. She almost froze. He never touched her like that.

He had become deranged.

'I see how it suits you, a child in your arms. As for the rest, for the hospital helpers, anybody can do that sort of thing.'

'Don't be ridiculous. You're embarrassing yourself,' she said. Then, more gently, 'Shall I fetch you a cool drink? Everything will fall into place again once you feel better.'

Felix asked her, 'You think the world of Samuel, don't you?'

There was a weight on her chest stopping the air from coming in.

He's a fine enough boy,' she said. When you're fighting to keep the water from your lungs, the truth is whatever you, whatever they, want it to be. 'But that is neither here nor there. This cannot happen. What does Violet have to say about it all?'

The mad words gushed out of Felix.

'I have decided. It's best all round. Violet is a sensible girl, wants the best for Samuel. As you said yourself, Miss Barnabas has agreed that the hospital will employ her, with suitable remuneration, while she studies at night to get a better qualification,' he said. 'Violet can live here with us a while longer, then perhaps in the nurses' quarters while she finds her feet. In the meanwhile, and for all time, Samuel will have all the benefits of you, my dear Ellen, his loving and beloved mother, here in our home, and later, a decent education as befits the son of a clergyman.'

Such deceit. Such disloyalty. It was unbelievable. It was exact. It was unforgivable. This scheme of theirs had all been worked out, decided, agreed upon and set in motion without so much as a whisper to her. One could imagine what it was that Violet had promised in return. The scandal all this would cause, that he would cause. She would not be party to this shame, could not stay and pretend all was well to cover his wrong-doing. She would disappear. She would join a Roman convent if that's what it took. Scandal enough in that.

Felix had denied her, had rejected her body all these years, those good years, her best years, the years that offered her any chance at all. He was too old for this sort of nonsense. Her hands rose to her mouth. She wanted to claw at her face. Her mind's eye designed a pattern to cut into the flesh of her face. She observed herself sitting in the garden, as though she were standing apart from herself, felt herself whirling about in the air. None of her selves could breathe. And all of them knew that Felix would not hear her say *no*.

'If you'll excuse me, the green-grocer has offered a basket of fruit for the tombola,' she said, standing up, smoothing her skirt. 'It won't walk here of its own accord, and I'd like to be back again before it rains.'

BANTLING

36 Violet. Stockwell. 1923.

Stockwell, London SW9, 15th June, Dear Mim & Da, You will have read the Vicar's letter by now. I hope you approve of the new arrangements. It has all happened so fast & will be a most awful wrench. You are right that it's my job to make sure Sammy is kept from harm & looked after as best as possible. I am resigned that I am not the person to do it. I cannot keep shilly-shallying. I keep telling myself it must all be for the best. Mrs H is quiet on the subject so it is difficult to tell what she thinks one way or another and she is such a busy bee already. I suppose the vicar has talked her round with his enthusiasm. He will dote on Sammy and they say boys do need a father. She can be strict, but she must be fond of Sammy in her own way & will make a decent mother to him, better than me surely. He will be at least safe with them. You talk about me getting a second chance, though I cannot see it like that. You should not get your hopes up about me & Stan. Too much water under burnt bridges for him & for me. Besides, even if, especially if, I am not to be a mother, I must start earning my keep, which is best done here in London. If all goes well, I shall start at the hospital just as soon as I can. I will be able to send money home to you. Also, Rev Holroyd says I can see Sammy from time to time, which is better than nothing. But if you think I should come & help look after Da for a bit, then I will do that, of course. Violet.

BANTLING

37 Ellen. Stockwell. 1923.

Violet had already sorted out the Bring-and-Buy money for her, putting the different coins into separate piles, and made a note of all the totals. She had put on a sour, sulky expression the whole time, all part of the act, but the duplicitous madam had made an efficient job of separating out the coins.

Ellen counted the money again, checking the totals. The pleasure of it. The relief of it. To have had such public support for her work was the most splendid of feelings.

Now this – hard solid cash – this was a real achievement. It meant assistance given and lives made better, even saved.

Ellen Holcroft. Inventive. Far-sighted. Visionary.

Who doubted her now? Who could possibly doubt?

She was not going to think about anything except the good her money could do. Certainly not about silly Felix and his blinding obsession with Violet and her baby. Whatever he said to anyone else, he could not force Ellen to mother that child.

The total now stood at over one hundred pounds. One hundred pounds, six shilling and thruppence halfpenny to be exact, with a few pledges still to be redeemed. The hospital will be delighted.

Even Felix had congratulated her. The Sale had passed off much more successfully than he'd anticipated. He was proud of her, he admitted. Of course, he'd spoiled it all by nattering on about putting the brat's name down for his old school. Where would they find the money, she'd wanted to know, and he'd shrugged in his *God will provide* manner. After that, he'd opened the newspaper and found something else to talk about. The Russian civil war had finally ground to a halt, but now the Communists were causing trouble in Germany.

Revolution was spreading, coming closer and closer. Hadn't Felix heard about all those poor people murdered in Russia just because of nothing at all and here he was wittering on about a single bastard child. She hadn't put it in quite those words, but she had mentioned about getting things in proportion. She sensed he'd taken her point.

Through the silence of the house, a thought, a wisp of a thought, was doing its best to distract her. An idle, impossible thought, not worth the time of day.

Felix would be gone the whole day, had all those everso important visits to make, would not be back until almost dark. For now, he had rushed Violet and her moodiness off to the hospital office, claiming someone there would show her the ropes. If indeed the hospital was where they had gone together. Funny but not amusing that they hadn't offered to wait until the cash was counted so they could carry it for her. Whatever it was, it didn't mean a thing. Not a thing. He would soon learn that Violet was making a fool of him, poor man.

Pay attention, Ellen. Concentrate. Who should decide how your money - the money - is to be spent? Should it be you? Should the lady visitors be given that honour, or at least a say? Voting might be too risky. Just look at what that sort of thinking has done for Russia. Perhaps Ellen could make a short list and seek opinions from those whose opinions she valued? Let's cross that bridge later. Should the money be put aside for coal for those households with new-borns? The warmer weather was here already, but extra money might be needed for heating water or cooking. Coins or tokens for gas meters? It was probably a waste to buy nappies. If they could only collect enough old towels ... But the hospital itself had first call on that sort of thing. Soap. Soap was universally needed.

The thought that wasn't worth the time of day had not given up, was still poking and nipping at her attention. Some storms you just have to ride out.

Nutritious foods were needed, that went without saying, though one had to be careful people did not take advantage. Milk. Eggs. Chocolate. Fares. The clinics could refund bus and tram fares in exchange for expectant or just-delivered women's tickets if circumstances prevented them from walking. Perhaps reimburse some of the less well-off volunteers too? A lesser priority. A hundred pounds would not solve the world's problems, but it would go some way to keeping her visiting scheme going. Lanolin. Talcum powder.

Her note-paper was covered with words, with notes and names, suggestions and ideas. Steaming ahead!

She shook her head to get rid of the prodding and prickling at the back of her mind. Whispering voices came from the shapes on the wall and had to be ignored. Pay attention, Ellen, concentrate. Money on the table or not, this is no time to slacken your efforts. Your next task is to get the cash to the safe at the hospital.

The cash was too heavy and bulky to put into her handbag. A shopping basket might be more suitable, but she didn't like the idea of carrying lots of jingling metal so openly through the streets all the way to the hospital. Too risky, by far. Felix could rabbit on about the locals being salt of the earth, but he'd not be caught carrying such large sums in the open.

Upstairs, the child started his shrill repetitive cries. He was laughing at her. At the first sound, the wallpaper leered at her. The thought she had turned her back upon all morning tapped her so hard on the shoulder that she jerked.

If she didn't put her foot down once and for all, the infant would put a stop to all her hard work.

She'd never do another thing except toil and clear up his mess and dirty nappies.

By the time it was over, she'd be too old for anything.

Violet would cut and run soon enough, just see if

she didn't, at liberty to do whatever she wanted now that she's leaving Ellen to pick up the mess. All that weeping and wailing about loving her child to the point of being frightened she couldn't look after him properly. Abandoning her responsibilities, Ellen had told her. Just buck up. But had the girl taken any notice of Ellen? Felix and Violet were in cahoots. What was good enough for Ellen was not good enough for Violet. Betrayal on all fronts. Who did they think they were to decide matters over her head? Nobody considered Ellen's feelings in all this. It was so hurtful, so very hurtful.

And it was wrong.

Felix, Violet – everybody, including the brat himself – had to learn that Ellen was at nobody's beck and call. Felix must have planned today, abandoning her, swanning off to the hospital office with Violet while Mrs Dawson was out running errands. He meant to leave her with her lap so weighted down that she was trapped. Well then, left to herself, Ellen would do as she thought best.

The brat could make himself useful for once. In the hall, she stashed the bags underneath the pram's mattress. Nobody would dare to even think of robbing a woman wheeling an infant.

Up the staircase. Stepping one two three, around the turn in the stairs. Tap tap tap along the passage to Violet's room. One foot in front of the other.

The house held its breath.

BANTLING

Samuel was red-faced and bawling, the room reeking of sour milk and excrement. It was as bad as the hole the Wingroves inhabited. It was what lay ahead for Ellen.

'Drat you,' she shouted, no-one there to hear her. She started to gather up what she'd need, decided to change him, if only because she it wouldn't do to take him into the hospital, not stinking like that.

She spread a towel on the bed and laid him on it. She bent over him. He thrashed his arms and legs, screwing up his face, generally kicking up a hullaballoo.

She scooped him up again. She was not going to spend her life doing this, whatever anybody said.

She pressed his face against her chest. His back arched and heaved. 'You stinking bag of shit.' Excuse her language. Squirming as he was, she was stronger. It was just a matter of putting her mind to it.

She put him down again. He glared at her with venom, recognising the one who dared to stand up to him.

The pillows were within her reach. It would be so easy. Too easy.

He was challenging her, pushing and provoking her, luring her into forgetting herself. If she gave into him, let herself be dragged into that tempting violence, he would have won. She knew then what he was, and for a moment the task of keeping safe the people she cared about overwhelmed her. Violet & Felix were just pawns in his game.

BANTLING

She took a deep breath. Steady, Ellen. Steady as you go.

She had got this far. The rest of the way would become clear.

She pulled off his shirt, his fingers catching at the sleeves, and took off his vest. His knitted drawers were next, wet, smelly, and heavy, the ammonia catching in her throat, stinging her eyes. She unpinned the nappy, shook the stinking contents into one covered pail, threw the soiled cloth into another. She held her breath for as long as she could.

So much wiping, so much mess. She would not let him burrow under her skin or provoke her, not now that she understood. She smoothed on the Vaseline, packaged him neatly back into a clean nappy and did not prick herself or him. She laid him in his cot.

To the bathroom, one two three, one two three. The waste from the bucket down the toilet, two three; the filthy lint into the bin, two three. She would leave a note for Mrs Dawson to empty it and clean everything up. She washed and scrubbed her hands until they were sore and almost clean enough. If she was not careful, the badness in the child might yet confound her. She could not, would not, let him win.

In the trunk room, she came across a few drops of medicine to take away the stench and clear her head for the battle to come. A little help, that's all she needed, for whatever was to happen. She stroked

BANTLING

Arthur's jacket, pressed her face into it, a moment only, for guidance and comfort.

Back to Violet's room, one two three, one two three. The baby was still lying in his basket, crying and hiccupping. Better take extra nappies and the bag of bits and pieces. Some clothes, too. He might need changing again by the time she reached the hospital, and she had to be prepared.

She opened the wardrobe, looking for something, nothing in particular. She pulled out the drawers of the dressing table. She had a perfect right, after all. There was nothing much there beyond Violet's smalls and baby clothes; knitted coatees, crepe flannel nightgowns, a shawl or two. The baby things she bundled together. In the bedside drawer, she happened across the birth certificate, a scrawled line, a blank, in the column where the father's name should have been. Very likely even Violet did not know who the father was.

The light through the window bouncing against the mirror stung her eyes, filling them with shards.

A sound downstairs, Mrs Dawson calling out that it was only her, back from the shops. Ellen picked everything up, walked down the stairs, oh so very careful not to trip.

'I'm off to the hospital,' she called from the hall. 'And I'm taking Baby for some fresh air.'

She pushed all the bits and bobs under the mattress. Back up the stairs to fetch him. Tuck him into the pram on top of them. He fixed her with his evil eye.

Mrs Dawson appeared in the hall and fussed over the pram.

'Only June and it's glaring hot out there. Humid too. Has Baby Samuel had his bottle yet? He'll need some water as well. Has he got his bonnet on? I'll help you with the pram down the front steps, saves him a bit of jolting. Oh, just look at that will you? He's got a grip on my finger. Couldn't do that yesterday, could you, mite?

'Mrs Dawson, you can be such a fuss-pot when you put your mind to it.'

Another one under his spell.

The sun dissolved the leaves into new colours and shapes, the whole world alive with possibilities and promises, although Ellen knew better than to let down her guard. In the house at night or on the streets in broad daylight made no difference. You never knew when malevolence would leap out at you, nor how.

There was the faint smell of tar and a slight tackiness in the tarmac underfoot as she crossed the road. The pram-wheels had minds of their own, catching and twisting every now and then. Steering was harder than she expected. The air became damper and heavier, the sky becoming a collection of silver-edged rags of wet grey felt. A figure at the end of the street floated in the lurid sunlight. She thought she recognised Nurse Henderson, and imagined telling her about the money she had raised, imagined the midwife's admiring expression, imagined her words of congratulation. But Nurse Henderson would not play her part, kept twisting words about, interrupting, telling her instead about Baby Samuel's mother, looking so very bonny and getting on so well with the Reverend, if she was not mistaken.

The other woman passed her by, not Nurse Henderson at all, nothing like her in fact, but no matter. Ellen had understood the message.

There was no point going to the hospital where Violet would be lording it over the cash-tin. Violet would set her envious prim little mouth, and all of Ellen's hard-earned money would slip unnoticed into the general funds. It would be far better to wait until Ellen could see Doctor McCall herself, even her deputy would do, someone who would appreciate what her hundred and six pounds meant. Perspiration itched the skin above her lips and around her chin. Such humidity.

Dizzy, she paused, trying to blink sense back into the street. She had wandered off her route, was in a rougher road. The purple-dark of the sky glowed in the sulphur-yellow light. Nothing was familiar. The road carried straight on and another ran across it. In the brooding light, the buildings looked as flat as a painted backcloth to a play. On all sides, cracked paint and grubby windows peered down on the street. Above and about her billowed a dirty-yellow brick wall.

BANTLING

She pressed herself against it, avoiding the inquisitive windows.

The paving stones carried their traces of long-ago currents, erased and criss-crossed by newer cracks, cuts and smoothings, their messages almost making sense. Otherwise, the street was as quiet as deceit. She waited in the strip of shadow.

Dark spots appeared on the pavement, fat and slow at first. She levered up the hood of the pram and fastened the gabardine cover. The drops fell faster, and the gusting wind slapped her skirt around her legs. Hail as large as peas. People had been killed, she'd read somewhere, by hail the size of bullets or eggs, but this storm didn't scare her. She held her hat and bent her head into the wind as the pram trembled and shook. She laughed. Water spread around her shoes; the gutters were overwhelmed in a moment.

The squall passed, runnels losing their energy, rippling away, only a few drips now from the pram and the brim of her hat.

A quivering procession appeared in the street when she looked up. Angels, troubadours or gypsies she couldn't tell.

She squinted into the sun.

The figures became more solid, recognisable. It was the Wingroves.

Henry Wingrove pushed a tottering pile of goods on a wooden pushcart. Alice drifted, ballasted by two cases hanging from her arms. Bertie carried a case and two baskets. Even Doris dragged a brolly like a broken wing. Who would have thought that malodorous room would have fitted so much?

Ellen wheeled the pram towards them.

She stopped in front of them, set the brake. Greetings were exchanged.

She released the hood and pulled it back.

The changeling blinked in the light and opened his mouth.

'Oh my, you poor little thing,' said Alice Wingrove.

She put her cardboard suitcases down gently onto the gleaming wet pavement. She bent forward, slowly, slowly, just as Ellen moved when she wanted to trap a spider under a glass, hoping it would not skitter away.

'Can I?'

Ellen nodded.

Alice laid one hand against his cheek.

'Hello, little lovely,' she said to him.

Ellen unpinned her hat and shook the water from it, replaced it on her head.

'Let's see if I can't make you comfier,' said Alice.

She unfastened the gabardine cover. She found a bottle of water tucked alongside him. His lips fastened on the teat. He sucked and sucked and sucked.

In front of Ellen's eyes, he was changing, his demon weakening, the human boy in him asserting itself at last. She let out her breath. She had found the right mother for the right child.

BANTLING

'Look, look, he's smiling at me, really and truly smiling,' said Alice.

'Don't be soft, girl, it's just wind,' said her husband.

'You don't see him like I can,' said Alice. 'This one knows me already, just like I know him.'

Ellen looked at Henry Wingrove. He was glowering at his wife, then at Ellen, his eyes furious. He shook his head at them both.

'Get along, Alice,' he said. 'No good can come of this. Leave the child to Mrs Holcroft. It's set to pour again and we've a way to go yet.'

'Where's that, Mr Wingrove?' asked Ellen.

'We're away to my brother's place in Peckham. More chance of work down by the canal. Get a move on, Alice. The kids can't stand here all day. Just look at that sky.'

Alice's arms curved around Samuel. For the first time since Ellen had known her, she stood straight. There was spanking new shine about her.

Ellen heard words coming from her mouth. 'This child ... the boy ... quite normal...healthy in every respect ... Abandoned by his mother, back in April, May, poor little chap ... Only three months old or so ... temporarily in my charge ... being offered for adoption before long ... almost immediately, in fact.'

'Adoption? Not to want a child like this. Poor girl. Poor little lad.'

'Alice. It's no concern of ours. Come on with you.'

'Every child should be loved.'

'The vicar and his wife will make sure he goes to a good home.'

'I could love him. Anybody would. Just look at him.'

An idea so clear, so precise she cannot mistake it or fumble with it, such an idea that only comes once in a lifetime, an idea that changes the everyday world, such an idea found her, claimed its home in Ellen.

'In view of your sad circumstances ... *very* irregular ... knowing your family as I do ... I'm minded to be charitable ... Lovely boy ... otherwise respectable family ... There would be some compensation for your kindness, of course.'

Violet could hardly complain. She'd been as keen as mustard to offload him a week back. In her place, Ellen couldn't be thankful enough.

Alice stared at her, comprehension and dark hope filling her eyes.

'Won't anybody miss him? His mam?'

'Better off starting over.'

Alice nodded, a woman accepting how hard the world could be.

'Pull yourself together, girl,' said Henry Wingrove. 'We've got enough on our plate as is. First off, you're not well in yourself.'

Ellen's stomach somersaulted.

'Look,' she said, lifting a corner of the bedding and extracted a bag of coins. 'This might help a bit. Quite a bit, I would think.'

Henry Wingrove looked at the money, glanced at

her, back to the money, muttering all the while about not needing a scrawny runt, another mouth to feed.

'Shush you,' said Alice. 'Only three months old and look at that head of hair. He's raring to go, just needs building up. I've no milk left in myself. But he must be used to that, if his mam's gone off and left him.'

'Not on your life,' said Henry Wingrove. 'Don't you give it another thought.'

'He already takes the bottle,' said Ellen. 'But I mustn't keep you.'

She bent, wretched as anything, to put the money back into the pram. She paused, hesitated.

'It's a crying shame all round. I know you'd care for him, bring him up as one of your own. Even his colouring's close enough to pass as your own.'

My oh my, she should have been on the stage.

'Please, Harry,' said Alice. 'He'll get me back on my feet proper, I know it.'

The new pinkness in Alice Wingrove's cheeks was not caused by the sun or rain. Her free hand rested on Bertie's head, slide to Doris'.

'Tell you what,' said Henry Wingrove. 'You take him back for now, missus and I'll sleep on it.'

He put his hands to the cart again and tilted it back onto its wheels. Alice's shoulders slumped, but otherwise she did not move. She did not put the brat back in the pram. Ellen caught her eye. They understood each other.

Alice bent down so little Doris and Bertie could take a good look at him.

People, some people, people like this man, they do almost anything for money. Not everyone was as principled about right and wrong as she was. It took a particular sort of person to stick to her guns, come what may. She'd think of it not so much as a bribe as a due reward, a contribution to expenses.

She kept her voice low, speaking only to Henry Wingrove.

'By tomorrow he'll be gone, put into an orphanage.' She would make it so, turn the lie to truth. 'It'll be too late after then. What if this infant could bring your wife back to herself?'

A few drops of rain fell.

It was true what they said about beggars and choosers.

She opened her umbrella.

'There's over a hundred pounds in the pram,' she said. It was a lot of money, too much probably, but needs must. She would stake it all. 'I know you'd use it well,' she said, wondering if he gambled or drank and to what extent.

He looked wary.

'I don't want any trouble with the authorities. What if the police come calling about the money?'

'They won't. You send them to me if they do. I'll tell them the money was honestly raised for a good cause and that's where it's gone. I'll deal with the authorities myself to make sure everything is ship-shape.' She'd got this far. She'd find a way to smooth everything over. Who would doubt a vicar's wife's intentions? 'All this will be our little secret. Not a word to anybody, if you please. No need to stir up unnecessary trouble.'

They both looked at his wife. She and the baby were gazing at each other as if they'd been reunited.

Another scatter of rain had Doris struggling with her brolly and Alice fumbling to shelter the baby with her body. Ellen pulled back the bedding and the mattress to show him all the pouches of coins sitting there. She opened the bags. She didn't have to; it was awkward with the umbrella handle tucked under her arm. It all took precious time, she was getting wet and was too close to the watchfulness of the houses, but she wanted Wingrove to know how much he owed her.

Lots of silver, even some crowns and half-crowns, bags of copper, a golden guinea, a few ten-shilling notes, several pound notes. One ten-pound note.

'A hundred pounds. More.'

More than he'd earned in the past year, she guessed. A great deal more.

He leaned over the pram, fingered the bags, weighed them in his hands, shuffled through the notes.

Henry Wingrove shrugged, a man giving up.

'Take the bloody kid if you're so set on him.'

Alice became a young woman, smiling and supple.

'Perfect,' Ellen heard herself trill. 'What good luck for us all that we ran into each other like this.'

BANTLING

'We'll give it a go,' he said to his wife. 'Just don't be expecting me to be doing what I can't. The truth is he isn't blood and never will be.'

'Harry Wingrove! Never you mind all that piffle. You'll treat him the same as our others, come what may.'

'All I'm saying is mine come first.'

Back over the bags of change went the bedding. The notes he pocketed quickly enough.

Splats of rain hit them.

The Wingroves were distracted now, reloading, rearranging their chattels.

She said firmly, 'I don't want Mrs Wingrove to risk an upset just because of a little paperwork, so I will take an address, just in case.'

Any nonsense about the brat would die down soon enough, but better safe than sorry.

She showed Alice what else was in the pram, thankful she'd thought to stuff his nappies and bottle and spare rubber teats and some vests and bonnets and the like into the pram. Alice wasn't paying much attention.

'I'm your ma, and this here's your dad and I'll have his guts for garters if he ever says differently,' said Alice Wingrove.

All the same, she gave her husband the sort of smile that shouldn't be seen in public and ran a hand down his arm to touch his wet hand, and his face softened at last.

BANTLING

'Got me round your little finger, you have,' he said, and patted her cheek. She giggled and blushed.

Ellen's heart pinched.

'Put our Doris into the pram,' said Alice. "She can hold our little one.'

He smiled at his daughter as he lifted her towards the pram, his bulk between Alice and the children. It was Ellen who saw him tug and handle the boy as she might have herself.

Not such a bad thing if his new father had the measure of him already.

'Best foot forward now, before we drown on our feet,' said Henry Wingrove.

Ellen had better get a move on too, before anyone changed their mind or asked more questions, before the windows in the street started to blink and notice what was happening.

It was a good day's work, by far the best solution all round. She might pass the bakery on her way home. In a little while, she would sit down with Violet. In her experience, which was considerable, there wasn't much in life that wasn't improved by a nice cup of tea and something sweet to nibble on. The madness that had come between them would pass. Together, they would weep a few tears for life's hard choices. Together, they would wipe their eyes, draw new breath and they would go on, side by side, a weight lifted from their shoulders, into their shining futures.

BANTLING

And for dinner? Which vegetables? Cauliflower always has a celebratory air.

BANTLING

38 Violet. Stockwell. 1923.

Stockwell, London SW9, 19th July, Dear Stel, I don't know if I am over the worst of the shock or not, but the fever has gone down. He wasn't with me so very long, but I was more attached to Sam than I have been to any living thing. I failed him in every way. She behaves as though I am doing everything just to be difficult. After what she did. The Reverend surprise surprise has gone to ground & I have not hardly seen him since. You cannot trust any man. I expect he still eats his breakfast each day, but I do not have the stomach to be in the same room as those people. I am worse than mouldy Mildred walking the streets from dawn, keeping hoping that I might catch sight of my Sam being wheeled about, but no such luck. Mim & Da say it's probably all for the best. What's the difference, they ask, I was going to give him up to him & her in any case & perhaps this is a cleaner break. She must have written to them to get her story in quick, but it's not the same, not the same at all. Mim & Da still think it means I have a chance with Stan. They don't understand that I cannot pretend any more. I can't stay here with these people any more. There's a chance they might let me stay in the Home for a while, but of course she won't give me a reference & I think she is letting people know I am likely to be a trouble-maker. She's too clever by half to let it look as though she's putting me out on my ear, but it's out on my ear all the same. Apart from

BANTLING

Hattie Dawson, who was here that day but needs to keep her job, nobody believes that the vicar's wife stole my baby. She took him to give him away, but sometimes in the night I wonder if she might have smothered him from spite. Other times I think I hear him crying & I am sure she has put him under the floorboards. She has convinced everyone that I got confused about them adopting Sam, that it's not unusual after having a baby to lose your mind for a bit, you make things up, you forget, you hear what you want to hear & you pay no attention to how things are. After all, she asks them, what would her & Felix want with my baby? As for him, he's gone quiet, doesn't say a word, even though it was all his idea, taking Sammy on I mean. I asked him straight out why he didn't back me up & he just said she did what she thought was best. Miss Barnabas at the hospital, she thinks I'm bright, but even she just looks embarrassed & says it's a shame I changed my mind again, but perhaps it's all for the best, it will be easier to get employment & make a fresh start & I'll feel better soon. Isn't that what they always say? So, in all events, she has me beaten. I deserved to be punished for the harm I nearly caused him, but this is not right. I have let him down more than anybody ever deserved. Oh Stel, whatever am I to do? Violet.

BANTLING

39 Ellen. Stockwell. 1923.

Downstairs the front door clicked open. It was well past midnight.

She waited for the slam.

One.

Two.

'What in God's name possessed you?'

Four.

For a religious man, Felix often couldn't tell when to hold his tongue.

Five. Six.

She was still waiting for the door to shut, so she didn't answer him. Seven. Eight. Besides, he already knew what she'd say. They'd gone over it enough times.

Nine.

He had blown out the candle, but even so she could see the dressing table, wardrobe and easy chair rising like reefs from the shadowed floor.

Ten. She sighed.

'Well?' he said again. He was shouting under his breath.

Eleven. Twelve.

The stairs creaked. Violet must be on her way up.

She pushed aside the covers, started to get out of bed. Somebody had to make sure they were not about to be murdered in their beds.

He held her arm.

'Leave her be. You've done quite enough.'

'The front door,' she said.

'It's locked. I heard her bolt it.'

'What is she doing out like this, traipsing about at all hours? It's been going on for weeks. She's so rude to me, never tells me anything.'

'Are you surprised, Ellen?'

She jerked her head.

'Manners cost nothing. You sound as though you approve of her making a spectacle of herself.'

'I hate to see her roaming about like this as much as you do. I'd never forgive myself if more harm came to her through us, the poor girl. But for the moment we must let her be.'

Under the sheet again, her nail pressed hard against her nipple.

'She'll be thanking me on her knees before long, you'll see. I told her, *'Free! You are free, Violet! You can soar wherever you please, do whatsoever you wish.'*'

Felix was behaving as though he couldn't hear her.

'So what did she do? Crushed me against the door-frame as she barged past, that's what. Caught me with her elbow, knocked the breath right out of me. So utterly thoughtless. I could show you my bruises.'

'She has some cause to be immoderate,' said Felix.

'Don't give me any of that nonsense. And don't pretend that you hadn't begun to think twice about that arrangement you charged into. Reckless.'

'It seemed for the best at the time.'

'It was not for the best. Not for you and me, not for her, not even for Samuel.'

Now he was gone, she could say his name without so much as a blink.

She took her hand away from her breast. She was fearless, renewed.

Felix tutted and clucked beside her.

'Surely it's not too late to undo all this?' he asked. 'Return the child?'

Felix's understanding of love was limited. Perhaps it came of being a man that he had no inkling that what seemed harsh now was the ferocity of her love rising to the challenges and threats that surrounded him and Violet.

'You're not thinking straight,' she said. 'How would that play with the bishop? That your wife stood accused of child-snatching and you agreed with her accusers?'

'An honest mistake, it would seem. A change of heart on Violet's part. No harm done.'

Water rumbled through the pipes. Violet was making her way to bed. Either that or creeping around laying traps.

'Have you heard what she's saying? All sorts of nonsense about betrayal and white slavery. *I trusted you. I trusted you.* Dreadful things she's telling them about me at the hospital, absolutely dreadful. Fortunately, of course, they still hold me in high regard there.'

Though not high enough at the moment, thanks to Violet's bleating. Mud sticks even to the innocent. There was a bit of an atmosphere about the Bring-and Buy money, even though she'd had a story all prepared about a special one-off case, had given them a receipt. She would have to make up for it, work harder, prove herself all over again.

'They think Violet's soft in the head and have told her they won't listen to a single word of her nonsense. Even so, she's spreading her lies all around the houses. How are you going to put a stop to that?'

'She'll calm down,' he said. 'Once she gets Samuel back. That's all she wants.'

'Are you trying to make me ill? Is that what you want?'

'She'll have learnt from her mistake.'

As stupid a platitude as she'd ever heard. Which mistake might that be? How many mistakes, the sort of mistakes that count, does one get the chance to not repeat? She, Ellen, had learned that she should never have married Felix. She'd give her right arm to have the chance not to make that mistake again.

A floor-board squeaked as Violet moved from the landing to the hallway. Then the house was quiet. Waiting.

'The child is not her plaything. He needs to be settled in one place, with a proper mother,' she said.

Alice Wingrove, for example, for whom getting a child meant reaching solid land. Two wrongs sometimes make a right. And as long as Henry Wingrove stayed put and didn't come back for more hand-outs, Samuel was safely out of sight.

'But ... but ...' said Felix.

'Do you want her to think she can hold what's happened over us to get her own way whenever she feels like it?'

'I'll have a word with her,' he said. 'She's not a malicious girl.'

She laughed out loud, a harsh bark in the dark. She couldn't help herself. The mistake she kept on making – you'd think she'd learn – was to forget how people, even Felix, most of all Felix, made life more difficult for themselves than it had to be.

'For Heaven's sake, Felix. I'm doing my best to protect you and your reputation. To say nothing of sparing your feelings. And all you can do is make excuses for the girl. People noticed the way she was making up to you, make no mistake. Even if we can stop all the rumours about who fathered her child – I hear things, Felix, things that you do not – she's shouting about promises she says you made to her. I see the looks, the tongues wagging behind the hands ... not a pretty sight.'

He sat up with a jerk, pulling the bedcovers with him.

'No. It's not possible that people would think that I ... that Violet's child ... She wouldn't do that.'

'It's a harsh, harsh world, Felix, more tattle-tongued than you care to admit. Even blameless men of God are not immune to gossip. We need to stick together now, you and me. Malicious tales will reach the bishop sooner or later and we must make sure he treats them with the contempt they deserve.'

She softened her voice.

'As you say, we live and learn. It's hard to admit, but I was naive in my initial hopes and expectations. You were right from the start. There would only be hardships ahead for Violet and the child. I know why you came up with your cock-eyed adoption plan. It was well-intended.'

He made a sound, it must be of assent, in the back of his throat,

'But the idea ...' She laid one hand on his arm. 'Think of the cost. Besides, we'd be elderly before Samuel was even at school.'

'I think as you as forever youthful, my dear,' he said. 'Wasn't a child what you wanted more than anything else?'

She felt sorry for him then, old and out of his depth. Angry with him, too. He'd only had to listen to her once in a while in all these years.

'I have my work,' she lied, 'and you have yours. It is enough.'

He had no real idea of what sacrifices she'd made

for them both. She had spared him that smarmy letter from the hospital. Thanks everso and cheerio. No place on their committee, after all. Perhaps another time. She'd been pushed aside for a benefactor with the deep pockets of her husband's cash. Ellen would eat her hat if that fine lady ever rolled up her sleeves and got her hands dirty.

'And Violet ... ?'

'She's young, she'll be right as rain before she knows it, marry, I expect, have more children.'

He was quiet again. She pressed on.

'In her present frame of mind, it's better if Violet doesn't stay here.'

'But where will she go? This is her home, at least for the present.'

'The Fellowship might be persuaded to be charitable for a few weeks, to find her a place in their Home until she perks up. And then I think back to her parents, don't you?'

There was a long pause.

'We have shaken a young woman loose from her moorings. God forgive us and help us in the dark waters we have entered,' said Felix.

He pushed away the covers. He put on his dressing gown, picked up a pillow and the counterpane hanging over the foot of the bed.

'I do believe you will be more comfortable if I sleep in my study.'

The old fusspot creaked slowly along the hall. She

listened, but his shuffling passed Violet's door without a pause and went on down the staircase. She pictured him guiding himself in the dark, hand on the wall, knocking the picture frames askew, feeling for each rug with his slippered feet. He'd be lucky if he didn't trip.

Ring out the bells! She'd be spared his fart-filling mornings. Good riddance.

Life would be clearer from now on. She was strong. Fingers crossed, thighs pricked with pins, skin squeezed until it bruised. She could pinch higher, even higher, right *up there,* when the storms were very bad indeed.

BANTLING

40 Violet. Streatham. 1923.

Streatham, London SW16, 17 October 1923, Dearest Stel, I will never forget your kindness. Four whole days here with me & you never said how you wangled the time & money to come to London. Now that you are back in Shanklin, I miss you more than I can say, but you have left behind some of your good sense. I did not tell you, perhaps you guessed, that before you arrived, I had given up on all fronts & was ready to pull the plug on myself. May you be spared such despair. Turning up out of the blue you pulled me back from the brink. I will not break my promise to you on that front. All the same, though I know you & Ma mean well, there is no going back to Cowes or Shanklin. On the other hand, you might be glad to hear that I have listened to your sensible advice about holding my tongue & eating humble-pie. Truly, it takes all my will & all my powers of deceit. At every turn I think 'How could she do it? I trusted her, I trusted them both, with the most precious thing I will ever have in my care. They broke that trust into particles too small to imagine and nothing, <u>nothing</u> will change that. But, as you advised, I sewed my lips together, I swallowed bile & I built walls between what I feel & what I say. I gave the Reverend all the assurances he wanted about 'not spreading rumours & lies' about that wife of his & so the references came from him & I started at the warehouse a few weeks back. Tedious it is, but will keep some sort *of roof over my head while I decide what to do next. The Fellowship doesn't mind me staying at the Home for a bit, especially since I have made a start on the wilderness at the back. I attack & hack at the brambles as if they are that creature herself, my eyes & nose streaming with bitter salt. Have you ever heard of people crying all the while, never mind what they are doing? That's how I am. Shrammed up in a pair of men's old trousers or old men's trousers I dig & tear & turn the soil, going like the clappers until it is pitch dark. Then as often as not I make a bonfire & sit outside come fine night or foul. I would sleep in the shed with the seeds & tools if I could, curled up in sacks, & not wake up until the spring. The other girls give me a wide berth at the weekends, their stares slipping away like fishes. Come Monday morning I am as primped & orderly as anyone. At the warehouse too, they think I am strange because I do not chat & gossip, not even to pass the time of day. I work work work. But honestly, Stel, I can't help it. I have nothing to say to anybody at all about anything at all. It is the only way I can stop myself crying all the time. Oh Stel, I can't believe I lost him. Whatever I did wrong I am sorry so sorry, but who can I tell? Perhaps I deserved it. The Police gave up on me long ago as a nuisance-maker & the hospital wants no more to do with me. There's no praying to be done these days & I am out of ideas of where & how to look, so cross your fingers (even tighter than that) & wish me well with all your might, from your most sisterly & affectionate friend, Violet. PS How goes it with that new young man of yours?*

BANTLING

41 Violet. Herne Hill. 1926.

Herne Hill, London SE24, 20 April 1926
  Dear Reverend and Mrs Holcroft,
  As ever, I do not know if it is possible for you to arrange for ~~Sammy~~ Samuel to receive the enclosed, now or at a later date, but please, if it is, it would mean so much to me.
  Yours sincerely,
  Violet Bantling

Herne Hill, London SE24, 20 April 1926
Darling Sammy, The Happiest Birthday in the World to you today, on your 3rd Birthday. Sammy, my dearest little boy. Three today! You will be walking & running & jumping & even talking sixteen to the dozen. I remember your skin was sheeny, like the faint colours you see on young petals & sometimes there seemed to be rainbows trapped inside your brand-new hair. You glowed from inside. We used to study each other for hours, though I know they say a baby cannot even focus. But to know the heart of someone is not the same as seeing them with the eye & I want to believe you saw the loving, fearful heart of me for those few weeks. As always, from Mummy with all her love.

BANTLING

42 Timmy. Peckham. 1926.

The sweet soapiness of her nightie and the lovely warm smell of her. The up-down in-out breath of her, in-out up-down, the same as his, his breath for hers, hers for him, her front touch-touch-touching his back, as if they are one and the same, as if he is a leaf and she is the tide and they are bob-bob-bobbing towards the secret island. His magic shoes will take him to the castle in the sunny patch, where Ma and him will live, and Bertie and Doris can come and visit and they'll all eat jam roly-poly and chicken every day. But for now, it's as good as it gets, just being here with Ma, thumb in mouth, safe between her and anything horrid, and on guard too, against wicked shouting giants and smoky dragons.

Nasty nippy draughts across his head. He scrunches even more into Ma; he'd melt into her if he could.

The clumping across the floor shakes all the way up the bed legs.

The shouting giant's back.

Ma shifts against his back and he makes himself as small and floppy and close as he can. Thump. Thump. It's shoes-on-the-floor time, smell-of-ashes-in-the-room time. Creak, groan, whumph goes the bed, like the barge when the crane dumps the load too fast and all on one side.

BANTLING

The mattress tilts and rocks. A gap opens between Ma and him.

Here's the stinkiness of beer and smoke. He's busting with not coughing. Dad's getting himself into bed, huffing and puffing like the Big Bad Wolf, not even caring if he wakes up Ma.

And Dad has woken up Ma, her breathing's different, she's shifting so the two of them are not all of a piece anymore.

'No, Harry. Give over,' Ma whispers. 'No, really. Don't. Harry. Not now.'

She's got her laughing voice on, very soft, the one that comes from the back of her throat. Her laugh isn't for him, though, she's shutting him out and she's stopped cuddling him. She's turned her back to him, is facing towards Dad. He's colder now, but it won't do to let them know he isn't asleep. It's so dark he can't even see the shininess of the eiderdown, so perhaps they'll forget he's here.

'Come on, girl,' says Dad. He's leaning all over her, blowing his smoking breath everywhere.

'Not with Timmy here,' she says. 'It's not right.'

'I'll fix that soon enough,' says Dad very loudly. 'The blighter should be in with Bertie in any case.'

'Let him be,' says Ma. 'Little lamb's sound asleep.'

'Then he won't notice,' says Dad.

He's up in the cold air and crying and grabbing for Ma, but none of it makes any difference because she's shushing him and telling him there, there, be her good boy, go back to sleep. Dad's grinning like the wolf that gobbled up Granny.

'I'll have your hide if I catch you in there bothering Ma again,' growls the giant wolf once they're out on the landing. 'You sleep in your own bed from now or I'll know why.'

He's in the shivery dark, dumped in with Bertie, all sharp bones, freezing feet and his brother's stinky breath.

43 Violet. Herne Hill. 1927.

Herne Hill, 13 April 1927
Reverend & Mrs Holcroft,

Four years and still I miss Samuel so very much. Do you make sure he is well-treated? To know he is healthy & loved, even to know if he is alive or dead would bring me some peace of mind, so I beg you again to please pass on any news you have of him.

Yours sincerely, Violet Bantling

BANTLING

44 Violet. Herne Hill. 1927.

Herne Hill, 13 April 1927, Dearest Stel, I do so appreciate your letters, even when (most of all when) my own are more than laggardly in coming. Your new job sounds not bad at all. Are you not so overcome with wanderlust for all those trips and places that you issue any old tickets to your travellers? Perhaps you will get the chance to pop along to Egypt with Mr Cook and dance the temple shimmy under the Eastern moon. Or perhaps Southampton is foreign and fast enough after Shanklin and Cowes. I'd love nothing more than to catch up with you again, but a visit to the island is not on the cards, not even to Southampton to see you, not with Mim still dead set against the sight of me. Perhaps she is right that Da fretted himself to death over me, but a body can bear only so much guilt. Things are not too bad here with me. I've been kept in shillings for the gas meter by several elderly ladies who trust a woman around their property more than they do some spotty lad – though some exclaim how slight I am & feel (though not for very long) they cannot ask me to do more than a little genteel weeding. They fear their sweet peas will suffer from weakly-dug & shallow trenches. More flatteringly (perhaps) they also think I must have a more sensitive & womanly eye for plantings. Needless to say, I always enjoy being asked for my suggestions & am recommending daphnes at the moment, for their heady scent during the bleakest months. I have been more than grateful for the wages & the privacy of their garden sheds where I do not have to chat & smoke with the municipal gardeners & generally behave like the lad I am not. But let us thank the gods of Corporation for keeping body & soul together. It's the parks & municipal gardens around Lambeth that have fed & watered me the past lean years & are still my bread & butter. This morning, I was tidying up, digging over & generally getting ready to plant bulbs outside the library in Brixton. All of a sudden, I remembered registering Sam's birth at the Town Hall. I felt seasick, as you do when a wave heaves & plunges, as if the wave is inside you. I braced myself to drown in anguish & remorse. It was only a moment, then the upheaval settled & me with it, leaving just some distant sadness & general philosophising. I scare myself thinking that if I don't agonise, then Sam will disappear from inside me as he has from my outside life. I still send cards of course & my usual notes to the Holcrofts, but I never hear back, not even from Hattie Dawson. At times, it seems a shame Stan wasn't his dad. He'd have stuck by me & made a fist of us being a family even if that was the last thing I wanted. I look back at being young & light-hearted even when I was expecting Sam. Even after he was born, I thought everything would come good. But as they say about split milk, you can't spend your life crying. All in all, life is more settled than I ever thought it could be 4 years ago. I would never have taken up the gardening if I was Mrs Stan or even Madam Widow as I suppose I would have

BANTLING

claimed on my own with Sam. I would be stuck in that dusty warehouse corner, scraping a living. Working out in the fresh air, solitary as it is, suits me well. You see how changed a woman I am when you learn I attend public talks for amusement. No dancing of a Friday night, but hard seats for me & harder facts at the local botanical institute. I sometimes pick up useful snippets at these lectures. They are more often scientific than they are horticultural, but all the same it's a night out. The audience is full of people more observant and valuing of mosses & dandelions than they are of fashion & other people's occupations or incomes. Or their past mistakes & their falls from grace. May you take pleasure designing travels for others and may the sun always shine on their destinations. Your sis, Violet.

BANTLING

45 Ellen. Stockwell. 1927.

Ellen's nerves have been playing up of late, the hospital full of whispers and rumours, nothing pinned down. When was it any different? All those women cooped up close together, it's hardly natural. They're bound to gossip and invent. Though the hospital ladies do good work, there's nothing so very special or trustworthy about women in themselves. She's learned a thing or two about how women can be, oh yes indeed. She doesn't let it stop her though. One thing she and Felix are agreed on, if on nothing else, is that personal feelings have no claim against the calls of duty. Busy, busy, always busy. Take that meeting this morning with a new volunteer. Hardly worth the effort, but yet a single new helper is better than none, especially as she's the first in a while. Let's hope she's got more staying power than some of the others.

Braid for armband.

Mrs Dawson brings in the post on the tray with the coffee, takes her time pouring it out. It'll be stone cold by the time Ellen gets to drink it. Ellen can see the handwriting on the top envelope. It's the same damned thing every year. The letters are on Felix's end of the table. She wouldn't put it past Mrs Dawson to do put them down there on purpose.

Copy a map for the new volunteer.
Paper.

BANTLING

Tracing paper.

Felix is occupied ladling marmalade onto his toast – two, no, three heaped spoonfuls, and most of that is bound to end up in his moustache. He's left her with the scrapings

She stretches out her hand.

'You might as well give the post to me,' she says. 'I'll sort them out.'

Mrs Dawson dawdles a moment.

'Now, if you please, Mrs Dawson.'

She's just in time. If Felix had been looking at her instead of his plate, Mrs Dawson would have put that envelope straight into his hands.

Felix has got his eye on Ellen now. He's pretending he hasn't, but she can tell. And there it is, marmalade, shiny and sticky in the stiff hairs around his mouth. You shouldn't have to tell a grown man how to use his napkin. Or how to eat his toast.

Coloured pencils.

She must open the envelope, she supposes. The wallpaper eyes glint and gleam at her while Felix watches her like the devil. Below the table edge, she holds the envelope's contents away from her, as if straining to read them.

Another blasted birthday card for the child. With the usual smarmy note. She is thinking, thinking about her day.

Thermometer? Is there someone who has a spare one for a volunteer?

'Anything of interest?' he asks.

'Not really.'

Apron pattern.

Linen. A yard and a quarter.

Though they are barely husband and wife even in name now that Felix sleeps in his study, she'll still not neglect his interests. No matter how bitter and high-handed Violet is, Ellen will rise above it, refuse to let Felix's ancient sores be picked, or give him the excuse for more dramatic sighs and pursed lips.

She fiddles with the envelope beneath the table.

Notebook. The new girl will need to make notes. *Write letters.*

Ellen adjusts her position slightly, puts most of the papers neatly on the table, out of Felix's reach, face down. In a moment, when he's distracted by something else, when Mrs Dawson is looking the other way, she'll slip Violet's letter into her pocket, hide it away with all the others.

Ellen looks down at her list. *Thermometers.* Or torches? Thermometers and torches both? The promise of one or both might help boost the numbers of helpers.

She must tell Mrs Dawson what they will eat for the rest of the week.

'Violet must say something in her letter, surely.'

He slurps some coffee and wipes the drips from his moustache. He'd spotted Violet's writing, after all.

It's a good thing she managed to pull that stupid

BANTLING

greeting card out without anyone noticing. She's sitting on it now.

Mrs Dawson is hovering.

On the other side of the window, there are daffodils and tulips, buds, bright hazy leaves, tight green pyramids on the lilac branches. Sunshine shows up the dust and smeary grime on the glass.

'These windows are filthy. Doesn't anything get cleaned around here? Do I have to see to everything myself?'

'Ellen, my dear. You hardly need to tell Mrs Dawson how to do her job.'

'The window-cleaner will be here next Monday, Mrs Holcroft.'

Mrs Dawson clangs and clunks cutlery and crockery.

'I get the impression Violet has married.' It's what he wants to hear, so where's the harm?

And she's right. See his face cheer up.

She chews very slowly, turning the slightly sweet, slightly tart mass to tasteless mush before swallowing it.

'At last! Excellent news. So, everything has turned out well for her.' Felix dabs his lips as though he's master of the Empire. 'You must write and congratulate her for both of us. I trust that she has forgiven us at last.'

Coffee?

The wallpaper rustles and smirks, but when she flicks a look to catch it out, it's as fixed as ever it was.

'There's nothing to forgive. We gave her an opportunity to keep the child. How many people would have done that? She decided it wasn't feasible for her to do so, so other arrangements were made, leaving her free to take her exams, if she wanted, to go on to better things or to do whatever she wished. We gave her the possibility of a future. No respectable man would have taken her with a fatherless child.'

'But I still wonder, I still wonder ... what happened to the child? Remind me how old Samuel would be.'

Felix has no sense of propriety, asking questions like that when Mrs Dawson's still hanging around with her big ears flapping.

'Some fresh water, Mrs Dawson. My coffee's nearly cold. Boiling water, if you would be so kind.'

As the door finally closes, she answers Felix.

'He'll be four this month.'

'Four already. What's become of him, I wonder?'

'He'll better off than he's any right to, certainly. I have no idea why on earth we're still talking about this. Violet sends her respects to you.'

Felix doesn't look convinced.

'Perhaps if I could visit him, reassure myself ...'

She twists the skin of her throat, right there in front of him. The faces in the wall whisper encouragement. They know this time she's not trying to keep them at bay. She is whirling, sick to her stomach. Let him watch how he makes her suffer. Twist, pinch. Let him see.

BANTLING

'Please, Ellen,' he says. His face is pink and contorted, like an ill-set blancmange. 'Please stop. Don't hurt yourself. I'm sorry. Best to let sleeping dogs lie. Stop that now. Forget I said anything. Please, dear.'

Nosy Mrs Dawson is back again with a jug of lukewarm water.

Felix is not finished yet. There's another trick up his sleeve.

'Open your other letter,' he instructs. He pulls his watch from his waistcoat pocket, frowns and puts it back.

'You need to leave?'

'Not just yet. Perhaps the other letter holds more good news?'

Across the table, he twitches like a cat on hot bricks. He is peering at her in his professionally sympathetic manner. Something's up. She twists and tugs at her the top of her thigh. However hard she tries, it doesn't hurt enough. It doesn't anchor her to Felix's world.

She unfolds the stiff paper. High quality, she notes. The hospital crest. A very effusive letter from Doctor and the head nurse, all thanks and curlicues, great strides made in their home visiting programme, thanks to her. Unforeseen benefits, marked improvements blah blah.

It's good to be appreciated, though in Ellen's opinion the number of women they visit and the number of volunteers is not increasing fast enough. It's been a bit of a worry and she's been meaning to do something about it. Her eyes skim down, down, onto the next page. A ceremonial dinner next month for all her heroic endeavours of the past four years. Above and beyond the call of duty. Guest of honour. Presentation. Thank you thank you thank you.

'They're dismissing me! They are taking my work – *my* work – and giving it to a new nurse. The best part of five years' dedication and all of a sudden they don't need me anymore. Just like that. I won't let them. It's not right.'

'You have done such sterling work, achieved so much,' Felix says smoothly. 'You've excelled all expectations. Truly. The whole endeavour has grown to such an extent it's more than one untrained person, even one as dedicated as yourself, should be asked to do. Especially on top of all your other responsibilities. And a little rest will do you no harm.'

He's had this speech prepared. She's clutching a fork in her lap, the tines pressing against her palm.

'Helping all those impoverished women in their own homes has succeeded to such an extent it needs to be part of the hospital's official activities. Please, dear, don't look for insult where none is intended. They are most tremendously grateful.'

'Nobody asked my opinion.'

He sighs.

There's blood on her palm.

BANTLING

'They wanted to give you a pleasant surprise, to express their appreciation.'

She looks down at the words on the page. The thick, deckle-edged stationery writhes. The world shakes and slithers away from her. There's nothing she or the fork can do to stop it. She is tumbling, plunging, or perhaps she's floating. It's as if the chair she's sitting on, and the floor the chair is standing upon, and the ground the house is built upon have all thinned to nothingness and she is fathoms deep.

The mocking mouths of the wallpaper are chattering so loudly that they block out everything else.

This is no way to live.

BANTLING

46 Violet. West Norwood. 1928.

West Norwood, London SE27, 16 July 1928, Dear Stel, Don't laugh as naturally it is not a light-hearted matter, but I am being courted. Blame it all on self-improvement and a homesick yen for the salty brine & all its treasures. Seaweeds, in short. It is surprisingly endearing when a man waxes giddy about bladderwrack. Much of the talk went over my head, so the only comment I could add afterwards was about using kelp on Mim's flowers & vegetables. Later, as I poured tea in the library, the speaker chatted to me about this & that, and I chatted back, about seashores & gardens, about Mims's potion for soothing a sore throat with orange juice & Irish moss, about I don't know what else. He was entertaining and made me feel the same. I suppose I get little conversation and less attention in the normal run of things. All of a sudden, there I was, an hour or so later, standing outside 'my' front gate (of 'my' rooming house) with an escort – nodding like a Chinaman, agreeing to meet him again, while my usual self stood to one side sputtering and helpless. And so we have met – several times to boot. He caught me off-guard, this amateur botanist. I am cautious. I am astonished. I confessed my history early on & told him about Sam. I thought it would put him off or make him sly about getting his wicked way with me. Of moral outrage, there appears none and he does not use it as a lever either. I even find he has a face I like to look at & nice little ways. I am more than astonished and more than wary. Leonard is a postman and likes being outdoors, as I do. I am watching him like a hawk and myself too. Am I any wiser these days? We will see what we will see. What do you think? Is it possible to start again, to be oneself renewed? And you, my glamorous Stel, private secretary at the aeroplane works. Back on the island, but the whole sky for your oyster. To have skimmed and raced across the sea like that and risen over the cliffs and fields. What an adventure. Were you scared? Were you exhilarated? Did it deafen you or take away your breath? Do you think you will get another trip? To sleep now as there is a whole new bed to be double-dug tomorrow. Your friend & sis, Violet.

47 Timmy. Peckham. 1931.

Jumping, bouncing, stretching up so far that he can almost touch the ceiling, flopping down, scrambling up, jumping, falling backwards, bouncing. Doris and Bertie are on the big bed with him. Bertie's laughing his head off, shouting at them all to go higher and higher. It's so springy. Doris is bouncing and laughing fit to burst. Bertie always has the best ideas. Bounce, bounce. Timmy's never had such a good time, not ever. Laughing so much that he keeps hiccupping and can't breathe and it doesn't matter, just laughing, mouth stretched and jumping more. Higher every time. Hard as he can. There. His fingers meet the ceiling.

Whooosh. Whoosh. Whoosh. Crunch. Crack. Everything's tipping, tilting, slipping topsy-turvy. Stopping still, except Doris is tumbling on top of him, squashing all his breath. There's a noise underneath the bed that he's never heard before. The corner of the bed bucks again and floor comes flying up. His open mouth whacks into its hardness, the whole lump of Doris thumping down on his head. All the soreness in the world is in his mouth. It hurts so much and tastes of salt and cold metal and is full of something thick and slimy. There's a giant roaring somewhere. There's dinning up the stairs. The room is full of Dad and Ma. Bert's nowhere to be seen,

BANTLING

but then there's his voice telling them it weren't his fault, honest. Someone's laughing, so it must be funny. Ma's laughing. No, Doris is the one laughing so close it makes his ears hurt. She's peering over at him, her eyes big and frightened. She's making such a tinny racket. She should shut up. It's not nice to laugh, not when he's trying to cough. He can't open his mouth. He's drowning. Someone slaps Doris and tells her to shut up, this ain't a laughing matter, but she doesn't stop. Dad's making such a row. Bertie's shouting that it's not his fault, he tried to stop them, honest, Timmy wouldn't listen and got Doris at it too.

He's on the floor and he can see Dad's big boot and the dirty thick sole and Dad's shouting rude words and calling him a bastard again. There's something about a hole in the floor that has to be fixed before they can get to bed tonight. Bertie's still spinning his tale about don't blame him, he tried to stop them, and they took no notice of him. It's all Timmy's fault. He's sure that's not right. Bertie had been egging them on, was jumping himself, big as he is.

He's lying against the floor and his eyes are closing. He tries to swallow whatever it is in his mouth, but there's more and more of it. Ma's sitting him up and got his face in his hand. Her face is all puckered up. He can't speak or move his lip, not even to cry. He can't swallow whatever's in his mouth. Ma's wiping his face with her apron. It hurts too much. Ma's yelling at Dad that shouting and swearing won't help, look at

BANTLING

Timmy, what's happened, where's all that blood coming from, what's done is done, the ceiling's down, but look at Timmy, he's choking and do something.

Dad's taken hold of his chin. His fingers are so close that Timmy can see the yellow where he holds his fags and black under his nails. He concentrates on Dad's red knuckles. He can't hardly feel anything because everything's so sore. He struggles. Dad's killing him. Ma can't stop him. Dad got him in a head lock. He can't move. His mouth's filling up with thickness that he can't swallow. Dad tugs at his face, pulls at the front of his lip. His face is on fire. Whatever's in his mouth comes out, soaking his front. His throat is on fire. He coughs and spits. He coughs and sicks up more nasties. It's dark and brownish and thick. Dad's swearing again and jumping out the way of all the reddish stuff. Ma's saying something about his tooth going right through his lip. The floor swallows the length of him.

BANTLING

48 Violet. Tulse Hill. 1931.

Tulse Hill, London SE25, 20 April 1931, Sam, my dearest little boy, Many Happy Returns for your 8th Birthday, my dear son. Eight today! Of course, any good coming out of what has happened is only if I make myself believe you are better off where you are. I am ashamed because it's hard enough to remember what you looked like and impossible to imagine you now. You would not know me either. So, having no choice, I trust it is true that you thrive wherever you are & that being so I try to count my blessings in our separation. I think of you each and every day. From your always loving mummy.

BANTLING

49 Timmy. Peckham. 1931.

'You just leave him be while he heals up,' Ma tells Bertie, as she tucks Timmy up in bed, his swollen lip all stiff with stitches and the rest of him as sore as if he's been put through her mangle.

For the life of him he can't get comfy. Ma props him up on pillows. All the pillows from the bed are behind him. Bertie's not looking happy about that.

Ma's not blind. 'None of your nonsense,' she warns Bertie, but the moment she's out of the room, he starts.

'Frogface, frogface, you've a face like an old toad,' Bertie chants. 'And don't think for one sodding second you're keeping those pillows tonight. Cry-baby, cry-baby. Wait 'til Dad gets his hands on you.'

Timmy does what he always does. He makes out he doesn't care.

Doris is everso kind – she usually is – helping him sip broth and cocoa from a tea-spoon, just about missing the moon-shaped cut under his lip where his tooth came all the way through. Everything that touches it, hot or cold, but hot most of all, stings like billy-oh.

Ma pops in to check on him from time to time, but she's got her hands full. A bible-basher in a dog-collar turns up from somewhere and sits on his bed for a few minutes reading a nursery tale to him. Ma hangs around all the time. He hears them talking on the landing afterwards before they shut the door, Ma

BANTLING

asking the man about his kind wife and saying how much Timmy means to her. Then there's Dad's voice going on and on about how much it's going to cost to fix the ceiling, never mind what the doctor's charging. Timmy feels sick. He's never going to be able to pay Dad back.

The vicar forgets his newspaper when he leaves. Timmy and Doris can read the numbers 1-9-3-1 on the front and she knows her months. September, she tells him. Then they look for the cartoons. There aren't any, only teeny squashed blotchy printed words. The best they see is a little map where the writing's bigger and a bit clearer. Doris helps him spell out *Chi-na*, where dragons and tea come from, and *U-S-S-R*, but that's not a word that makes any sense, even to Doris. She can make out *Ja-pan*, too, where Ma's told him they make gardens out of stones and cherry trees. All those places are very far away. Other words, like *Man-chur-i-a* and *in-vas-ion* are too long even for Doris to know.

The other thing the vicar leaves behind is a card, happy birthday to somebody called Sammy. Timmy's sorry for Sammy because he won't get the greeting from his always loving mummy. Doris thinks the card is pretty and takes it away for her scrap book.

Once the stitches come out, he cops it from Dad, with a whacking on his backside so bad he has to lie on his tummy to get to sleep. Bertie tells him he's lucky that's all he gets, bringing the house down around their ears. Ma whispers to cheer up, it's not as bad as it could be. Dad's not going to make him work off the cost of the damage after all.

BANTLING

50 Violet. Kentish Town. 1931.

Kentish Town, London NW5, December 22nd 1931, My dear Stel, Merry Christmas to you & may all jollities and good things attend you & yours in 1932. Your young man sounds like just the ticket. Ralph must be very bright mechanically, working on the planes & in demand hither & yon, but you will be more than a match for him on that score. Make sure he does right by you & does not just entrap you with the glamour of 2 wings or 4. By right, of course, I mean suppers of peeled grapes & beds of rose petals. All change here with me too. Len & I are moving up North. He is being transferred & will be Under-Manager at a sorting office in Hull. Lots of seaweeds for him near there I expect & more regular hours. I don't mind leaving London, in fact I am looking forward to being nearer the sea again. It is sad to be moving so much further away from you & Mim. I gave up hope of stumbling across Sam a long time ago, though I will probably needle at the Holcrofts from time to time. You just never know. Len is determined to make an honest woman of me. We take the plunge next week. In the nick of time as, dear Sis, I am expecting. I am so very happy. I never thought I would have the heart for happiness again. Let's enjoy it while it lasts. Wish me luck on the next part of the helter-skelter. I am thinking of you, as ever. Love Violet.

BANTLING

51 Ellen. Stockwell. 1933.

Nobody can be trusted. No-one at all. That's what the wallpaper tells her, and it never lies. All those years she'd thought the sprites and goblins were malevolent, were out to get her, and all that time they'd been trying to warn her.

Felix has a sneaky look about him tonight. He's digging in his heels about not telling her something or other.

She doesn't give a hoot. Let him have his secrets. She's got better ones.

Mrs Dawson's prepared coley in parsley sauce.

'Invalid food,' says Felix. He stops mid-moan. He'll have remembered his unfortunates. The food doesn't matter to her. It all tastes the same these days. And it slides down easily enough.

Organise flower rota.
Order raffle tickets.
Polish pews.

'Don't forget our soup kitchen, dear.'

Unemployment soup. It's his favourite new undertaking, part of the endless work he has her do. It's one thing to find people to do the church flowers, though that's hard enough these days. The soup-making is another kettle of fish altogether. Felix almost had a fit when she suggested they get some of the women and men who queue for handouts to do some of the cooking. Something about treading on Mrs Dawson's toes, as if she's going to be doing this sort of work from the goodness of her heart. So, as ever, it's Ellen who's picking up the slack. She hates it, going around begging scraps and discards from butchers and grocers and having the kitchen full of greasy steam and miserable people traipsing in and out the whole time. Some of them are women she knows from before, and their skinny shadow-eyed children. Better off if they'd not been born for the most part. She keeps her thoughts to herself and makes her notes.

Bones.

Soup rota.

For pudding there's semolina with a dollop of jam. It's a bit of a treat.

Brandy for medicine cabinet.

A little brandy is always handy to have around the house. Anything that bucks her up a bit must be a good thing. Not that Felix would see it like that. He's watching every penny they spend as though self-deprivation could cure unemployment and the Depression on its own.

~~Brandy for medicine cabinet.~~

Felix has farted again. These stinks over dinner have been going on for months. Perhaps he saves them up for her in the evening. The only dignified thing is to ignore then.

Pins.

Lace pins are the best by far. So long and fine and

pretty too with their coloured glass beads at the tips, they are sharpest by far, piercing her skin so easily. A cheap luxury, all things considered.

In a while, she'll go and put on Arthur's jacket. It's lovely being able to keep it in her bedroom since Felix took to having his own room. She can keep anything she wants with her now. Anything else is safely tucked away, out of sight, out of mind.

BANTLING

52 Violet. Hull. 1934.

Hull, E. Yorkshire, 20th April 1934, Dearest Sam, today you are eleven. Many Happy Returns to you. Have you enjoyed your day? Did you have cake & presents? Did they sing to you & take you out for a treat? I hope it was a lovely time. Please understand you have family with us if you ever want it. Len would have been just as kind towards you as he has been to me & just as good a father to you as he has been to his own daughter. Your sister, my dark-eyed Stella, is playing with her friend from 2 doors down. They have been making a mess of the sitting room, turning it into a Bedouin camp, with blankets & tablecloths & the like stretched from the table & across some chairs. They are crawling in & out & will take their naps under there. Stella is coming up for three & even though you are so much older, I like to think you would have joined in too, directing operations & laughing with them. Perhaps you are doing something similar with brothers & sisters wherever you are. There was a new book in the children's library that made me think of you, about a young elephant. Of course, being a book, it all ends happily with him becoming king. It is very prettily drawn & coloured. I brought it home to read to your sister & she was surprised to see her mother wiping her eyes & she cried too, for Barbar, the little motherless elephant. Do you like to read? I enjoyed the Peter Rabbit & the Just So stories & anything by Edith Nesbit when I *was younger, though they perhaps have more appeal for girls. Very possibly you prefer more dashing tales. I wish I could make sure you do your lessons & behave yourself. I cannot be there to watch over you, but I have to believe that someone loving & sensible stands in my place. I have not given up all hope of knowing something about you & your life, but I do not expect it to be anytime soon. I like to imagine that if we passed on the street, blood would call out to blood & I would know you from all the rest & you would recognise me too, but life is not like that. At least, I have not found it so. Do you think that thoughts can travel through air & time to the person we are thinking about? I do believe it to be so, sometimes, with enough effort. I am thinking so hard about you now, at this moment, that some faint ripple might well reach you & you will know at least that you are loved & missed still. I did not want to part with you, but our life together would have been harsh. The manner of you being taken from me was out of my hands, but at that moment it all seemed too much for one young person to take on. I was so, so confused then and still am when I look back at that time. And frightened, I remember, so frightened that you would not be safe in my care. Perhaps those feelings would have settled down – I did not have the chance to find out. How we were separated was not done with my agreement – I knew nothing about it until afterwards. Even so, I had begun to doubt I had the strength to do what I had hoped for and perhaps the way we were split was my punishment for my weakness. I am trying to be honest, so if ever you see these letters you will understand something about me. A flawed person trying to recall her younger self. I was less fearful then, but much more ignorant. I thought it would be an easy thing to keep a child, or if not easy, possible without delivering you to hardship. Now I find it takes both Len and me to care for Stella, especially in these lean times. Of course, some lucky girls manage by themselves & perhaps I would have too. Naïve as I was, I wanted to give it my best efforts, Sam, so even if I failed later, I would have known & you would have known that it was not through laziness or cowardice that your mother relinquished you. I would have been the best mother I could have been. I hope you sense or find out I did not give you up willingly & that you do not hate me. Now I do my best for Stella & the new one on his or her way, but there is still an emptiness in me that has your shape, my ocean-eyed lad. I cross my fingers & pray that your family is managing. We are lucky that Leonard earns enough to keep us warm & dry & to put food in the larder. I make sure meals are ready on time & on a clean table & Stella is dressed & healthy. I grow what I can in the garden for us to eat. From time to time, people give me their accounts book to help with, so I bring in a little extra cash like that. Oh, I do hope you have your health, it is a great blessing. I fretted so much about you not having my milk when you were taken away so suddenly & whether you would suffer for lack of it. I thought it was so cruel, not even to let me wean you properly once you & I were used to feeding together. Here I am, complaining again for myself about old history, when I had the idea of telling you about myself (a person's complaints might say much about them, but it is not always what they would want to be judged upon). I am sad not to see you grow up, even though I am thankful & grateful for the life I have now. I don't know how you might ever come by these letters, but if by some miracle it ever happens, please know that Leonard & I would both welcome you with open arms. He is not your real father, of course & I wish I could tell you different, or give you some tragic, uplifting story about the man who was. But that one was a chancer, quite a bit up the social ladder from me, very charming and not to be trusted. My friend Estelle, like a sister she's been to me, sent me an announcement from the Times newspaper not so long ago. He married money. It comes as no surprise. I understand now that he was a low individual & you & I are both better off without him. I hope you have not taken much after him. I do not think you would. Now my Bedouins are calling for refreshments in their caravanserai, so I must put this away. Goodbye, my lovely. Be brave & loyal & honour those kind people who, I am sure, love you like their own. As ever, your mummy, Violet.*

BANTLING

53 Timmy. Peckham. 1935.

'You tell him or I will.' Dad's rough voice.

The door to the kitchen is open, just a bit, and the hall's heavy with the smell of pease pudding and the scorchy smell of ironing. He's not meant to hear whatever it is. He shuts the front door very quietly and listens.

Ma coughs. She's got a bit of a wheeze.

Dad says, 'You coming down with something?'

'Mustn't grumble.'

He hears the iron clank back on the range.

'That's Mr Jackson's shirts done.'

'You take it easy now, Alice.'

A match strikes the box, then there's the gentle fizz of its flare and Ma taking her time blowing out the first smoke.

'Time's still not right, Harry. Leave it to me. I'll do it when I think fit. Promise you'll leave it to me, you won't say nothing. You promise?'

'Just don't leave it too long.'

Ma blows out another long breath, as though something was settled.

'The kids'll all be back soonest. I'd best get on with the tea.'

He skips down the hall, no point creeping about any more, they're done with secrets for the moment, clickety-click, practising the footwork and punches he's learning at the club, huffing as he jabs and hooks and dances.

Dad comes out of the kitchen with a scowly face, sees him bobbing and ducking and comes at him with a snappy straight left. Dad's not messing around. His great bunched fist is tight and hard.

Timmy sways, bends and Dad's fist just misses him. Dad looks as though he's narked about that, but all he is says is, 'Duck and weave, duck and weave. All you can do, is it? You got to learn to take the blows and dish them out as well. And you'd best learn to roll with the punches. But not too bad for a maggoty little thing like you.'

Boxing's the only thing he does that Dad doesn't give him a hard time about.

'That you Timmy?' Ma calls out. 'Put these shirts in the other room for me before they reek of onions and call the others. I'm dishing up. Wash your hands first.'

Whatever it was they were muttering about, she's not telling.

BANTLING

54 Violet. Hull. 1936.

Hull, E. Yorks, May 23rd 1936 Dearest Stel, Yes yes yes yes of course I will be your matron of honour & not before time. I wouldn't miss your wedding for the world. The children & I will get to Cowes on the Wednesday & come back again on Saturday, if that is still alright with Mim. Len would give his eye teeth to come & meet you both in joyous celebration, but there's no hope of him getting off work. He sends his best. Times are not so tough with us that you have to stand me the train fare, so please not to mention it again. It will be like olden days, catching up with you again, even for a couple of nights. Even better to be with you getting married. Nobody deserves happiness more than you. You have been the best and truest of friends. Billy is beside himself, being at that age of things mechanical. The thought of the trains from Hull and London and the ferry from Southampton is excitement enough, or should be, but he keeps asking if he will ride in a plane, seeing as how Ralph works on them. I've told him fat chance, but perhaps you could ask Ralph if we could peek in at the hangar. It'd make a small boy very happy. If you'll let me, I'll bring 'the something old' for you to wear. It was the 'something blue' I wore when I married Len – the satin ribbon garter that you made for me. I can't wait. Much love, your sis Violet

55 Timmy. Peckham. 1937.

'Fat load of good books'll do you down the docks, even if you're that lucky,' Dad shouts, and swipes everything off the table with his dirty fist.

They're in a tumble on the floor, open higgledy-piggledy, pages scrunched.

Timmy stacks the books back on the table, smoothing out the pages and trying to rub off the dirty marks. Dad's just an ignorant savage. A stupid ignorant savage.

Dad comes out with, 'You think you're so much better than the rest of us, you little maggot.' It's like Dad can read his mind.

Ma favours them both with one of her looks. 'Pack it in, you two,' she says. 'Harry. Don't you start.' It sounds like a warning. 'I don't want the library coming after me for fines, saying I don't know how to treat books.'

He's checking them to see if they're torn or had their spines broken. The library books are one thing, taken out on Ma's ticket. On top of that, Miss Barnes isn't keen on getting school property back in a worse state than she's handed it out. And she's lent these ones to him special. He doesn't have much time left, only a few weeks, then he has to leave school for ever. If Dad doesn't calm down, he'll have to try and work in the parlour, where it's freezing and the

BANTLING

lightbulb is the dimmest in the whole world. There's no chance of doing homework in the bedroom, not while Bertie's ruling the roost, with his ponging socks, stabbing cigarettes, noisy, messy wanking and all that racket he makes, calls it singing ha-ha, louder and more horrid when Timmy's around just to make him go away. The kitchen's not quiet either, not with Dad in it, but at least Ma keeps the range going in here to dry the washing. There are shirts hanging up above their heads today, and women's underwear. He wants to look at the secret female shapes, but doesn't want a slap around the head for taking liberties.

'There's no harm in being able to read and count more than elementary,' says Ma.

'You're the one for all that,' says Dad. 'Reading the papers and managing the house-keeping. It beats me what him and you do down the library at all hours. You'll make him even softer than he already is.'

He'd blow his top if he knew they pop into the art gallery next to the School of Arts every now and then coming back from the market to take a gander at whatever pictures are up that week.

Dad lights himself a fag off the end of his old one and offers it to Ma.

She takes a puff and hands it back.

'There's more troublesome places to be than a warm library,' she says. 'Asides, the more kids know these days, the better. If all ours had his head for learning, they might afford to keep us in a grand old manner in our dotage.'

Dad huffs through his nose, the way he does when he thinks something's stupid.

'You don't need to be putting ideas into his head. He can't stay on idling at school forever.' Dad circles the cigarette a few inches away from Timmy's face. 'Fourteen and you're out of there, laddie.'

Talk about the obvious. Everyone leaves school around their birthday, knuckles down to earn their keep.

'Careful with that fag,' warns Ma. 'I don't want no burn holes in Mrs Fleece's bloomers and girdles.'

She's being bold. She won't usually mention unmentionables, not by name.

They all turn their heads up at the articles in question. He sees pink corsets, like gigantic Elastoplast bandages, hanging flat over the wooden hoist, their big pointed cups with stitches going round and round like contours on a map and the suspenders hanging down. Some of the panels look as though they've had a good stretch on Mrs Fleece, because they've already gone baggy where her bum would be. He thinks that Ma and Dad are probably thinking the same as him, of Mrs Fleece squashing herself into and out of all that tight pinkness. Her slips are silky and shiny, with lace around the hems. Her baggy-legged knickers are getting a bit grey and worn now. Ma's folded them so you can't see between the legs, but the sight makes them all laugh in any case.

The mood doesn't last, not with Dad around.

'There's better lessons to be had than from some sorry spinster in a schoolroom,' says Dad.

Timmy's never thought of Miss Barnes as a sorry spinster. She knows about where rubber comes from and about Rudyard Kipling. She took the class, all forty-odd of them, up to the new museum to look at a huge painting, so big there's no wall in his whole house that would fit it. Across the great width of it was a line of soldiers, bandages over their eyes, one hand on the shoulder of the man in front. The more you looked at the painting the more blind soldiers you saw standing in line, or lying there in the mud. Behind them, other soldiers played football as though nothing had happened. From the look on Miss Barnes' face, you'd think she'd known them all.

'Harry, just let him get on with his books. It's only for another couple of months, if that. And Timmy love, you get finished quick as you can. I'll be needing the table for a load more ironing tonight.'

Miss Barnes had explained how the artist used pink for the morning light. He meant that all the young soldiers should have been in the rosy dawn of their lives. Instead, they were facing a dark future. The yellow he'd chosen where light strikes their uniforms was the colour of mustard gas. Putting the colours together in the painting contrasted how the young men's lives should have been with how things had really turned out for them. All without putting it into so many words. Timmy had said he thought it was a bit like magic, like the conjuror's tricks at the Christmas show, making you see something that wasn't really there. Miss Barnes had been pleased with him in front of the whole class.

Timmy answers Dad back for once, says about how Miss Barnes thinks he's fit for more than fetching and carrying in the shipyards. She's recommending – he loves that word – recommending him to a firm she knows.

'In a textile warehouse, Harry, just think of that!'

It's better paid, clerking, than labouring down the wharfs, and cleaner. And more regular. In any case, it's a fine thing to at least have the know-how to read the lading notices or add up how much timber you carried in a day and not have to trust the clerk that Dad is always moaning about cheating him.

Dad looks as though he's going to bust a gut. He comes over and sticks his head into Timmy's face.

'You saying I can't read or write?'

Timmy stares back, won't look away, tries to pretend he can't see Dad's ugly mug. If atmosphere is colour, Dad's mood is the dark green of poison bottles. Dad flicks him under his jaw with a finger. 'Cheer up, maggot.'

He tries to remember that the painting made him feel sorry for Dad, because Ma had told him Dad had been in that war. She blames it for the way his nerves are.

Ma says, 'I haven't got time to listen to you two squabbling again.'

'All in all, we've not done too badly, have we, Alice? One way or another.'

Dad gestures around the kitchen, but he means the whole house. He's got it right. Even though the place is only rented, and Timmy's heard some people say the whole terrace is a slum, an eyesore and should be pulled down, it's Ma's pride and joy. Oh, but she keeps it spic and span, even with other people's clothes drying all over the place the whole time.

'As far as it goes.' She puts one hand very gently on Dad's arm. 'I'm not complaining. But kids should outdo their parents, not be happy with the same.'

'And what's wrong now?' Dad shouts. 'What else do you want?'

It's hard to remember to feel sorry for Dad when he's like this, his face blotchy, yelling at Ma.

Quietly, Ma shakes her head. She's so patient with him and his loud mouth.

'Harry, there's nothing in the world I'd change about you, you know that. You work all the hours God provides and you're still the finest-looking man I know.' She strokes his chin and Timmy has to look somewhere else. 'But you're always scrabbling around for the next job, queuing up, seeing if they need an extra hand that day. You can never be certain that something will come up.'

'Something always does come up. I make sure of that,' he shouts. His spit is flying about. 'Everyone knows me. All up and down the canal they know me for a good worker. That's why they always pick me. Even now, when you see grown men queuing just for the dole, I've got work most days.'

'Ma's doing all that laundry, that's heavy work. Boiling the copper and putting everything through the mangle. I give her a hand with that. Bertie's labouring when he can. Doris's cleaning houses when she can get it. Her and me, we do our bit too,' says Timmy. He can't help himself.

Dad snorts.

'No more than you ought. Bertie's big enough to start pulling his weight. At least he's willing to get his hands dirty, not too proud. And Doris, it's only right she helps out your mother, though God knows I'd rather you didn't have to do it, Alice. But you, you little maggot! What do you bring in? Pennies, if anything.' Dad's voice was snarly. 'And don't think I don't know you spend as much as you hand over. Picture-houses and sweets and other nonsense while your mother works her fingers to the bone.'

He gives Timmy his look that means he'd happily knock him through the wall. Timmy stares back at him, then looks away at the steamed-up window. It always upsets Ma when him and Dad have a go at each other. One day he'll not give way.

'Leave him be,' Ma says. Perhaps she saw the look too. 'He earns his keep. Always has done. One way or another.'

Dad opens his mouth and shuts it again. Ma and Dad catch each other's eye. Ma carries on speaking, but her voice is higher, sharper than he likes. There's a touch of mustard-gas yellow about her tone, something not quite right. Something's going on and he can't work it out.

'Anyhows, his bits of wood and lumber keep the copper going half the time. And where would we be these days if I couldn't fire that up every day? Scrabbling around more than we are or on the charity, that's where. I'd rather do the laundry. I'll not have the means-test man in here, telling us we live too grand for their hand-outs.'

He doesn't want to feel as though he's hiding behind Ma's apron the whole time. If it gets much worse, he could take Dad on. He might be shorter and lighter, but he's faster on his feet than Dad. Even Dad calls him nimble, only compliment he'd ever had from him. He can use his head too when it comes to punches, doesn't just lash out. Even if he gets thrashed, it'd be better than just looking scared.

Ma's as fierce as he's ever seen her. 'I just want our kids not to have it so hard as we have.'

'What we need's another war. That'd shape him up.'

Ma puts her arm around Timmy and looks around as though she might find Bertie in the room too.

'Don't you ever say that again.'

'I say it as I see it. No beating around the bush. There should be more plain speaking around here. You take my meaning, Alice.'

BANTLING

56 Ellen. Stockwell. 1938.

Arthur is as sweet-faced as he ever was, beside her in the perfect warmth of the perfect sunshine. She can feel him, breath in his closeness. Around them, as far as she can see, lilac-blue, green-hazed hills and shallow valleys. Everything so lovely, so fresh and clear and jewel-like that she could almost sit and gaze at it forever. Except she cannot keep still enough; she is more lively than she has ever felt before. The turf cries out for them to run and run. So, they do, hand-in-hand, almost flying, they are so light, so fast.

The kites, yellow and red, are high and proud, floating in a sky of infinite blue. She's remembered how to laugh, what it means to laugh with your whole heart, until the laughing takes you over. She's hardly able to breathe for happiness.

They are swooping and sailing, the ground rushing away in a blur of colour.

This is what happiness is. Your heart beating so high and free in your chest and you hardly able to breathe for it, but no matter because the one you love is breathing for you, you for him. You are breathing each for the other. And with each breath you are more vivid, more your loving self.

Even with the return of daylight, after scrubbing and scouring herself *down there* until it's raw, it is Felix who is colourless, a hardly-there, foggy ghost.

BANTLING

And it's cold, so cold.
Pins. Pins. Pins.

BANTLING

57 Timmy. Whitechapel. 1939.

There are a fair few people in here, in this place that looks more warehouse than exhibition room that Ma's dragged him to. She wriggles them to the front, smiling and elbowing and holding tight to him. His eyes move from the mound of boots up to the painting and back to the boots on the floor. Boots, painting, boots, painting, boots. A shabby man is adding another pair to the pile.

It's easier to keep his eyes on the boots than look at the painting. Ma has been mad keen to come. She'd read about this strange painting hanging in Whitechapel and how working people were bringing stout shoes for the people fighting in Spain as their price of admission. She'd gone round all the neighbours collecting pennies and then snaffled a pair of broken-down old boots from a totter she caught at a weak moment. She'd persuaded the cobbler, God knows how, that it was his Christian or working man's duty to put them together again. Dad went on at her about charity beginning at home and about this new-fangled art being nonsense and about it being no business of hers what went on in Spain. She'd said there was nothing wrong in making up her own mind. She'd dragged Timmy along with her and here they are in front of this picture that doesn't look like any painting Miss Barnes ever showed him.

BANTLING

Dad's right for once. It's all of a jumble of grey and black shapes and cartoon figures. He's never seen anything like it before. He wonders what Ma makes of it. He almost has to look at it sideways, out of the corner of his eye. Just look at the peculiar thing. That's a horse's neck in the middle, big ugly teeth like something from the Beano, and a bull's head on the left, but what's the rest? He can just about tell there are people, or bits and pieces of people, but Timmy's seen seven-year-old kids draw better than this bloke. And what's the jagged eye shape with the light bulb at the top meant to mean? With a painting that big, you'd think the artist, if you can call him that, could have spread it out a bit more, not squash and cram it all in like that so that you feel you're trapped in there as well. He might have done better to make a smaller painting and spend the savings on coloured paints.

'Bombs, they always come at night,' says Ma. She's leaning more than usual on his arm. '1916 it was. I was at my aunt's house near Streatham Common station when the Zeppelins came, quiet as smog.'

'I never knew that, Ma.'

'You don't ever want to hear sounds like the ones a bomb makes. One moment I was sound asleep, then *flash flash*, so bright it blinds you, so dark it blinds you, just like the painting tells. Shapes keep jumping out at you, but there's no time to make sense of them. Even if the roof's not falling in on top of you, you think it is. You don't know where to turn, where to hide. It makes you dizzy, worse than dizzy, like a headless chicken.'

He doesn't know what to say.

'The stables across the road from us were hit and poor Mrs Chadwick was killed in her house. The sound of those poor beasts, it's not something you ever forget, not really. Folk clinging onto each other if they could and crying out. This painting's got it to a tee.'

Ma, who never cries, is dabbing away at her eyes.

'We all worked in the almost pitch-dark to help dig out people, even me, kid that I was, too scared to make more light for fear of more bombs or setting fire to the gas.'

He looks back at the picture. He's trying to see what she can. It's making him shiver. How can it do that? There are only different greys and different whites and different blacks, laid side by side with no shading, and forming a sort of triangle of legs, arms, odd-shaped heads. All those gaping, screaming mouths. All those people trapped in the space. And right in the middle, on top of them, is the screaming horse.

'Terrifying they were, those Zeppelins. No warning. We thought England was a fortress until then. After that I was always looking up at the sky, not knowing what I might see. Scared stiff.' She points her chin towards the canvas. 'He knows how bad it is, that painter, you can tell. Those brave souls in Spain, standing up for themselves. Look what's happening to them. It's us women and children and animals that get it in the neck when they start bombing homes. Not a quarter of a century gone and it'll be happening again here soon enough, God help us, never mind Chamberlain's nonsense in Munich. You best put our boots with the rest. Little enough, but you can only do what you can do.'

She's as angry and sad as he's ever seen her. She shakes her head and breathes deeply.

'Let's make a day of it, Timmy. We'll go up West, do some window shopping. See what we'll buy when our ship comes in.'

Ma lays her fingers against the window as though she can touch the fabrics through it. He's glad that the January sales are over and there's something half-way decent in the windows for her to look at.

'Imagine wearing them,' she says. 'That gorgeous blue. And what about that green? Real silk, it says it is.'

'Fine and bright as pond-weed,' he says.

She elbows him.

'Pond-weed, my foot. Crown jewels more like. You got no respect.'

He knows she doesn't mean it. And he's right about the colour and the gloss.

'See that red and white polka dot over there?' He presses his finger against the glass. 'They call that vermilion. That exact red, with the touch of orange. Vermilion.'

'Get you. When did you grow to be so clever and know so much?'

Vermilion. He's proud of the word. He's practised it in secret until he can say it as though he was born with it and others in his mouth, long words, unusual words, words that crack open the greyness he mostly sees around him.

Vermilion.

Azure.

Magenta.

Emerald.

Pistachio.

There's no such thing as one be-all and end-all colour, not really, only thousands and thousands of different colours, variations laid on top of differences, so many that lots of colours don't even have a name. Reds are very special. Add white to dark blue, ultramarine, say, or cobalt, add more and more white, the blue becomes a paler and paler blue. Not that ultramarine and cobalt make the same range of blues. But add white to any red and *hey presto!* You get pinks, not pale reds. And every single red makes a pink different from the last.

'Vermilion.' She coughs, pulls a hanky from her pocket, turns away from him and spits into it. She doesn't like a fuss, so he pretends it's nothing.

'Red like a post-box,' she says, 'not like a strawberry or a robin redbreast,' and he knows she understands.

'That one over there, with the triangles and circles. See the colour of them circles. They're cerise. That means *cherry* in France.'

'Oh, yes?'

'Ken in the workshop told me.' Ken was still proud as Punch because once he'd gone with the owner to some silk factories way over in France.

'Ken? He's the one with the big family, that right? You went for tea that time.'

'That's the one.'

'Hope you minded your manners.'

Ken Bailey's family is like a tangle of puppies, touching and nudging and roaring with noise. They were all crammed into one of the flats in a block in Bethnal Green, three rooms running together front to back and a bathroom outside on the landing. It was a bit hard to remember everybody's names and get them in the right order, and to work out who lived there and who didn't. Some of them were cousins and other relatives, but of Ken's own, Sam could place Don, the eldest. Sally was about ten. Cora, he knew, was fourteen, closest to his own age, and had taken him under her wing for a bit, made sure he'd got bread and butter on his plate, that sort of thing. The way they'd all got on, felt free to say what they thought, arguing their pitch even if Ken didn't agree, it was an eye-opener. They made a racket, but he'd liked it, wanted to be part of it, felt left on the outside at first, but then he made them laugh a couple of times, and Mrs Bailey had cut him a whopping slice of cake. He hopes they'll ask him to tea again.

Ma's attention's somewhere else now.

'Oh, would you look at that one over there? Wouldn't I look grand up the butchers in that? You wouldn't be ashamed to be seen with your old Ma if she was wearing that.'

She's nodding towards a silk chiffon, pretty enough but not one of his favourites. He prefers the heavier fabrics with the more intense colours, like some of the taffetas that shine with at least two colours depending on the light.

Her nose and mouth are so close to the glass that the window's steaming up as she breathes. She wipes a spy-hole with her glove. She has another coughing fit, a bad one this time, one that goes on and on, makes her body judder the whole length of her. Even the fabric on the other side of the plate glass seems to ripple. She puts her hand against the window to steady herself, and he puts his arm around her.

'It's too cold for you. I should never have let you stay out.'

She shrugs.

'I know,' he says. 'Mustn't grumble.'

'Light us a fag.'

She drives him mad sometimes, the way she always pretends she's just dandy. She sounds better once she takes a drag, and carries on where she'd left off. She points the cigarette towards the display.

'I'd feel like the cat's whiskers if I ever had the chance to wear something like that, I can't pretend different. One of those weddings you see in the papers, something like that. Or when the King makes a lord of our Harry.'

'That's the ticket.'

'Do you think chiffon would suit me? Or should I go for one of the heavier silks? Which one do you think I'd get more use out of? I do love the flimsy one though, like petals on grass. Perhaps I should go for both, hedge my bets with the weather?'

Timmy says, 'Ma, you'd hardly know you had that chiffon on. It's like fairy gossamer, so soft you think you're dreaming when you touch it.'

She turns to him. She looks comical, she's that surprised. One day, he'll buy her all the beautiful things she wants, so she can dress in silk and lawn and pretty hats and never have to scrub a step or deal with other people's dirty underwear ever again in her whole life.

'You've felt it? Yourself? They actually let you?' She turns to stare at it again. 'With your grubby mitts?'

'I help pack that sort of thing. They make us wear gloves to handle the rolls, but when no-one was looking, I put the end of it across my face. It was like looking at the factory through a rosy sky, hardly there, but prettier than it ever is in real life. Just floating on my face.'

She looks worried now.

'Why did you go and do that? You best watch it. You don't want them catching you behaving like a skiver. Asides, you could snag it or stain it or something and then you'd be out on your ear.'

'I'm always careful, Ma. They're not going to chuck me out.'

He's got his fingers crossed in his pocket.

'There's plenty want your job if you slip up. And it's not so easy to get another. No Miss Barnes to put in a good word for you again if you let her down on this one. We need all you can bring in nowadays.'

It makes him feel good and proud, that they need his wages at home. Even if Dad takes no notice, it's what Ma thinks that matters. Perhaps one day, perhaps next Christmas, or even better, in time for Ma's birthday, they'll let him have a piece, an offcut, which Ma could use as a scarf. Enough for a pretty hankie at least.

'I'll take care, Ma, don't fret. And we're upping production, well, of some things. Cutting back on the dress materials and curtains, but making lots of silk for the government.' He says it very softly, though there's no-one near them on this chilly Saturday afternoon, the shops all closed since three hours ago. 'Some say it's for …'

He leans even closer towards her and whispers, '… they say it's for parachutes.'

'Parachutes?'

She shakes her head as though to clear it and sucks air through her teeth, just like she did in front of the painting.

She rubs her finger – it's rougher than silk chiffon – against his chin.

'1939 already. You'll be sixteen before we know it. Let's hope it's all over before you're old enough. They'll take Bertie, he's that age already.' She looks as though she might cry, gives him a funny sad smile. 'Did Dad show you the razor yet?'

He wriggles away.

'Course he did, Ma. A while ago.'

Not that he's had much call to use it as yet.

'That's alright then.'

Then she turns and hugs him, right there on the street.

'My sweet baby. Look at you. I've been so lucky with you. Did I ever tell you that you brought me back from the dead when we got you? Promise me you'll grow up just as slowly as you can. Don't be in a rush to leave your old Ma, whatever happens.'

He can see her eyes are watering. She's in a funny mood. It's that painting that's brought back all sorts of memories and worries. Even if the war happens, it can't be that bad. He's got more sense than to say that to her. He doesn't want her to start coughing again.

'You're getting chilly, Ma. Let's go home.'

'I'd rather walk on a bit. Ciggie's warmed me

up. Liberty's just down the road. We can pick me a hat to go with the frock.'

The olde-worlde building, all its complicated old-fashioned windows and black and white decoration, is theirs to enjoy. The wind is starting up again. It's almost dark already. Dust and leaves skitter around their feet.

'I remember them building this,' she says. 'You was a tiny nipper, we'd only had you a few months. Brought us luck, you did, our summer baby. Remember that, whatever happens. See the beams round the side? After you came along, Harry got a job working down the dock where they broke up one of them ships for the timbers.'

'That right, Ma?'

He wishes she didn't have to bring up Dad's name every other moment. It was bad enough they have to live with him and his temper. He'd rather have had Ken for a dad. But he wouldn't swap Ma for anyone else.

She tugs her hat down and put her arm through his so they're close as peas. Her coat seems loose on her. He's sure the buttons used to be tight across her middle.

'You're right,' she said, though he hadn't said a word. 'No use picking over the past.'

He's just about the same height as her now. He feels like a man, big enough to look after her. Soon, another year and a half, he reckons, and he'll be earning proper money.

'It's nippy, fair enough,' she says. 'Let's find a bus back now. I'll do us a fried egg sandwich for tea.'

BANTLING

58 Violet. Hull. 1939.

Hull, E. Yorks, 17 February 1939, Ahoy there dearest Sis, I'm back on my feet & fighting fit. I have a little girl, Lily. I will bring her with me when you're due. Mim expects me around the end of next month, but I'll wait for the exact date or good as from you to make sure I am with you. Send me a telegram & hang the expense! The other children will stay here with Len. I will see to Mim & pack up her place. Things are getting on top of her, so much so that she has agreed to come north to live with us. Well, at least we will all be together if & when the inevitable happens. All this talk of Czechoslovakia. We can't trust Hitler an inch. Barely 20 years since the Great War ended & here we are, looking at it happening all over again. I can't imagine it's much cheerier down south, especially where you are. Make sure you plant things you can eat in any space you can find. Spuds and sprouts will see you right. Remember how hungry we were the last time? Looks like I might be getting back to more than rootling in my own garden. I have put myself forward to the council to (help!) make plans for growing vegetables in the parks & other open land not already dug up last year for trenches. The biggish houses & gardens along the Avenues apart, most people here live in 2 up 2 downs with barely a backyard between them, so any soil we can lay claim to will be useful. They're used to catching fish up here, but not to setting potatoes and cabbages. Len sends his best. You, Ralph & the kids are in our thoughts. In a few weeks I shall see your lovely face again & your little son or daughter. Until then, do take care. You cannot be too careful. As ever, Violet.

BANTLING

59 Timmy. Peckham. 1939.

There's a bowl of batter by the stove. Ma and Dad sitting at the table. That one's looking as angry as ever and Ma's been crying. He must have been giving her an earful worse than usual about something.

Tim puts his two pounds, his wages, or the best part of them, on the table for Ma, like he does every week. It's regular money, not bad for someone who's doesn't turn sixteen for another week.

'The firm says I'll have to get my number and card from the Social once I turn sixteen. Then I'll be a proper working man.

Ma and Dad don't say anything

'They reckon they're increasing production.'

And some of the blokes only a couple of years older than him are already doing their military training. Like Bertie. If the war happens, more like when it happens, those blokes might be off before long. There've been hints Timmy might get a raise come his birthday to help him decide to stick around, but he's not counting his chickens.

This week, Ma doesn't pick up the money and put it in her tin. She looks set to start crying again. Dad says, 'I'll tell him if you won't,' and he thinks that someone's died or been hurt. Please don't let it be Doris. Ma pulls herself together and tells Dad to sling his hook for a bit, which, glory be, he does.

BANTLING

She wipes her face with her apron and her hands. Her eyes are very red, and her nose too. It looks as though she's been crying for a while.

'What's happened, Ma? What's he been doing to you? What's he been saying? He's not hit you, has he? I'll kill him.'

She stands up, puts a frying pan to heat on the stove, doesn't say a word.

He's as jumpy as a scalded rat.

'Ma? What's happened? Has Doris or Bert had an accident? Is that it?'

She dollops some thick batter into the pan, watches it sizzle.

'Nothing's happened, not as such. Sit yourself down.'

She flips the batter. The smell from the pan is fit for a king.

She puts a couple of drop-scones onto a plate, hands it to him.

'It's not my birthday yet, Ma. Not for another couple of weeks.'

'I know full well when your birthday is. Sixteen. Like you said, you'll get your number and your card from the Social, start paying your stamps.'

'It's a bit more than that, Ma.'

He doesn't know if he should tell her about the raise. It would cheer her up. Then again, if it doesn't come off …

'What's going on, Ma?'

BANTLING

'Can't your old Ma give her boy a treat when she wants?'

She flips another hot scone onto his plate.

'Eat up, Timmy. I know they're your favourites.'

'You're making me nervous, Ma. Sixteen, it's not that big a change. Though they might give me a raise at work, fingers crossed.'

'Touch wood.'

She's still got her back to him.

'I was never one for many words,' she says. 'Harry even less.'

That's not the way he sees Dad, but he lets it go.

'You know you're my special lad, don't you? Perhaps Harry was right. Everything catches up with you sooner or later. Perhaps I should have told you sooner.'

Splat, sizzle-sizzle.

She's making drop-scones as though her life depends on it and he can't see her face. Perhaps Bertie's got his orders already, is off to get ready for the war.

'Told me what, Ma?'

He's lost his taste for drop-scones. Whatever's in his mouth feels like Plaster of Paris, getting thicker all the time and impossible to swallow.

Her shoulders are shaking.

He gets up and turns off the gas and puts his arms around her.

'Is it Bertie? Have they called him up already?'

She shakes her head, tight and fast. When she turns

around her face is a mess. She looks smaller. He's never seen her like this. It's frightening.

'You've been happy here, haven't you? I've done my best to be a good mother to you, and you've made it easy.'

'You're the best Ma, the only Ma for me in the whole world.'

He's thinking that it's her dying, that's what she's finding so hard to tell him.

'I'll look after you,' he promises. 'I won't let you die.'

She stops and looks at him.

'Oh, my lovely, that's not it.'

They sit down and she holds his hands tight. She closes her eyes and takes a breath.

'There's no easy way to say this. Harry's right about that. No use beating about the bush no more. I thought it best you hear it from me. You'd be finding out in any case before the month's out once your papers come from the Social.'

'Spit it out, Ma.'

'I never said anything before because it makes no difference to me and I didn't want it to make no difference to you. Now the Welfare's been in touch. They'll be writing to you soon enough. I always knew it was too good to be true and I might lose you. Promise me I won't.'

He promises her because he'd tell her anything to take away that look on her face. He's sick to his stomach.

BANTLING

'The truth is, Timmy love, Harry and me, we're not your real Ma and dad. You wasn't born a Wingrove. We got you out of the blue when you were just a tiny thing and then you were one of us. My miracle baby. It never made no difference, not to me. It still don't. You're my Timmy, always will be. Plain and simple. Whatever the Welfare people say.'

He hears the words, but they don't really make sense. Then they start to make sense. Then they don't again.

He's the cuckoo in the nest.

How can he not be Timmy?

Of course he's Timmy.

He understands the words in themselves, but they still don't mean anything. How can Ma not be his Ma?

'It was like I said, a miracle,' she said. 'You looked at me and I looked at you and that was that. You brought me back to the land of the living when I couldn't see the point of it.'

He doesn't belong.

It's all been a lie.

He's never belonged.

Everything's been a great big whopping lie.

Ma's lied. Even Ma. Ma most of all. At least Dad's never pretended to give a hoot.

His mind is rocking like water shaken in a tight-screwed jar. He might as well be in a drowning ship. All the air's been sucked out of the room.

On the table there's a pile of congealing of batter on

a chipped plate. There's his green pound note and two reddish-brown ten-shilling ones.

'If I'm not Timmy, who am I?'

'You're the same as ever.'

'Have I got another name? What am I called?'

'Far as I'm concerned, it's Timothy Wingrove. Please, love.'

'But it's not, is it? Not really?'

His hands are on the edge of the table, pushing it away.

If he isn't Timmy, then who is he? He's a hollow man, a puppet. A different name, it stands for a different life. He's like a ball shot into dark space and there's no gravity and no light to bring him back again.

On the other side of the table, Ma put her fists to her mouth and he wonders what's frightening her so.

'I'm a bloody nobody, just like dad always said.'

He shoves the table so hard that the edge catches Ma in her middle and knocks the breath out of her as he stands up. Her chair rocks back and she grabs the table to stop herself falling backwards. He wouldn't hurt her for the world, but he's not himself.

'Timmy! Come back, love. Timmy! A name's of no matter. You're my boy, blood or not. Timmy!'

Dad's smirking in the hallway. Must have heard everything. Not Dad anymore.

He pushes past him, past Harry.

Harry shouts. 'Going to get yourself down the Labour Exchange, are you? Have to register for your stamps, in your real name, your slut mother's name. Whatever that is. Think labouring's too good for you, don't you? You'll be grateful to get anything as a no-name, mark me.'

Ma's behind him, crying and trying to get Harry to shut up.

What's he going to tell them at work? What will they say? What will they do? Christ, if he hasn't got a job …

'Better any name than yours,' he shouts back. 'Wingrove never was a good fit.'

Harry's face twists. He's laughing, that horrible mocking wheezing sound.

'You ungrateful little bastard. Your mother was a common tart. That do-good vicar's wife was trying to get rid of you for her, paid me a best part of a hundred quid to take you off her hands. She got the best of that bargain, let me tell you.'

'Stop it. Stop it both of you. Harry, you promised.'

It's come to this, then, after all this time, the two of them locked and struggling in the cramped space, crashing from wall to wall and stumbling over the rug. Dad – Harry – is stronger than he is, but if he's learned anything from him, it's to not give way. He doesn't care if he ends up dead, not now.

She's yelling out, 'Wash your mouth out, Harry, and behave yourself. His mother was just a chit of girl who couldn't cope.'

She's whacking them both on their backs and shoulders.

They've sent the coat stand flying and their feet are kicking around in a tangle of overcoats, scarves and hats.

Doris is screaming blue murder from the stairs.

Ma's coughing again. Damned if either of them will be the first to let go. They clutch and twist, chest to chest. He's pretty sure it's Dad's – Harry's – elbow that gets Ma in the throat because he sees her jerk backwards.

Harry's pressing his arm across his windpipe, and it takes more than he thought he had to push away and let himself fall so Harry can see Ma for himself. Harry gives him a God almighty kick as he goes down. It just about knocks the stuffing out of him, but mostly he's still got his mind on Ma.

She's slipping down the wall, coughing her heart out, sucking, sucking at the air, trying to get it into her. Doris is doing her best to push past them both to get to her.

All of a sudden, Harry's giving Ma a hand, got his arm around her. Harry looks over at him.

'This is all down to you,' he says. 'Your fault, upsetting her like this, you misbegotten bastard.'

That's a load of codswallop. If there's anyone to blame, it's Harry, and once he gets his wind back, he tells him so, says Harry's likely to kill Ma with all his yelling and stupidity and never looking out for her and he doesn't deserve her, never has, never will, is worth less than her little finger and he wishes Harry was dead.

Harry looks as furious as all get out.

'Get up. Scram and don't bother to come back, you little bastard.'

'Dad!' That's Doris. Much good she'll do.

Ma makes the smallest movement with her hand, so feeble they can both pretend they haven't seen it. He'll take himself off to Aunt Flo's, just for the night, just until he can work something out. Flo must be in on the secret too, but she's always treated him fair. Tomorrow he'll see if someone at work knows a room. Maybe Ken can help.

He starts to scrabble around for his coat, snot and tears all over his face. He has to step over her legs, squeeze past Harry who's not going to make anything easier for him. Doris is grabbing at him. She must have known all this time too. No wonder Bert's never really given him the time of day.

Ma makes the movement again and this time she opens her eyes. They neither of them can ignore it, glare at each other as they might.

'Timmy.' It's more a croak than anything. 'Harry.'

All right. He'll stay until morning, make sure she's alright. He doesn't want her upset more than she is, but he needs to know which do-gooding vicar's wife Harry's talking about.

60 Sam. Stockwell. 1939.

He feels sick and shaky, so jittery that he walks past the gate, once, twice. It had taken some doing to squeeze the address out of Harry, for no other reason than the old devil's pig-headedness. Ma made him do it in the end, like a woman with nothing to lose. Broken-hearted. Timmy promised her it'd make no difference what he found out, that she'd always be his Ma. She said, but you're going ahead, it's made a difference already, so where was the truth in all that?

Pull yourself together, Timmy. Or whatever your name is. *Nothing ventured, nothing gained.* You won't feel any better however many times you walk around the block.

It's an elderly man in a dog collar who opens the door, smiles politely at him, invites him in. Down a hall covered in the sort of wallpaper that would make Ma throw a fit, into a study stuffed with books, the window half-covered by some bush grown out of control. Everything's pretty shabby. Not that he's used to much better, but it's a surprise here. He's offered a seat and apologies that the housekeeper is out so there's no tea to be had, asked what the vicar can do to help him.

He takes a deep breath, hopes his voice doesn't shake too much.

'I'm after some information. It's your wife who can help me better, I suppose. From what I've been told.'

'Mrs Holcroft's not available.'

That's not the first thing he wants to hear.

'Why don't you start at the beginning, lad?' says the vicar. 'You don't have to tell me your name, not everyone does, but anything told to me here stays between you and me.'

Where to start?

Deep breath. Look the man in the eye. Might learn something that way.

'I've answered to Timothy Wingrove for as long as I can remember.'

'Ah.'

Is it his imagination or does the man blink?

'It's not my real name.'

The man nods. He looks wary now. He doesn't say anything.

It's like wading through glue.

'I never was a Wingrove, it turns out. But none of us know any other name for me. I was hoping you or your wife might help me. If you were here in 1923. April 1923.'

The vicar's face is blank, but in the end he nods again.

'We were here.'

The room is quiet. Outside, the bush shakes as a bird flies out of it.

'Tell me what you think you know,' the vicar says at last.

'My mother – Mrs Wingrove ... Ma ... who brought me up ... she told me she got me from your wife after she lost her own baby. She wasn't expecting it. Harry – Mr Wingrove said much the same. I only heard all this last week. I don't know anything else. I don't even know if any of it's true.'

A slow nod.

'You and this Mrs Wingrove, you're fond of each other, I think?'

He shrugs, nods. It's too complicated. And it's none of the vicar's business.

He's really shaking now, so much he grips his hands. They're all sweaty. He hopes the vicar can't tell what a state he's in.

'Yes,' said the Vicar. 'Mrs Holcroft thought it would work out well.'

Then the quiet again.

He can see how this is going to go. The bugger won't give anything away. He's going to have to gnaw away at him.

'Did you meet her, whoever she was? Did you know her to talk to?'

It doesn't seem fair to call this other person his real mother.

Reverend Holcroft stares at his hands. He's not looking that comfortable himself.

'Violet? Yes, I knew Violet. She lived here for a little while, just before the birth. Before you were born, I should say.'

BANTLING

Violet.

'Violet? Violet what? Did she have a family? A name? Did she care enough to give me a name of my own?'

The vicar looks startled, goes bright pink.

'I'm sorry, I forgot you don't know. Of course, of course she cared. Her name was Violet Bantling and she named you Samuel. That was many years ago. A name can't make that much difference, not after all this time.'

'It does to me,' he says, feeling as fierce as he sounds. He has to sit on his hands to stop them shaking.

Samuel Bantling. Sam. It sounds fine to him. The only thing this Violet has left him with. It fits him well enough.

Except it's someone else's name, belongs to someone else's life. A life that hasn't happened because Timothy Wingrove came along.

The man is fidgeting, rubbing the thumb of one hand along the little finger of the other.

'What else?'

'It was all so long ago,' says the vicar. His voice is soft. 'It's all best left alone. For everyone's sake. It wasn't a happy time.'

'I just want to know.'

He doesn't like the whining, desperate sound of his voice, loud in this quiet house.

'I'll thank you to keep you voice down,' said the vicar. 'There's nothing to be gained by shouting.'

BANTLING

They stare at each other. He's either going to blub or hit the bloke. Or something.

The vicar puts his hands in his lap, out of sight. He's frowning. He chews on his lips. He looks more unhappy than angry, as though he doesn't know what to say or do.

It's like scratching salt from rock.

'And?'

'Violet was a kindly person. Very lively for the most part. I grew fond of her. She had a good way with figures and a lot of common-sense. You have something of her colouring.'

There has to be more. He nods, more like a jerk. Nodding is what Ma does when she wants people to carry on chatting, though her neck probably doesn't feel as stiff as his does.

'You have to understand, lad. It was a different time. Attitudes might have changed somewhat, but it's always been hard for a young woman on her own with a baby. We'd all hoped and prayed for a different outcome, that you and she could stay together, but Violet was a sensible girl, could see it wasn't a good idea.'

What would he be like now if he'd grown up as Sam Bantling? Would he like the same food, think the same thoughts? He'd not have had to put up with Harry. What sort of work would he be doing? Would he have ever looked at Picasso's painting? Or would

BANTLING

he be someone else altogether? It's a puzzle he can't begin to answer.

A conundrum.

'We considered ... the long and short of it is that my wife settled on the Wingrove family for one reason or another. And it sounds as though Mrs Wingrove made as good a mother as you could wish for. You wouldn't want to hurt her, I'm sure. My wife will be glad it all worked out so well.'

He gives this nonsense as much attention as it's worth. Except for the part about hurting Ma. The thought of Ma not bringing him up, not being his Ma, was impossible.

'What else about Violet Bantling? Do you know where she might be nowadays?'

His head is tight and sore.

Footsteps cross the floor upstairs. A door opens and shuts somewhere.

The vicar sits up as though a wasp has stung his bum.

'No, I certainly don't have any information like that. You should be getting on. I've a lot to do.'

He stares at the vicar, shakes his head. It's rude, behaving like this. Ma wouldn't approve, but he's not going to budge.

'You can't be thinking of getting in touch with her?' The vicar looks shocked. 'She's built another life, married as far as I know. Just think of the harm you might do. No, no, it's out of the question. Much better to let sleeping dogs lie. Besides, there's been hardly a word from her since she went away. I have no idea where she is.'

He's not going to let it go like that. Timmy Wingrove's life is for the birds. He's history. Sam Bantling's life is standing in front of him, waiting to be claimed. There will always be room for Ma.

Distantly, a toilet flushes. The vicar jumps at the sound. What's he so nervous about?

'Perhaps Mrs Holcroft might remember something else. When would it convenient to see her?'

He's doing his best to be polite. The vicar should be jumping through hoops helping him put the pieces together, not acting as though he's the last defence at Mafeking.

'I'm afraid it's not possible to see her,' says the vicar. 'My wife's health is not the best. She keeps to her bed most of the time and has very few visitors these days. I'm sorry, lad, I can't help you further. My advice is to be grateful for what you have and make the best of it.'

'Ma's not at all well either.' He means that he knows how to behave around sick people, but the vicar misses the point. Probably because his voice came out trembly.

The man looks truly sorrowful. 'I am so sorry to hear that,' he says. 'She struck me as a fine person.'

He fishes around in his desk drawer, pulls out a whole tenner and pushes into Sam's hand. When they stand up, he shakes Sam's hand with both of his, really pumps it up and down. His eyes are watery

'I'm glad to meet you, I really am. It's a weight off my mind to see how you've turned out. Good luck. I'll pray for you tonight. And for Violet.'

61 Sam. Peckham. 1939.

Greys that fade into mauve. A streak across the top of Ma's nose that runs from butter-yellow to the faintest blue. Brownish-yellows in the hollows of her cheeks and under her jaw. Green, like a light chartreuse, between her nose and lips. A shadowy bruised red around her closed eyes. The colours change all the time, so gradually he can hardly see it happening. But he does, all the same. How can her face, that tiny space, hold so much and never hold still? A patch on her cheek that had been the colour of curdled milk has a blueish tinge now. Planes are shifting too, her mouth slipping open, her nose getting sharper. Her breath is changing. He keeps thinking it's stopped, that's it all over. And then it comes again. Stops again. Comes again. Not that quietly. It sounds as though there's some piece of strange water-logged machinery inside her, dragging the air in, dragging it out.

He should probably wake up the others to say goodbye to her.

In a little while.

He watches her, not believing, wondering what sort of monster he is that can sit and watch his own Ma dying, and still see, and, even worse, name, the changing colours of her face. They're all turning to one sort of yellow or another now. It's a good thing he kept his own mouth shut the past few weeks, so she always thought of him as Timmy, as her Timmy. She never knew him as Sam, but Timmy will die with her. He's kept some sort of promise. No other Ma but her, not while she was alive.

He takes her hand with its papery skin and twisty, sticking-up veins, presses it gently. If he sets his mind to it, she'll know he's here. The thin bands of gold and small luminous opals are loose even on her middle finger. He'd never noticed when her fingers got so wasted that she'd had to change even how she wore her wedding ring.

All around her eyes, her skin is darker now, ochre and livid purple and dark ash grey. Her lips look dusty, paler than he's ever seen, vanishing. Her mouth's becoming a gaping void.

Oh Ma, let there be flowery meadows and sunshine and people you love coming to meet you.

There's a draught on his back. Harry's standing in the open doorway. Sam's got no idea how long he's been there. It could just be the gloom or Sam's eyes playing silly buggers, but Harry looks rough as hell. His face, the way the skin is stretched tight across the bones and the way his lips have shrunk to a dark line, almost make Sam feel sorry for the man. It's what Ma would want, the two of them burying the hatchet and he gets up to let Harry know, he'll even call him Dad if it helps, gets up to let him sit by Ma and say good-bye to her.

'Well. That's that, then. Satisfied now, are we?'

He's not got the faintest what Harry means.

Harry drops his fag onto the polished lino.

'No skirts to hide behind now, maggot.'

The whole time Harry's talking he's looking at his boot grinding the butt into the floor. There's a whiff of scorch.

'You'd best be packing your bag. I want you gone by the time the others are up. Us family have a lot to sort out today.'

BANTLING

62 Sam. Stockwell. 1939.

A lady opens the vicarage door this time. She looks a bit untidy and her clothes are old-fashioned. She's topped them off with a funny old tweed jacket that's miles too big for her, and that even the rag-and-bone man would sniff at. It's not for him to judge, but he can't help but notice wafts of stale body smell and sugar-sweet talc. He supposes she's a charity case. He takes off his hat.

'I wonder if you can help me, please Miss.'

He deserves some answers. More answers than the vicar gave him last time. *A kindly person. Good with figures. Something of her colouring.* It's thin gruel. That's why he's back. Everyone else is somebody's son or brother or cousin. That's what he wants too. It's not so much to ask. Sam needs some answers. There's nowhere else to try. He doesn't know why he feels scared, but he does.

'That's Mrs Holcroft to you, if you don't mind, young man.'

The vicar's not about, she tells him, and he takes a breath, says he's just as happy to see her, that's better, in fact.

She starts to close the door, but he puts a hand against it and smiles as nicely as he knows how. He can't quite believe this musty-smelling, distracted creature is the vicar's wife.

BANTLING

'This is to do with something that happened quite a while ago. Sixteen years ago.'

'I don't know, I don't know,' she says. She's rubbing her hands very hard together and they are already red-raw and sore. 'I can't remember. It's so long ago. What did you say your name was?'

He takes a deep breath.

'Samuel Bantling. But I grew up as Timothy Wingrove.'

The letter from the Welfare people is in his pocket, so he knows there's no mistake.

She's gone everso pale, and starts to sag. He grips her elbow to steady her.

'Sorry, Mrs Holcroft. I didn't mean to startle you. Perhaps you should sit down.'

There's a chair in the hallway, and he helps her to it.

'Why are you here? Who sent you? Nobody was meant to know.'

'Know what, Mrs Holcroft? I'm trying to find Violet Bantling. It's a long time ago, but if you can remember anything ...'

She glares at him with a fury like Harry's own.

'Who are you? Where are you from? I warn you, my husband will be home soon.'

She starts to cry.

'I always did my best. They were all scheming against me. Felix was bewitched by that Violet.'

His breath stops. This old witch-woman has spoken the name. *Bewitched.* Is that what the vicar meant when he said he was fond of Violet Bantling?

BANTLING

'I treated her like a daughter, but she was a viper in my bosom. We might all have been destroyed. I had to look after everybody.'

She's picking and twisting the skin of her hands and wrists.

'Was I so wrong?' She looks up at him, her face smeary with tears. 'What would you have done?'

She's as nutty as a fruitcake.

She zigzags her finger towards the wall.

'They're not deaf, you know. They listen and they hear and then they talk about it between themselves. They tried to warn me.'

She looks around the hall and fixes on the patterned wallpaper. He follows her gaze. The hall looks as though it hadn't seen a coat of paint or change of paper for thirty years. It's ugly paper, but he can't make out whatever it is she can see there.

He tries again. 'Do you know where Violet Bantling is? Where she went from here?'

He's come to a dead-end if she can't help him, or won't.

'I don't know anything. Get away from me.'

She's on a par with Harry, all spite and rage. Sam's out on his ear already, never mind Harry's promises to Ma. The minute Ma died, the same minute, Harry flipped his wig and chucked him out. Doris did her best to put in a word for him, but blood's blood after all and Harry wasn't listening to anyone. Doris cried when she said goodbye, but she went back inside to make Harry's breakfast all the same. He's on borrowed time at Flo's, and it's making him twitchy, answering to two names.

'I don't know you,' the lady screams.

He's scared someone will hear her. The front door's still open and a passing policeman or busybody might believe he means her harm.

'You must know something,' he pleads. 'You recognise her name. Violet Bantling. Please help me.'

Finding her, finding out about her is the key to who he's going to be.

The lady's mouth twists.

'Gone and taken her troubles with her,' she says very faintly. 'I kept my end of that bargain.' She blinks up at him, her forehead wrinkling, 'Do you know where Arthur is? We're to be married when I'm old enough, you know. He said we could walk down to the river after lunch if Mama agreed.'

Her mouth takes on the shape of a coy smile. She puts one finger across it and leans towards him.

'I'm might let him kiss me. What do you think of that?'

She blinks at him.

'Are you Arthur? How old are you now?'

'I'm sixteen as of a few weeks ago, Mrs Holcroft.'

'Do you want to kiss me?'

He's heard a slap can bring people back to themselves. At least, that's Harry's line. He's tempted because he doesn't know what else to do. This one's off with the fairies. Harry also says you shouldn't hit a woman, but he never really said what made the difference between hitting and slapping.

He puts his hands into his pockets.

'That can't be right. You don't look much like Arthur. My eyes are not what they were.'

She blinks at him.

'Are you my dear and lovely Arthur? Why won't you kiss me?'

He takes a step back. She scowls.

'Is he coming? What have you done with him?'

He shakes his head and backs out through the door, keeping his eye on her, like you do with a snarling dog. The lady is humming to herself and swaying gently on the chair. She really and truly gives him the creeps. Perhaps he shouldn't leave her on her own. On the other hand, he's scared stiff of hanging around and what she might do next.

Yards down the street, he turns to look over his shoulder. Another woman has stopped as she opens the gate, and has her eyes fixed on him. He dithers for a moment, almost goes back, but one mad woman in a day is enough. If a storm blows up, there's no port to shelter him. The lady on the chair might accuse him of anything. The other might be even worse. He starts to run. It's all so bloody unfair.

BANTLING

63 Violet. Hull. 1940.

Hull 1ˢᵗ November 1940
Dear Reverend and Mrs Holcroft,
It is some years since I last wrote to you, but at this time of national danger, I am writing to appeal to you for any information about my son, Samuel Bantling. Do you know where he is or might be? Or do you know of anybody who might be able to help me? In a few months he will be old enough to be called-up & the thought that he might be injured or perhaps die without knowing that I have never ceased to think about him keeps me awake at night. My husband is a good and understanding person, so I do not need any secrecy – I have not needed it for a long time, if ever, so do not worry about that.

With greater dangers looming, I can now appreciate that whatever you did back in 1923, you did in the probable belief that it was for my benefit & for Sam's. I have told myself over the years that I am sure he found a loving home – who could not have loved him? – but now he is almost a man & about to face the hardships that so many young men are enduring for their country. I am fortunate that my other children are still young. They have gone into the countryside with my elderly mother, away from the immediate dangers of the city, though any war threatens all of us, wherever we are. I however, am staying, making myself as useful as I can. If by any chance, Sam has no family, perhaps the knowledge of his mother's affection will give him courage or at least something to fight for. Please, if you can give me any indication, never mind how old or vague your information is, I will never trouble you again if I can help it. I beg you to help me.

I hope for your well-being and safety through these difficult times.

Violet Landon

64 Sam. Balham. 1941.

Out of Balham tube. Onto the High Street. Not sure which way to go. A shivery feeling – mustn't give it the time of day – being out in the open, a sitting duck, though all things considered, it's probably safer here than back at camp.

A decorated branch sits in a pot by the door of the bank. Someone's made an effort with old tinsel, newspaper chains and pinkish-red tape. Noël. Noël. There are shrouded shops up and down the High Road and rooms above them, and stalls off the side and a few people selling stuff any old how along the pavement. Shoppers muddle around, getting what they can before everything closes, more people out and about than he's seen for ages. The yellowy-grey scudding sky makes the street seem too exposed, impossible to protect.

Get a grip. No point being nervy, that's not how he wants to be.

Every so often there are shored-up ruins with blackened brickwork and jutting beams like broken spars. He should be used to it by now, but they still give him the willies. Everything gone, bang, just like that. When a building vanishes there's nowhere to come back to, not in the same way as before, so everything you think you'll always remember and the people who should be there get lost along the way as well.

Funny old mood he's caught. Could be he's just done in, what with the journey and all.

He'd like to stay where he is, being part of the crowd, listening to everyone. It's not just the accent, but the way people talk to each other that's making him feel he's back where he belongs. If only Bert or Doris happened by and took him home. Or even Harry. They could go to the pub, catch up with each other on neutral territory.

In the butcher's shop opposite the station the women behind the counter exchange a glance when he asks if they can find something for him, and they pull a rabbit from under the counter. They'll sell him half as a favour, and he thinks, why not, it's only money and a bunny could come in handy. He has to look away while they skin it, gut it, chop it into pieces. God help him if he's getting squeamish. The one with the bloodiest apron, who's handy with the cleaver, rolls her eyes and says something to the other one about them looking younger all the time. Her workmate – wide pale face and powerful arms –says that she likes them a bit fresh and that he looks old enough to her. His uniform suits him a treat. Navy, is it? He knows he's blushing, but he is old enough, it's true. Fleet Air Arm, miss, and it's her turn to colour up, especially when he salutes her. He tells them he's nineteen, and he really will be in another couple of months.

BANTLING

Outside again. Almost dark. The street is just about packed up. Balham's making its way home. He buys a scrap of mistletoe from a skinny cold kid in the doorway of a boarded-up shop, for no particular reason. Just because. The two of them wish each other merry this and happy that as if they're related.

The air carries the smoky smell of chestnuts roasting somewhere nearby. Sixpence worth would have bought him directions as well, along the station wall, straight over at the cross road, then left somewhere opposite the common, except the old bloke looks him up and down, gives him the chestnuts in a twist of paper and the instructions and then his coin back as well. Happy Christmas, sailor, make the most of it.

He starts to walk. Most of the shops are shut and even if they're not, blackout means they're pretty dim. There's hardly any light and it's getting colder by the minute. The road off the High Street is quietish. Not quite empty though, and he wishes everyone he sees a Merry Christmas and they say the same back and it is all very jolly and he has made the right decision to come here, never mind all the travelling back and forth, three out of his five days' leave, all told. Everything will be fine, better than fine, it's the season for it. Mind you, he'd feel happier if Harry had bothered to reply to his letter.

Not that Harry was ever a great one for the writing.

He peels the chestnuts as he walks, burning his fingertips and blowing on them before putting them

BANTLING

into his mouth, feeling them warm him all the way down. Ma went for chestnuts as well, so he feels he's enjoying them for her too. There again, she said herself, it doesn't do to pick over the past.

Perhaps they'll all be waiting for him at Harry's. Well, not just sitting around, hands in their laps, they'll be getting on with things, of course, but expecting him, looking forward to seeing him. It would be a real treat to see Bert if he's on leave too, and Doris, or even just find out what they've been up to. Fingers crossed he's got enough presents for everyone. Hope they'll like them. Harry's at least should go down a treat. It'll show Harry he's serious about making up the trouble between them. They both said things they shouldn't have, but he can put them to one side, if Harry can.

Past a pub. A street of houses. The houses all dark, of course, as though everybody has gone away or died. Part of the terrace has disappeared into a jumble of bricks and spars. The smell of ashes still hangs around. Bare shrubs are frosty already. The chestnuts are finished now and he's feeling empty and still a bit jumpy.

Wood-smoke has a kindly smell. Other lives, other times, eh? Brothers and sisters pinning up holly, dads opening the beer, mum rinsing out the trifle bowl, the lot of them all together again for Christmas. He'd bet it's like that at Ken's today, or as like it as can be these days.

His boots are loud on the glistening pavement and

his kitbag's squeaking against his coat and digging into his shoulder. It's gone cold enough to make his fingers ache.

With any luck, if Harry's having a get-together, they'll all have pooled their coupons to get something half-way decent, a bit like in the old days. How decent depends on who's doing the cooking. Not Harry, that would just be a waste. The slop he used to serve up in those first weeks after Ma took bad. Worse than bilge-water. Doing his best. Let bygones be bygones. He could do it if Harry could. For Ma's sake.

There's dark, roughed-up land to his right now, trees, little huts and flung-together fences between him and the railway embankment. Whiffs of ammonia, chicken shit, decaying vegetables. Dogs barking and going quiet again as long as he doesn't stop to nick a cabbage or whatever they're guarding.

They can rest easy, he tells them, he's got enough in his bag to bring to the table.

Trees make black tracery against a rich dark sky. It's as though a light has been switched on behind it, making all the blues glow and run into each other, from quite dark to almost black. It's beautiful.

Haverhill Road is off to the left, just as the bloke back at the station said. Twice as wide as Stanton Street and then some again. Stanton Street and everything left of Ma in the old house is gone good and proper now. The slum clearance men got you if Hitler missed.

Number 58 is as quiet and sombre as the rest. By the

BANTLING

look of it, Harry's come up a bit in the world. Come up quite a bit. This new place must be double the size of the old one, bigger, even just looking from the outside, even if there's eight of them living in there. Which there isn't, as far as he knows. Then again, he doesn't know much about Harry these days. Bay windows up and down, a porch, a neat brick wall between them and the rest of us. There's a bit of garden out front, just scrappy dead flower heads and miserable shrivelled stalks inside the gate.

The gate latch clangs loud behind him and he gropes for the knocker. When it opens, even though it's just about dark, he knows he's never clapped eyes on her before.

'Merry Christmas, Miss,' he says. 'I'm looking for Harry Wingrove. Is he here?'

She shines a shaded torch into his face.

'Depends who's asking.'

He doesn't know her, so he holds his tongue. In any case, it's hard to explain. At least he's found the right place.

'You can tell him it's Tim asking for him.'

Then she says, 'Well, well. I might have guessed.'

Whoever she is, she doesn't seem surprised he's on the doorstep, but she's not welcoming him in either. That way she's standing with the door almost shut, blocking the hall, it's not very friendly.

'He'll know who you mean,' he says.

His name's the only thing his mother left him - it's

on his birth certificate and call-up papers - so he's not about to give it up. But for Ma's sake he'll be Tim for Harry.

For the moment.

He gives her his smile, the one that had the butcher blushing.

He slips the kitbag off his shoulder at last and the blood rushes in like needles. She still doesn't bother to introduce herself.

There's a blare of radio music. She turns and shouts back to keep the kitchen door shut and that there's nobody to speak of at the front door and the hallway goes quiet again.

'He's not expecting you,' she says.

'I wrote to him. The post's up the spout.'

Perhaps she screws up her mouth or perhaps she smiles, but the torchlight makes shadows over her face so that it looks as savage as a mask.

'Let's just say, he didn't get no letter from you.'

'Doesn't matter. I'm here now. Better to do it all face to face in any case.'

'From what I heard, you've done enough damage to last a lifetime. Things have changed around here. He's got me looking out for him now. See this.'

She turns the torch beam onto her hand.

He looks at the tiny opals, the worn-down gold.

'Ma's rings,' he says.

It doesn't seem right, seeing them on someone else's finger.

'Harry give them to me.'

'So you're Mrs Wingrove these days?'

'As good as.'

'Congratulations.'

He's getting chilled, and she should let him in so they can sort things out in the warm. He opens the top of the kitbag, gropes around the bottle and shows her the whisky.

'It's for Harry. If he's not in, I'll just wait.'

She pulls the bottle out of his hand eager enough. It cost him a fortune and took weeks to get hold of, but she shoves it into the pocket of her pinny as if it's nothing more than a thermos of cold tea.

'He'll get it.'

He hadn't meant to give it to her, but wouldn't be polite to snatch it back, not from a woman.

'It looks like I'm heading out before too long,' he says.

She shrugs. 'You're not the first to go and you won't be the last. Harry's frantic enough about Bert getting hurt without being upset by your tricks. I don't want him getting all worked up again, not at Christmas.'

'Bert got hurt? How bad?'

'None of your business.'

'He's my brother, for God's sake.

'Brother. That's rich, coming from you. Family sticks together. Henry Wingrove, Bert, me, that's family. Doris and her lot.'

BANTLING

'Bert and me, we've got no argument with each other.'

It's no use. He feels shrunken and cold, like he used to a kid. The rabbit is beginning to ooze through its newspaper, and its gaminess makes him feel a bit sick. Coming back wasn't meant to be like this.

'I want to set things to rights with Harry before I ship out,' he says.

'There's things been said that can't be unsaid. Can't be forgotten neither.'

She presses herself behind the door.

'Here's me standing here letting all the heat out. Like I said, you burned your boats good and proper.'

He leans against the door before it shuts. He's bigger than her, and stronger too. Dad, Harry, taught him never to use force against a woman, but this is different. She's got no right.

'Let Harry tell me himself. I just want to talk to him. Where's the harm in that?'

'Well, pardon me, but he doesn't care to talk to you or hear your excuses.'

Fair's fair, there had been harsh words all round, but it's not her he needs to sort it out with. He pushes onto the door and feels it start to give.

'What I've got to say to him is between him and me,' he says. 'I daresay he's got things he could say to me as well.'

She heaves back and the door quivers between them. She's tougher than she looks.

BANTLING

'And so you think you can just turn up and call the tune? He took you in for Alice's sake and you threw it back in his face and there's an end to it. Now sling your hook.'

He doesn't budge. He can stay here all night, foot jammed in the door, if that's what it takes.

'All right,' she says. 'Suit yourself. Harry!'

He hears the radio come and go, and heavy footsteps along the hall. Then there's Harry, looming out of the dark, as hatchet-faced as ever. Harry doesn't say anything, just puts his arm around her. She looks like the cat that got the cream.

Sam holds out his hand all the same, gives Harry a smile.

'Hello Harry. You're looking well. Sorry to hear about Bert. Give him my best.'

Harry gives a little snort.

'I came to put things right between us. It'd break Ma's heart to see us like this.'

The pair of them stare at him. He thinks that Harry might have made some move, and that she might have put a quick stop to it, but if it happens at all it takes no time to speak of, and it might only be his eyes or his mind playing tricks.

'You should have thought of that before,' she butts in. 'Telling Harry he good as killed his own wife.'

'I was only a kid, and I spoke out of turn and I'm sorry for it.'

BANTLING

He bit his tongue about Harry making the same accusation.

'Asides, Alice was no more your mother than I am, just a poor woman gone soft in the head.'

He can't understand why Harry doesn't say anything, not even to defend Ma's memory.

'You can't talk about Ma like that,' he says. 'Tell her, Harry. Tell her she can't hold a candle to Ma.'

He wants to thump her one and it probably shows in his face.

Neither of them says a thing.

So this is how it is going to be. They both deserve a punch. Harry taught him how. He puts both his hands back into his pockets. The rabbit is cold and clammy.

Now he is really feeling rough, wobbly in the legs and everything. He should never have eaten that sandwich on the train. He puts one hand on the wall to steady himself.

'Shut the door, Jessie love. Dinner's getting cold.'

The door closes quietly in his face.

It's like saying goodbye to Ma all over again.

He squats down in the dark, all fingers and thumbs with the kitbag cords. The door opens again and he hates his own hopefulness. An envelope drops onto his bag. It's addressed to Harry. It takes a few moments for it to sink in that's it's his handwriting on the front.

'Don't bother writing to him again,' says Jessie. 'Waste of good paper. Like I said, he won't get to read them.'

BANTLING

All the way back to the tube he is listening for a shout and for feet running towards him to turn him round and take him home. If Harry had answered the door first, or Doris, if Bert had been around, it would all have been different. Might have been different. He could have said what he had to say before they all got so het up. That Jessie. Setting herself up to take Ma's place, turning Harry against him even more.

The cold stings his eyes hot and watery.

He should have done it different. He could have insisted himself through the door and into the kitchen and then what? He must be mad to think for a moment that Harry had an ounce of fairness in him. If she's what Harry wants, they deserve each other.

He runs into the mistletoe kid again and makes him take the rabbit. Merry Christmas and here's to peace in 1942. Every cloud, as they say. He could have taken the rabbit to Ken's, but the feel of it in his pocket was making him retch.

Harry didn't use his name, not either of them. That's that then. Over and done with. Done and dusted.

He's not due back at camp for three days. It doesn't seem right to impose on Ken and his lot, not for that long. The place they're in these days, since the old block copped it last year, is just a small back-to-back, not so different to Stanton Street. After that scene with Harry, it feels even more like a cheek to roll up there out of the blue. Not that they'd mind, most likely.

BANTLING

The signs back at camp were that they're probably headed north and onto Atlantic convoy duty, though all anyone can do is guess. Whatever happens, at least now he doesn't have to worry about the people at home fearing for him or praying for him or crying when he doesn't make it back again.

Except, perhaps, Cora. She'll miss him. Might miss him. For a little while.

And Ken. Ken's been a good mate.

BANTLING

65 Violet. Hull. 1942.

Hull, 12 February 1942, Dear Stel, Thanks for your letter. The post gets through even now! Len would be proud. It is a relief to know you are away from the coast & are as safe & comfortable as can be expected or hoped for these days. I am sure Ralph's family is glad to have you there. You could never be a burden. Mim & the kids have gone to the countryside as well & they seem finally to have settled a bit. For myself, I am staying put for the moment. I'm as busy as can be, keeping an eye on allotment committees (mostly women & bossy old men who always know best), writing pamphlets & demonstrating how to grow food in the smallest spaces & receptacles. Throughout Hull we have a fair amount of land under cultivation these days, parks of course & using all sorts of scraps & corners, even between craters & bomb rubble, ~~of which we have our fair share~~. I feel I am doing something useful, ~~especially as the fishing has been so affected~~. Len of course is away too, heavens knows where. As far as I can tell he is doing work in the forces not a million miles different to his old job, but different conditions, different times. It makes me watch what I write in my letters as I imagine him looking over my shoulder. If I keep as busy as I can, I have less time for worry & am so tired I sleep though almost anything & everything. Love, Vi

BANTLING

66 Ellen. Stockwell. 1943.

'Time for a little break, Mrs Holcroft. I'll bring in the refreshments.'

She gives Mrs Dawson and her refreshments about as much attention as they deserve. Which is to say not very much at all. It's no fun these days.

Look at those two respectable ladies, so straight and upright on her sofa, pretending not to stare at her, waiting like Harpies to use up her tea rations. Felix lets them get away with it because he doesn't like her being on her own. Doesn't trust her, more like. It doesn't mean she has to pretend to enjoy jailers in her sitting room, click-click-clicking away with their long needles.

Smile at them, Ellen. Don't give anything away.

The door opens again and bone china clinks.

Is she imagining the smell? Where on earth has Mrs Dawson managed to find coffee? Her eyes water. It's been like gold-dust, harder to get hold of than if it had been rationed. Mrs Dawson must know someone working on the sly.

'One of my relatives,' says Mrs Dawson. Has she taken to reading minds now, or has Ellen spoken out loud? 'Works down the docks. I thought we could do with a treat. All above board, honestly. Have to drink it the way foreigners do, though. Unless you ladies have brought your own sugar with you.'

And they have and Mrs Dawson's heated the milk

and slips a sliver of sugar into Ellen's cup and it is really rather wonderful, in spite of the circumstances. And even if it's on the black market, well, let that be on Mrs Dawson's conscience.

Even the condemned man can take pleasure in the little things.

Forever collecting and knitting, unravelling the old and making up again. She's always been thrifty, nobody can accuse her of being profligate, but this make and mend, make and mend, turning sock heel after sock heel never stops. It goes on and on and on. Felix's mind is set on sending off a parcel to his boys in the forces every week or so. Socks, scarves, gloves, long-johns, vests. It's endless. Old garments, odd parts of balls of wool, grubby baby jackets, they arrive at the vicarage every day. Who has to sort it all? Why, Ellen of course, dutiful wife and devoted servant that she is. Tasks were so much more fun with Violet, once upon a time. They used to have a laugh. Nowadays, the wool gets up her nose and what with the blunt needles and all the unpicking her fingers are raw. Still, it keeps her hands busy.

It's all they let her do these days.

Smile, simper. Express wonder and thankfulness. That's enough, Ellen. Don't overdo it.

Remember how she used to make stock for somebody or other, oh ages ago? She can almost smell and taste even now. She could do with a nice bowl of it tonight. Fat chance of that. *Don't you know there's a war on, Ellen?*

These days, there's hardly a moment when there's not someone with her if she's got knitting needles in her hands. Mrs Dawson or a parish stalwart with inquisitive, pitiless eyes, just waiting to pounce if it looks as though she might prod herself with one. Even worse is them looking pityingly at her when they think she's taking no notice. Everyone chats to everyone else as though there's nothing amiss, as though she's not in the room, has never existed.

She is floating away again.

Why had she thought something was all Violet's fault? It's too long ago now to remember what happened, or why.

'You look as though you enjoyed that, Mrs Holcroft. Another cup, dear?'

She holds out her cup and puts on her sweetest face.

They're all done for the day. Same time tomorrow, Mrs Holcroft? So kind of you and the vicar to let us use the room. Delicious coffee, a real treat, Mrs Dawson.

Mrs Dawson whisks away the wool and the needles to somewhere she thinks Ellen won't find them. Ellen makes up new bundles to post.

And so it goes on.

BANTLING

67 Sam. North Atlantic. 1943.

Even salt water freezes, freezes harder than fresh. Sea and ship, both weighted down with thickened ice. Most of the time it's hard to tell them apart. Grey-white, blue-white, green-white, grey-grey, blue-grey, green-grey, black-grey. Along the masts and rigging, snow and ice pile and creak. The cold numbs whatever brains he's got left. Sam and Streaky go aft to the guns and depth charges, crawling along, clinging to lifelines to stop themselves sliding overboard. He wonders if the powers-that-be see them as disposable men. Twice, as the ship lurches and grinds forward, he's ended up hanging on the end of a cable, twisting his arms around the metal strands above the greedy waves and the surging pack-ice, hanging on for grim life, counting seconds that seem like weeks, feeling his clothes riding up his body, willing the ship to right itself, sick with not knowing if he'll land back on deck again. A couple of times he's hauled Streaky back to safety, too, if the frozen deck counts as safety.

His eyes are swollen from the freezing wind. Ice and snow are forever blowing into them. He daren't rub them. His eyelashes are like needles.

They have to attack the remorseless, indifferent ice and snow with axes, steam, and shovels, chopping and hacking to keep the ship lighter and upright. All the while, he waits for a torpedo to strike them or for fire and bombs to drop from the clouds and fog around them. All the while, the cold sets up home inside him.

The ships rolls and pitches all the time, thirty degrees port and then thirty starboard. Port, starboard, port, time after time after time. Waiting for the return like his own heartbeat. He can't help but think about sea spray growing solid over the decks and rigging, over the wings and bodies of the Hurricanes, the Albacores and the Fulmars, of snow settling, dense as concrete, of the ship becoming more and more top-heavy, of its pitching reaching the tipping point and toppling, toppling, so him and Streaky and all the others fall into the cavernous sea. It's not as though he hasn't seen it happen. The best anyone can say is that it's fast drowning in a frozen ocean. He remembers choking on his own blood when his tooth went through his lip, and imagines the water, cold beyond understanding, paralysing him inside and out. He'll never learn to swim, it'd just make it worse.

'Look at that, would you? Engagement dairy. What the heck's that when it's at home?'

'Diary, Streaky, it's a diary. You know, where you write down who you're meeting for luncheon and when you're due for a manicure.'

Streaky's holding the small book as though it's something nasty from another planet.

Sam unwraps the small parcel he's picked from the Santa sack. Small and heavy.

BANTLING

Streaky's face is puffed and tight. He's upset, no two ways about it. Christmas in the middle of nowhere, seas too rough to get mail, a lucky dip in the mess deck and the poor sod has pulled out a lady's dainty calendar. White, gold lettering on the front and a white ribbon marker. In his cracked hands, it seems like a nasty joke.

'Dairy, diary, who cares what it's called? Who'd send it to a sailor for a Christmas draw? And what office idiot would send it on here? What am I meant to do with it?'

'Perhaps Modom would care for a light?'

Sam clicks his new lighter. Blue flame flares. Streaky's cigarette glows.

Streaky sucks in the smoke, breaths it out into the close air of the mess deck.

'A lighter, now, that's not bad. That's worth pulling out of the barrel, you lucky bastard.'

It's fair to say that it's a nice piece. Heavy enough, not bulky, just the right size for his palm. He fingers its smoothness and reads the cover of Streaky's winnings.

'Could be worse. At least it's next year's. You might've had to remember all of last year.'

'Christmas, eh? What's the point? What a laugh.'

Streaky pushes congealing food around his plate.

It's not like his mate to be off his food. It's not like any of them.

'Bet they're not eating this muck in the officers'

mess. Bet they've got all the trimmings. Bet they've got letters from home too,' says Streaky.

Streaky looks so very young. Much younger than Sam feels. Like a scared little boy who can't find his way home.

'Bet Santa Claus and Rudolph are up there scoffing milk and custard creams with the captain as well,' says Sam.

Streaky's fidgeting with Sam's lighter, turning it this way and that, staring off at nothing.

'They'll land the mailbags soon. You'll get your mum's letters in a day or so. You'll see,' says Sam.

He picks up the diary. He'd be hard pushed to say where he'd been or what he'd been doing on any of those days last year. All he knows is that most of it hadn't been what he'd have chosen. And if he couldn't even remember it, it meant the time had been stolen from him twice.

Not that there's room to go to town. A week per page, half an inch a day, even less, Saturday and Sunday lumped together. He could give it a whirl. It'd cheer Streaky up a bit.

'Tell you what, Streaky,' he says. 'Pretend it's Christmas. I'll swap you.'

BANTLING

68 Sam. HMAC Victorious. 1944.

Fri 9 June 1944 *Completed our last operation in Home Fleet. HM Aircraft Carrier Victorious now on way to Greenock from Norway.*

Mon 12 June 1944 *Saw my last of Britain for a while, watched Jura and Islay disappear over horizon. Ship turned Sth. Streaky's 19th birthday today. Lots of buzzes about where we're going, nothing certain. Captain says Gib, Casablanca, Azores or Freetown. Hope it's Casablanca.*

Thurs 15 June 1944 *Rather calm, Captain says we're likely to end up at Dakar, Bermuda or Algiers. That's 7 names on the list now. Algiers is favourite. It's been beautiful weather all day, lovely azure sky. Sunbathing prohibited until 16.00 hrs from now onwards. "Bar" open now. Only sells very weak lime juice. P.T every night.*

Sat 17 June 1944 *Saw Tangiers on the starboard side. Also Alexandria and small towns. We came through Straits of Gib, lovely scenery on both sides, especially Spanish Morocco side. Enjoyed P.T. tonight with music supplied by Marines Band. Beginning to tan nicely. Captain spoke just now. He says we are due in Algiers tomorrow morning at 08.00hrs. He also gave us a word of warning about Algiers "red wine". He said 'It is not beer repeat not beer and cannot repeat cannot be drunk like beer'. Bad ending today: - On watch all night. Midnight salt spray bath.*

BANTLING

Sat 18 June 1944 *Spent a wonderful day ashore. Got dressed in tropical rig, proceeded ashore about 13.30hr, travelled through nearly all the main roads in Algiers. Some beautiful streets and some horrid smells. The most beautiful street was Rue de Constantine, but I heard poultry cackling in the second floor flat of one of the classy-looking buildings. A novelty to use different money and argue with hawkers for a lower price. Picked up a few French phrases. Had some lovely muscatel wine, also ice-cream with milk in. Vin de Rouge is lousy, something like Red Burgundy. Met a Cockney bloke who took Jock, Streaky and me round the town. Didn't go far into the Kasbah, too dodgy. There were clean Arabs, dirty Arabs, women wearing veils and European men and ladies {mainly French}, in lovely fashionable outfits, and a few street vendors.*

Sat 19 June 1944 *On duty. Bought some fruit, plums and apricots from a small boat alongside us. Listened to marine band on flight deck at dinner time. Now heading E. Watched Algiers become smaller in the distance. Could only see one building clearly:- Hotel Aletti, Casino Municipal. Wrote to Ken and family.*

Tues 20 June 1944 *Passing along North African coast. Large tracts of beautiful white sand. Mountains. Small islands. Passed Malta. Later Captain spoke, says we're bound for port, maybe Alexandria, Tunis or Cyprus.*

Wed 21 June 1944 *Passed Tripoli. Funeral service for Air Crew on Flight Deck. RIP.*

BANTLING

Fri 23 June 1944 Alexandria. Proceeded ashore with Streaky at 13.30hr. We hired a carriage that took us through the native quarters to the town centre. Mohamed Ali Square is a lovely sight, palms etc. Had our photographs taken there. Ate chicken, eggs, bananas and lots of peace-time luxuries.

BANTLING

69 Ellen. Stockwell. 1944.

She raises her face to the warm sunshine for the first time in months, letting it bathe her eyelids, her cheeks and – oh sod it for once, let's unpin the damn thing – her hatless head. When she opens her eyes again, who's there but Arthur, on the other side of the road, beaming at her, nodding his approval, his amusement at her boldness. There's still late blossom on the trees behind him. He has a fine-shaped figure and he's looking at her full-face with so much love it takes her breath away. She waves her hat at him. It's as though somebody has lit a beacon inside him. She can feel the same pure fire within herself.

He's gone.

Her heart stops.

She cannot breathe.

There he is again, popping out from behind a passing tram. He's laughing at her, smiling at her, delighted that he's caught her unawares. He's playing such a lovely trick on her. He's the best-looking man on the street, has the broadest shoulders, the thickest, shiniest hair.

And it's such a beautiful day. There's nothing better than an early summer day. And if she hadn't been so determined, so clever, she'd still be holed up in the house with Mrs Dawson making out she's not Ellen's jailer.

BANTLING

She can't help herself. She waves her hat at Arthur again, a big, broad, heart-felt swing that uses her whole arm, that knocks the hat of the person standing next to her and earns her a few grumpy mutters. They should understand. Arthur is back from the war! At last! Her cheers are the least he deserves.

Sod them all.

Fancy Felix thinking he can keep her prisoner. What a ridiculous man he is. And what a ridiculous way for her to live, always scurrying around him, knitting, knitting and pretending not to notice the smells he makes. Now here is Arthur, finally come to rescue her, here on funny old Kennington Park Road. And not a moment too soon. Poor Felix. He'll miss her. Perhaps Mrs Dawson will comfort him.

It's too warm for her overcoat. Why on earth did she put it on? Most likely some busybody made her do it.

Another tram and a cart heaped with God-knows-what make a wall between them again. It's like playing cuckoo with a child, ducking behind your hands and popping your face out from different sides of your palms, making the child squeal with delight. Ellen will play that game with her own little ones, one day. One day soon.

Somebody tries to give her back her coat, keeps telling her she's dropped it, as though she didn't know, as though that wasn't what she meant to do. She won't need it where she's going.

BANTLING

Arthur's there again, still there, still waiting. It's no dream, and he's laughing at the fuss people are making around her.

It's the best birthday present she could have.

She'd forgotten it was her birthday. And so had that other man. Felix, he calls himself, though there's nothing cheerful about him. Trust Arthur to remember her special day.

He's as young as ever, but he's filled out, become a man, a man to share her bed. And about time. Eighteen she might be, but she's a woman now and has waited far too long.

Arthur's gone again. Whenever did Kennington Park Road get so busy? Don't they know there's a war on? Why is everyone glaring at her? Surely they've heard that laughter is the best medicine for life's ills?

There he is again, still laughing sweetly at her surprise, as handsome as he ever was. He's calling her. He's holding a bunch of glittery balloons. In her silliness, she'd mistaken them for those barrage whatsits hanging above the city to confuse the enemy. But for the life of her she cannot recall who the enemy is these days, nor why they are at war. It is beyond her why people should hate each other when it is so easy to feel nothing but warmth and affection for the whole world.

How on earth could she have forgotten her eighteenth birthday? Arthur has remembered, bless him. This time, Ellen will put her foot down, her dainty pretty foot that Arthur so admires, and demand that Mother allow the engagement. Ellen has learnt from her mistakes, has been given a second a chance. This time she chooses Arthur, come what may. She will not marry Felix this time. History will not repeat itself.

Arthur's beckoning her now, stepping towards her. Since he went away, she's put up with more than a person should. She's kept her own counsel, done her duty. She's turned the other cheek. Arthur understands how she's forgiven Violet. You have to forgive the ones you love.

Arthur is closer now. He means for her to meet him half-way. There is a tiny sliver of space separating them. The rest is up to her. She only has to cross the glittering tracks.

Courage, Ellen.

You're almost here, Arthur is telling her. Don't take any notice of the fusspots in the crowd.

She's not scared, not in the slightest. There's nothing to be afraid of. The voices are just senseless buzzings in the air, flies to be swatted away.

She waves to him with both arms.

'I'm coming, I'm coming.'

Precious Arthur, you put your finger to your lips and all the silly chatter stops. Calm and quietness, that's what you bring me. The silence to be myself.

Don't waste any more time, Ellen. Step lightly and quickly. Live the life you were always meant to live.

She runs towards him, one step, two steps,

three. There's yelping and blurting, an annoying racket from those who know no better. She bats away the clutching, jealous hands that try to stop her. There's a sudden crack that comes perhaps from inside her, perhaps not, and the air is sucked from her. There is joy and brightness and Arthur's arms wide open to catch her.

BANTLING

70 Sam. HMAC Victorious. 1944.

Sat 24 June 1944 Left Alexandria this morning. Port Said visible now, but darkness setting in. Reached the Canal as darkness fell. Most wonderful evening ever, neither hot nor cold, couldn't feel the air. The sky almost all black velvet, except for a small streak of purple which changed gradually to green and red on the Western horizon. New moon and four stars. Lovely violet searchlight from ship. Saw a few palm silhouettes. Entrancing. Wrote to Ken and family.
Mon 26 June 1944 No land in sight, sea very calm. Had a scrap up - RAF Beaufighters sent up. Lots of flying fish.
Tues 27 June 1944 Still cruising along. The water is covered in yellow and green slime. Hellish heat. Atmosphere dense with vapour. FED UP.

A sickly ocean as lifeless as worn aluminium, air that smothers like wet flannel, heat that forces his eyelids down, slimes his face and his arse and makes his tools slip loose of his hands. He's melting in the heat. The sea, pressed flat enough to walk on, creeps past the ship. It's only when he goes below to the hangars that he gets a sense of how deep the ocean is, feels the ship resonating around him, hot as Hades. It's as though the sea is at boiling point, as if he could be cooked alive if he slipped into it. All sorts of strange animals and fish must inhabit it, with coloured stripes and waving tentacles, sucker mouths and revolving eyes. But there's nothing that breaks the surface, no life, no currents, no breeze. It's just them in the Victorious, marooned on the yellow-green sludge.

Sat 30 June 1944 *Got paid.*

Mon 2 July 1944 *Rough seas and wet weather. Drew my first tot. Seasick. Heading for Bombay. Captain says HMS Victorious adopted by War Savings Committee of India, so to be polite. Expect to be in harbour tomorrow.*

Lying in his hammock with a porthole close by. Sunshine on his chest and outside, stonework and the glinting slant of a mooring cable. They've docked in the night and he never noticed.

It's so quiet and so still, and there's a perfume in the air like every promise come good. He's died and come to the place that he doesn't believe in.

The perfume is like nothing he's come across before. Its headiness follows him around the ship until he loses it in the smell of men and the engines' hot grease. He picks it up again on the portside decks, wafting from tiny, white starry flowers growing along the harbour walls.

Mon 3 July 1944 *In harbour 09.00 hrs. Beautiful hills with lots of palms all over the place. Hundreds of islands. Leave to Port Watch. The Town looks okay from here. Daily orders: - All money must be changed before proceeding ashore. Currency is the Rupee and Anna. Rupee = 1s 6d. Exports: - Cotton, tea, rice, silk, ivory etc. Imports: -beer. Birthplace of Rudyard Kipling.*

Tues 4 July 1944 *Independence Day. Shore leave to*

BANTLING

*Starboard watch. Went ashore with Streaky. Had a most wonderful time in Bombay. Had eggs, ham and chips for tea. Bought some sweet limes, oranges, bananas and mangos. Wish I had more cash. The shops and stalls all very interesting. Ivory, silk and other goods.
Fri 7 July 1944 Arrived in Colombo tonight. Different coinage. Bloody nuisance changing money around. Shore leave to Port Watch. Colombo looks okay from the harbour.*
Sat 8 July 1944 *Shore leave to Starboard Watch. Broke. Didn't go ashore. Letter from Mrs Bailey yesterday.*

It's decent of Mrs B to write and she does her best with her letters. He'd rather get them than not, because it's always good to know he's missed, but they make for pretty glum reading. There's probably not a lot of cheery news, though at least there's been no more really heavy bombing in London. Cora's posted out of London, on gun sites in the thick of it. Seems she doesn't mind the ATS, though Mrs B can't help but worry for her. She tells him where to send letters that will get through to her. Ken's away most of the time too, what with the firm being evacuated to make sure they keep going, but loose lips in mind, Mrs B can't say where or what sort of work. Her Don's somewhere in the Far East, she thinks. He hopes they've not got too much cause for worry where Don's concerned. He's got a lot of time for Cora's brother. Don never kicked up a fuss when Ken decided Sam could lodge with them after Harry threw him out, let Sam share his room, even his saggy bed and his eternal snuffling and bad jokes. Good luck, mate.

Sun 9 July 1944 *Same routine as Saturday. Wrote to Ken, Mrs Bailey and family. Wrote to Cora. Victorious set out on 6th operation with 3 other carriers. Indomitable, Indefatigable & Illustrious. Heavy swell. Heading E.*

BANTLING

71 Felix. Stockwell. 1944.

Stockwell, London SW9, 19th September 1944
Dear Mrs Landon, my dear Violet,
I have only recently seen your letter dated November 1940. To my knowledge, you never had a reply, for which please accept my heartfelt apologies. I have of course heard of the poundings delivered to Hull and I pray this letter will reach you despite the unimaginable turmoil and upheaval in that poor city. I would be so grateful to hear that you and your family are safe and well.

My wife passed away recently. I came across your letters while clearing her effects. For whatever reason, I had not seen them before. In the most recent one, as in all of them, you ask for news of your son. I do not believe in stirring up the past unnecessarily, but as you say, we live in uncertain times. Also, you are old enough to know your own mind, as is Samuel. He came to see me shortly before hostilities were declared, seeking information about his origins. Though not quite sixteen he had recently discovered he was not who he had grown up thinking himself to be. I could not tell him very much at all, as I did not know where you were nor if you would welcome him looking for you. I told him his name, and yours, and some thin facts about you. He went away rather disappointed. I had the impression of a sensitive young man turned out into an indifferent world.

I believe he returned and met Mrs Holcroft shortly

afterwards. Her mind was somewhat confused by then, and I fear he did not learn much from her either.

I am happy to share the little I know. The Wingrove family lived almost alongside the canal in Peckham, an area of warehouses and ship-building, in Stanton Street, number 5. I visited them once many years ago, but I can no longer remember what prompted me to do so. Forgive an old man for keeping this information to himself. I did not know your whereabouts. Perhaps I feared to prod the tiger. I had promised my wife to respect her decision about a clean break being the best for all concerned. I saw Samuel – he must have been about seven or eight – and he seemed to be doing well. He was recovering from an incident where the children playing on a bed upstairs had caused it to collapse, causing him a minor injury. I 'lent' the family £2.0s.0d to help towards the repairs, as Samuel seemed to be the main culprit, according to Mr Wingrove. I did not try to get it back. It was you who taught me to keep those records, and Mrs Dawson (do you remember her?) was able to put her hand on them the other day and so I was reminded of the incident.

Mrs Wingrove doted on Samuel – Mrs Holcroft was not mistaken about that. I might be confused with the passage of time, but I seem to recall that Mrs Wingrove told me that Samuel, Timmy as they called him, brought her back from deathly anguish after a still-birth. It was clear when he visited me many years later that Samuel cared deeply for her, less so perhaps for her husband, though Mr Wingrove was a decent man from what I remember, a hard worker and former soldier and I am sure he did all he could to provide for his family. They were not well-off, and the area was run-down, but the home was clean and Mrs Wingrove was a regular user of the lending library and made sure Samuel did his homework.

Before the war there was talk of clearances of some humbler dwellings and slums around the canal. Estates of bright new accommodation were planned. Of course, since then, Hitler has had his go at London too. I went back Stanton Street yesterday, but the family is long gone, as are most of the houses. Apparently, Alice Wingrove passed away soon after Samuel's visit to me and the family moved, together or separately, the few remaining residents of the street did not know nor where to.

I wish you all the best in your search, and hope it does not bring you more heartbreak. In my experience, reunions such as you seek are rare and often painful for one, both or all parties.

With the benefit of hindsight, Mrs Holcroft and I perhaps acted hastily, making such a decision on your behalf. I comfort myself that some good came out of it, that you made a happy marriage and created a family, which Mrs Holcroft anticipated so many years ago.

I do remember the shock hit you hard at the time. Please forgive an old man for any unintentional distress he might have caused, and please let me know how you get on. Hattie Dawson asks to be remembered to you. You, Samuel and your family are in my prayers.

BANTLING

*Yours most sincerely,
Reverend Felix Holcroft*

BANTLING

72 Sam. HMAC Victorious. 1945.

Tues 2 January 1945 *Duty mechanic tonight. To bed very late. Fed up.*
Wed 3 January 1945 *Nice and calm. Had another touch of sunburn. Air Sea patrol took off on catapult accelerator. Bombed-up ready for action early tomorrow. 2000lb bomb loads. 19 bomber Avengers, 35 Corsair fighters.*
Thurs 4 January 1945 *04.30 Wakey-Wakey. Action stations 05.20. Torpedo Bomber Reconnaissance Avengers took off 6.50. Was in Stand-By Action Crash Party. No crashes. One TBR Avenger lost, crew safe, picked up by destroyer. Jap aircraft – bogeys – flying nearby. Action very successful. First degree of readiness for enemy attack. 7 Jap Aircraft. Only 4 bombs dropped. Guns opened up and then our fighters went into the chase. Bombs landed ¼ mile starboard side.*
Fri 5 Jan 1945 *Steering back. Uneventful. Plenty corn beef.*
Sat 6 Jan 1945 *All day at sea. Still steering back. Small flying programme. Duty mechanic. HARD WORK. Wrote to Ken and family. Wrote to Cora. Water rationing for second day. Heat on mess deck is hellish, hangars worse. Expect to be in harbour tomorrow. Letter from Cora. Yahoo! Most beautiful sunset. Pictures at night in hangar "Lady in the Dark." WOW! Head down at 23.00 hrs.*

BANTLING

Wed 17 Jan 1945 7th operation. Torrential rain. A/craft carriers Indomitable, Illustrious, Indefatigable and us. K.G.V. cruisers, destroyers. Our biggest operation so far.

Thurs 18 Jan 1945 Crossed equator for 4th time. Hellish weather. Wet! Ops continue against refineries in Sumatra. HMS Ceylon caught up with us. Brought our mail. Too rough to receive it. Fed up.

Fri 19 Jan 1945 Refuelled at Freemantle after ops, then returned and continued with bombardment. 3rd and worst day of torrential rain, never seen so much, ever. No flying.

Sat 20 January 1945 Captain says:- 'Very hard times ahead.' Can't see how it can get much worse. Third day of water controls. Still rough weather. RAIN & RAIN. Embarked mail from destroyer. Letter from Cora. Don a POW, poor sod. All cruisers and destroyers oiling. Expect to strike on Monday. Biggest operation Fleet Air Arm ever had.

Cora's life can't be a bed of roses, but she fills up the pages with news and gossip about the other ack-ack girls and what a laugh they have. He doesn't know any of their names, has to look back at her earlier letters to make sense of her tales. Sometimes the earlier letter gets to him weeks afterwards. She goes on about catching up with her mum and dad from time to time. On a bad day, he feels – he knows it's not fair – he feels he's out in the cold staring at happy families cuddled up together on the other side of a brightly lit window. Then his mood lifts and her letters are a door onto her life that she's opening for him, inviting him inside.

Sat 27 January 1945 *Saw good film last night "Destination Tokyo" while sailing into vicinity of North Java. Been refuelling all day. Returning now to attack same objective as before. Enemy aircraft scare. Captain says we won't leave until Mana is obliterated completely. Water supply not too good.*

BANTLING

73 Sam. Sydney. 1945.

Sun 11 Feb 1945 Entered Sydney harbour. Looks like a marvellous place. Huge bridge. Lots of trees, beaches.
Tues 13 Feb 1945 Hospitality everywhere. Plenty beer! Wine! Got drunk. Sherry. Muscatel. Port. Ate every kind of fruit. Went to the Trocadero. Had to sleep on the jetty at Woolloomooloo.
Sun 18 Feb 1945 On board. Broke. Fed up. Make and mend.
Wed 21 Feb 1945 Invited to spend day at Kogarah Bay with Mr and Mrs Hartley, part of hospitality group. He's on a few days' leave too. Had a lovely time. Swimming. Ice-cream. Fruit. Milkshakes
Sat 24 Feb 1945 Photographs, drinking at Russian Club with Reg and Eve H, sightseeing, sun bathing and long lie-ins. Leave is just marvellous. 2 letters from Cora.

The basement of an office block just down the road from a big station seems a strange place to have a nightclub. There again, what does he know about nightclubs? Lock-ins down the Old Kent Road and standing to attention outside officers' parties on the ship are about the size of it for him.

'Mr and Mrs Hartley, you are very, very velcome,' says the woman inside the door. She's the most regal-looking creature he's ever been within a mile of, tons more imperious-looking than the pictures he's seen of the royal family. A streak of white hair in a jet-black mass and the face of a thoroughbred, as Ma might have said, all sharp bones and hollow cheeks, no flab under her chin, head balanced high on the straightest back he's seen out of uniform and wearing clothes of the sort usually modelled on the other side of plate glass. She'd have given the French ladies in Algiers a fair run for their money. And he reckons she knows it, too.

Reggo puts his lips to her hand. 'Mrs Koslova', he says. 'As beautiful as the night is promising.'

She's looking the three of them over. Reggo is in his Australian army uniform and Mrs Hartley is well-turned out, trim in a powder-blue suit, a little hat on her wavy blond hair. He thinks that he won't pass muster in his rig, he's no officer after all, that she'll not let him in. Instead, she raises a single eyebrow at Reg, kisses Mrs Hartley on both cheeks, just like the French women in Algiers greeted each other, then ushers them all through draped curtains. He gives her his smile and starts to salute, but she's already turned around & snapped her fingers.

'Valentina!'

Her voice is deep and she speaks imperious English with a heavy foreign accent.

She's beckoning a girl in a fancy-dress peasant costume, all ribbons and embroidered flowers and flowery doo-das on her head. Underneath the artificial flowers her hair's so black it's almost blue and as straight as can be. It's a pretty ropey cut though, as though someone has upturned the proverbial on her head and chopped around it.

Behind the curtain, it's less like black-out and more like one of those American movies they show onboard. Assorted small tables, dim lighting, drifting blue smoke from women with cigarette holders and a little stage with an upright piano on it.

The young woman leads them across the nightclub and seats them near the piano. Almost the only lighting comes from low lamps on the tables, beaded pink cloths draped over the shades.

Mrs Hartley orders up little bits of this and that for them.

'You're our guest, Sammy,' they both insist, and though he's not used to not paying his way, it doesn't feel right to say no.

Pickled fish so much sweeter than soused herrings, pickled mushrooms, a salad of cooked peas, carrots, potatoes and beetroot, bowls of purple-red soup. She tells him it's made from beetroot and cabbage, but it's so tasty it can't possibly be true. Mind you, he'd eat almost anything these days after the miserable grub on the Victorious. He'd be happy with the bread and butter by itself. It's the real McCoy after all those months of hard sea biscuits and half-cooked dough. He can't get enough of it.

He watches Mrs Koslova progress around the room like an empress, a word here and there to the favoured few, topping up glasses and calling orders over her shoulder. She gets a lot of attention. She's been a beauty in her time, and doesn't she half know it.

All around, there are conversations in foreign languages, people making themselves understood one way or another, serious looks, a few wide-open laughs and loud toasts to world peace, international co-operation and the end of dictatorships, and quieter, sadder discussions. It's not what he's used to, but he doesn't feel as out of place as he probably should.

It turns out that the girl slaving away on a Saturday night in the peasant get-up is Mrs Koslova's daughter. Funny, that.

It's a bit of a surprise when the girl sits down during her break to have a cigarette with them. Valya, she calls herself.

In the pinkish lighting, such as it is, there's something Chinese or Japanese about her, a touch of the Orient about the girl's colouring and the delicacy of the bones shaping her cheeks and nose. She's not showy, but pretty enough in her own sort of way. Nice mouth, full and luscious.

It might be a story the Hartley's have heard before, but he wants to know where Valentina ... sorry, Valya ... and her parents come from, how they ended up where they have, what brought them so far.

Hmmm. Valya was too little at the time to remember much about the old days. For all she was born in Siberia, she's grown up in Sydney for the most part. Her parents lived aristocratic lives before the revolution, that much she's had drummed into her, with servants and carriages and a goldmine near Chita that made Momma's father's fortune. He put some of his money into good works, founding an orphanage and a school in Chita and so forth. He was mayor, at some point.

'Poppa was a cavalry officer, from a military family stretching back to Peter the Great. He commanded the Czar's troops during the Patriotic War from nineteen fourteen to nineteen eighteen and afterwards he went to Siberia to join the Cossacks fighting the Bolsheviks. He crossed Lake Baikal when it was frozen solid. He's still got his curved sabre and his rifle with its mother-of-pearl decoration.'

There's lemonade and coffee on offer, and tea with lemon or milk.

'My grandfather, Momma's father, had bought land in Manchuria, miles of forest and plains, so the whole family escaped there when the Whites realised that they'd lost the war. My grand-parents, my mother's sisters, their husbands. My mother's younger brother. Poppa. Servants. And me. I was just a toddler.'

It's like a fairy-tale, a magical world he might have dreamt up way back when.

Valya's face becomes dreamy. There was a beloved gardener and a dog she adored and endless waving grass. She was happy while they stayed.

'Cucumbers fresh from the vines. I've not tasted their

like since. It didn't last, of course, and we were lucky to get out of there ahead of the Japanese. Momma's father died. Some of the family went back to Russia, some of us washed up in Sydney or Melbourne. The others are dead or scattered on the four winds. I'll always be thankful to Australia for taking us in, Chinky-looking reffos that we are.'

Mrs Hartley tuts and shakes her head. Reg looks embarrassed.

'Don't say that,' says Reg. 'Nobody thinks that of any of you. I'd call you glamorous and exotic.'

'You might have been refugees,' says Sam. 'Once, not any more,' and he believes it while he's saying the words. But one glance from Valya and he feels like a fool. Once an outsider, always an outsider. He of all people should know that. It's crying shame she's had to learn it too.

Knowing that you don't fit in. She and he have that in common. Perhaps it's not always such a bad place to be, not if there are other people on the outside with you

'The main thing, the only thing that counts, is being safe,' continues Valya. 'In Manchuria, we were running away from the Bolshevists. Only moments later we were running from the Japanese. Like most of the people in this room, we ended up here by chance. Virtually the only things my parents brought with them were a couple of astrakhan jackets, Momma's hatbox from St Petersburg and Poppa's stash of White Russian bonds for when the

BANTLING

counter-revolutionaries get the upper hand again. Plus his surveying kit. He worked on building the Harbour Bridge, you know.'

He can't help smiling. It's so foreign, a world apart. Yet, here he is, Sam Bantling, pushing up into the middle of it. As Valya talks, he imagines the blue-shadowed snow, the elegant soirées, plains and forests and high grasses, the loyalties and dreams that can't be set aside no matter how events turn out.

'One day, when all this is over, I want to travel to Europe, America, everywhere,' she says. 'If you come from somewhere else, if you're different, if you don't belong anywhere in particular, you can fit in everywhere. I've always dreamed of England, of London. When the war's over, I want to go there, to see all the culture, the pretty places I've read about. Belsize Park, Kensington, Harrow-on-the-Hill, Richmond.'

The London she imagines from her books might exist, or have existed once upon a time, but it's not the town he knows. It never was. He looks down at his plate. Butter. Tomatoes. Mincemeat. They've got it easy here, a better class of make-and-mend. He's a long way from home, whatever, wherever, that might be.

He's not got the sense to bite his tongue, to keep the words to himself.

'London's dark all the time. Bomb sites, empty museums, blacked out windows, families split up. Everyone's always on edge, wondering if and when the bombing might start up again. Not giving up, not at all, don't get me wrong, but tired, getting more tired. And hungry. Rationing's working, I suppose, more or less, but there's never enough. Having to grow vegetables on every skerrick of land. Never, ever having enough. And I'm not just talking about London.'

'We have worries here in Sydney, too,' Mrs Hartley points out. 'Enemy submarines spotted in the harbour. Darwin's been just about bombed off the map, the Jap subs have more or less blocked us off to the north and our boys are out there fighting alongside your mob.'

'Not to mention bloody bombings in Broome,' mutters Reg.

'It's not the same,' he says. 'In London, all over the country, there's wreckage.'

'But life, even survival itself, is more than air and food. People are still hungry for music and theatre and paintings,' says Valya. 'To be with other people and be part of something older and grander than the difficult present. We hear about them on the news, the concerts, the theatres carrying on. It gives some meaning to all this sacrifice.'

He ploughs on as though he hasn't heard. 'Lives, homes, businesses, parks, tube stations, roads, hospitals, everything so battered and changed that even if you used to know the place like the back of your hand you can't find your way around anymore. Hardly anybody's got time for museums and the like. They can't be bothered.'

BANTLING

There's a horrible silence. Him and his big mouth.

Valya stands up. She turns her head away from him. She's not very good at hiding what she feels. 'You're so ungrateful, you English,' she says. 'You never change.'

He starts to apologise, to say that he's talking through his hat, that she's right, people are packing into concerts at lunchtime, helping to keep their spirits up, reminding them there's something worth fighting for. He tries to tell her about going with Ma and all those other people to see Picasso's painting about war.

She's faster, scraping the chair legs against the floor.

'All those young Australian men sacrificing themselves for England,' says Valya. She looks furious. 'What about them? What's England ever done for them? Do you even remember all the Australians who died at Gallipoli?'

Now, if you'll excuse her, she's got to get back to work.

'She had bad news about a friend last week,' says Mrs Hartley as they watch her walk away

'And she's got a point as lots of Aussies see it,' says Reg. 'A lot of our boys, New Zealanders as well, are in Burma and thereabouts, hand-to-hand with the enemy. An awful lot of them have been taken prisoner or worse.'

He's been a rat and it's too late to say sorry.

He tries to catch Valya's eye once or twice. Putting down drinks or picking them up from their table she manages not to look at him. Even if they never meet again, he can't leave it like this.

He corners her before he heads off, tells her he's been a lout. It was frustration and tiredness talking, but it's no excuse. He's sorry about her friend. He's lost mates too. It's a filthy business. It gets him down sometimes. Please say she won't think too badly of him.

When she looks at him, her eyes are as grey as a hillside in November rain. They're too sad for a bloke with only a couple of days' leave in front of him, and anyway, he gets the impression she's off limits and so is he, in a manner of speaking, of course, though Cora's a world away and it's anyone's guess what will happen next week, let alone once all this ugliness is finally done and dusted.

He holds out his hand. She'll tell him to stow it if she's got any sense.

Valya looks him over. Her eyebrows slide together as she concentrates. He wonders who it is that she sees with that cool grey gaze.

She covers his hand with hers. A more generous heart than his own.

BANTLING

74 Sam. HMAC Victorious. 1945.

Mon 19 March 1945 *Cleared lower deck. Addressed by Admiral Vian.*
Tues 20 March 1945 *Set out on operation "Iceberg", in conjunction with the Americans. US Taskforce 57.*
Wed 21 March 1945 *Expect to be 1 month or 18 days at sea. Objective: – to prevent Jap aircraft from being used. Heading north of Formosa*
Fri 23 March 1945 *Longer Action Stations expected from now.*
Sat 24 March 1945 *Worked hard. D-Day tomorrow Monday. Action crash party. Spent evening listening to Streaky playing guitar in the battery room.*
Sun 25 March 1945 *Lots of church services. Wrote to Cora and Ken & Mrs Bailey. Spent evening with Streaky and Jock. Spoke about days gone by.*

Against the noise of the engines and the banging and booming of the ocean around the ship and the smells of hot metal and oil he lists the games of his boyhood. Head under blanket to shut out the bulkhead lights, too bright for sleep, too dim if you're making your way around. If he can list all the games, he might sleep. He might at least not think about what's coming tomorrow.

When they'd had a few pennies, he and Bertie used to toss them against a wall to see whose landed closest, and then that person would throw them all in the air and collect the ones that came down heads up. Tails went to the other one. Wonder where Bert is now? Spansy was better, more skill involved, tossing your coins against the wall to land close enough to the other bloke's so you could span from your money to his with your hand. Mind you, you had to make sure the other lad's hand wasn't a deal bigger than your own. Cards. Brag when there was a gang of them, playing for whatever they had to hand. And Banker. Tops, of course, whipping them with a shoelace tied to a stick, and seeing whose spun the longest. Marbles. Whatever happened to his lucky marble, the one like a tiger's eye?

Sometimes they'd make their way up the towpath to Rotherhithe and Cherry Garden Pier and clamber about seeing what they could find that the porters had dropped. Peanuts in their figure of eight shells, mostly. They'd watch the sticklebacks and sometimes on a hot day some of the lads would dive in. Not him. Not since he jumped off the wharf and had to be pulled out more dead than alive. He'd sunk like a stone.

Keep thinking about on sitting on Platform Wharf in the sunshine and watching the others lark around in the river.

Don't think about the waters around you now, just a sheet of metal between you and the deep.

It's best he never learned to swim. If he goes over the side or the ship goes down it'll all be over that much quicker.

BANTLING

Cricket, with that funny crooked old bat.

Leapfrog, over the posts along the side of the street.

Throwing tennis balls over the roofs of the terrace.

The hammock swings, and something on the floor rolls away and dings against the bulkhead. At least he's found a place to hang his hammock tonight, but the space is too short and he can't stretch out.

Where'd he get to?

Catching birds with a trap made from old bricks and pieces of wood over on the wasteland. Kicking balls around, of course, and swinging your leg, left then right then left then right over a bouncing ball until you were out. Some rhyme went with it. Skipping with the girls when you were just a little tyke, but only when the other lads weren't around to call you a sissy. Messing around in the aireys that ran between and in front of the terraces, tying door knockers together across from one side of the alley to the other. Lift, bang, lift, bang, from side to the other as one woman answered the knock, then closed her door and started the banging off across the way. Bicycles, when they could lay their hands on one. Sixpence to hire an old heap. No brakes except your foot on the front wheel. Scooters that he and Bertie, well mostly Bertie, knocked together from two planks of wood, some screw-eyes, a nut, a bolt and two ball-bearing for wheels. Sneaking in the back way to the picture houses when they could. The Tower, the Gaumont and the Peckham Odeon at Goose Green. Swings and the pole in the park, one arm in the sling of the rope, whirling round and round in the air for a long while if you got a good run at it. Or you could stand and watch the girls and try to see their knickers as they whizzed by. Hanging onto the backs of carts and trams and riding for free. Gobbing contests. Ice-creams from Giuliano's. Water ice and milk ice, a penny a wafer. What was that damn rhyme that went with the ball game? *One two three a lairy, my ball's down the airey.* Bert was bigger than him, but the so-called maggot was quicker and lighter on his feet. Used to drive Bert crazy. Where was Bert these days? He'd never know, if Harry had anything to do with it. Bert could be a mean bastard, but he wasn't going to get another brother in a hurry. They used to mess around on the towpath and in the timber yards where they weren't meant to be, keeping the local rozzer on his toes, and the water bailiffs too. Poor old Ma, she must have been worried sick about them half the time. Swapping cigarette cards of footballers, actresses and flash cars.

Jumping on Ma and Harry's bed. Did that count? Him and Doris used to do that, until the bed leg went through the ceiling and Harry near enough skinned him alive. Even Ma couldn't save him from that thrashing, not once his lip had healed. Fetching beer home in a jug from the Swan, scooping up the foamy head with one finger and hoping no-one would notice. Picking up the scraps of wood along the canal path and in the wood yards to heat Ma's copper or to hawk around the houses at a half-penny a bundle.

Snakes and ladders. Ludo.

Sometimes they'd sweet-talk road-workers into letting them have tarry logs to burn, even going up to the Council Yard every now and then if they could get their hands on a pram. That's where the old logs were stored until they were reused, but the ones that weren't good enough for the roads were sold off for tuppence a sackload and they'd load them into the pram. What a stink they made. Put out a good heat, but even now just the thought makes his nose crinkle. Funny, he can hear all the bells and sirens though he doesn't remember them. Perhaps the yardmen think they've nicked the decent logs. They're making a bloody racket.

Sweet Jesus, it's wakey-wakey. Already. He's sick to his stomach.

Mon 26 March 1945 *Action Stations. Bombed islands between Formosa and Japan. Sailing 130 miles from Japan, ran into typhoon.*
Tues 27 March 1945 *Action stations. Still making a nuisance of ourselves. Bombed Jap Aerodrome. No Jap bogeys.*
Wed 28 March 1945 *Sailing to meet oilers to refuel. Sighted oilers. Uneventful. Liberators sighted.*
Fri 30 March 1945 *Full speed, heading back. Kind of rough.*
Sat 31 March 1945 *Left school this day 1937. Action*

stations. Indefatigable got a suicide bomber. Damage negligible. Plenty enemy bombing, one destroyer damaged. Jap aerodromes bombed. Action successful.

Cora's got into his blood. *Darling*, she writes. *Dearest darling. Sweet pea, sweetheart, my life, my love*, they write to each other. *I miss you.* As soon as he's read one letter, he's waiting for the next, mixed blessing that they are

If he gets out of this alive, he'll make a bee-line for Cora and settle down with her. He doesn't want to raise her hopes. *If* is a big, big words these days, and there's no use her making too many plans. It would only be the worse for her if he never makes it home.

My sweet, he writes back. *Sweet baby.*

Do your chances get better or worse the longer you don't bite the dust?

Sun 1 April 1945 *Easter Day. ACTION STATIONS. Americans landed Okinawa. Suicide bomber grazed port side forward. No damage done. 3 casualties. Jap a/craft shot up.*
Mon 2 April 1945 *Heading back to oilers. Very rough. Still in Jap waters. Hope to have decent sleep tonight! 14th day at sea.*
Thurs 5 April 1945 *Heading back for another dig. Action tomorrow early 0.4.30 hrs. Grub not bad. No water rationing.*
Fri 6 April 1945 *Action stations. Avenger crashed on*

BANTLING

crane and jumbo. Plenty bogeys. 4 Japs shot down. 1 sea-fire near Illustrious. More airfields bombed. A/craft strafed. Two twin engine bombers shot down

Sat 14 April 1945 *Somewhere South of Formosa. Illustrious left for home. HMAC Formidable joined us today. Posted letters. Jam Session on mess deck. Drums piano bass trumpet. Streaky played a 'blues' song that a Negro US Marine taught him. First one I've ever heard.*

Mon 16 April 1945 *ACTION STATIONS. Bombed Ishigaki. Americans on Iwo Jima opened fire on some bogeys. Also told about NEW TYPE of weapon: - flying bomb cum suicide plane.*

Tues 17 April *ACTION STATIONS. This new Jap weapon has been launched against us quite a bit, but no bad damage yet. Heading back to oilers. Task forces 57 & 58 have now accounted for 1600 Japanese aircraft.*

Wed 18 April *Rest of fleet oiled today. Nothing special happened. Make & mend. Jam session this evening with drums, guitar, piano, trumpet. Captain spoke to us.*

Fri 20 April 1945 *Happy 22nd birthday, Sam. Joined Fleet Air Arm this day in 1941. Sucker. ACTION STATIONS. No sign of Japs today. WEATHER CHOPPY. Finished reading book – 'She' – Rider Haggard. Passed it on to Streaky.*

Sat 21 April 1945 *Heading back for Philippine Islands. Getting warm now. Corn beef today. Bread's just dough. Water rationed again.*

Sun 22 April 1945 *Fed up. Got last month's pay.*

BANTLING

Wed 25 April 1945 *Got mail. Received two bottles of beer. Two Corsairs – 137-138 joining 1836 squadron.*
Fri 27 April 1945 *Got two bottles of beer. Saw movie picture COVER GIRL. First dame I've seen for ages.*
Sat 28 April 1945 *Air raid last night*
Sun 29 April 1945
HMS Deerhound –V– HMS Victorious

Tug O'War	*Won*
Fencing	*Won*
Uckers	*Lost*
Darts	*Lost*
Deck Hockey	*Won*

Thurs 3 May 1945 *Captain spoke. Going into action tomorrow, bombarding Okinawa. Wrote some letters tonight.*
Fri 4 May 1945 *Action stations. Both kites up. Formidable and Indomitable struck by suicide bombers. Indefatigable grazed by suicide bomber. Considerable damage. Op successful.*
Sat 5 May 1945 *ACTION STATIONS. Cora's Birthday. Many happy returns, my darling.*
Tues 8 May 1945 *Action Stations. Weather too bad. Ops. postponed. Fed up. Corn dog for grub.*
Wed 9 May 1945 *ACTION STATIONS. Kamikazes struck us, one forward, one aft. Casualties. Struck Formidable. Fire. Bloody mess. 3 funeral Services. Op successful.*

BANTLING

75 Sam. HMAC Victorious. 1945.

The planes are ripping at him from two directions. Two of the buggers, out of the sky like shot from a catapult. The ship's right there in the middle, a sitting duck. One of the planes is heading for him, much too close for comfort, so huge it's blocked out the sun, filled the sky. There's that moment, even less, just before it hits the flight-deck, when he could swear he sees a human-shaped mass inside.

Get your head down, maggot. Hit the deck and roll with the punches. It comes out of the blue, but there's no mistaking that voice.

The flight-deck has stretched as vast as the ocean. It's shrunk to nothing. Falling metal. Noise noise noise noise.

Nowhere to hide. Nowhere to hide.

Weightless, twisting, falling, stretching through nothingness, the deck flying up towards him.

'*Duck and weave, maggot. Roll with the punches.*'

And he takes the advice for what it's worth, so he's curled up when he hits the ground, skittering across the deck, arms snagged around his head.

He can hardly hear anything, only a soft booming on the other side of his skull, that's nothing to do with him, nothing that gives him any sense of up, down, front or back. Smoke as thick and dark as oil. A monstrous roaring. He's digging himself safe

BANTLING

now. Clawing and scratching to make a crawl-hole, away from the flames. He's burning up, on his knees, flaming, inside and out, his eyes about to melt.

He scrapes, burrows, pounds. He can't see a thing, but something's got to give. He's a dead man if there isn't a way through into there, out of here.

Somewhere not far away somebody's calling for their Ma. If there ever was a time for her to lend a hand, this is it.

Snot's streaming out of his nose and mouth. His mouth's full of blood. If he opens his eyes, they sting to hell. Makes no difference in any case. He can't see his hands or what they're doing.

He can't feel a door, a hatch, nothing. He can't find the give in the seam between the solid steel sides of the island and the solid steel of the deck. He turns to water, grinds his head against the wall. He's choking on whatever's in his mouth. Why isn't Ma helping to get rid of it?

And now some bastard, it must be Dad, nobody else would want to stop him and where's Ma when you need her? Dad has his arms around him, is doing his damnedest to drag him away. He knows Sam's near the bolt-hole, that he's on the right track. Dad wants it for himself.

He fights back for all his worth, all elbows and knees and choking for his breath, but it's not a fair fight, the stuffing's still knocked out him. *Hey, hey, hey, easy there.* He's being dragged along the ground, hooked under the arms, bum bouncing and scraping against all manner of God knows what until he's dropped, face flat to the boards, weight on his back. He's heaving and bucking to get Dad, get Harry, off his back.

'Take it easy, Sam, keep breathing.'

Harry has never called him Sam before. Something must be up.

The smoke's clearing in patches.

Metal stretches away in front of his face. He sees running legs and piles of clothing, flames and bits of metal and whipping hoses aslant and skew-whiff and everything out of kilter.

There's air again, but it's hardly worth the candle to breath. There's a mallet banging against his back, making him cough in spite of himself. His throat's full of razor blades and blood.

There's a pair of boots almost up against his face.

He's on his knees, sobbing, retching, trying to breathe, sounding as though something's backfiring inside him. He must be coughing up lumps of lung.

He's flat on his back on the deck. Metal, paint, rubber, wood, grease, vomit, fuel are making a stinking fog all round him and boom-boom-boom go his ears. He rolls over, making himself more comfortable on his side.

If he can lie down, go to sleep, perhaps it will all be over when he wakes up. If he doesn't wake up, it'll be over in any case.

BANTLING

'Sam! Get up, mate,' comes a voice from a million miles away.

Why can't they leave him in peace? He's doing no harm, lying here watching the show.

Sirens sound the all-clear, which must be wrong. The sizzle and roar of water hitting metal glowing through its own steam. Flames flickering inside the smoke over towards port. The tannoy is shouting orders, megaphones blurring the sounds. Officers and crew yelling. Feet pounding across the deck, equipment and machines being dragged and wheeled and pushed.

He's yanked up to sitting. Streaky is in front of him, shaking sense into him, looking as worried as hell.

He's starting to join up the dots.

Two wrecked Jap planes, one towards the stern, one near the bow, sending great thick black plumes up into the sky and swirling across the decks.

He's starting to get his bearings.

Over there, one of his Corsairs has been knocked sideways. The lift down to the hangar might have taken a knock as well. There's steam above his head from pipes that dangle free. On the deck, firemen in asbestos suits, docs, stretchers, deck-hands, scorch-marks, hoses, boots, scattered mounds of trousers.

They're not empty heaps of clothing. There are deck-hands inside them. Blokes like him. Used to be blokes like him.

He tests his ankles, bends and straightens his

legs, rolls onto his knees. Streaky grabs his armpits and hauls.

'One, two, three, oop-la.'

On his feet now, throwing up again, Streaky jumping away and swearing at him. That's more like it.

How could you do it? Aim your plane, aim yourself straight at a ship, watch it rushing towards you, never having the faintest chance of making it, and not turn aside, not give yourself even that tiny, useless chance? Thurs 10 May 1945 *Refuelled today. Mail from destroyer. Wounded taken off. Flight deck patched up. Officer died today. Both legs crushed. RIP.*
Fri 11 May 1945 *Fleet still refuelling from oilers. Heading back to attack again. Action tomorrow early. Keep them crossed.*

Streaky has had a letter from home and he's let it get under his skin. He misses his mum, worries about never seeing her again. Sam tells him to buck up. Adds that mothers aren't always what they're cracked up to be, have been known to bugger off before you've begun, not like some others he could name. He doesn't mean anything by it, just that it's good to have mates who watch out for you, but Streaky takes it the wrong way, thinks Sam's having a go at his mum and he's bloody well not standing for that.

BANTLING

76 Violet. London. 1945.

Euston Station, London, 12th May 1945. Dear Stel, I want you to sit down while you read this. You know I came to London to see if I can find any trace of Sam, but I had another mission too, one that concerned you. I did not tell you beforehand, the chances being it would come to nothing. So dear pal & sister mine, sit down now. The Red Cross has news of your Ralph (nothing about Sam). I have been from pillar to post here in London & hung around in more queues than a shopping bag, but it's been worth it. They tell me he is – was – taken prisoner. Alive. The last they heard he was in Germany. 2 months ago, in March, he appears on their lists of men seen & spoken to by a Red Cross visitor. He was in a hospital, sick, but recovering. The reason you have not heard is probably because of all the moving around you've done in this shemozzle. They say a letter was sent to the old address after the MIA from the army. I told them where you are now, so you will doubtless hear from the authorities in the fullness of time. The address that you can write to is on the piece of paper in this letter. The Red Cross will send letters on. They are hoping to get everyone home soon, but can't say when exactly as it's such early days & prisoners have been moved around by the Germans, so nobody knows where everybody is. All the same, I could hardly believe it when his name showed up on their lists. Oh, Stel, I burst out crying with joy & relief. It's

BANTLING

the first half-way decent news in a long while, though as they made clear, no-one is out of the woods yet. We must hold our breath yet awhile, make do & mend. And wait. As far as my own search goes, there is little enough news. Stanton Street no longer exists. Most of Peckham has been flattened. Everything has gone that might have been there. London is awash with bunting and victory delight, but otherwise sad these days, hardly even patched together over the breaks, though overall it's probably nowhere as shot to pieces as Hull. I walked as much along the canal as I could & spoke to a couple of bargemen, but they didn't know anything. I made my way up & down, over & across the rubble where Stanton Street used to be, hoping that some fragment might call out to me, that the stones would carry some message. Nothing. The closest I got was a pub a few streets away, where the landlord's mum is helping out. She & her husband used to have the pub in Stanton Street itself. The Swan, it was called. She thought she remembered Sam ('Timmy') coming to collect jugs of beer for his 'dad' before the hostilities. She also recalled the wife collecting for the Spanish Republicans, so I felt he was brought up by someone with her heart in the right place. She had an inkling the dad had moved to Balham or thereabouts. There was no-one at the vicarage. I called twice, but the place was shuttered up. No sign of anyone, not even Hattie Dawson. The pretty front garden was a tangle of weeds and flowers gone wild as they want. Somebody's been growing veg in the middle of the little circus, but not yesterday. The

BANTLING

church is in one piece, but had props against it & the windows were boarded up. I suppose they can take those down now. Though the door was open & there were fresh flowers inside, it was empty both times I visited. Reverend H must be getting on. Perhaps he's dead too, it being more than 20 years since I last clapped eyes on him & a while since he wrote. I don't know what I'd say in any case. The old hospital has lost a wing & most of its records. Or at least, they claimed not to have any papers from my time. From there I got myself to Balham. The underground trains are still running & have been all along, what a marvel. No stones singing out to me in Balham any more than in Peckham, but I had a thought about electoral rolls. Blow me down, the library was open, in a way. The lady in charge was kind. She'd never heard of the Wingrove family, no way of locating them without more information. I suppose I looked so aghast she thought I should see for myself & pointed me over to the shelves where they keep the electoral rolls. Oh my, Balham is bigger than you might think. It was chilly sitting there, even in my coat, with the light going, but she let me stay & let me look through them until she closed up shop. Of course, she knew her business. It was hopeless. Stel, I'd been so sure I'd find a trace, some clue or another. Nothing. You'd never believe there are so many streets & they all have a hundred houses or so & every house has two families at least. Of course, on top of that, the electoral rolls haven't changed for the duration, even if I'd known where to start looking. Needles &

BANTLING

haystacks come to mind. But I couldn't stop. I was like a madwoman, turning pages & running my fingers down all the lists of people. All the time I wondered how many are still alive, how many will come back from wherever they are & where is Sam? Where is Sam? I was cross-eyed & a right smeary, blubbing mess by the time she closed up. I was near to missing the train, especially after I stopped by the vicarage again on the off-chance. It was hard enough getting just the Monday off work & I don't know what I'd do if I lost this job. The librarian must have thought I was a charity case, forcing my name & address onto her & making her promise that she'd write to me if she heard anything. Poor woman. All she wanted was to go home & make herself a cup of tea & a hot water bottle & to warm up a bit. Even so, I was glad I'd done it all. I'm not sure I know why – you could say it was all a waste of time, but walking around Peckham, seeing the canalside, crossing over one of the few bridges still left standing, at least I saw some of where he grew up. There's greenery sprouting across the rubble, buddleia and nettles and rosebay willow-herb, nature and spring making a stand in spite of man's worst. I don't know, Stel. I just don't know. Balancing the past, the present & the future, it's an impossible slippery job. I miss my lovelies now I'm away from them, even for just a couple of days. I thank my lucky stars this war, or the most part of it, is over before Billy's old enough to see active service. Just as long as they finish it off in the Pacific soon. Stella's big enough now to look after everyone for a day or so,

BANTLING

can you believe it & manages to keep Lily and George in line. I miss their funny little ways & their different smells. I think I miss Sam, too, but perhaps I have just missed out with him. How can you miss what you've never known? There's a place inside me kept for him, but it's anyone's guess if the real Sam would even want to try & fit it. Perhaps it's the only shadow of a space & now it's filled by my real-life children. I know I've got a lot to be grateful for, especially having not the same worry for Leonard as you have for Ralph. You will let me know as soon as you hear anything, won't you? Probably I should just be happy with what I have, keep my mind on Leonard & our four & not keep fretting about what I haven't got. Nothing's simple, is it Stel? Yours, Violet

BANTLING

77 Sam. HMAC Victorious. 1945.

Wed 16 May 1945 *ACTION STATIONS. Lost my A/C raft No. 138 "Kay". Pilot seen in dinghy 1 mile off coast. Op. successful. Bogeys around.*

He's teamed with Streaky today. Him and Streaky, the two of them and the other mechanics, they just keep at it and at it, going and going and going. There's a raid happening, an air attack, the ship's closed up to action stations, the planes keep coming down off the deck, red-hot some of them, needing to be checked and turned around and sent out again. The hangar's like a tin box on a stove at the best of times. In the heat of the Pacific, it's an inferno. The sweat's pouring off him. Working inside an oven couldn't be worse. The guns going off on deck turn the hangar into a deafening sound-box. He can hardly hear the tannoy above the din. The stink of hot metal and oil gets stuck in his nose and mouth. Even with a rag wrapped around his head, he's blinking stinging sweat away from his eyes as fast as he can. He keeps another rag for that, but it's so smeared with grease and the rest that it's no better than useless.

There's one poor bugger in a Corsair that comes down from the flight deck. His rubber suit is full of holes and leaking blood all over the shop. A couple of blokes heave and drag him out to the casualty station in the washroom flats, blood slopping all over the floor as the ship pitches.

They're up and down from the flight deck, pushing and dragging planes. They're checking struts and tightening nuts, loading bombs and patching holes.

The mess bell sounds. His throat is scorched with thirst. Everyone's going like the clappers. He catches sight of Streaky. He's as red as they come. Sam gestures to him to go get his tea, he'll cover for 5 minutes, but Streaky is still playing silly buggers over that nonsense about mothers, isn't taking any favours from Sam. Cutting off his nose. Now there's no chance of getting to the canteen.

That's makes it the second tea break he's missed. Bugger it. They're down to their overalls and if you didn't need to keep your tools somewhere close, he'd have those off too. Except when you're crawling over planes as hot as frying pans you need something between you and sheet metal. But he's sweating less, so he must be getting used to it. That's good, because you need your eyes and wits about you if you're sending blokes back up in these tin canisters. Come the next break through, he'll make a dash for tea. There might be a lull by then. Come to think of it, he hasn't needed to piss for a while. Must have sweated it all out.

Streaky flakes out and gets carted away. Now there's even more to do. That's the third bell for tea gone west. His head's pounding.

The tools are hot in his hand and there are burn

BANTLING

stripes up his forearms, like Ma used to have from pulling pans from the oven.

Things have slowed. It's dark on deck. They've been at it all day, but the planes are still coming in. He's feeling a bit woozy. He steps back and his hand opens of its own accord, bloody stupid, then his fool legs give way.

He comes to with a whacking great tube sticking out of his nose and his arse burning. He can smell piss. His throat is on fire and he can't speak and all around his bum is sore and raw. Someone's taken sandpaper to his privates.

There's a bloke's face above him, telling him to take it easy, sailor, take it easy. Bloody easy thing for him to say. He feels like he's choking. The doc tells him *big breath in, big breath out*, holds him down with one hand and rips out his nose and his throat with the other. That's what it feels like. He's coughing and rasping. The tube's gone. Someone's got their arm around his back, sitting him up, and there's a mug of tea being held in front of him. He sips. It's hot and sweet, too hot and it scalds when he swallows, but he's greedy for it, for the sweetness, for the wetness.

'Not too fast, lad.'

He's stark bollock naked, sitting in pools of piss on a rubber sheet. When he's able, they get him up and sponge him down. They use sea-water that stings like nettles. Then they put him into a berth, the first proper one he's ever had on board, with a jug of water and a bottle to piss into, telling him he's out of the woods, but not home and dry yet. Keep drinking. Keep pissing. He does what he's told. Hot as it is and as much water as he gets down himself, there's not a trace of sweat on him.

He doesn't know it then, but he finds out. He's been lying in the casualty station being pumped with water for the best part of a day and night. They shake their heads when he asks about Streaky. He doesn't believe them at first.

Nine hours later he's back on duty.

Friday 18 May 1945 *RIP Streaky. ACTION STATIONS. 4 planes crashed on deck yesterday, 1 pilot lost overboard, 3 deck hands killed. Other minor injuries. No bogeys hit us. Water controlled for 6th day. Received my first driving lesson. Lieut. Banning died of injuries. Good officer. Better than most of the rest. RIP.*

Sun 20 May – Wed 23 May *Operations. Operations. Operations. All the bloody time. Have not been ashore since 27th February. No mail. BLOODY FED UP.*

Tues 12 June 1945 *Left Greenock this day 1944. 1st year foreign service completed.*

Thurs 5 July 1945 *Terrific heat. Left Manus. Admiralty Islands. Ops again. Destination Japan. Heading North. Wrote to Cora.*

Fri 6 July 1945. *Still heading North. Wrote to Cora.*

He writes to Cora every chance he gets, sends her

a photo of himself with the other lads in front of one of the Corsairs he looks after. He's never felt further away. It'll be a miracle if that one scrap of paper, folded inside another scrap, in a sack along with thousands of others, swung from the hold of one ship to another, steaming north through all the Jap defences and attacks, crossing the equator, through ports that have been bombed and into London stations much the same, and through the hands of people who've got other things on their mind than whether his letter arrives or not, ever makes it to Poplar, let alone to wherever she's stationed.

And the thought of it finally making it all the way there only makes him feel further away than ever. But writing it reminds him that Sam Bantling, somewhere or other, one time or another, has got a life with his own name on it. In that life, he's not just Air Mechanic FX 98737. That other Sam Bantling sleeps in a bed of his own, can walk out of a thankless job, go to a library with more than 10 books in it and break bread with people who give a toss about him.

Except, as often as not, thinking about how things could be different is the last thing he needs. This is his war, too. Much as he hates it, scared as he is, he reckons he's on the right side. More to the point, those Japanese bogeys are aimed at him just as much as anybody else. The only way out of this mess is with everyone else on board.

What you have to do is not think too much except

about what's on your plate at this very moment. If you fill your head with day-dreams, take your eye off the ball, you'll forget to keep your head down, you'll not know which way to jump when the shit hits the fan.

Then again, writing to Cora, even when there's nothing much to say, reminds him that he hasn't always been in this hell-hole and he might get out one day. It's a thin, tight thread. The letters could end up in a fish's belly. So could he. And it might not even make such a big difference to her. Not in the long run.

Sat 7 July 1945 *Heading North. Lost my life-belt and one flash gear. Have to replace on tick until next pay. Wrote to Cora.*
Sun 8 July 1945 *Oiled at sea. Wrote to Cora tonight.*
Mon 9 July 1945 *Heading North. Wrote to Cora.*
Tues 10 July 1945 *Heading North. Wrote to Cora.*
Sat 14 July 1945 *Expecting to meet Yanks tomorrow. Wrote to Cora tonight.*
Sun 15 July 1945 *Sighted American Fleet. Umpteen carriers. Captain spoke. Now heading for Japanese coast.*
Mon 16 July 1945 *90 miles from Jap coast. 150 miles from Tokyo. Action Stations. No signs of Japs.*
Tues 17 July 1945 *Action Stations. Visibility very bad. Ran into typhoon. One Jap bomber.*
Wed 18 July 1945 *Back to oiling rendezvous. Received one letter from Cora. Posted 3.*
Thurs 19 July 1945 *Left oilers. Heading back for Honshu coast. Passed through typhoon.*

BANTLING

Fri 20 July 1945 *ACTION STATIONS. Visibility bad. Postponed 6 hrs. Fighter strikers flew off. No bogeys.*
Sat 21 July 1945 *ACTION STATIONS*.
Sun 22 July 1945 *FED UP*.
Mon 23 July 1945 *ACTION STATIONS Plenty activity. Plenty Japs.*
Tues 24 July 1945 *ACTION STATIONS. Not very successful due to bad weather. No bogeys.*
Wed 25 July 1945 *ACTION STATIONS. One Jap Zeke crashed about ½ mile starboard beam. Night flying from HMS Formidable.*
Thurs 26 July 1945 *Back to oiling rendezvous. Received letter from Cora. Posted letters. Fed up.*
Fri 27 July 1945 *Oiling at sea. Heading back. Waiting for Japs' answer to surrender offer.*
Sat 28 July 1945 *ACTION STATIONS*
Sun 29 July 1945 *Action Stations. No bogeys. Rather quiet.*
Mon 30 July 1945 *Action Stations Action Stations Action Stations Action Stations. Hellish Hellish HELLISH*
Tues 31 July 1945 *Hanging around. Weather bad. No Japs.*
Wed 1 Aug 1945 *Action Stations. Plenty crashes.*
Thurs 9 August 1945 *ACTION STATIONS. Op not so successful. No bogeys.*
Sat 11 August 1945 *Oiled ready for operation. Op postponed due to typhoon. Captain said 2 new bombs dropped by the Americans. Expect Japs to pack it in.*

BANTLING

Sun 12 August 1945 *Japs surrendered. Captain said we are leaving op area, proceeding to Manus to top up with oil. Either to go to Sydney or go to Japanese port to take over from Japs.*
Sun 19 August 1945 *Manus, Admiralty Islands.*
Fri 24 August 1945 *Arrived Sydney. Shore leave. Up to Kogarah Bay to see the Hartleys. Welcomed like a long-lost little brother. Nice soft bed, clean cool sheets. Eating lots of oysters. Drinking plenty milkshakes.*

BANTLING

78 Sam. Sydney. 1945.

Celebrating at the Russian Club. This time there are no blackout curtains and he's got cash in his pocket. It's less like a nightclub, more like a wedding reception, men mostly in uniforms, some in smart suits, women in flounced-up hats and wearing their furs against the August chills. Reggo is due to go to Burma in a couple of days to repatriate Australian PoWs so he's making the most of his leave. People are milling about between the tables, looking to be in the most wonderful mood. It's like the bleeding League of Nations. The flags and colours of Australia, USSR, America, Canada, France, India, plus more than a few he doesn't recognise, hang side by side all over the club mixed in with Union Jacks. Imperial eagles and photographs of the martyred Tsar and his family hang side by side with the hammer and sickle.

Mostly everyone's a stranger one way or another and everyone's at home and they are all toasting the peace.

There's beer on the menu, which he likes better than the wine even if it's nothing like a decent bitter, as pale as piss and so cold it's got no taste at all. There's muscatel and burgundy, both made in Australia and no worse than Algiers's Vin de Rouge. He'll try anything. The word is there will be no six o'clock shutdown tonight. The bottles will be on the table for as long it takes and the Police won't get a look-in.

Mrs Koslova circulates, posing for photographs with person after person, group after group, table after table, with the clusters of people that include priests in high black headgear, impressive beards and large crosses gleaming on their black-robed chests. Mrs Koslova holds her chin high, doesn't smile for the camera and makes sure she's only photographed from one direction.

'Only ever show your best side,' whispers Valya behind him. 'And you must never be photographed laughing, dahlink. It distorts your face, after all.'

She gives him a big smile that doesn't do her face any harm at all. She'll take a few minutes break with them if they don't mind. He offers her a light.

What would happen if he tried the Algiers' cheek-kissing routine with her?

'This club – Momma was one of the people to really get it going – helped the Medical Aid and Comforts Committee raise almost a million pounds for Russian war relief. Doesn't matter that it's for the communists, not for the moment, not as long as they're her Russian communists.'

Reggo pours her a glass from the icy bottle of vodka.

'For Momma, it's my Russia, right or wrong,' Valya says, blowing smoke over her shoulder.

'Even the Church made its peace with Stalin during the war,' adds Reg. 'They bought tanks for the army.'

BANTLING

'Now everyone's a winner. Holy Russia, Mother Russia, Russia Eternal. Momma's done well by her beloved Russia.'

'And they've done well by us. The Allies couldn't have swung it without them,' says Sam, lifting his glass to hers. 'Here's to all our Russian brothers and sisters, communists and the rest.'

Mrs Hartley, Reggo and Sam all raise their glasses. Valya joins in, toasting thanks to all the brave young men who have sacrificed so much.

He's getting used to this frozen vodka lark. There's a delicious heat as it goes down. Yes, go on then, pour him another, why not?

Why would anybody let themselves be pulled into a war? But what else could they have done, could he have done? You can't just stand by and say it's nothing to do with you. Wouldn't want to, even if they'd let you.

He hears people talking about what they're going to do now they can get on with their lives again. Get an education. Get qualified. Find a girl. Get in touch with the Red Cross. Find a husband. Find a job. Start a business. Start a family. Track down relatives. See the world.

His thoughts, his feelings, foreign or familiar, slip and slither, change their shape, spring up, here then gone, before he can pin down any single one. It's like everything, good or bad. What you take for granted slides away while you blink. All the rules change in a

BANTLING

flash. What's normal one day is turned on its head the next. He can remember what it's like to be under fire, or dreading it, of course he can, he probably won't ever forget, but now it's over he can't imagine being back in the thick of it, not really, even though he can't believe it won't start all over again any minute now. Cora's a long way away. He's got no sense of who or how or where he might be a year from now.

'Here's to being able to take a breather at last,' says Valya. 'You servicemen more than deserve it.'

'Not for all of us,' says Reg. 'Not quite yet. The fat lady might have sung, but someone still has to clear up the stage.'

'To your bright eyes, darling,' chips in Mrs Hartley. 'To everyone's bright eyes.'

'To friends, absent and present.' That's Valya.

She always makes a toast before she so much as takes a sip. And her eyes are very bright. She doesn't look anything like the girls he's known back in England, or seen around. She's a different type altogether. By rights and by old-fashioned rules, given what she's said about herself, given the slant of her cheekbones and the sheer blackness of her hair, she should seem foreign, be out of place. But he can't imagine her being anywhere else but here.

Valya's playing the piano now and another lass is singing along. He doesn't know the tune. All the Russians have joined in the singing, even the sombre-draped priests, and everyone else is clapping along. It's a bit gloomy for his taste, hardly festive, too close to the part of him that wants to have a bit of a cry.

Valya's face is mysterious, full of curves and depths that draw him in the more he looks at her. She seems to sum up something new and modern. She may look foreign on the surface, though even that is less and less clear to him, but she's part of the mix. That's how things should be, will be, from now on. All sorts of people will be, are already, joined up together, like the flags draped around the room. With any luck, it won't matter so much where a bloke sets out from. Or it will, because you can't be yourself without everything you've gone through, but all that old stuff, country, class, money and the rest of it, won't be the be all and end all of it. Touch wood.

He watches her hands. She doesn't have long fingers, but her hands are efficient, capable, strong, dancing their way across black and white keys.

When the music changes, so does the mood. *Rule Britannia. Waltzing Matilda. Australia Song. God Save the King. Advance Australia Fair.* Everyone is as cheery as chips. He flicks through the sheets of music on top of the piano, comes across a few old songs that he knows. He reckons a bit of the old country will go down a treat and he's got a voice that holds enough of a tune. Valya raises her eyebrows when he puts the music on her stand. Never mind the quality, he tells her. Just let it rip. She gives it a go. Her playing's a bit neat and tidy to start with, but after he leads them all in a couple of rounds of *I'm only a Bird in a Gilded Cage* and *Maybe it's because I'm a Londoner*, she loosens up. She's swaying with the music, her fingers going like the clappers and she's grinning away. She's enjoying herself, he can tell. He starts on *My Old Man's a Dustman*.

Mrs Koslova appears by the piano, like an unpleasant magic trick. She says something to her daughter. She's not shouting, but she's not exactly whispering either, and he's close enough to hear her tell *Valentina* that she shouldn't play the piano, that she's not very good, that it doesn't *become* her. It's not a nice tone of voice and it puts an end to the Old Kent Road in Little Russia. Valya closes the piano lid. Momma waits. She doesn't so much as glance at Sam. There's a superior little smile twisting up the beauty of her face. She reminds him of Harry, always cutting him down to size, never liking to see him enjoying himself. It's a bloody shame a girl like Valya has to put up with it too. She's not tough enough.

Now Mrs Koslova turns to Sam and thanks him for his *interesting* songs. Someone calls for more music, and she smiles and puts one elegant hand on her well-shaped chest. *Me?* She graciously agrees, sits down and starts to play another slow dirge. For all he knows, Mrs Koslova is a better musician than her daughter, but that's hardly the point. They're perhaps more alike than they seem, Valya and him. He backs off to their table and Reggo pours him another drink.

BANTLING

Valya stands awkwardly, her face stiffened and blotched red and white.

'Poor girl,' Reggo says. 'That mother of hers leads her a rough dance.'

She sees Sam looking at her, and her face goes even stiffer. He knows it's worse for her that somebody has noticed what's going on. And if he hadn't pushed her, she'd never have belted out those tunes as if she was playing a musical-hall joanna.

She turns and walks very stiffly into the back, and she doesn't come out again before he has to leave.

Mon 3 September 1945… … . *A marvellous time … … … … … … … … .*

… … … . a wonderful time … … … … … … A terrific time … … … … … … . Gee! This Is Great!. … … … … … What a country … … … .!

Wed 12 September 1945 *Spent day out in bush stamping to scare away snakes.*

Fri 14 September 1945 … … … … … … . *What … … … … … . People! More oysters!……………more milkshakes … … … … … more wine … … … . Burgundy … … … … … . more steak, eggs … … … … … Utopia … … … … … … … … … …*

Sat 22 September 1945 *No more cash. It was good while it lasted.*

Sun 23 September 1945 *Become due for Leading Air Mechanic.*

Mon 24 September 1945 *My last Day in Australia (Sydney) Letter from Cora. Can't wait to see her.*

BANTLING

Tues 25 September 1945 *Goodbye Reg and Eve. Bye-bye Sydney, T.T.F.N. Tearful farewell as we sailed out of Woolloomooloo. Marine Band played "Auld Lang Syne", "Now is the Hour" and "Waltzing Matilda." Banners and streamers on the quay.*

They're heading north. Going home, says the captain. It takes a while to sink in. He's come out of it in one piece and with something and someone to head back towards.

Wed 26 September 1945... ... ...   At. ... .. *S E A* ... ... *Show me the Way to go Home*... ... ... *Home* ... ... *Home* ... ... *Home*

79 Sam. London. 1946.

All through October and even into November, London light is as pink as candyfloss. He'd never noticed before, but now he can't miss the sheer pinkness of it. Everywhere he looks, pink. It first hits him walking over the river one late afternoon. It's not just the sky and clouds, but the building and stones and bricks and pavements, as well, even the damaged ones. For weeks, it's like looking through a soft rosy veil. It's not at all like the brazen blue white yellow harshness down on the other side of the world.

It's February 1946 by the time he gets his temporary release. His demob suit isn't bad, wide collar and chalk stripes on navy. He feels pretty damn smart in it. His first drink as a free man tastes special, that's for sure. For longer than he can remember, he's not wearing out his shoulder carting around his damn kitbag.

It's pretty good, even with the feeling that the peace could all come crashing down around his ears, that it'll turn out to be a mistake or a trick. Any moment now he'll find himself frizzling on red-hot planes and dodging the kamikazes again. Just thinking of it churns his guts. It's taking a while not to take so much notice of feeling jumpy all the sodding time.

Winter or habit puts paid to London's pinkness. The

BANTLING

town's as cold and dirty and full of queues as ever. No heating in the trains, no food in the shops. He's living squashed in a hostel.

There are two Londons now. Probably more. He's not even thinking about the haves and have-nots. It's the layout of the place that throws him. In the old London, the one whose alleyways, bus routes, short cuts, landmarks he'd grown up with, he knew how to find suits, favours, pals, a decent pint. The new city has been thrown down on top, like a torn and rumpled cloth skew-wiff on top of another. He sets off to find his way across town, and it all seems fine, he knows exactly where he is and where he's going, then suddenly he doesn't. It's as though the city, *his* city, is playing nasty little tricks on him. Plus, there are not enough jobs to go round. Doesn't mean he's not looking though. Something will come up sooner or later. He'll make sure of it.

Cora's been discharged as well. She and her bunch are beside themselves to see him safe and sound. She's so pleased to see him, keeps staring at him and stroking his hand. Seeing him with all his fingers and toes in one piece means a lot to them, because not all of theirs made it. Ken has lost his older brother and two nephews, merchant seamen in the convoys all three of them. Much worse, worst of all, Ken's own boy, Cora's brother, Sam's mate, Don, captured by the Japs, was beheaded only a couple of days before the A-Bomb was dropped. It gives him the heebie-jeebies just to think about it. God knows what it does to Ken and Mrs Bailey. Six months later, they've both still got that dazed unbelieving look about them when they're not putting on a face for other folk. Sometimes he catches Mrs Bailey looking at him, and he knows she's asking herself how come Sam made it back to her kitchen and her Don didn't. She won't go out unless she really has to. The radio's always on so loud it echoes up and down the stairs and into all the rooms. Mostly, she makes sure that Cora's around, or that her youngest, Sally, is in whatever room that her mother is. She feels safer with Cora and Sally in her sights.

Ken's different. He's like a tap that's been turned off. He's still with the old firm. He's not done too badly on that score. His know-how came in handy when they had to reset all the winders and looms for the new synthetic threads and fabrics for parachutes when the silk supplies dried up. He manages the workshops out of town and three warehouses now, and they're talking about changing some of the machines back to silk production come next year. It means he's still away, out of London for four or five nights out of seven. He doesn't seem to mind. He doesn't seem to mind very much at all these days, just says that it's good to keep busy.

Sam's not sure how or if it makes any difference, but when Ken's around the two of them spend a lot of time together, just the two of them, getting out of the house. It's as though Sam's a piece of tissue paper Ken's wrapped himself in. He stands Ken a pint when he's got the readies – 'Thanks son' – in one pub or another where they're less likely to bump into anyone Ken knew before. They'll make a beer last all night, play shove-ha'penny or backgammon. Or they wander around, end up leaning against the river wall, having a smoke and looking down at the littered foreshore, the filthy water. It's suits them both, not talking about the things you can't talk about, even if they're just about the only things you can think about. Mostly they both keep schtum. When they speak, if they do, it's about football, a neighbour's pigeons, what's been washed up by the river today.

Keeping an eye on Ken, keeping an eye out for him, it's the least Sam can do. It's the most he can do.

'The company might have you back, son, and not just because our lords and masters at Westminster want jobs for the boys coming home,' Ken says one day out of the blue.

He'd only been a kid when he left in '41, he can see that now. He's come back knowing there's more to the world and to himself. What's on offer, something like Ken's life, seems cramped. He doesn't want to be a man doing a boy's job, but he knows enough to know that sometimes that's the only way.

'I'll give it a go. Thanks, Ken,'

The truth is, the thought of the old firm makes him feel as though life's closing in on him, blocking off the chance to strike out, forcing him into the same old patterns. And he doesn't fancy the idea of being ordered about again, and being told what to do and when and where. He had a gutful of all that on board ship, enough to last him life-time.

Still, it's good of Ken to put himself to the bother.

'That's the spirit,' says Ken. 'Mind, the industry's not like it was, but it'll pick up again.'

He's not looking as keen as he might, because Ken squints at him for a bit.

'If you don't mind moving about, they're looking for a salesman to cover the regions. Should make for a change.'

It would suit his itchy feet.

'Fancy yourself as a bit of a mind-reader these days, do you, Ken?'

'It'd mean living out of a suitcase. Can't promise anything, mind. I'll put in a word, then we'll have to wait and see.'

Ken and Mrs Bailey let him stay over sometimes while he finds his feet. On the sofa, it goes without saying, no funny business with Cora, if you please. In any case, it's a break from the hostel. A few times, Aunt Flo in Lewisham gives him a bed and a meal. Flo's fond of him for Alice's sake.

'I never had much time for Harry, especially since he teamed up with that stuck-up cow, Jessie,' she says every time she sees him. It sounds like Harry's not bothered about Flo, either.

He hears that Doris went off to the States with a G.I., and that Bertie was invalided out. He's been training as an electrician and is settled somewhere out in Essex. Sam's glad to hear they're doing all right for themselves, but that's about it. He thinks he probably won't look Bertie up, after all, and Flo nods and says it's probably all for the best.

There's a lot of talk at the Bailey's about a fresh start, meaning him and Cora, but he hardly ever sees her on his own, not for more than a minute or two, when he sneaks up on her doing the washing up or walks to the shops with her. When they get the chance, which is not often enough, he and Cora sit holding hands or feel each other up in the cinema. It's not so easy when Cora's sister, Sally – 'but, she's going to be your sister, too, Sam, you can't mind her coming along' – or one of the cousins is bouncing on the seats next to them or leaning over from behind or kicking the seat backs. Sometimes Mrs Bailey comes with them.

'We can't leave mum at home on her ownsome, can we?'

Those times they sit one on each side of her and there's no chance of any sort of messing around.

The firm comes good. He gets the job, and he's only been back in civvie-street a few months. It's much more than most have got if they weren't born sucking a silver spoon.

On the day before he starts, he and Cora stroll around Victoria Park. Late March, and every week it's looking that little bit different. Some days the frosty grass crunches underneath. Other days, it's as fresh and beautiful as an English spring can be, even here in the battered old park. Cora points out where the gun emplacements were. At one point she'd been based that close to home, but she was still barracked on-site. She'd done everything except fire the bloody guns, she said. Cleaned them, loaded them, operated the searchlights. A few of the girls in her unit had been killed on duty.

The area's still pretty bare and choppy in places, but all around, the trees and grass are brimming with so many greens that they make his eyes water. He'd made himself forget all this softness in the Arctic and down south. He can smell the earth coming back to life, feel the softness in the air when the wind dies down.

'Oh Sam,' she says when he tucks his coat around her, 'I missed you ever so much. I'm dead proud of you, helping to drop that bomb and teaching those Japs a lesson after they did what they did to our Don.'

He doesn't feel quite the same. Perhaps he should. He hated those kamikaze pilots dive-bombing him, hated them so much he could see himself pulling out their innards with his bare hands. He still imagines doing it, given half a chance. The thought of what happened to Don makes his stomach heave. The A-bombs ended the war, no doubt about it. He would most likely be dead otherwise, so he's got to be grateful. But it's a hard circle to square. He's seen photos of those two Japanese cities by now, buildings and people turned to ash and shadows, and he's not sure in his heart it was the right thing to do.

But he can't say that, of course, so he hugs her back.

'It was your letters kept me going through it all, made sure I came back.'

He knows it was only the luck of the draw, but it's what he thinks she wants to hear, and she seems ready enough to believe him. She doesn't seem to notice that he feels on edge most of the time. That's a relief, because he'll stop feeling hemmed in once he's used to being back.

The wind comes up again and the park turns grey. It's bloody cold most of the time and the sun never seems to rise, not properly or for long enough, and the afternoon sky hangs low and heavy enough to crush the pair of them.

Being a travelling rep isn't too bad. Flo's place is only a bus ride from the terminus, for the odd night he's in London, but it's a bit awkward there all the same, and he doesn't want to cause more ructions than he already has. Besides, she's knocking on a bit and he's a bit of a bother, he reckons, especially if he's out late. He never quite knows when he'll be in London, what with one thing and another. His visits tail off.

Life's a bit hand-to-mouth. Mustn't grumble, eh?

His discharge becomes permanent three days after he turns twenty-three. He can breathe easy, at least for the moment, and he wangles being back in London on a Saturday, wants to take Cora dancing. It'll be just him and her, for once, swinging to the band, celebrating his discharge and the future he's got in mind for them both.

It makes for their first proper argument. She's more like her mum than he thought, always has to have a crowd around her. She'd rather make up a party with some of the girls she knows and their blokes. Her old mates are headed back home from their factories in Luton and Huddersfield and they might as well make merry now they're together again after all this time. After all, they're freeing up jobs for blokes like him.

'I can't tell them not to come now, can I? How would that look?'

'As though you and me want to be together. They won't mind the once.'

'And when you're not here, which you aren't most of the time, what then? I'm not going to sit around like a lemon. Life's too short for that. I want to be out with my pals, having a laugh. I can't just drop them, pick them up again, drop them again whenever you breeze in. You've got to pack in what you can while you can. It might not last.'

'It's only the once,' he says. 'A special occasion.'

'Besides, I want you and them to know each other. They like you. I thought you liked them too.'

'I do. Of course, I do.'

She puts up with him reading poems to her or paragraphs out of the papers every now and then, but it's not really her cup of tea. She's more interested in the new bikini shown in Paris – 'them French!' – and Howard Hughes's plane crash than she is in Churchill's worries about what he calls an 'iron curtain descending across the continent,' or Atlee's austerity programme. These are things that will make a difference to us, he tries to tell her, will change the world our kids will grow up in, but she laughs and rubs her fingers into his curly hair, and tells him the only thing that matters is that they're together, and they end up cuddling. Which is not bad in its own way.

He's hungry all the time and rationing's worse than ever. If he tells people about Australia, about mangoes and oysters and steak and milkshakes, they look sad and envious. Some of the places he has to stay when he's travelling make his hair curl. Cold, dirty and little enough to eat, even with his ration cards.

He'll cheer up when he and Cora are married, he tells himself, and they've got a place on their tod. One's likely to happen before the other. Mrs Bailey's offered them a room in the house to start married life. He's not sure how he feels about that. Grateful, of course, but with a horrible tight feeling in his chest. He misses the rough and tumble there used to be in Ken's house, so many people milling about and sitting down together to eat, but now there's fewer of them, they press against each other more closely trying to close up the gaps. They're sticking to each other like glue, and he's part of the plan, but he feels trapped. It's not a nice feeling, and he's not proud of it, but he can't shake it off. Ken's family want something from him that he's not sure he's got.

On top of that, he's restless. More than restless. He feels disconnected, as though some mooring rope's been cut. Everyone's lost someone, but most people at least know where they come from, who they belong to and what they've lost. They can point to a photograph or a grave or a place on a map and have it mean something. It gives them history and a place in the world. It's not the same for him, and it's biting at him more and more. There's something he has to give one more try. It's probably a dead-end, but nothing ventured, nothing gained.

BANTLING

80 Sam. Stockwell. 1946.

The vicarage looks shabbier than last time he was here. The window frames are peeling, the front garden's a mess of plants gone to seed and the door needs more than a lick of paint. When it opens, it's not the mad woman standing there, nor the old vicar, thank God. This woman's just in there clearing up before the new vicar moves in, then she'll be gone too, she tells him. Reverend Holcroft passed away a few months ago, she says, and his wife, well, she died in the early days of the war. He starts to move away and she asks him what it was he wanted. She's Mrs Dawson, by the way, worked here since before the old vicar arrived, way back in the early twenties.

His heart is pounding, but he can't get his hopes up again. He comes straight out with it.

'I was looking for someone who used to live here. Did you ever know a Violet Bantling?'

She sucks in her breath, stares into his face.

'You're her boy?' she asks. 'You're Samuel?'

She puts her hands on either side of his shoulders, the first time he's been touched in recognition of being Sam.

'Little Samuel. I remember the night you were born. I never thought I'd see you grown.'

He's shocked into silence.

'Come in, come in. You'll have some tea, won't

you? I'll tell you what I can, though it's not much. You came once before, I think.'

He nods.

'I saw you running off and I wondered even then. You must have spoken to poor Mrs Holcroft. She wasn't at all well by that time.'

His legs could be filled with jelly for all the good they are. She leads him down the hallway to a big old-fashioned kitchen, a bit like the one Ma used to have, but four times the size. It's cold and been emptied out and smells of old soot and grease. She puts a kettle onto a plug-in electric ring.

'Tell me about Violet Bantling.' What else could he call her? 'Do you know where she is or what happened to her?'

She shakes her head. 'Sorry, love. Not for a long time. She used to write here for a while. For a good long while, she used to write around your birthday. I'd see the envelopes from time to time, but never the letters themselves. And believe me, I used to look for them. I would've written to Violet myself. After Mrs Holcroft passed away, the vicar found them stashed away. He'd never seen them before, though some had his name on the envelopes. There were a few tears shed that day, let me tell you. He was old by then, but still bright as a button, you know. He said something about a place in Peckham.'

'Stanton Street?'

When the kettle boils, she tops up the teapot.

BANTLING

'That's the one.'

'I grew up in Stanton Street. But it all came down ages ago.'

'Soon as he found the letters, he sent off the address to Violet. He'd gone there once, when you were a nipper, to check for himself that you were all right.'

The vicar had kept that piece of information to himself. Never said a word when Sam was sitting right in front of him.

'Let me see, must have been late summer 1944 when he wrote to Violet. He was trying to make amends. He never made his peace with his wife giving you over like that.'

'So do you have an address for her?'

Mrs Dawson pours tea into two thick blue and white striped mugs, shaking her head from side to side.

'Look at that tea. Like gnat's piss. Won the war we did over the best part of a year ago and we're still scraping the barrel for tea leaves.'

He mumbles something about it being enough for him that it's hot and wet.

'Where was I? We never heard back from Violet that time. He wrote to that last address, but it was nearly four years old by then. In Hull, it was. The place had been more or less blown to smithereens by the time he found her letter.'

She sits back heavily. She's an old woman. She pats his hand across the table.

'Violet's boy sitting in my kitchen. Well,

well. After all this time. And with a moustache, to boot. Handsome as all get-out. Anyone tell you that you're a ringer for that Ronald Coleman? You've got something of your mother's look, too. I always had a soft spot for that girl. She had guts and grace and not a lot of luck. She was here because she wanted to keep you with her. Reverend and Mrs Holcroft were meant to help her and they let her down.'

'She wanted to keep me?'

She leans across again and grips his arm. He looks at her hand and thinks that it held him when he was a baby. The thought makes him float.

'Always, always she wanted you. Before you was born and afterwards. She was mad for you.'

It doesn't make sense. It's not what the vicar said or Ma thought.

'But she gave me away!' He sounds like a cry-baby.

'You listen to me. Violet and me, we'd chat from time to time. She was dead set on bringing you up herself, had a job more or less lined up, everything. Then at some point everything got on top of her, it's true.'

She stares at the greasy wall, her hands around the mug.

'There were troubles back home, too, I seem to recall.' She shrugs her shoulders and shakes her head. 'Doesn't matter now. Given time, it most likely would've found its level. Anyway, the Reverend took a real shine to you. I remember that taking us all by surprise. He came up with the bright idea of adopting you. Violet went along with it. For your sake. She was quite low by then, didn't feel she had much choice, what with one thing and another. Mrs Holcroft, she wasn't so keen. One thundery summer's day we all came home and you was gone.' She snapped her fingers. 'Poof! Just like that.'

So Harry had been telling the truth, or close enough.

'Mrs Holcroft was drunk on duty in my opinion. She thought I didn't notice the sherry and brandy going down in their bottles. That day she stank of those cachous she used to suck, rabbiting on about how she'd solved everyone's problems. Violet didn't know a thing 'til it was over and done with. It near sent her round the twist, poor girlie.'

He rolls himself a fag, or tries to, shreds of tobacco dropping onto the table.

'I'll have one those while you're at it,' she says, and he obliges, best he can.

The smoke hits his lungs, calms him. The room and everything in it become a bit sharper.

She puffs at her fag. 'You should never smoke in a kitchen,' she said, 'but what the heck. It's all going to be stripped out and redone. Out with the old, eh? It was a mean thing that Mrs Holcroft did, giving you away like that and she twisted herself up trying to square it with herself.'

She hesitates for a moment. 'Sugar?'

People don't offer strangers sugar every day.

'I don't mind if I do. If it's going spare.'

'Chance would be a fine thing.' She waves her roll-up. 'Still. Fair exchange and all that.'

She stirs a small spoonful into both mugs.

'Thanks.'

He picks up his mug. The tea trembles inside it and nearly slops over. He holds it tight with both hands.

'Losing you sent Violet off the deep end for a bit. She wandered the streets at all hours looking for you, making people get their babies out of prams and all sorts. Then her money ran out, and the hope. I lost sight of her after she left here. Was thrown out, more like. From the letter I saw, it seems she got married and moved north with him. Hull, as I said, but I've no idea of her hubbie's name. She had a child. Children, more than two, I seem to recall.'

Mrs Dawson looks around the kitchen with a puzzled expression.

'Hang on. I might still have something somewhere. I remember now, I helped him write that letter. His eyes weren't so good by then and he was still shaken up by Mrs Holcroft's accident.'

'Accident?'

'It was horrid. She was quite doolally by then, poor lady. I tried to tell her, what's done is done, live with it, but it ate away at her more and more. She never saw she'd done wrong, mind you, just that everyone blamed her, that she hadn't been able to make them see the sense of it. In the end, she walked in front of a tram on the Stockwell Road. People that saw it happen said she knew what she was doing, that she waited until the tram was so close it couldn't stop, but I don't buy that. I think she was just distracted. And that's what the enquiry said, too.'

He waits while she drinks some tea. He tries to himself, but though his mouth is dry as anything, he can't swallow.

She looks up, startled and blinking.

'You were saying,' he reminds her.

'Where was I? Violet, that's right. She stuck to her guns, I'll give her that. She wrote to them on your birthday most years. Trying to grind them down, I suppose. I think she hoped Mrs Holcroft would have a change of heart or that the Reverend knew more than he was letting on and would break ranks. But I'll tell you for free, he never saw those letters, not until after she passed away. None except the one I got to before her and gave to him. She hid the all rest away. Shame. If I'd have known you'd turn up, I could've kept them for you. Hang on a tick.'

She potters around the kitchen, opening drawers and cupboards. From time to time she mutters, pulls out a bent spoon or rusted lid, puts them on the table or draining board.

'I don't know, I don't know. We wrote the reply at this table. Last I saw of her letter, it was in here somewhere. Must be a good couple of years ago now. Let me see. Broke my heart when we never heard from her again. '

He should have come back before, before everyone lost their marbles or popped their clogs or cleared the house.

He's parched now, drains his mug, wishes there was more tea on offer.

He coughs and she looks up. 'I'm sure it was in here somewhere.' She turns out the drawer at her end of the table. 'Have a look at your end,' she tells him. His drawer is more or less empty. A scrappy piece of newspaper for lining, sticky crumbs and a few rotted rubber bands. She leans across him and crumples the newspaper before she tosses it away, crumbs and all.

She's breathing deeply, probing around the inside. Her rough fingers stretch into the corners, then she pulls the whole thing out and shakes it.

'Like I said, don't ever get your hopes up,' she says, at last. 'The letter's gone, everything's gone. Reverend Holcroft tried to find her afterwards, contacted the Red Cross, even went up to Hull himself, but nothing came of it. Perhaps he took the letter with him. There was nothing to say one way or another what had happened to her. The street was off, let me think, it ran off one of the long roads, he said, that's right, I remember now, Beverley, like my niece, not far from the docks and the centre. The house got a direct hit. The Reverend told me the whole place was flattened. We hoped for the best, but you have to face facts. He couldn't find anyone who knew her, not even pulling all the strings a vicar has. He kept trying, more or less until he died. Shame. She was a sweet girl. I'm the only one left now of them all. Funny to think of that.'

Mrs Dawson thinks Violet's dead, but he's pounding with hope. He's been playing lost and found with the people in this house for years and he's not giving up today.

BANTLING

81 Sam. Poplar. 1946.

He and Ken are sitting in the lean-to shed at the back of the house. It's only just turned September, but outside it's chilly and damp. Miserable as sin. Inside Ken's cosied it up with a couple of Tilley lamps and some old carpet he's found somewhere. The hissing lamps and the glow coming off them makes the shed seem warmer than it is. The damp smell is turning into a cheerful fug of paraffin, glue and cigarette smoke. Ken's working on his model of the old London Bridge. Arches, houses, shops, spikes and all. He's got a couple of old pictures of the bridge as it used to be, but mostly he's making it up as he goes along. Sam's giving him a hand. At least, that's the story. It's mostly made out of used matches, and it's as good an excuse as any to have a smoke.

Ken dips one side of a match into glue. Using tweezers, he gently adds it to one of the bridge columns.

'It'll look a treat when it's finished,' Sam says.

He reckons it'll take Ken years at this rate.

Ken gives him one of his quiet looks.

'It'll need painting before it's done,' he says. 'Every little edge of it. That'll keep me out of her hair for a fair while.'

Sam's working out what Ken's telling him.

Different strokes for different folks. Sam can't see himself gluing matches together in his spare time, sitting by himself in the cold. Ken and Mrs Bailey, they've lost Don, which is bad enough. Worse than bad. But it looks like they've lost each other too. What's the point of marriage and kids if you just want to get away from each other? What about enjoying yourselves together, for better and worse, though thick and thin? Like him and Ma used to. Isn't that how family should be?

'Mrs Bailey and me, we're looking forward to having you in the family,' says Ken.

There's not quite enough air again.

'Me too,' he says. Too soon? Too slow? 'You've been a good mate, Ken. All you've done for me. Pulled me out of a few holes.'

It's true what they say, friends being as good as family. Or better.

Ken waves his tweezers. 'Get on with you. Pass us another match.'

Sam takes a breath. 'I might've got a lead on my mother. She was in Hull in 1940. I've got brothers and sisters too, it looks like. Half-ones, at least. If I'm ever I'm up that way for work, I'll try to track them down.'

Even if he has to make a special trip. Just the thought makes him warm all the way through.

In the lamplight, Ken's face is shadowy.

'That's six years and a lot of war ago. Even if you do find something, you might be poking a snake's nest,' he says. 'You know what they say about sleeping dogs. I wouldn't want to see you hurt. All that business about not having your own people doesn't mean a thing to us. You're a second son to me and Mrs Bailey.'

There's a Don-shaped hole in this family going begging and Sam doesn't want to let anyone down. If he holds his breath, squeezes and shoves and doesn't mind shaving off some his edges, he'll fit in nicely.

BANTLING

82 Sam. Hull. 1946.

He fetches up in Hull early one Saturday afternoon, sooner than he expected, getting the bus across country from Leeds after a morning in the outskirts, doing the rounds of shops and workshops until they all shut up shop at mid-day. Got a couple of orders too, though he had to cut his whack to the bone. Worth it all the same.

The bus trundles across miles of flat fields, the never-ending grey sky pressing heavy as lead onto the soggy ground.

Everywhere in England that he's been has had it rough. Hull doesn't look too bad, not at first, but that's only because so much has been knocked down. The closer to town they get, the worse it is. You don't have to be a genius or to have known the place beforehand to see that Hull's been blasted almost to Kingdom Come.

There's a long way yet to go, years and years of work, to make good the damage. Acres of lumpy waste ground, blocks of land scattered with propped-up buildings. It's so flat and flattened that he can see for what seems like miles around. Boarded windows. Empty windows. Tatters of papered roses and cornflowers around suspended fireplaces. Cracked sills and wooden props. Allotments in cleared patches. Rosebay willow-herb fluffing silver among the brick and stone rubble. Collapsed roofs and rusting barbed wire. Broken chimneys and missing bricks. There's something about the levelness of Hull that stretches out the damage. He hasn't seen a building yet, not a house, not a shop, not a chapel, not a pub, not a warehouse, not a shed, not even a telephone box that looks as if it got off scot-free.

The closer they get to town, the more prefabs there are, some used as shops or workshops. People live in others, grey-faced men and women smoking in doorways. Or just standing and talking. He stares at women in their forties, wondering, hoping. And in their thirties and fifties too, because with the war and rationing he can't really tell anyone's age these days. But slow as the bus moves, it's travelling too fast and most of the women have their heads covered with a scarf and it's pointless to ask himself if she'd still have hair as dark as his.

The bus ends up, in what was once the city centre, one flat, quiet, empty space next to the train station. He finds a hostel close by, puts his case into a locker and gets going.

Right here, in the middle, it's so cleared-up it looks bare, like a room after everything in it's been broken and then thrown out, or a hospital ward where the mutilations are tidied away behind bandages and tightly-tucked sheets. There's not much else to see. Half the time, he can't even tell where the old streets might have been.

All the same, he starts wandering around. Down

by the river, the mixed-up smells of fish and tar, boiling bones, salt and timber mix with the slaps and snaps and scrapes and clicks of rigging and masts and hulls. Scale apart, it's not so different to the canal behind Stanton Street. There's activity of a sort going on, boats moored where parts of the wooden docks seem repaired, where one or two hoists and cranes are in working order and some of the brick ruins along the quay are doing limited warehouse service.

Away across the mud and water, there's Lincolnshire.

Beverley Road or thereabouts was where Mrs Dawson had mentioned Violet living. A policeman points him away from the docks, back up through the dead heart of town, straight past the station, tells him to just keep going if he wants to see it all. Only nine miles to Beverly itself. He starts walking. He has a ridiculous hope, he knows it's ridiculous, that if Mrs Dawson is right about Violet caring about him so much, there will be some sort of clue, signs he can read. The stones and streets, the destroyed areas, should show him something if there's any justice, should somehow point him in the right direction.

The streets are narrow, knocked-about terraces of two-up, two-downs, not very different to the one he grew up in. The doors open straight onto the street, and people gossip and smoke and yell at their kids. He moves from doorstep to doorstep, asking his questions.

'Does anyone remember a woman called Violet? She wasn't from around here. Moved up a bit before the war. Might have been bombed out. She'd have had a southern accent.'

Someone will remember her, surely. He stops a man with a ferret in his pocket and a woman too old to be the mother of the baby she's lugging about. Everyone's kind enough, even the ones with accents so thick he can hardly understand them. They look at him, shrug their shoulders, shake their heads, tell him about the firestorm and the countless raids and so many people dying or becoming refugees in their own city. Over a hundred and fifty thousand people lost their homes in those six years, half the people who lived in the city. It's hardly surprising that nobody recalls anything that might help. He goes into the one corner shop still not shuttered this time of the afternoon. The man in the corner shop sells him a glass of fizzy drink, a sweet-sour concoction he brews out the back, and wishes him the best of luck. The Northern Cemetery, the man tells him, is where a lot of them, not all, mind you, were laid to rest, some in marked graves, a lot of them buried together and never named.

It's getting dark fast. When the pubs open, he'll try one or two of those as well, but half the town seems to have disappeared into rubble and thin air.

It doesn't help that he doesn't know the name his mother married into. *Mother*. The word feels strange and he can't help but wonder what Ma would make of it. *One Ma not enough for you?* It's not that, he tells her. Don't get the hump.

BANTLING

He's never felt lonelier.

Sunday afternoon he ends up sitting on a bench in a park. He's walked the streets – Springbank, Trafalgar Street, Providence Row, Wellington Lane – both sides of the Beverley Road as far as Pearson Avenue, and covered a fair amount of the cross-streets to boot. Knocking and getting nowhere.

It's only a mile's straight walk from the station to Pearson Avenue up the Beverley Road, but countless streets, lanes and alleys off on either side. Even going nowhere as far as Beverley itself, there must be miles more of the Beverly Road in Hull. Even with the amount of damage, all the gaps between buildings, it's impossible to cover the ground.

His feet are sore and his shoulders ache from carrying his case all day. There's nothing open, not even a pub. He'd best start hitching back to Leeds soon if he wants to get his train tonight.

He's run out of time. It's the end of the road. Mrs Dawson was right. The vicar was right. He could come back again, even carry on tomorrow though it might cost him his job, but what's the use? He's an orphan and no mistake. There's no point feeling sorry for himself, crying for what he never had. He's dead sure he's not Timmy, but he's not the Sam he's been hoping for either. He's on a hiding to nowhere if he carries on scrabbling around, reading the ruins for clues and signs.

He sits and looks around at the damaged park, at

the churned-up earth that's just beginning to settle, at patches of struggling grass, at new-dug beds and fenced off vegetable patches. No rosebay willow herb to be seen here. The whole park looks orderly and useful, or heading that way. He watches groups and families chatting or playing or just making their way across the open space, going to and fro, knowing where they're headed.

About a hundred feet away, a couple of rugged-up women are digging in some shrubs, tamping down the soil around the roots. It's corny, but the sight gives him a sense of perspective, of hope, the town repairing itself, people knuckling down to it. Perhaps he'll have a garden one day himself, grow roses and sweet peas just for their smell.

It's not possible to walk straight through walls or solid buildings or barbed wire or deep water. You have to find your way past them or round them or across them, along corridors, down lanes and streets, however twisty or shadowy, across parks, gardens and bomb-sites, through unexpected gaps. Perhaps it's the same with life. Perhaps the worst parts of a life, like never knowing Violet Bantling, like the years in the Arctic and Pacific, are not barriers for beating your brains against, but pathways towards being yourself, just as the good things are, like Ma and flying fish and Miss Barnes. Destruction smashes down what you know, takes out people whether you care about them or not. It can cut you loose of your old self too, for better or worse. Losing what you've grown up with or what you thought you knew makes you look at everything, even yourself, yourself most of all, differently.

He's awash with emotions. Mostly sadness. Sad for everyone. For himself, both selves, Timmy and Sam. For Violet Bantling, because Hattie Dawson cared about him though she didn't know him from Adam, just because she'd liked his mother.

The women finish, scraping mud from their spades and boots, picking up their tools, walking away across the park.

There's more than sadness for Streaky, Lieutenant Banning, the pilots and deckhands on the Victorious, for Don and his uncle and cousins and all the ones buried here and buried at sea and in Burma and France and Greece and wherever else they died or were killed. Slaughtered, a lot of them. Turned to smoke and ash. Germany. Japan. All those who never even got a grave or made it onto a memorial. The sheer numbers. The loss and waste. All those people. All their secrets and sadness and hopes blown away. It isn't fair.

It's miraculous that he made it. *You're my miracle baby*. He hadn't expected to live to see the end of the war, though he'd never said that out loud to anyone. But here he is, and hard though it is, it's a sight better than the alternative. The war chucked everything into a whirlwind. The old ways of doing things, the servile expectations, the childish hopes he had a million years ago, all up into the wind. What's coming down is landing higgledy-piggledy. It looks like a jumble, but it's making new patterns and puzzles, leaving great cleared swathes. Where he comes from doesn't have to be where he ends up.

If he and Cora get married – *if?* – they'll find their own way of belonging and sharing. Her family think of him as one of their own, and that's fine as far as it goes, it's a compliment, but he wants more, something that's separate from the Baileys as well as connected. A wife to call his own, that goes without saying, somebody he can look after properly and for whom he'll be the most important person ever. And children, as many as they can afford. But kin shouldn't be the be-all and end-all. They shouldn't keep you apart from everybody else, because you can't ever guarantee that blood will be thicker than water. The family he's got in mind isn't blood-narrow. If he hasn't got parents, brothers, sisters or cousins, he wants good mates, foul-weather friends, like Ken and Streaky, who see you through thick and thin. Him and Cora, they'll make a family by choice as well as by chance.

BANTLING

83 Sam. Poplar. 1946.

Cora has unbuttoned her coat and snuggled herself against him. He pulls her inside his coat, wraps it round so they're squashed into each other. The chill of the wall is seeping into his back already, but all down his front he glows where they're pressed together. He lights a cigarette and puts it to her lips, then draws on it himself. He saves the match for Ken. The two of them blow warm, sweet, smoky breath around each other. Over her shoulder he can see the steamed-up kitchen window between the gaps in the curtains. Another Christmas almost on them. Funny how quick you get used to things. Only a year or so ago you'd never have seen a window lit up like that. Everything would have been blacked out. Now glowing yellow windows look more or less normal. When the electric's on, that is, what with coal strikes and power cuts every two minutes. Here he is with the sort of family Christmas he envied back in 1941, a tree in the front room, paper-chains they've been making for the past couple of weeks hanging off the picture rails and from the lampshades. Glass and china being shined up. Everyone with something to do and he's part of it all

It feels good, but it's not enough. None of it feels like it's really his.

BANTLING

'What do you want?' he asks her. 'Deep down in here.'

He touches her with one finger just above her heart.

'I want a lovely blue dress. A new dress, not a make-and-mend, with enough material for a decent skirt and collar and plenty left over for trimming a hat.'

'Is that forget-me-not or bluebell? *Je Reviens* or sailor suit?'

'Silly thing.' Her voice is just the right side of affectionate. 'Blue. You know. Just blue. Ah well. Fat chance, you don't have to tell me, not this year.'

Or next, if things don't pick up soon.

'And apart from Christmas,' he says. 'For you and me?'

Let her want what he wants.

She squeezes him tight and puts her head against his chest.

He hugs her. She wriggles and presses herself against his hardness.

'There's this,' she says.

'That feels good.' He gives a little grunt and settles himself against her. He's losing track of what they're talking about.

'On top of all this. Next year, I mean, and for the rest of our lives?'

He wants her to say that she'll go anywhere, do anything that has to be done, as long as they can be together, make a better life, whatever that might be. He wants her to say that nothing in the world is as important as he is to her. He wants her to say that she knows what's on his mind and that anything he decides is good by her. He wants her to be as fidgety as he is, to want as much as he does to make a place of their own.

If she says that, he's got her the perfect present.

She kisses him. His mouth feels chilly when she pulls away.

'I want us to get married quick. Two can live cheap as one,' she says. 'I want to do it proper, though. Church and all that. Other than that, just be grateful for what we've got. Me, I've got everything I want for now. You, mum and dad, Sally. I want a load of kids, though, I warn you.'

'A big family's fine by me,' he replies. And it is. One day. Not quite yet.

'We can live here for a bit. Mum says there's even room for a baby while we're saving up. We're set up, we are.'

She hasn't got the point, and any moment now, someone will put their head out of the back door and call them inside. Or come outside for a smoke themselves.

'Save up,' he says. 'Set up. That's a laugh. I've been back the best part of a year now, more or less just on commission-only for sales, and any spare jobs they've got going, fixing machines, writing up the ledgers, helping out in the warehouse. With the miners on strike and the docks closed half-the time, it's short hours coming up for everyone however you look at it. Even if they keep me on after Christmas, it's not enough. Not to get married on. We've said all this before.'

'Things'll get better', she says. 'You'll see. You're a hard worker and you'll get a break. It's rough all round at the moment, but we'll do all right in the end. We've got more than many as it is.'

Listening to her is like falling into a clay pit.

He puts the fag between her lips again and nuzzles her neck.

'Wake up, Cora. Take a look around. There's sod all here in England for a bloke like me. I want us to do more than scrape by.'

It was true. You freeze your arse off in the Arctic, you broil below decks in the Pacific, you eat their hard weevilly biscuits, shower in sea-water, put up with their ranks and distinctions and rules, their them and us, you see your mates pulped and burned, and every moment you're either dying of boredom or faced with dying for good, and then, when it's all over, they kick you in the balls. Or grind you down, one way or another. The coldest winter anyone can remember, the miners on strike and coal as rare as hen's teeth.

'I want my kids to have more than I did, to have a better start than I did.'

And he wants more for himself than he's had so far. A working man should be more than a work-horse.

'I want the best for my kids too, Sam. And they'll get it if you and me have anything to do with it.

BANTLING

He runs the tip of his nose down the side of her throat.

'So, you'll come then?'

'You're freezing,' she squeals, and he slowly breathes out warm air. She's teasing him, making him work for his passage.

'I don't mind breaking my back, but it won't get us anywhere here.' He nuzzles her again. 'There are other places in the world, where what you do and how hard you work count for something, places you can make yourself into who you want to be. Places where you can look up and the sky isn't always murky yellow.'

He's over-egging the pudding, so he shuts up. He's said most of it before, in any case. He gives her the last drag of the cigarette and throws away the butt. It arcs orange-red before it hits the ground and sizzles out on the damp earth.

There are other things he wants too, the chance to read and not be laughed at, and to see some of the art he knows is out there, but that sort of thing doesn't cut much ice with her. An hour in the National Gallery where they're putting the paintings back on the walls, and she'd been pulling on his arm for a cup of tea and complaining that when he'd said he'd show her some pictures, she thought he'd meant the moving kind. She giggled and tutted when they walked past any nudes. She wouldn't look at them straight on, didn't know where put herself, all those men and women with their bits hanging out.

Wasn't much keen on the rest, either.

'Life's too short to spend it looking at all that rubbish. I'd rather have a nice photograph. Like that one you sent me from your ship.'

It had been a shame and waste of time to take her, but it's no reason not to marry the girl.

'You're not still going on about Australia, are you? Other side of the bleeding world, that it is, in case you forgot.'

'Think about it, Cora. We'll get cheap passage because we're both ex-services. We'll get married before we sail, next week if you like. I've spoken to my boss. They've got a branch in Sydney – I came across the warehouse when I was there. They'll give me a reference. It'd be a shoo-in. At least, it'd be a fighting chance. But we have to do it soon. I've wasted so much time already.'

'You've got it all thought out. The land of milk and honey.'

There's an edge to her voice that gets on his nerves.

'I never said that. There are homes in the city with dirt floors and outdoor toilets that you have to empty into the dunny-cart.'

'Oooo, lovely things you've got planned for us,' she says. 'Doesn't sound like my cup of tea.'

He ploughs on. 'Men are out of work there too. But nobody laughs at you for trying to better yourself. And they're not rationing bread. Nor a whole lot else for that matter, not compared to here. Think of it, Cora. Bananas. Steak. *Grapes.*'

He blows warm air onto her ears in a white mist. He has got it all planned out, she's right. He's applied for their passages. Any moment now, he'll hear back. He's leaning against the wall and she's leaning forward against him. She makes a little sigh and slips her hands down his back under his trouser belt. There's cold air and there's her warm hands and there's him getting hotter, just in that one place.

'We'll be as warm as toast there. We won't need overcoats. And there's space and land enough for us to have a house with a proper garden. We can grow our own grapes and oranges and jasmine. And, Cora, you should see the harbour. You won't believe your eyes, it's so lovely.'

Even through all their layers of jumpers and coats he can feel the soft give of her breasts. Her legs are parted and so are his and she's moving against him.

'Hot as furnace you are there,' she says.

He's aching and losing his thread, but he's pretty sure he's winning the argument.

The back door's opening and she takes back some of her weight.

Light gleams dull on the wet ground.

He rubs her back with his cold hands and tries to keep hold of her. She's scared of taking the plunge, but he's seen a bit of life, knows there's more to be had, more that he and Cora can do to grab it. It's up to him.

Her mum calls out, 'Cora love, come and have your turn with the pudding for luck. You too, Sam. You can scrape out the bowl after.'

'And,' he adds, 'We'll have more than three minutes at a stretch for ourselves without looking over our shoulders all the time. It's a whole new, modern world, Cora. Where we come from doesn't have to be where we end up. Say you'll come with me.'

'We best go back inside.' She stirs the front of his trousers with the tips of her fingers, giggling. 'That's your lot for today, greedy.' She pulls away and tugs her coat up round her ears. Her face becomes serious. 'I wish you could just settle down and be happy with what we've got here. Now Don's gone, mum and dad need me and Sally both. And while I'm on the subject of family, I want you to make it up with Mr and Mrs Wingrove. It'll look funny if you've got no-one on your side at the wedding. I think a June ceremony would be nice.'

'Cora! Can you hear me?' calls Mrs Bailey.

No bloody coal to be found for love nor money, but the taste in his mouth is of soot and ashes.

'Go on in. Mustn't keep your mum waiting,' he says and lights another fag, cold, softening and shrivelling in the icy air.

BANTLING

84 Violet. Hull. 1947.

Hull, 27th March 1947 Dear Stel, so glad to get your news about Ralph being home at last. It sounds as though he's had it quite bad & it must be tough on you as well. Here's hoping he'll settle down soon & be the old Ralphie again, once you feed him up a bit & he gets some loving attention. After all, he's been through a lot & so have you. One day the twain will meet & you will get back your family life again. Everyone's been patient for so long, waiting for it to be over & all we want is ourselves and our loved ones back as we once were. Can you remember when we were young, bright, affectionate and simple? Not afraid nor wounded in body or spirit? I can't. The moving finger etcetera. Believe me, Stel, if you're still breathing you can adjust to anything & make something worthwhile of it. Don't give up. Give Ralph time & give yourself a break. It must be hard on the kids too, not knowing their dad from Adam & him not knowing them. I have that worry to come. Leonard's still over in Germany with all those displaced people, so no telling when he'll be released from duty. The children ask after him, but I know he won't be as we all remember. And neither will he recognise us at first. Billy was a child 7 years ago & now he's overseas, in Egypt, holding the fort as the lads who saw action are sent home. But however the dice fall, I want him back. It can't be that long now, surely? He's done his bit & then some. He has some horrible tales to tell, though I know he keeps most of it to himself. Meanwhile, I am kept on at the Parks Department, though it's just a matter of time until they get a serviceman who knows the ropes to take over getting the parks back on their feet. Then I'll be out on my ear. I'll miss being the person with a bit of clout. And of course, I like being in charge of my own purse-strings too. Would you believe I've heard from that librarian in Balham? She kept my address all this time & kept in mind what I was after. She wrote to say they're making a new electoral register & that I should come and look them over sometime when they're done. If I'm still interested. Chance would be a fine thing to get away during the week. I'm only hanging on at work because they find me so obliging & I never ask for time off and I weigh cheap for the job I do until they find someone else. Besides, perhaps I should let sleeping dogs lie, turn my face to the future, build a hero's new home for Leonard & the kids. There's probably no trace of the Wingroves even now. And even if there is, it'd take a life-time, a week at least, to check all the addresses. Perhaps they would refuse to speak to me. There's nowhere for me to stay in London unless it's a hotel that I can't afford. Excuses, excuses. I don't want to hear that Sam's missing or worse, plain and simple. I would rather not know. Thank God Ralph & Leonard both made it through, one way or another. Give Ralphie & Viola a hug from me. My brood send their fondest thoughts too, your Violet.

BANTLING

85 Sam. Sydney. 1947.

There are big, grandly-built sandstone houses up on Sydney's Darling Point. Mansions, a person might call them and not be lying. Turrets, columns, huge windows, ironwork and curlicues like negligee trimmings. Most of them have seen better times, have been turned into boarding houses or have rooms to let, shared bathrooms and a couple of gas rings on the landing to cook with. It's an ill wind ...

His rented room, it's bigger than any he's ever had to himself. A bed, a cupboard, a chest of drawers. An apology of a table plus a chair or two. None of it matches and the best said of the paintwork is that it's not half as old as the house. The window's all the decoration he needs, though. Given half a chance, he can sit and look out of it for hours.

There are wide, overhanging trees in the gardens outside. Magnolias with dense shiny leaves and huge, sweet, waxy flowers. Birds that whirl and whirrup and whistle and laugh like roisterers out on the town. Across to the left are the jacarandas he walks under to the bus-stop, flounced with mauve, as ridiculous as a whore's underwear. He can look out and across at the harbour turning to silver, steel and aluminium, the light bouncing into his eyes, ever-changing shimmery golds, greens, blues. Some days, the water looks as dense and powdery as asbestos roofing, on others it's like crumpled glass or delicate, shifting petals or the cutting edges of mirror shards. Some days it's covered in whitecaps, as choppy as you like. Evenings approach in smoky turquoises, Prussian blues, translucent indigos and fierce oranges. He can see the dark massed clouds barrelling in with the extravagant drama of the electrical storms. Tiny lights punctuate the night-time harbour like pinheads.

There's another young bloke in the boarding house, Robby. He's English too, a Londoner, a Cockney, did his time in the army. They run into each other heating baked beans on the gas ring on the landing. Sometimes they eat together in one room or the other. Robbie legged it down to Sydney after being sent by the Immigration to shear sheep in his Zoot suit in some godforsaken hole in the middle of nowhere. Not a hope he'd stay out there. He's a city boy, born and bred.

Sam knows what he means. Sam lives where he does because he doesn't feel at home in the streets of neat family bungalows everywhere else. He fits in here where the houses have a bit of height to them, one or two floors at least. He fits in here where he doesn't stand out.

From his flat high up on Darling Point, Sam's able to walk down to the park in Rushcutters Bay past the smoothly twisted columns of the Moreton Bay figs, stroll around the slapping curve of water, climb the steep, worn stone steps and come up to a street of terraces. They're a bit tatty on the outside and the ironwork balconies upstairs have been turned into makeshift rooms with bits of board and glass. He passes taller, more ornate buildings, gone up before the war, and secretive, opulent piles with big gardens, high white walls and green-tiled roofs, that look as though film stars live there. Perhaps they do.

At the top of the slope, and off to the right, Macleay Street heads down to Woolloomooloo, where the Victorious used to berth, to the piers, warehouses, dockers' pubs, naval base and Harry's all-night pie van. If he goes left instead, he's in Kings Cross. There's not one, but two, glossy curved and geometric cinemas, one white, one black. There's Repin's tiny café where the Russians gather. He always looks through the window, but never sees anyone he recognises. He thinks about Valya, her grey eyes, her kindness. Her unhappiness. There's a shop selling pickled fish and rye bread and another with olive oil, bitter, salty olives and chunks of real parmesan cheese. There are stalls of bright fruit and vegetables, a milliner, night clubs, a fancy baker, French dressmakers, a big Woolworths store, swish blocks of flats, some Deco, some with steps and Greek columns that could have been dropped from Manhattan or South Ken. There are rooms let by the hour, glamorous bars in stylish hotels, dives in the backstreets where Black sailors go. There are jazz musicians and artists, the sort they call bohemians, men and women changing the world on soapboxes, and people of all sorts in strange clothes and haircuts that make him blink. Day or night, King's Cross is as good as the paying pictures.

And then there's everything else. The orange-umber-russet-cream tiger stripes of the wave-shaped Tamarama rocks and the fine sand that sticks to his skin and turns up even in his face-flannel and best suit. Rationing so light it hardly counts. The netted tangle of tram wires over the crossroads in the city.

He drinks milkshakes by the barrel. Vanilla, chocolate, green lime. There are goodies Sam and Robbie can still hardly believe are there for the taking. Bananas on tap and pineapple that doesn't come from a tin. Girls by the yard toasting in the sun in two-piece costumes. Oysters to be prised off the rocks.

It's magical, even if he hardly knows a soul and his girl stayed put in London and is not going to change her mind. Robbie says that's how it is sometimes, no use crying over spilt milk.

She should have come. Silly, blinkered creature. Ignorant and selfish and scared. She'd have thought Sydney was a grand place if she'd bothered to give it half a chance. Bonzer. That's what the locals say. Sydney's a bonzer place. Him and Cora would have made a bonzer team, planning and pulling in the same direction. Sod her. Not that he says that to her, of course. If he writes – when he writes – he's careful to leave her room to change her mind. You never know.

BANTLING

In the meantime, he's giving Sydney his best shot. The old firm came good for him over here, thank his lucky stars. For someone in the fabrics industry, he was lucky with his timing, what with clothes rationing ending just after he stepped off the boat. Helping out at the warehouse at first while they got the measure of him, then trudging the outer suburbs and towns further away within the reach of clattering trains.

He must have done something right. These days he drives – *a car! The new firm loans him a car!* He drives southwards and west as well, to Parramatta and beyond, towards and across the mountains and it is hundreds of miles sometimes to see a customer. Always on the go, working all hours, the sunsets and sunrises blazing along those flat horizons.

Some days it seems he's making a future. Other days he wonders who he's doing it for and why. It would make more sense if Cora was here with him, pulling her weight, cheering him on. That girl could put her shoulder to the wheel with the best of them, wasn't afraid of getting her hands dirty. It's one of the things he likes – liked – about her, but in the end, it turned out she only wanted a comfier version of what she already had. Didn't, doesn't trust him enough or love him enough to take a punt on him. On the two of them.

It comes up out of nowhere, the anger and hurt, and he calls her all manner of names in his mind and can't get his thoughts off those useless high, idiotic hopes he had. So, he posts her yet another card of the big, proud buildings or the esplanades lined with Norfolk pines or the Three Sisters at Katoomba or of Bondi Beach crowded with bathers.

When he's driving, the wideness, the space and the great big skies set off a longing inside him he didn't know he had, and he feels he could drive into the horizon for ever. He notices the subtle changes of colour in the soil and the rocks, the direction of the light and the smells of the land, the different shapes of the birds on the wires and the flashing brilliance of flocks in the distance.

His mood flips like a beached fish. Like the blasted August weather, it can turn foul on a sixpence. He never knows if he's going to like the same thing twice or what he'll see in it the next time round. The bloody birds shriek and howl like banshees, jeer and take the piss out of him. The cicadas sound as though they're drilling into the insides of his head. When it rains for days, everything in his room smells of mould.

At these times, it's as though someone turns two pages by mistake and everything's wrong. The monotony of browns and reds and greys and dull flat greens, the dust dust dust dust everywhere, all those bloody flies and the inside of his hat getting greasy the minute he puts it on makes him long for anything with a bit of bloody variety or familiarity. East Street market. A couple of geraniums in a pot. The sun setting from

BANTLING

Waterloo Bridge and turning the grey stone into the rose-pink city.

He's been around enough to know nobody in their right mind would want to end up in those bleached little towns out west in the middle of woop-woop where his Pommy accent is sometimes grounds for suspicion, puts them off the cottons he's touting, and makes them scorn these lovely new fabrics that hardly need ironing, missus, you just wash them, hang them out, they dry in a flash and bob's your uncle, they're ready to slip right back on again. These are flat, dry, spread-out places where the men and women have faces like shrivelled prunes and axe blades, where there's only a pub and an apology of a general store for entertainment if you're lucky, and you don't know if today you'll be one of the crowd, a mate, or if the bar will fall silent when you walk in, where Aborigines sit or stand to one side of the street like shadows, bunched silently together or calling out to each other in a strange language. Or maybe more than one language. He's got no way of knowing.

He buys fresh peaches and apples by the roadside.

Out on the road, they all look out for each other, will stop to help a stranger change a tyre or drive him to the nearest petrol. Most of the time, and in spite of the empty miles they drive, most of them have never seen the snow in their own State.

Kangaroos stand and scratch their balls or bound along like cartoon drawings.

BANTLING

Late one afternoon, between a lake and the ocean where the bushes and grasses meet the hard dust road, the shadows in front turn to petrol blue, turquoise, pondweed gloss. It's the same around the next bend and the one after. Birds with under-feathers like sun on oil on water scatter in front of his windscreen.

He always carries more than one spare tyre because the roads are covered with sharp little stones and he's forever in the middle of nowhere and he might not see another car for hours. *Don't forget your water bottle, mate.* On the far side of the mountains, heading towards Orange or Broken Hill, some nights he sleeps in the car, or on its roof, to save money. Out there, he watches the sky turning, is dizzied by the earth reeling through space.

He could die out here from snakes or spiders and nobody would know and fewer would care.

He is a scrap of tissue, part of this vast beauty. Amongst all the foreign constellations, the Milky Way hangs so low and so bright a taller man could reach out and grab it.

Sharing some of the newness, the excitement, the unfamiliarity with Robbie is fine as far as it goes. He's grateful, don't get him wrong. Robbie's a good mate in lots of ways that count. All the same, it'd be a whole lot better if his girl was here to mosey around with, work out how they do things differently here and decide together what sort of future he and she could make. Not that Cora was ever that curious about anything beyond her own front door. He's not heard from her for months now. To be honest, he misses smoking in Ken's shed, watching Ken work and the talks they used to have, more than any single thing about Cora.

'Forget her,' says Robbie. 'She's just a bint. You'll find another one, easy as anything. Plenty more fish in the sea'.

He'll probably not bother keeping up the box at the Post Office much longer. Robbie's right. He should stop pretending there's anything else to be had from the old country. If Cora's not in touch, nobody else will be.

BANTLING

86   Violet. London 1948.

London, 14th November 1948 Dearest Stel, You have seen me all the way through the sorry saga of the Wriggler & me. Leonard, bless him, is at home looking after the children (who, truth to tell, need little looking after these days. I trust they are looking after him) I am finally here in London, where it all begins and ends. That librarian, Gladys is her name, took on my search as her own. Against my expectations, we found Henry Wingrove's address without much bother in the new voter listings. He lives only ten minutes or so from the library. I swear Gladys would have come with me, but it was better I went on my own. Henry Wingrove is old & bumbling. Sam's name agitated him. His wife, the second Mrs Wingrove it seems, treated me like the dirt on her shoes, keeping me on the doorstep as we talked. I begged her for news of Sam, anything at all. She said they hadn't seen hide nor hair of the, in her words, ungrateful wretch since 1941 & good riddance. He'd nearly been the death of her husband, he had, more than once, never mind helping the first Mrs Wingrove into an early grave. But what could one expect, what with his beginnings? And so on & so forth. Who was I to come weeping & wailing after all these years? Who did I think had put food in his mouth all those years & a roof over his head? She moaned that he had used their address for his official post until after he was safely demobbed, though he had nothing else to do with them, not even their name. Did that mean Sam was alive, that Sam came back? I asked. I was saying his name as much as I could to hold onto the Samness of him. She looked sour as spit, as though I'd tricked her into giving away a state secret. Finally, she gave me another address, way over east in Poplar. Just to get rid of me, I got the feeling. She hissed mean words as I walked away. I was halfway back to the station when a youngish woman caught up with me. Doris. She'd grown up with Sam, except she called him Timmy. Sam, I reminded her. He'd been her little brother until Henry threw him out after her ma passed away. Hadn't seen Timmy for years, what with the war & getting married, not that it had worked out. Sam, I told her again. I was to pass on her best if I caught up with him, with Sam, tell him he was an uncle now. She wished she'd been more like her ma & able to stand up for him against her dad. Truth be told, she'd been a bit jealous, her brother even more, their ma doted on Sam so. It was all water under the bridge now. She was crying & saying sorry sorry. I told her she'd done me no harm, she had no call to apologise to me. For anyone or anything else, she had to make her own peace, as we all do. She went back & I went on. I was shaking, Stel, I don't mind admitting it, crying sorry sorry too, to nobody in particular & to everyone. I got myself to Poplar all the same. The Baileys are very nice people, him especially. Mr Bailey seemed fondest of Sam, had thought of him as a second son, had hoped he'd marry their daughter. Funny, we might have been in-laws. Can you believe it, Sam went looking for me in Hull? Found nothing, of course. But he went looking. Now he is somewhere in Australia. Not enough to keep him here, said Cora, the daughter, shrugging. Cora had too much here to let her leave, said her dad. She should have cut herself loose, gone with Sam, not stayed with her old mum and dad, stuck in the past. The girl sat on the arm of her mother's chair & they clutched each other's hands as though the other might float away. Who of us knows what the right choice is? I said. We can only do the best we can at the time. At least Sam seems not to have been crushed by the bitter Wingroves. He is his own man, I have to believe. But he & I have passed each by. Only by moments, as counted against a lifetime, but nothing to be done now. When was life ever fair? It takes away & it gives back. Cora, the daughter, gave me a photograph. She didn't need it. She & Sam have lost touch. Do you remember I was going to get Sam photographed after he was born, but I never had the chance? Now I look at a young man in his naval hat & white shorts, standing at ease, arms behind his back, head slightly to one side, in front of an aeroplane on a ship's deck. He has the sun in his face & his eyes are in shadow. It is a sweet face, handsome, shy. I don't think he has his father's look, nor mine either particularly. He is smiling. I stare & stare at this boy, but I cannot pull him to me from where he stands. He is in his world & I am in mine. As ever, your sis, Violet

BANTLING

87 Sam. Sydney. 1949.

Of course, it's not all oysters on the rocks, beers on the beach and red skies at night. It's bloody hard work being a stranger, the odd one out, learning new words for cuts of meat and measures of beer, getting to grips with seasons and celebrations being out of kilter, being the one with the mockable posh accent because mostly their ears can't tell a Kennington bloke from a Kensington one. Even with all the trimmings on offer, he and Robbie don't buy into the God's Own malarkey. They're forever running into people telling them they're lucky Poms, bloody lucky Poms at that, to have landed on their feet here in Australia. Others – the same ones more often than not – talk longingly about England or Scotland or Wales, about how things are done back home in the Old Country, about going home one day. It makes him laugh. If they didn't land with the last boat like him, there's hardly ever a family member who's even set foot in England or Wales or wherever.

To his mind, anybody with any sense knows that England never did a great deal for working-class men. Send them to war and sling them on the scrap heap. Look at Harry. Look at Streaky. Look at Sam. Unless you're lucky enough to get a hand up or strong enough to haul yourself up over everyone else and never mind whose skull your foot's crushing, you can forget it. Robbie can get pretty noisy on the subject, about the only thing the Old Country doing well is keeping the proletariat in its place. That's to say, pressing their face into the mud with the heel of its boot.

All the same, there are times when a cold, misty drizzle or a trick of the light like a lingering summery night makes him suddenly feel that he's made a mistake, that he's in the wrong place. Robbie and he moan to each other about the Sydney pubs, like whopping big piss-parlours, all white tiles from floor to ceiling, filled with blokes knocking it back before closing time at six o'clock. And on a Saturday afternoon in town, it's so dead that you could fire a cannon down Pitt Street and not hit a soul.

It's not the Promised Land for everybody. Hard voices scrape on about wogs and Poms flooding in now the war's over, getting away from the problems in Europe, looking for an easy life. Believe him, a step away from the old colonial buildings in the middle of the city, Balmain and Surrey Hills are as grim as Peckham or Bethnal Green ever were. Houses with mud floors, dunnies in the back yards, whole families in single rooms.

He glimpses thin, dark refugees murmuring in foreign languages on street corners, their women in headscarves always carrying children and bundles as though ready to move on again at any time. Like his, the men's shabby suits were made for colder climates.

BANTLING

There's rough talk about the reffos from some of the locals, though that's nothing compared to what most of them have to say about the Abos, the blackfellas, which beggars belief. Most of them don't even think the blackfellas are human, let alone Australian, whatever that is when it's at home. They can't even vote, for Chrissakes, or collect their own dole.

As far as he's concerned, there but for the grace of God go him and Robbie, side-lined in the country they were born into, flotsam and jetsam from the wreckage of war. Nobody here is exactly popping a silver spoon into his mouth, but he knows he's lucky. At least he has the right-coloured skin to pass in the crowd – until he opens his mouth, at least. Even then, he speaks the lingo. And he's got a job he's hanging onto.

One Saturday morning he's heading though King's Cross before the shops shut to stock up on smokes, tinned sardines, bread, a couple of pounds of fat, scarlet tomatoes and a bunch of flowers to take up to Eve Hartley tomorrow. The sun's already warm on his head and shoulders. He's thinking about nothing very much at all, just this and that, a bit undecided about the flowers. They ship them in from the cooler regions in the south. The names are familiar from back home, but somehow not quite right in the Australian light. Frail freesias that look insipid, and the coarser varieties of roses, scentless carnations and harsh, funereal chrysanthemums. Evie likes delicate colours, light blues, lilacs and pale rose-pinks. Yellow chrysanthemums won't do the trick. Perhaps he'll find a potted scented camellia, though the petals are likely to bruise during the long bus ride up to Kogarah.

The samovar in the window of Repin's Restaurant is gleaming and steaming and the unbelievable smell of roasting coffee floats out of the open door. He glances in. There's nobody familiar in there, no Mrs Koslova, no Valya. He hopes somebody has made those grey eyes less sad these days. He wonders about finding his way to the Russian Club again. There's no harm in suggesting it to Reggo and Evie over lunch.

The florist is helpful and Sam is lucky. He leaves the shop with sweet-peas all the way from Tasmania and a twist of greenery, the last two bunches in the pail, for the price of one and a half. Even so, it's almost an arm and leg that he pays, but Reggo and Evie, they're proper friends, generous with him from the off, the sort of people it's good to have on his side. It's worth finding something a bit special for them. The flowers are gorgeous, colour upon colour upon colour and perhaps, just perhaps, there's a bit of sweetness in the air around them as well. If they arrive in Kogarah in one piece, they'll be just the ticket.

'Put them in water in some dark place. Maybe ice-cubes? Or put in frigo. Tomorrow, you wrap in wet paper,' says the man in the flower-shop. 'Lady will love them, I promise.' He's come from somewhere else too, by the look and voice of him.

BANTLING

New lives all around, old lives made over.

He should drop Ken a word, except mate though Ken is, his loyalty is with his daughter. Which is how it should be. He hasn't heard from Cora for, what, eight months? Ten? Not surprising, really. She doesn't have his address and he's given up the P.O box. Perhaps he'll send the Baileys a Christmas card. Or more likely he won't. Perhaps Cora will be sorry then, realise that she's missed a trick. It isn't fair. She was meant to be his girl, but in the end, she didn't even kick up much of a fuss about him taking off. She'd just let him go.

He can't breathe all of a sudden. He's stopped in his tracks, as though he's walked into a punch-bag, except it doesn't hurt. He simply can't move.

She'd just let him go.

There's not room enough inside him for both ordinary air and this glow that's filling him up. It's not a feeling he's rubbed up against very often, but there's no question what it is. It's happiness. He feels happy. That's it, plain and simple. Not just airy-fairy-thank-you-Lord-for-what-we-have gratitude. He's not sure yet what it means, but he's just been handed something he's missed all his life.

In the muddle of Saturday people, this is a rock hard, spit-on-your-hand, full-to-the-brim, specific blessing, a fairy godmother's good spell in a square foot of stained pavement.

He dares not move in case it goes away, in case he's suddenly out in the cold again. It's better than booze, this airiness of heart that goes to his head and to his feet, that spins and dizzies inside him. It's not complicated by any ifs or buts or maybes.

She just let him go.

Exhilaration sweeps over him like a floodlight. It's blindingly obvious where it's come from. Cora meant her promises, of course she did, but she couldn't deliver. He was just the same, put like that. It wasn't her fault. It wasn't his. She loved the person he couldn't be. She hasn't forced a deal out of him or held him to ransom or squeezed him into her mould. In the end, for better or worse, she's let him go his own sweet way and not charged him a penny. In a sense, he owes her. Or rather, he doesn't owe her, he doesn't owe her a button. That's her gift to him. Gratis. On the house. No strings.

Everyone is wonderful.

Everything is wonderful.

He's blocking the busy pavement, picking up the smells of frying fish and gasoline, dogshit, perfume, stale beer and hair oil, the tang of mangoes and cigarettes, of sweet peas warming in the open air. Women anxious to finish their weekend shop, dog-walkers, street-walkers, sailors on leave, men aiming for a pint, they all weave around him.

He'll remember it, this lighting up inside like a Roman Candle, will warm himself with it another time, because even now the intensity and beauty and clarity are jumbling, thinning.

BANTLING

He stares at the pavement as he starts to walk. He recognises sandstone, a swirl of dusty greys, streaky pinks and flaring orange-browns, marking the ebbs and flows over the shores and dunes they must once have been. Out of time and place, transplanted, hardly recognisable, they look almost at home, ocean beds lining city streets.

He grabs hold of the thought, tries to put it into words he'll remember. The shifting sands of time don't always blow away and disappear into nothing. They don't always bury and suffocate everything, everybody in sight. They can become, they really are, solid enough to bear his weight, these ancient tides beneath his feet.

Acknowledgements

Many people contributed to the genesis or writing of this book. Firstly, my father, Ron Russell, whose sparsely-documented and outwardly bleak early life prompted my curiosity about how he became such a well-rounded and generous spirit. His friend, Andrew Fisher-Hyde, gave me his own wartime diaries for the time he served on HMAC Victorious. Andrew's wife, Mary, fed me stories of post-war Sydney that were detailed, evocative and frequently hilarious. Lambeth Library Services, in the form of the Lambeth Archives at Minet Road, filled many gaps in my knowledge and visualisation of south London in the 1920s and 1930s. I was lucky enough to visit the Annie McCall Hospital, formerly the Clapham Maternity Hospital, when it was still artists' studios and architecturally almost intact, and to speak to archivist, Beryll Barrow, about its history.

Thanks also to Linda Leatherbarrow for criticism and comments, to friends (you know who you are) who have encouraged me in one way or another and Alan Slingsby for the final push and technical know-how.

BANTLING

Author's note

Our culture places a high value of the family in forming personal identity. Many people, perhaps most of us, have a less than perfect experience of family life, whether as adults or children. Doubtless, it's that less than perfect experience that makes us both mysterious and inquisitive in our connections to other people.

But some people have a much, much harder time of it.

I was intrigued by the apparent contradiction between my father's generous, creative and widely-loved persona and the meagre known facts of his bleak childhood. These facts seemed to signpost 'anti-social loner', and raised broader questions for me. How do you know who you are if you don't know where you come from? Where do you stand in society if you don't have a family? Is it possible to create a whole and loving person from a neglected child?

I was even more fascinated when I realised that he was born in the Clapham Maternity Hospital (later the Annie McCall Hospital), set up by radical, pioneering doctor, Annie McCall in the late C19th. As described in *Bantling*, they not only offered services to the many impoverished women of Clapham and surrounds, but also to otherwise respectable unmarried women expecting their first child. My grandmother, a book-keeper from the Isle of Wight, fitted this description. How, I wondered, would a young woman from such humble origins find herself at this hospital in the 1920s?

Without necessarily wanting factually true or definitively final answers, I invented, imagined, conjured a narrative about an unmarried woman, a child raised in poverty and the people around them.

Bantling is a work of fiction, an historical novel. It is not a biography or a psychological portrait, imaginative or otherwise, of the person I knew as my father. The broad trajectory of Sam's life (Peckham, wartime Fleet Air Arm, post-war emigration to Australia) follows that of my father's, but that's about it. I've tried to pin the narrative into a social and historical setting that rings true, at least from the perspective of the characters, and to then let the characters wander around that landscape and make it their own. I have stolen certain 'facts' from the historical record (census, trade directories, annual reports), borrowed heavily from a personal record of time aboard the HMAC Victorious and helped myself to the memories and reminiscences of an earlier generation. Equally, I have made up many, many things.

It was by making things up, by changing names that I was able to separate what I knew about my family history from what I was inventing. Named for themselves, the characters were able to become themselves, creating their own relationships, making their own decisions and living with the consequences.

BANTLING

And yet. And yet, I feel as though I have been able to explore and experience at level more emotional than academic some of the restrictions and assumptions that a woman like Violet might have collided with or the impact that poverty might have on a family. Some sort of melding, an emotional accommodation between the fictional, the real and the (mis)remembered has taken place.

Printed in Great Britain
by Amazon